Dedicated to the memory of Wendy O. Williams

Upon completion of his own memoirs, the Provost Marshal commissioned the establishment of the Black Book of the house of law, being a record of the exploits and achievements of the Queen's Men. Here begins the first volume.

Since immemorial times the courtesan has proved an invaluable
instrument of espionage.
　　　　　　　　　—*With Our Army in Flanders*,
　　　　　　　　　G. Valentine Williams (1916)

Chapter 1

Why hope to be happy? That's a fool's errand. Only hope to survive.

That's all Our Lady offers, or so they say at temple.

'Can you believe this horseshit?' spat Caromir, brandishing the news sheet in his fist.

'What is it *this* time?' Eline asked with a weary sigh as she turned from the fire to face her husband. 'Every day it's something. Every morning you rage at the sheets, and more days than not it's reason enough to drink when you could be working.'

Oh, he had been handsome once, had her Caromir. Handsome with his thick moustache and thicker muscles. Now his chest drooped with flab, and his moustache was grey and stiff with neglect and flaking skin, and 'once' was long, long ago.

'That bastard of a councillor,' Caromir continued. 'He's only gone and made himself the fucking Prince Regent! The whole country's going to the whores, I tell you!'

Eline sighed again. She couldn't care less who the Prince Regent was. She had never set eyes on the last one, nor the queen he had replaced. *Someone* was in charge, that was all that really mattered. Someone was always in charge, that was just how it worked. She had always been far too concerned about how to put food on the table for her children and herself and her excuse of a husband to care who it was.

Of course, she had married young. She'd been only fifteen when Caromir had come swaggering home from his turn in the army with thirty years to him, his corporal's stripes gleaming on his sleeve and a medal on his chest. He had been so dashing, then. Now he was fifty to her thirty-five, and their children were grown and gone. Her precious boy was signed up in the army just like his father, and her daughter off in service to be some lady's maid. The age of majority was thirteen, after all, and past that their mistakes were their own to make.

'It's a fucking disgrace,' he snarled, still raging at the paper in his hand.

Caromir had been enough to turn a young girl's head and no mistake, then. He'd been young to have joined up, too young in truth with only ten years to him at the time, but then after victory at Krathzgrad a lot of lads had lied about their ages to join up and win their honour and earn the respect of their peers and a bit of coin. He had his twenty years' service now, and his pension. All the same, it had taken all Eline's wits and wiles to keep their heads above water on his meagre income. She was no fool, unlike her brutal oaf of a husband, but it could be done if you cultivated friendships with the right people. Just about, anyway. At least he'd mustered out before the carnage at Messia and Abingon, but that, too, had been long, long ago.

'Oh well,' she said.

That, as it turned out, as it so often turned out, was exactly the wrong thing to say. Caromir reared up to his feet from behind their roughly made kitchen table and raised his hand. He raised his hand to her as he had done so many times before, and something changed.

Something changed for Eline right then; Eline who had been knocked to the flagstones by that hand times beyond counting. That had been her married life.

Beaten.

Battered.

Bloodied.

But unbroken.

The dam that had held back the tide of rage for so, so long finally shattered. Eline screamed, but not in fear. She was done with fearing Caromir. She was done with *him*.

Her good kitchen knife was right there, right by her own hand, and as he swung for her she grabbed it up and shoved it through his neck.

Enough, she remembered thinking, long after it was over. She had little memory of the event itself, only the rush of hot wetness, and the sense of overwhelming relief.

Rid of him. She was rid of him at last.

Amid all the drama, the fear and the shock and the fury of it all, she had never noticed the little urchin girl staring in through the kitchen window.

*

2

The Guard caught up with her after a while, of course. Drathburg was not the capital, and it could have been worse, but there was still the City Guard and there were still Queen's Men.

A Queen's Man, anyway, and if perhaps he was the only one in the city then it wouldn't have mattered. In Dannsburg she would probably already have been hanged, after Jottie next door ratted her out to the Guard, but here it was different. Jottie of all people, who she had used to babysit for and who had minded her own children in her turn. Eline had thought better of her than that. Friendships made out of mutual need, she was forced to admit, probably didn't mean much when one of you didn't need the other anymore. The Guard still had a gaol in Drathburg, of course, and the gallows, but she wasn't there. Instead she was in the back room of a nondescript house talking to the fat man who had come and quietly taken her away.

Eline wondered why that was.

'Killed your husband, then,' the fat man said, and it wasn't a question. His words didn't sound like they had any judgement in them either; a simple statement of fact, not like he cared much one way or the other. He was perhaps forty years of age, and she supposed that made him a veteran of Abingon. 'I looked at the scene, and the body, after my little spy came to tell me what she'd seen through your kitchen window. No defence wounds. Clean work, that.'

My little spy. So it had been some child agent of the Queen's Men who had told the fat man, then. Not Jottie or her daughter as she had originally supposed, although they had obviously sold her out to the Guard in the first place. The Queen's Men had eyes and ears everywhere, that was well known enough, but left to the Guard she would simply have hanged for murder, of course, and not be sitting here now.

'So I'll hang, then,' Eline said, resigned.

He had already shown her the Queen's Warrant that he carried, the thick piece of folded leather that contained the seal of the royal arms, a white-gold rose set upon a golden crown. She knew what that meant. Judge, jury, executioner. The Queen's Men were above the law, the absolute authority of the Crown's justice. The only question she had left was why she was getting his personal attention in what should have been a simple matter for the Guard.

'Don't have to,' he said.

Eline blinked.

'How do you mean?'

The fat man's face creased into a smile.

'I want a thing doing,' he said, 'and I want it doing quiet, like. Cleanly, you might say.'

'Oh?'

'There's a woman who killed a man,' he said. 'She's a madam, runs the poshest stew in the city. It's expensive and guarded by as many thugs as I've got guardsmen, just about. There's no taking her by assault, not easy anyway and definitely not quiet. So here's the thing. You've what, thirty years to you?'

Eline, who was older than that but looked good for it and knew she did, nodded.

'About that,' she said cautiously, wondering where he was going with this.

He looked at her for a long moment, and she wondered if she was fooling him after all.

'Aye. So you sign on as a tart. I can arrange the paperwork and the bawd's knot to say you're licensed. I've got a very good forger. You do the work, and when you get the chance you kill her for me.'

Eline's face fell.

He wanted her to be a whore? To sell her body, for coin?

Ma used to dance for money, but she had been very strict on this point: *Dancing is all it is.* She had made that very clear. *Never sell your body, Eline. There's no greater sin in the eyes of the gods. You'll save yourself for your husband or damn yourself, so you will.*

Eline, who had been very young then, hadn't really understood her words at the time. She only had one body, as far as she was concerned, and if she sold it where was she supposed to live?

Much later, after they had settled in Drathburg, she came to finally understand what Ma had meant. She saw the working girls, the scrubs standing on the street corners with their skirts hitched high and the glaze of the poppy in their eyes and she resolved that no, she would never do that.

But then of course she had met and married Caromir and that had ended how it had, and now it seemed she was going to have to do it anyway. She had saved herself for her husband, as Ma had wanted, and look how *that* had turned out.

Could this really be any worse?

'Why?'

'She's wanted for murder,' he said. 'She killed a man, after all.'

'I killed my *husband*, you fucking well know that,' Eline snapped. 'Now I get a job and she gets the end of a knife, how's that justice?'

'I'm not concerned with justice,' the fat man said with a cold smile. 'I am concerned with the law, and the will of the Crown. Different thing altogether.'

'How do you work that out?'

'You killed your husband, but I didn't care about him. Sounds like he needed killing, from what your neighbours have told my little birds, so no fucking loss there. Her though, she killed a duke. That . . . that I *do* have to care about. Dannsburg says so.'

Dannsburg.

Even the name of the capital city made Eline shiver in fear. Everyone knew about Dannsburg, or thought they did anyway.

'Why do *I* have to care?' Eline shot back. 'I'm not a murderess.'

'Overlooking the fact that you obviously *are*,' the fat man said, 'you'll hang if you refuse me. But maybe you don't care about that either, after what you did. There's your boy, though. Thirteen and a man grown, past his age of majority and signed up in the army like a good lad should be. He's in basic training right now, in fact. Dangerous, that is. Can be, anyway. A lot of lads have accidents in training. Fatal ones.'

Eline stared at him, and felt a sick knot clench in her stomach.

'How—'

'I'm a Queen's Man,' he said. 'Assume I know everything, and you'll never be caught in a lie. You don't want to lie to me, Eline.'

'No,' she admitted, defeated. Her precious boy. 'No, I won't lie to you.'

She had never lied to Caromir either, not about anything that mattered at least, which meant anything he might find out about. Little things – things he was too stupid to notice, like where those coppers had gone when she had needed them to buy needles and thread to mend her son's britches or buy her daughter the necessary things for her personal hygiene – yes. Those things she had lied about, and got away with. The thing about Eline was, she knew how far she could push her luck. With this man, she realised, that was not an inch. No, she was no fool and she knew *exactly* what sort of man she was looking at.

She nodded curtly.

'That's done then,' he said.

He gave her a piece of paper with an address written on it in an untidy scrawl. The stew where she was to work, and eventually kill. The House of Silver Bells, apparently. How charming.

He also passed her five silver marks, more money than she had ever had all of her own in her entire life. Caromir's army pension had been two marks a month, and she had seen precious little of that. Barely enough to feed them and her beloved children, in truth. Although when he came home stinking drunk on a Coinsday night and passed out in their bed she was quick enough to sweep up and hide whatever coin he had left, if any. Come Godsday morning she knew he would never remember how much he had drunk and how much he had spent the night before, so what matter if some of it went missing? He was never going to suspect and that was a big part of how she kept their poverty-stricken household together. Times were hard, and a wife had to do what was necessary to keep body and soul together for her family.

'First month's pay,' he said. 'You work for me now.'

Eline took the money and tucked it away in her pouch. She would not, it seemed, hang at dawn as she had expected when she had been arrested. She took a breath and prepared herself for her new life as a whore, and as a killer for the Queen's Men.

She would protect her son, whatever it took. Nothing else mattered. She was a mother, after all. Keeping her children safe was what she was *for*. At any cost, and fuck the consequences. Her own mother had moved heaven and earth for her, and she would never forget that.

She was allowed to leave after that, to return home in the gathering dusk, although the house she had shared with Caromir no longer felt like a home to her. It hadn't for a long time, in truth. After years of abuse in that house, of course it didn't. She realised now as she let herself in that it had become only the place where she had murdered her husband.

Eline started to shake then, and had to sit down quickly. She leaned forward and pressed her face to the kitchen table as the tremors overcame her.

She had killed Caromir. Earlier, after her early morning flight from the house and eventual arrest and everything that had come after it, she didn't think that had really sunk in until now. Arrested for murder.

I killed a man, she thought. *I took a life.*

It had been a long, long time since she had loved Caromir, if she ever really had, but *this*? Her vision was blurred, her hands shaking uncontrollably.

I killed a man.

She felt a bead of sweat break from her hairline and run down her face as she shook and shuddered at the table. To kill was something outside of her experience, until that morning. To take up a knife and ram it into a man's neck, whoever he had been and whatever he had done to her, was just not something she did or had ever done before. She wondered how soldiers could do it over and over, how anyone could harden their hearts to stick a length of sharpened metal into a stranger's guts and take their life away. At least she had had a reason, but them? She had no idea. And that was to be her son's future?

I'm not a murderess.

You obviously are.

A sob escaped her. Not for Caromir, perhaps, but for what she had done. Had she damned herself, in the eyes of the gods? Eline wasn't overly religious, but *murder*? She had committed murder, right there in that very room. The Guard had at least taken the body away and cleaned up the worst of the blood; she supposed that was something. One less chore for her to do. She had been forever clearing up behind Caromir, but cleaning a murder scene was somewhat beyond her experience.

A murder scene, that was what it was.

I killed a man.

She sucked in a breath, feeling as though her throat was closing up, feeling like there wasn't enough air in the room. She lurched to her feet and hurled herself out of the back door and into the small yard behind the house where the shithouse was, sure she was about to vomit. The shithouse and its cesspit was shared by the four houses in her row, and Jottie was just coming out of it.

'Why the fuck aren't you in gaol?' her shrew of a neighbour demanded, going wide-eyed with surprise.

Eline's nausea turned to anger all at once as she glared at the other woman and took a step towards her.

'They let me go,' she said. 'It was self-defence, which is something you need to learn right now, you *rat*.'

Her blow was so quick Jottie didn't have time to react, and Eline's fist cracked into her jaw and sent the other woman sprawling in the dirt. Eline stood over her, shaking again and trying not to cry. Yes, they had minded each other's children. Yes, she had counted the woman something along the lines of a friend, but friends didn't snitch to the *fucking* Guard.

She cradled her throbbing fist in her other hand and fought back the urge to start kicking. The need to hurt was almost overwhelming. The need to hurt someone else, *anyone* else, to take her own pain away.

What the fuck is wrong with me?

I killed a man.

You obviously are.

Eline fought it down. She'd had disagreements with some of the other children a time or two back on the wagons, physical ones, but her mother had taught her when to walk away from a fight.

If they're on the floor, you're done, her mother had told her. *Time to leave it there, Eline.*

'You fucking bitch,' Jottie spat as she got to her feet, rubbing her jaw. 'I wasn't to know, was I? Lots of husbands have heavy hands, I didn't know he was trying to fucking *kill* you.'

That was just the story the fat man had given her, of course, but Eline realised then that Caromir had been killing her for years. It *had* been self-defence, in a way. No wife should have to put up with what she had been through. All the same, she had taken a human life and that wasn't an easy thing to make your peace with.

Especially now she was expected to do it again.

Chapter 2

A messenger came to the house at dawn and rapped on the door while Eline was lighting the fire in the kitchen hearth. There had been a little bacon left in the meat safe, put aside for Caromir's breakfast. Normally she would have contented herself with bread with a smear of butter and a little sage, but he was gone now, and it would have been a shame to waste it.

Oh yes, he was gone now.

She had spent an uneasy night alone in their bed, part missing the warmth of his body but mostly grateful for the absence of his rough hands, his slurred speech, his endless drunken snoring. She would take cold blankets over those things any night of the week, but all the same she had found sleep hard to reach.

I killed a man.

In the cold light of the next day she still couldn't fully believe it had happened, or that she had been arrested for murder and then taken away by a Queen's Man who apparently had a job for her in exchange for her life. For her *son's* life. To whore herself and shame her mother's name, and to kill again. The thought was so abhorrent that Eline had to admit had it only been her own life at stake she would probably have chosen the gallows and been done with it, but her son?

I murdered my husband.

Her two children were the only good things to have come out of her miserable marriage. She couldn't, she *would not*, endanger them. As a mother her focus, her purpose, her whole reason for existing, was to protect her children. That was what she was *for.*

If that meant working for the Queen's Men then so be it.

She looked at the raw bacon and the still-cold pan and sighed, and went to open the door.

9

There was a woman there, little more than a girl really, with perhaps eighteen or nineteen years to her, but she wore the bawd's knot on her left shoulder bold as brass. The intricately tied yellow cord stood out against her otherwise demure grey kirtle, fit to tell the whole world who and what she was. A whore, and not just some common street scrub. The bawd's knot was granted by city ordinance and that meant she was licensed, and at least in theory clean and better trained than some back-alley tart. She was dark-skinned and dark-haired and dark-eyed, and those things indicated she was Alarian.

Alaria was away across the seas to the east, Eline knew that, where the precious silk and tea and the forbidden poppy resin came from. Silk and tea were expensive and poppy resin illegal and worth even more than tea was. Merchants who sailed the Tea Winds made good coin indeed, and in the process had brought thousands of Alarian immigrants into the country over the previous fifty or so years. The Poppy Winds, those were called by many, and that meant something else entirely. The same trade routes, yes, but different cargoes, different destinations. Poppy resin was a major problem in the cities. It had followed the soldiers home from their wars, where it had been used to relieve the pain of the grievously wounded. Then men had realised that smoking poppy resin when you weren't half dead from wounds made you feel good. Eventually they discovered that once you start smoking poppy resin, you can't stop.

Then there had been trouble, but that was no fault of this girl's.

Many immigrants were second or even third generation now, as this one perhaps was, born here and knowing little to nothing of their own land. Some had done very well for themselves, others less so. It seemed this girl had fared less well than others, if she wore the knot.

'You're Eline,' the girl said, and it wasn't a question. 'He sent me. You'll let me in, if you're wise.'

Eline just nodded and stood aside to let the girl into her house.

'Aye,' she said, for want of anything better.

'I'm Nama,' the girl said as the door shut behind her. 'I work for the madam. At the Silver Bells, where you're to work.'

'And you also work for *him*, obviously,' Eline said. 'As apparently I do too, now. Do you know who he is?'

'Not rightly, no,' Nama admitted. 'An important man, though. A man with money. Sometimes he pays me to do things that don't involve lying on my back or sucking cocks, and I'm all in favour of that. Easier money than whoring, innit? Today he paid me to bring you this, and teach you how to tie it.'

She reached into her pouch, pulled out a length of stout yellow cord and passed it to Eline.

'For the bawd's knot,' Eline said.

'Aye,' Nama agreed. 'We all wear the knot, at the house. Madame doesn't take on anyone unlicensed. Here, there's this too. Paperwork that says you're licensed.'

She handed Eline a folded paper sealed with an ornate sigil impressed into red wax, the mark of the city council of Drathburg. It seemed the fat man hadn't been misleading her about the quality of his forger.

'Thank you,' Eline said, as she took the paperwork and tucked it carefully into her pouch.

'You ain't though, are you?'

Eline blinked at the girl and wondered briefly how she could plausibly deny it before she realised that she simply couldn't. More to the point she wondered how much she could trust her, then decided she would just have to, to an extent at least. She didn't have anybody else, after all.

'Not as such, no,' she confessed. 'I've been married though, I'll get by.'

'You know how to fuck, is that what you're saying?' Nama said, and laughed. 'There's more to it than that, lady. You've got to make them feel special. Got to make them believe you enjoyed it, even though you didn't, and did you ever bother with that with your husband?'

Eline smiled, and found herself warming to the Alarian girl.

'Not as such,' she said again, and this time they laughed together. 'I've got a bit of bacon ready to go on, if you're hungry. Not a lot, but I'll share if you want some.'

It was still very early, after all, and she couldn't imagine the girl had breakfasted yet.

'Kind of you,' Nama said, and followed her into the kitchen.

Eline put the pan over the fire with a knob of butter in and pushed the bacon about with a wooden spoon until it started to sizzle. They would be working together, she had realised, and she thought it would be no bad thing to have a friend in the house. Especially if she could establish herself early as the older woman and therefore the senior partner in their friendship, if not their profession. Always be the older and wiser woman and that would serve you well. It was always good to have a friend, she knew that from experience. Especially a younger one who maybe looked up to you. There had been Nettie at the market, the fishmonger's daughter, who Eline had befriended. Her fish had then been that little bit cheaper than everyone else's, and even a little bit made a difference when the purse strings were as tight as hers had always had to be. Nettie had been a good girl, but then Nettie had died in childbirth with her first baby and that had been the end of their friendship and of cheap fish. Such was the world, in those days.

'There's bread on the side and platters in the cupboard,' she said. 'Off you go.'

It was like she was talking to her own daughter, before she had left home and gone to make her own way in the world in service. Nama just nodded and went to cut the bread, which was in all honesty a bit stale by now but not mouldy yet, and Eline knew it would probably be all right with the bacon fat on it to soften it up.

'You've been married, you said,' Nama said. 'What happened?'

'He died,' Eline said shortly, and that gave her pause. Aye, he had died, that was truth enough. She remembered her knife plunging into his neck, the fountain of blood. She forced her hands not to start shaking. 'I'm a widow now, with a need to make my way in the world. Our friend got me a job, that's all.'

'Aye, we've all that need,' Nama agreed. 'You miss him?'

'No,' Eline said shortly, and the Alarian girl laughed.

'I've heard that one before, from some of the others,' she said. 'Might be you will, once you've been working a few months.'

'I very much doubt it,' Eline said, and something in her voice made Nama look at her.

'He wasn't good to you, then?'

'No.'

She snorted back snot and left it at that, still trying to stop her hand from shaking as she turned the bacon over.

'Right, right,' Nama said. 'I've heard that before, too. Married life ain't always what it's cracked up to be, is it?'

'No,' Eline said again, desperately looking for a way to change the subject. 'How's the whoring life?'

'Shit,' Nama snapped at her. 'But then you'd know that if you were licensed and experienced like your papers say you are, wouldn't you?'

Eline sighed. She supposed she would, at that.

'Nama, look . . .'

'I know,' the girl interrupted. 'It's a put-up job. Something *he's* cooked up, for whatever reason. I know how he is. Thinks he's clever but he ain't really, not without direct orders anyway. You do realise you'll actually have to do it, don't you? This isn't a mummers' show or however he's sold it to you. Fuck knows why he wants you in that house and I know you won't tell me, but whatever it is you'll actually be whoring yourself like the rest of us. You ain't no better than we are, whatever he's told you.'

'I know,' Eline said, but all the same she wondered.

Not without direct orders. From who, exactly? From Dannsburg, she thought with a shudder. Did she really understand who she was working for here? A Queen's Man, yes, but by the sounds of it a fairly junior one, in however they ranked seniority. She had no idea, but then no one knew how the Queen's Men worked. They didn't even officially exist, for the love of the gods, although of course everyone knew that they very much did. There was a children's rhyme she remembered from when she was a girl, one her own son had used to torment his little sister:

Here comes the boggart to snip off your head,
Here comes a Queen's Man,
And you're better off dead.

The boggart wasn't real, of course, just a monster from folklore and children's stories, but the Queen's Men very much were. They were untouchable. Above the law. The word of a Queen's Man was a direct order from the Crown itself, for all that they didn't even have a queen anymore and hadn't done for almost two years now. It had come to the point where it simply didn't matter. Authority was what it was, and with that warrant backed by the might of the City Guard and even the army if it came to it, who was to argue with them?

'Bacon's done,' she said, wanting to think about anything other than the Queen's Men.

Nama put platters of lightly buttered bread down on the table, smeared with what little there had been left, and Eline shared out the meagre portion of bacon between them. Nama took hers up gratefully and took a bite.

'Thank you,' she said, and she sounded like she meant it. 'Madame does actually feed us well in truth, but I had to be up early to run this bloody errand, so I missed breakfast.'

'Sorry there's no small beer,' Eline said, eyeing the empty short barrel on its stand beside the back door. 'Caromir, well—'

'Drank it all,' Nama finished for her. 'Oh aye, I've heard *that* more times than I can count. You know what, I think you'll actually be better off at the Silver Bells than it sounds like you were here with him.'

Eline looked around her small, dirty, kitchen, and winced as a rat scurried out of a hole behind the cupboard and through into the cold parlour where she seldom went for lack of fuel for the fireplace. Nama tracked it with her gaze, but said nothing.

'I think I agree,' she said.

After breakfast she left Caromir's house with Nama and together they made their way to the House of Silver Bells. She had with her a leather travelling bag containing her worldly possessions: three kirtles and a spare cloak, all the smallclothes she had, a few pots of carefully rationed paints and powders for her face, a little wooden carving of a cat that her father had made for her when she had been a girl, the things she needed for personal hygiene and the knife she had killed her husband with. She didn't really own anything else except her kitchen pots and pans, and she knew she wouldn't be needing those again. She doubted she would ever be going back to Caromir's house. Fuck it, she would just let the lease lapse. It really didn't matter now.

He wasn't there any more, after all.

I killed a man. I took a life.

I murdered my husband.

Nama had shown her how to tie the knot on her shoulder and now they both wore them boldly as they made their way through the crowds of early morning Drathburg traffic. They had to stop once for a column of geese being carefully marched to market, and again for a herd of sheep harried along by the shepherd's dogs and boys. There was no trouble, and they received no abuse from anyone.

In Drathburg, and no doubt anywhere else in the country, that knot meant they worked for someone who mattered. Someone who would ruin your life if you hurt one of their girls. It was, she had to admit, one of the safest disguises there was.

If only a disguise was *all* it was. But it wasn't, Eline knew that. She was doing this for real. She tried to think what it would be like, to lie with a stranger for coin, and soon came to the realisation that it couldn't possibly be worse than lying with Caromir for free had been, or more likely for yet another fucking beating when he couldn't perform the act. Perhaps things were looking up after all.

14

Chapter 3

The house Nama led her to was impressive, large and set back from the road with walls around it and guards on the gate. Big men, those, tough-looking, and visibly armed. It was the sort of house the rich folks lived in up in the north quarter of the city, far away from Eline's neighbourhood of itinerant workers, poor Alarian immigrants and broken-down retired soldiers.

Like Caromir had been.

They were the lords and ladies with a 'Lan' in their name, their houses places Eline had only ever seen from the street. She had certainly never been inside one. People like her only went into houses like that if they managed to get a job as a servant, and even that had been beyond her reach.

Nama walked up to that gate bold as brass and showed the guards her dazzling smile. They obviously knew her by sight, but looked a question at her as they saw Eline at her side.

'All right, Nama?' one of them said, one with the look of the boss of them about him. 'And who's this then?'

'My friend Eline,' Nama said. 'She's licensed, and looking for work. Thought I'd introduce her to Madame, see what's going.'

The guard's gaze lingered briefly on the knot on Eline's shoulder, longer on her chest.

'Aye well, she's come to the right place,' he allowed after a moment. 'We'll let her in then, won't we, lads?'

'Fucking right,' one of the others said, and grabbed his crotch in a way that made Eline feel a bit sick.

Perhaps things weren't looking up quite as much as she had hoped.

All the same they opened the gates, and Nama led her quickly past the leering guardsmen and up the sweeping gravel path that led to the front door.

'Don't mind them,' she said, once they were safely out of earshot. 'Madame would have any guard who touched one of us without paying skinned alive, and yes I do actually mean that literally.'

'Um,' Eline said, wondering whether that was reassuring or not. 'I see.'

Nama snorted. 'No, you don't,' she said, and that was *definitely* not reassuring.

She put a hand on Eline's shoulder to halt her before they reached the front door, and spoke quietly.

'There's Marcoss. He does that sort of thing for her, believe you me. Right, it's like this,' she said. 'You're my mate from drinking together in the Grey Rat in our off hours. It's a tavern a few streets away. You used to work at the Golden Petal before it burned down. Their madam and most of the staff and girls died in the fire and the others have legged it out of the city, so there's no one to say otherwise. You weren't there that night, off visiting your sick mother, so you survived what happened. You've been grieving for your dead friends, but now your money's run out and you need to work again. You understand me?'

Eline nodded. It was probably as good a cover story as she was going to get, she supposed. She wondered if it was the fat man's invention, or Nama's own. There was one thing, though.

'Why did the Golden Petal burn down?'

'Why does anything in this city burn down?' Nama countered. 'Some cunt set fire to it. Don't know who, no one does. Don't worry about that. Madame will buy it.'

Eline gave her a look.

'She'd better,' she said, 'or by the sounds of it this Marcoss will have *both* our skins off.'

'Fucking right he will,' Nama said, 'so don't you dare fuck this up. The fat bloke doesn't pay me *that* much.'

Eline nodded.

'Let's do this then.'

Nama gave her a short nod and opened the front door.

Eline started as she found herself suddenly staring at a loaded crossbow that was pointed right at her.

'Who are you?' the man behind it asked.

'Fuck's sake, Loran, she's my mate,' Nama said. 'Gorath on the gate let us in, so what's your problem? She's looking for work, that's all. I'm introducing her to Madame.'

16

'No you ain't,' Loran said, and his crossbow never wavered. 'Not until Marcoss has checked her over.'

This Loran, it occurred to Eline then, was obviously junior to Gorath on the gate. He might be trusted with the front door but Gorath clearly had the authority to make decisions for himself where it seemed Loran hadn't. There was a definite hierarchy here, and she knew it would serve her well to understand it, and fast. She understood hierarchy from the wagons, and how the menfolk and the matriarchs had had their orders of deference and respect. She could see that this was going to be no different.

'She's my mate,' Nama protested again, but the man shook his head.

'No one sees Madame until Marcoss says its safe. You fucking well know that, you silly tart. You think anyone trusts *your* word?'

The look on Nama's face said that she had thought they did, actually, but there was nothing to be done about that.

'Who's Marcoss?' Eline asked, to break the tension as much as anything.

She had never been there before, after all, and some natural curiosity was only to be expected. So she hoped, anyway.

'The captain of Madame's household guard,' Nama said. 'You'll show him some respect if you're wise.'

'Heed that advice, lass,' said Loran, for all that he was probably younger than Eline. 'He's a nasty bastard when he wants to be.'

Boss of the pair of them, then, Eline thought. It sounded like this Marcoss was a man she would have to watch carefully, if she was to hope to succeed here. Or even survive.

'I'm sure he is,' Eline said quietly.

'You'll wait here,' Loran said.

He shifted one hand off the crossbow and put two fingers to his mouth, but still the weapon didn't waver from its steady aim. He whistled a piercing note, and a moment later yet another armed thug came out of a side room and looked a question at him. He really was young, this one, but already his face bore the scars of hard-won fights.

It's expensive and guarded by as many thugs as I've got guardsmen, just about.

Eline was starting to see the truth of that, and already she found herself wondering why. She knew little of whorehouses, but all the same this seemed an excessive amount of security for what was basically just a stew, however exclusive it was.

One frequented by dukes, apparently, she thought, and perhaps that explained it.

Perhaps.

All the same, she wasn't convinced. There was something else, something she wasn't quite grasping . . .

'New tart wanting to see Madame,' Loran said. 'Go fetch the guv'nor, will you?'

'Aye, boss,' the new arrival said, and marched off like a soldier who had just received orders from his general.

He's no one, then. Just a grunt.

'Do we really have to?' Nama protested. 'I've known her for fucking years, Loran.'

'Oh aye, where from?'

'The Rat, mostly,' Nama said. 'She used to work at the Petal, you know?'

'Horseshit, she's alive. Can't have done.'

'They weren't *all* there, that night,' she protested. 'Why does no cunt in this place ever believe a word I say?'

'Because you talk a lot of shit, by and large,' a new voice said, and Eline looked up to see an older man coming down the stairs.

He was grey-haired and broad-shouldered and his posture and his stride said *veteran* as loud as if he had been shouting it. He was well dressed, in a fine coat and doublet and britches, but he had a short sword at his left hip and a dagger at his right and the look in his eyes was hard and sharp as flint.

Nama bobbed a short curtsey, and after a moment Eline realised she was supposed to do the same, so she did.

'Marcoss,' the Alarian girl said. 'This is my friend Eline, late of the Petal. She's licensed and looking for work, so I said I'd introduce her to Madame. Get her a job and that.'

'Oh, did you now?' Marcoss said, giving Eline a long look. 'That ain't fucking up to you, is it?'

'No, Marcoss,' Nama said quietly, and there was something in her voice, something cowed, something *owned*, that made Eline's skin rise in goosebumps.

No, Caromir. How many times, how many *fucking* times had she said that, to try to stave off the anger, the blows, the beating that was sure to follow?

I killed a man.

He fucking deserved it, a part of her said. Eline swallowed, not sure how much she believed that. He had been awful to her, yes, but had he deserved to *die*? And at her own hand, at that? Perhaps he had, but she still wasn't at all easy with what she had done.

She forced down a shuddering breath and clenched her hands together in front of her to keep them from shaking.

'Please,' she made herself say, hating the tone of supplication in her voice. 'How do I get to see Madame?'

Marcoss gave her another look.

'First you put the fucking bag down,' he said, and Eline dropped it to the floor at her feet at once, horribly aware of the kitchen knife hidden in there, wrapped up in her spare cloak. 'Then I search you.'

'There's no need for—' Nama started, but he silenced her with a glare.

'It's all right,' Eline said, before he had the chance to start on the younger woman. 'Do what he says.'

Establish yourself, Eline, she told herself. If she was really to be the senior partner between them, and she meant to be, she needed Nama doing what she said and right now. This was Nettie at the market all over again, and Eline knew that what had worked once would work again. Make friends, be accommodating, but always be in charge. That was the way it was done.

I need to keep her safe too, Eline realised, although she wasn't quite sure why. The girl was a professional and clearly had some connection to the Queen's Men, so surely she could look after herself. But she was barely four or five years older than her own daughter and it just felt . . . right. Like something she should do.

She knew men like Marcoss. He reminded her far too much of Caromir. Oh, he had heavy hands this one, she could tell, but according to the fat man, the House of Silver Bells was famously expensive, and who would pay silver for a bruised and battered woman? She had no doubt he was a violent man, but she very much doubted he was allowed to hit Madame's *merchandise*. From what Nama had told her, Eline suspected that wouldn't be good for his health.

Not at all it wouldn't. He might well be a nasty bastard, but she was already forming the opinion that Madame herself would be worse.

Much, much worse.

Hierarchy, always, and there was oh so often a matriarch at the top of it. That had been the way of the wagons, at least; for all the men's swagger

19

and bravado, they had all respected and perhaps feared the grandmothers who basically ran their entire culture.

All the same Marcoss searched her, and his hands lingered too long in places where they weren't welcome, roaming up her thighs under her kirtle and around her smallclothes. She was unarmed, of course, apart from the kitchen knife hidden in her bag, and eventually he was satisfied of that fact.

'So you're licensed then, you say?' he asked when he was finally satisfied. 'Can you prove it? Any scrub can buy a length of yellow cord.'

'I'm licensed,' Eline said, and fished the sealed paperwork out of her pouch to offer to him.

He gave it a brief glance and cleared his throat.

'That's for Madame to decide,' he said, and Eline realised he probably couldn't read.

A lot of people couldn't. Caromir had learned in the army and that let him read the news sheets, and by the gods she wished he hadn't. In truth she only could herself because her mother had taught her to read her herbalism books when she had been a girl with the travelling wagons, before economic necessity had driven them to settle in a city. In Drathburg. Before she had met Caromir, and effectively thrown her life away.

No, not thrown it away, she told herself. Without Caromir she wouldn't have had her children, after all.

I killed a man.

Aye, she had done that, but she had borne two beautiful children too. She supposed some prices were perhaps worth paying. For a while, anyway.

'So, I can see her then?' she ventured.

Marcoss gave her another long look.

'Aye, I reckon. You're a bit too fucking old for a working girl but we'll see what she says. Come with me. You, fuck off to your room and earn some fucking money. There's punters coming later so go and make yourself presentable.'

'Yes, Marcoss,' Nama said, but she gave Eline a conspiratorial wink before she turned and headed up the staircase.

There at least, Eline thought, she was already making progress. Always cultivate someone, always make an ally and preferably a subordinate one. That maxim had served her well among the wagons, and even better in the slums. Here, in this strange new environment she knew next to nothing about, she thought it would serve her better than ever.

This was about survival now, and if there was one thing Eline knew well how to do it was *survive*.

Eline in her turn followed the guard captain down the hall and deeper into the house, until they reached a door right at the rear of the large building. He turned and treated her to another glare.

'You be fucking respectful now,' he said. 'Madame is one of the richest women in this miserable city, and she don't owe you nothing. If you want a job here, a roof over your head and the chance to earn food in your belly you'll fucking well work for it, you understand me?'

'Yes, Marcoss,' she said quietly, and wondered if in the fullness of time the fat man would allow her to kill him too.

She hated the idea of killing again, but Caromir had proven to her that she could do it once and to her mind that meant she could probably do it again, given reason enough. This woman who called herself Madame had done nothing to her and that might be different, but Marcoss? She saw enough of Caromir in him that she was already wondering how it would feel to ram her knife through *his* neck.

What in the names of the gods is wrong with me?

Her hands were shaking again, and once more she clasped them demurely together in front of her kirtle to hide it. Normal people just didn't have fantasies about killing other folk they had only just met, did they? He might have a family, for all she knew. He might be a loving husband, might have children of his own even. What gave her the right to want to kill him?

I killed my husband.

She looked out of the corner of her eye at Marcoss as he raised a hand and knocked on the door. Aye, he might well be a loving husband and father.

But she fucking doubted it.

Chapter 4

'Come,' the voice snapped from within the room, and Marcoss turned the handle and opened the door.

He strode into a well-appointed study with Eline following in his wake, and offered a bow to the woman seated behind the wide oak desk where two more thugs stood guard behind her.

She was in her late middle years, pale-skinned and dark-haired and wearing an obviously expensive dress of crushed and ruffled red silk, with a generous display of ample if somewhat crinkled cleavage. Her black hair was voluminous and pinned up at the sides to make it cascade down her back in thick waves, and there was a great deal of paint and powder on her face that did less than she probably thought to disguise her at least fifty years.

'Marcoss,' she stated, rather unnecessarily in Eline's opinion. 'And a whore. Who are you? You're not one of mine.'

'No, ma'am,' Eline said, and dipped her a small curtsey. 'My name is Eline. I was at the Golden Petal. I'm friends with Nama, from the Rat. After what happened . . . I didn't work for a while. Now I need to, for the coin. Nama brought me here; she said there might be a place going for me?'

Madame looked a question at Marcoss.

'She wears the knot and she's got papers,' he said. 'Nama vouches for her, for what that's worth.'

'That's not worth the steam off my piss and you know it,' Madame snapped at him. 'Girl, show me these papers of yours.'

Eline met the woman's eyes for a moment, hard as nails, and shakily opened her pouch. If Madame saw through the fat man's falsehood she doubted she would be leaving this house alive. There was something about this place, something far more sinister than any normal stew. Yes, there was a probably a lot of money involved, but even so she couldn't shake the feeling that anywhere this heavily guarded was more than it seemed at first look.

Her heart almost stopped as the Madame broke the intricate seal of her papers with a long, lacquered thumbnail and slowly read whatever was inside, but it seemed the fat man's forgery passed muster. After a while she smiled in a way that reminded Eline of a predatory cat, got to her feet and came around the desk to stand in front of Eline as though to inspect her more closely.

'Well, dear, your paperwork seems to be in order and you do wear the knot, as I should hope, but aren't you a little old for a working whore?'

Eline flushed slightly, not least because she knew it was true.

'I'm still comely enough,' she said, hating the defensive tone in her voice. 'I . . . I need the money, ma'am.'

Madame, who had fifteen years on her at least if not twenty, showed her a sad smile as though addressing a simpleton.

'For now you are comely enough, yes. But in another five years' time? In ten? Oh dear me, no. And yet . . .'

'And yet?' Eline prompted, when this woman she had sworn to murder fell silent.

'Look to your left,' the woman said.

Eline blinked in surprise, but turned her head to do as she was told. The woman's fingers grasped her chin with unexpected speed, and slowly turned her head the other way, examining her like a wealthy gentleman of learning might examine an interesting specimen under the brass microscope in his study.

'Hmmm,' she said. 'What do you think, Marcoss?'

Her captain of the guard regarded Eline for far too long, in a way that made her feel he was undressing her with his eyes.

I am to be a whore for the Queen's Men, she reminded herself. *I suppose I have to learn to put up with this sort of thing, to protect my son.*

Whatever it takes.

Anything to protect her son, that was all that mattered. She knew she had to remember that, keep it at the front of her mind. Nothing else mattered. Not her, not what was left of her dignity, *nothing.*

His life before mine, she told herself.

A mother's duty, after all.

'I'd do her,' he said, and Eline felt a little bit sick at the prospect.

'You absolutely would not,' Madame said, as a slow smile started to spread across her face. 'I intend to make sure that you couldn't possibly afford to, not on what I pay you, and I pay you extremely well. Eline, my dear, do you know what a courtesan is?'

'A posh whore, I'd always thought,' Eline said. 'An expensive one, anyway.'

Madame laughed.

'Oh, how the streets speak truth to the euphemisms of society,' she said. 'You are not entirely wrong, of course, but there is much more to it than that. So much more. Some courtesans never even need to sleep with their patrons. Find the right sort of gentleman, perhaps one who is too elderly to be capable or one who doesn't like women in that way but doesn't want the fact widely known, and you've won the game.'

'I don't . . . then what's the point?' Eline faltered.

'My dear, at society occasions it is convention that gentlemen and ladies come in pairs. It is well known that many gentlemen are widowers, for the birthing bed is not kind. So, too, are many ladies widows, for the battlefield can be even less so. Sometimes they make accord between them, but family rivalries being what they are in society, often not. Then of course as I have said there are men who don't care for female company in that way at all, and probably as many ladies who feel the same way about men. But in society, gentlemen and ladies *always* come in pairs. Anything else could cause a scandal, and few in this world can afford scandal in their lives. That is where the courtesan comes in, and I suppose her male counterpart, although I will allow I know little enough of that side of the business.'

'So . . .' Eline faltered, 'so I don't have to be a whore after all?'

Madame laughed again.

'You have the cheekbones of a duchess, common though I know you to be,' she said. 'You are too old to be a viable whore for more than a year or two longer, and Nama bloody well knows that, but no duke or general can expect to be taken seriously with a slip of a twenty year old on his arm. No, they want to rent a woman of distinction, an actual adult and one with at least the vague plausibility of aristocracy about them. I think I can make a courtesan out of you, my dear, given time.'

She thought about it for a moment, and the implications of it. 'Oh, thank the gods.'

'Thank no one yet, girl,' Madame said. 'Yes, yes there is a place for you here, but you are *common*. Most whores are, after all. We need to work to hide that. You will need to learn society etiquette, elocution, deportment, dining, manners, dance, music, the language of fans and so much more. All these things I can teach you, but it will take months and no one dines for free under my roof. In the intervening time while you are still just about saleable you will whore yourself *raw* for me to pay for this. Do we have a deal?'

Eline looked into Madame's pitiless stare, and realised she had no choice.

Anything at all to protect my son.

It couldn't be any worse than it had been with Caromir, could it?

'Deal,' she said.

It was worse than it had been with Caromir. Half the nights he had been incapable on account of the drink, and most of the rest of them he would spend down her leg before they even got that far. She was grateful for those nights, when he would roll off her and fall asleep almost instantly, and leave her to wash herself in peace. It was the nights he had been incapable that she feared the aftermath of, the making it her fault and the beating that would follow.

It was a miracle they had the two precious children that they did, but that too of course had been long, long ago.

These men now, these men who *rented* her, as Madame had phrased it, she regarded them how she had regarded Caromir in the last years of their marriage.

With disgust.

With rage.

With fear.

She was ashamed of the last, but she couldn't shake it. Her customers scared her, and there was no way around that. Aye, she had the odd beardless boy paid for by his friends to lose his virginity and become a man, and the occasional old fellow who just wanted to remember what a woman felt like, and she supposed they were harmless enough in their way and at least quick, but on the whole her customers were absolute bastards.

Callous men who treated her like a piece of equipment, like a *thing* they had rented for an hour or two to use as they willed, not any semblance of an actual person. At least there were no beatings, that was something. The house was very strict about that, and the one time a punter had raised his hand to her she'd only had to shout and Loran had burst through the door of the room where she worked and broken the man's head with a wooden club. He'd been thrown into the alley behind the house where the rats were the size of cats, and who knew what had happened to him? There, at least, the house looked after its girls.

Wouldn't want any damage to the fucking merchandise, *would they?*

Bitter though the thought was, she knew that was the truth of it. No, they would not. Madame was nothing if not protective of her girls, of her investment. Understanding, however?

No.

'A whore is not a person,' Madame had explained to her, the morning after the first time this happened. 'A whore is a whore. A disposable toy. A courtesan *is* a person, a treasured work of art and a status symbol in society. Now that you have finally made me some money, shall we begin your training?'

Eline stared at Madame, at the cold indifference in her eyes. She *was* a fucking person, whatever this ghastly harridan had to say about it, and so was Nama. She and the Alarian girl had been building a solid friendship over the last few days, albeit one built largely on shared experiences of misery and suffering.

'Yes please, ma'am,' Eline said.

Madame backhanded her across the face hard enough to knock her to the floor.

'What do you, a courtesan, do if a client does that to you?' she demanded, before Eline could speak.

'Report him to Marcoss and—' she started.

'Put another hundred marks on the bill, you stupid girl,' Madame spat at her. 'Gods, don't you know what a courtesan *costs*?'

Eline didn't, but she knew her father had been a master carpenter before he died and a month when he had brought home four silver marks had been a good month's pay indeed. Another *hundred marks*? On top of *how* much, exactly? For a hundred marks she could have sent her son to the university in Dannsburg for an entire term, and spared him the army and all its dangers and horrors.

Also, it occurred to her then, while customers might not be allowed to hit the girls it appeared that Madame very much was. This was Madame's realm, and here it seemed she could do anything she pleased.

Anything at all.

Oh yes, she was the matriarch here and there could be no doubt about that. Hers would have been the lead wagon in the convoy, had they been on the road together, and the most brightly painted. Eline had known women like her when she had been a child, and she had both respected and feared them.

Mostly feared, in all honesty, but she had only been a little girl then. Now she was a woman grown, and she thought that might be beginning to change.

'The house takes ninety percent, of course, for your board, lodging, training and introductions. You're hardly likely to arrange an assignation with a duke yourself, are you, dear?'

Eline knew she wasn't, but all the same she knew when she was being exploited. The house dealt in hundreds of marks, perhaps even *thousands*, and it took *ninety percent*?

That didn't seem fair, to her, but then little enough in life was. What had *fair* ever had to do with anything? Little enough, she knew that from bitter experience.

Life was not fair and it never had been, and that was the simple fact of the matter. Life on the road had not been fair. Life in the slums of Drathburg even less so, and she had learned from those things. She looked up at Madame from where she lay sprawled on the floor, and thought again of the day she could kill her. She had been dreading the task, but no longer. Now she found she was beginning to look forward to it.

'Get up,' Madame said to her.

Eline pulled herself to her feet, and Madame put a folded fan in her hand.

'Do you know anything of the language of fans?' Madame asked her.

'I . . . I don't think so,' Eline faltered, looking down at the finely crafted thing in her hand, a confection of bone spines and black silk. She had obviously never owned a lady's fan in her life, not on Caromir's money she hadn't.

'I don't *fink* so,' Madame mocked her. 'Your elocution is shocking, Eline. Put your tongue between your teeth and say *th*. We really do need to work on this. Now listen to me, and repeat my words very closely after me. And repeat them *properly*. You must learn to *enunciate*, girl. You are supposed to be a lady, not a guttersnipe. You must learn to speak like one, act like one, dance like one, threaten like one. It is all acting, dear, but you must learn to do it *properly*.'

Madame opened her fan and held it close beneath her chin, then snapped it shut very abruptly and rested it gently against her lips.

'I do not speak to you,' she said, and made Eline repeat it three times until she was satisfied with her enunciation.

She touched a closed fan to her right cheek and said 'Yes', and she was happy enough with Eline's response to that. Then to her left cheek and said 'No.'

'Now, like this,' Madame said, and slowly wafted her fan up and down before her in the gesture that said 'I do not care about you'.

She touched her finger to the tip of the closed fan in her hand and said, 'I wish to speak to you.'

Again, Eline mimicked her movements and repeated her words.

'Yes, hold it to your right cheek for assent,' Madame went on. 'You'll probably need that more than any other. And this, you may need someday. Not soon, perhaps, but someday.'

She held her closed fan in her right hand and drew it slowly and deliberately through her left.

'And what does that mean?' Eline asked.

'I am superior to you,' Madame said.

She nodded to acknowledge the other woman's acceptance of her teaching. If Eline was supposed to feel honoured then she didn't, but she *did* feel she had learned something that evening.

'One more message,' Madame said, 'and again you will repeat the words after me until you speak them clearly in an acceptable accent.'

She passed the fan to her left hand. Holding it near her left ear, she held Eline's eyes. 'I can destroy you,' she said.

Maybe, she thought then, training under Madame wouldn't be so awful after all.

Chapter 5

'Are you religious, girl?' Madame asked her on her sixth day of employ-ment at the House of Silver Bells, late on Coinsday afternoon.

It was the busiest night of the week at the Bells, or so Nama had told her. This would be her first Coinsday in the house. Madame had accosted Eline on her way into the common room and seized her by the elbow to ask her questions while her ever-present bodyguards waited in the shadows behind her. She looked at her employer, and swallowed as she realised Madame was still waiting for an answer, looking at her like she thought Eline might be some sort of simpleton.

'I hold little enough with gods and religion, I must admit,' Eline said, although she had a feeling this might not be the right answer to give. 'The Storm Lord rules the winds, but I'm not a sailor. The Forge Father is the Master Maker, but I'm not a smith or a carpenter or a seamstress. The Harvest Maiden brings in the crops, but I'm not a farmer. What are they to me? I suppose there's Our Lady of Eternal Sorrows, who all face in the end; She and Her Ascended Martyr cannot be denied, however much we may wish it otherwise. But why would anyone worship the Lady of Death before their time comes to stand before Her?'

'Exactly,' Madame said. 'However, we hold to the Harvest Maiden here at the Bells, girl. She may bring in the crops but She's also the goddess of fertil-ity and love and sex. The patron goddess of whores, in a way. We hold to Her as our goddess here, and you'll do the same if you know what's good for you.'

Eline bowed her head, and tried not to sigh.

Whatever it takes.

'Yes, ma'am,' she said.

'See that you're ready in the morning, then,' Madame said. 'We all go to temple together. This is not negotiable. Wear something demure, and no knot. We do not advertise what we are outside of the house, in general, and *definitely* not at temple.'

'Ma'am,' Eline said, and dipped her head.

What else could she do?

The next day would be Godsday, of course, the traditional sabbath and day of rest when the faithful visited the temples of the city to worship and say their confessions. In theory at least no one worked on Godsday, but when times were hard and folk had to work if they wanted to eat, well, most priests were prepared to overlook that. All the same, temple was broadly observed by those who could afford to take a day off, whichever of the numerous gods they held to. Many of the gods had their own temples around the city's more affluent districts, and of course Drathburg's Great Temple of All Gods had a shrine and a chapel for each of them, the same as every city did. The Church was nothing if not rich, after all.

So rich, when most of the city was so, so poor. Eline had a personal issue with that, but honestly what could she do about it?

She ate her dinner and was glad for it, stewed mutton and vegetable pottage that was hot and filling, then sighed and went up to her room to work.

Later, when it was mercifully over, she sought out Nama in her room.

The Silver Bells was finally closed for the night by then, and the girl was sitting on the end of her bed washing her paint and powder from her face before she retired for the night. Without it she looked ten years younger, if not more.

Barely older than my own daughter, Eline thought, and the thought was an uncomfortable one. She remembered when her daughter had become a woman, shortly after her twelfth birthday when her first bloods had come, and how Eline had suddenly had two women's hygiene things to provide for a month instead of just her own. That had meant even more work, but there was no way she could have told Caromir, of course, or even remotely expected him to understand if she had. He would probably have told the poor girl to do without.

Her life with Caromir, trying to raise their children on next to nothing, had taught her to be furtive indeed, and be quiet and nimble with her fingers. He had made her quite the thief, all things considered, if driven only by pure necessity.

I will provide for my children, whatever it takes.

That is what a mother is for. Gods, I really am too old to be here, she thought, although that didn't seem to put her clients off. Madame was right though, she couldn't have got away with this for many more years. Not that she wanted to, of course. Besides, she had a job to do.

A job of murder.

'Nama?' she asked, and peered through the half-open door before tapping on it. 'Can I talk to you?'

'Come in, Eline,' the younger woman said without looking up from her mirror of tarnished silver that stood propped up above her washstand. 'Of course you can. How was your night?'

'Shit,' Eline said shortly. 'You had the right assessment of the whoring life, I have to give you that.'

Nama snorted. 'I've been doing this a sight longer than you have, whatever your dodgy paperwork might have said. I know how it is.'

'Aye,' Eline had to allow. 'I had a right one tonight, some merchant from Kastavia. A rich man, obviously. I overcharged him, if I'm honest, but Marcoss gave me the nod that said I could do that. He paid all the same, tipped as well even, but . . .'

Overcharging paid her an extra percentage under the rules of the house, but she could only do that with Marcoss's say-so. How he knew who she could get away with it with and who she couldn't was a mystery to her, but the man had to have *some* use to him beyond looming and bossing the other guards around. It seemed that was one of them. He certainly had the shrewdness of a businessman about him, and the brutality too. There was something about Marcoss that gave her the creeping horrors, even if she couldn't have rightly said what.

'You don't have to tell me if you don't want to,' Nama said, when she fell silent. 'Sometimes we compare notes on clients, aye, but sometimes . . . sometimes you don't want to think about it. Sometimes you just want to forget it. I know. I get that. Did he hurt you?'

'Fuck no, or I'd have shouted for Loran and had his head kicked in,' Eline said. 'I'm not having that. Never again. Not . . . No, he didn't *hurt* me, as such, but . . .'

'Aye,' Nama said. 'Some things are worse, ain't they?'

'In a way,' Eline said, and she cringed a little at the memory of what the merchant had wanted her to do. What she had *done*, to help her pay for her future training. Still, that was a lot less coin she owed Madame, she supposed, and what had it truly cost her? Not pain, only dignity.

What dignity did I ever have?

She winced, and sat down uninvited on the edge of Nama's bed. A moment later she had her head in her hands, and she realised she was crying.

Nama had her arms around her a moment later, like a daughter comforting her grieving mother.

'Gods, what did he *do* to you?'

'Nothing,' Eline confessed around her snotty sniffles. 'It's what he wanted me to do to *him*. Seriously, Nama, what the fuck is *wrong* with men?'

'Only some men,' Nama said. 'You have to remember that, or you'll go mad. Most of them just like to fuck and have their cock sucked, and that's normal enough.'

'Aye, I suppose so,' she said. 'But he wanted me to . . .'

She started crying again.

Get a hold of yourself, woman, she shouted at herself in her mind. She had killed her husband. She had taken a life. What was pissing on a man's face, if that was what he wanted?

What was that, when that was what he was paying her for? He hadn't even fucked her, for the love of the gods, just taken his faceful of piss and made himself happy while she was doing it. On balance he had been easier than a normal punter, but . . . Aye, fucking *but*.

That wasn't something she'd ever thought she would find herself doing with a man, for coin or not. Whoring was definitely not how she had expected it to be. Caromir had been the only man she had ever lain down with in her life before this, and it seemed he had been relatively straightforward to please compared to some of her customers now. She'd had another who liked to call her 'Ma' while he sucked on her tits, and she really hadn't known what to do with that either except humour him and wait for it to be over. Which it had been, quite quickly. Easy money, aye, but at what cost?

She shuddered, and sniffed back the snot and tears of absolute misery. It couldn't be any worse than it had been with Caromir? Oh yes, yes it fucking well could and she was only now finding that out. The life of a whore was absolute shit, and she had to admit that Nama had had the right of that. At least it wasn't that anyone hurt her because they didn't or Loran would kick their head in, and fucking was just fucking, but it was everything *else*. It was the perversions. The degradation. The fact that she was just an object, a thing to be *rented*, to be *used*. She hated that more than she could put into words even in her own mind. Sex was just sex and no, that wasn't any worse than it had been with Caromir, but the rest of it?

A whore is not a person.

Yes I fucking well am!

She thought the trauma of killing Caromir had affected her more than perhaps she had expected it to.

Not that she'd *had* expectations, of course. It wasn't like she'd planned to kill him, it had just . . . happened. The knife, right there beside her. His raised hand. The flashing memories of all the other times it had happened, the other beatings, year after year of them, sparking in her memory like lightning on a dark night.

Frozen visions of suffering.

Staccato images, one after another after another. Time after time after time.

The sudden thought that it was fucking *enough.*

Her mother would have been appalled by this new life she was making for herself in the Silver Bells, by what she was doing. *The lowest form of degradation,* Ma would have reminded her, but what choice had she had? Caromir would have killed her in the end, she knew he would, and if she hadn't taken the fat man's offer she would have been hanged.

Sorry, Ma, she thought, *but when the alternative is being dead it doesn't look so bad, does it?*

I killed a man. I took a life.

She broke. All at once, she broke and it came spilling out of her.

'I murdered my husband!' she confessed, in a great sobbing rush.

'Aye,' Nama said, and left it at that.

'*Aye?* What the fuck does that mean, Nama?'

'Means I guessed, didn't I?' Nama said. 'You work for *him,* same as I do. He had to have something over you. That's how he does stuff. He's got something over all of us.'

'Oh aye? And what's he got over *you?*'

'That's my business, innit?' Nama said, but all the same she stroked Eline's hair as the older woman cried into her shoulder.

After a moment Eline felt wet drops falling into her hair, and she realised they were Nama's own tears.

That was how it was, in Drathburg in those days.

That Godsday morning found them all lined up in the common room dressed in their Godsday best, ready for temple. The common room was for the girls, and while it was clean it was plain, too, nothing like the

35

salon that was reserved for the punters. That was opulent as a palace, as might be expected for the prices the place charged. Madame was there at the head of the line, holding a small silver cup not much bigger than a thimble in one hand and an unlabelled black glass bottle in the other.

Eline watched in confusion as Madame poured from the bottle into the cup, and passed it to the first girl in line. She took it without question and drank it down, made a face and stepped aside while Madame poured again for the next girl, and so it went.

'The fuck's this?' Eline whispered to Nama who was stood just ahead of her.

'Medicine, every Godsday,' Nama said. 'Just drink it. It's vile, but Madame will raise the gods over it if you make a fuss.'

'Medicine? For what?'

'Stops us getting the pox, or in the family way. It's some sort of alchemy, apparently. Madame buys it at the market.'

Eline snorted. There were no alchemists in Drathburg that she knew of, so unless it was imported at great cost, which she fucking doubted, then that was a tiny little bit unlikely as far as she could see.

'You sure?'

'No. Just put your big girl drawers on and drink it, Eline.'

Eline sighed, but Nama did it and when her turn came she swallowed the stuff in her turn without complaint. It tasted somewhere between lamp oil and vomit, but she made herself choke it down and stepped aside to make way for the woman behind her.

Eventually they were done and finally in the temple of the Harvest Maiden, the goddess of farmers and family, love and sex and fertility who Madame held to. They were all there, from the lowest whore to the grandest courtesan, every woman who made her way under that roof and a good deal of the men, too. Madame's will was law in this, it seemed.

Madame herself wore a sombre black kirtle that morning, with a lot less cleavage on show than her normal attire afforded. She looked almost respectable, in fact, although she still wore far too much paint and powder to pass in public as anything but what she was. Perhaps she didn't realise, or didn't care, Eline really wouldn't know. Either way none of them wore the knot that morning, and she had seen Madame greet the priest with a warm familiarity as they filed obediently into the temple behind her.

The temple itself was small and on Spicer's Row not far from the house, not one of the chapels in the Great Temple of All Gods. It was bedecked with the idols of the Harvest Maiden, the icons of Her faith. There were the plentiful sheaves of wheat and bunches of grapes, obviously, but the rest were all carvings of the exaggerated genitalia of both sexes. Everything a whore did not need to see on her day off, to Eline's mind. Still, it seemed this really wasn't optional.

She leaned close to Nama and whispered in her ear.

'Bit creepy this, isn't it?'

Nama shrugged.

'Madame likes it,' she said. 'All this "holy sex" nonsense. I reckon she thinks she's some kind of vocational priestess, like.'

'But it's horseshit, isn't it?' Eline whispered.

'Of course it's horseshit,' Nama whispered back. 'Show me a fucking religion that isn't. Now shut up and try to look pious. An hour or so of this, two tops, and then we get Godsday lunch. Best meal of the week, that is. It's worth it, for that at least.'

Aye, perhaps it was. Eline hadn't had a proper Godsday lunch in a long time, not since she had left her mother's house to marry Caromir and discovered they had even less money to live on than her mother had. She found she was looking forward to it. She sat back against the hard wooden pew and let her eyes slowly close as she thought once again how she could kill the madam. Pious, yes. She supposed she could look pious when she had to. It was just another act, like everything else. But she thought that perhaps she would be pious before a different goddess than this, one more fitting to her new purpose than the Harvest Maiden.

In Our Lady's name.

Chapter 6

'Cor, look at him,' Nama said. 'Ain't he smashing?'

The two of them had gone out drinking together after Godsday lunch, making the most of their day off. Eline found she rather liked the Alarian girl, although the younger woman's taste in men was truly atrocious.

They were sitting at a table together in the Grey Rat where they had supposedly first met during Eline's entirely fictitious employment at the Golden Petal. It was a tavern a couple of streets away from the House of Silver Bells that was actually a lot nicer than the name made it sound, although it was on the edge of the rough part of town that bordered the street where the Bells stood. They weren't allowed to go far on their own, not without Madame's permission and a guard or two with them, but according to Nama the Rat was just about close enough to get away with.

Neither of them wore the bawd's knot on her shoulder now that they were away from the house. The knot attracted attention, of course it did, and that afternoon both of them just wanted to be left alone. Godsday, after temple anyway, gave them that. Eline flicked her hair back and chanced a look over her shoulder to see who Nama was talking about.

The young man was striking enough, she supposed, although he was far too young for her, but there was something strangely unpleasant about him all the same. He strongly resembled a rat himself, to Eline's mind. Too groomed, too sleek for these parts, hair all slicked back with oil and a silver chain across his doublet. He had money, that one, and on those streets that made him conspicuous. He was also obviously quite mad.

'They call me the Rat King,' he proclaimed to the group of young oiks who clustered around him at the bar like barnacles on the hull of one of the barges that sailed the city's river.

'Once I was but the twinkle in a cunning man's eye; a mad delusion some might call it, but it fucking worked. Aye, it fucking worked, my lovely boys. A few days in the alleys until I found a canny lad like one of you, then I fucking pounced! And now here I am, in beautiful Drathburg, and we start all over again.'

'The Rat King?' one of them scoffed, and Eline hid a smirk of her own as he downed his beer. 'You're fucking mental is what you are, mate. Cunning man? You pounced? Aye course you fucking did, and I'm the captain of the City Guard. What the fuck are you on about, you halfwit? And I'm not calling you that. What's your proper name, you fucking ponce?'

'Aye well,' said the sleek young man, 'I reckon a canny lad like you can call me Kurt. And he can show me some fucking respect, too.'

'Kurt, aye? And why should we listen to you, on my streets? You ain't right in the head, are you?'

'Well, it's like this, my boy,' the oily lad said, and he drew the other one into a conspiratorial hug that wasn't reciprocated. 'Last time around I was interested in helping not hurting, but then I met my god. This time, well. This time I think it's fair to say that I fucking well ain't.'

'Who *is* that?' Nama whispered across the table.

Eline just shrugged.

'Some prick,' she said. 'I don't know. He sounds like he's mad, to me. Met his god? Did he fuck, as like. No one's ever done that, not since the Time of Saints anyway, and even the Temple ain't too clear on whether that's actually true or not, or if it ever even really happened. And you need to have a word with yourself about your taste in blokes.'

'Aye, that's as maybe, but *look* at him,' Nama said. 'There's something about him, like. He *shines*.'

Eline blinked at her.

'What?'

'Can't you see it?' Nama asked. 'He's shining!'

'He's oily, I'll give you that,' Eline said. 'Beyond that, I've no idea what the fuck you're talking about.'

'He . . . some people just do, you know what I mean? Shine, that is. I ain't never met anyone else who can see it. Maybe *I'm* a bit mad, I don't know. Sometimes – not often, mind, but *sometimes* – I see someone in a crowd or whatever and they . . . they just shine. I don't know how to explain it.'

Eline cleared her throat and wondered if perhaps the younger woman couldn't hold her drink. They were on the wine and they'd only had three or four cups each, but Nama seemed to have suddenly started talking utter horseshit, as far as she was concerned.

Maybe five cups, if she was honest about it. She had more money in her purse than she'd ever had before, even after paying Madame her tithe, and what else was she going to spend it on?

Wine made it better.

Wine blotted it out, and anything that could do that was good, as far as she was concerned.

'Aye, right, if you say so,' she said eventually.

'Nah, it's like –' Nama said, gesticulating wildly, and it was that exact moment that she knocked her cup over.

The cheap tin cup of even cheaper wine spilled on the table, then rolled off it and hit the floor with a clang.

'Oh bollocks!' Nama exclaimed.

The lads at the bar turned to look, to point and laugh, but the sleek young man wasn't laughing. The supposed Rat King was regarding them with narrowed eyes. A minute later he was beside their table with a fresh cup of wine for Nama in his hand.

'Allow me,' he said, and showed her a smile that displayed surprisingly good teeth. They looked sharp, those teeth, but they were reasonably white and looked strong enough to gnaw through a ship's rope. 'May I?'

He pulled a vacant stool over from the next table and joined them at theirs without waiting for an answer. He fixed Nama with a look.

'My name's Kurt,' he said. 'And who might you be?'

'I'm Nama,' she said, and to Eline's ears she sounded almost shy.

Eline he ignored completely, which she was both glad of and a bit offended by all at once.

'You shine,' he said bluntly. 'Just like me.'

'*What?*' Nama said. 'You . . . you can see that too? And . . . and *I* shine? How can I, I'm not anyone.'

'Oh,' said Kurt, 'I assure you that you very much are, my girl.'

'She's not *your girl*,' Eline interjected, 'she's my mate, and you're spoiling our fucking afternoon.'

'Oh, leave off, Eline,' Nama said, but the young man just smiled and spread his hands.

'I wouldn't want to come between you two lovely ladies' mother and daughter time,' he said.

That was a deliberate insult, as Eline was both not old enough to be

Nama's mother and she obviously was not Alarian, either. Not *quite* old enough, anyway. He smirked at the look on her face, then reached into his pouch and pulled out a stiff card which he handed to Nama before he flourished a seated mockery of a courtly bow.

'I can be found at this address, should you ever wish to talk,' he said.

Nama clutched the card and just stared stupidly after him as he swaggered back to the bar and his cluster of young pricks.

'No,' Eline said at once, the moment he was out of earshot. 'Bad idea, Nama.'

Nama showed her a half-shrug that could have meant anything, but she tucked the card into her pouch anyway. She lifted the cup of wine this Kurt had bought her and took a sip, then set it on the table and met Eline's eyes.

'You're not my ma,' she said softly. 'You don't get to tell me "no".'

'No,' Eline had to allow. 'No, I'm not your ma. But I'm a lot older than you, more so than you probably think, and I know a man who's a fucking bad idea when I see one. I should know; I married one, after all.'

'Aye well, that's your opinion,' Nama said. 'Don't mean I'm going to listen to it.'

Eline sighed and gave it up for a bad job.

If the girl wanted to go and get herself hurt by that oily prick and their shared delusions of shining people then honestly what business was it of hers? They whored together at the Bells and apparently they both worked for the fat man as well, but that was it. They weren't even really friends, as such, they just worked together and that was all.

Last night I was sobbing into her shoulder, Eline thought. *We cried together. I told her what I had done, and she held me as I wept for it.*

'Look, Nama,' she said. 'I'm sorry. I'm not trying to tell you how to live your life, it's just ... that bloke. There's something about him I don't like.'

'Well, there's something about him I *do* like,' the younger woman countered, and Eline raised a hand in surrender.

'All right, all right,' she said. 'That's your business, then. I don't want us to fall out over it.'

Nama looked at her for a long moment then smiled and drained her wine.

'Nah, nor do I,' she said. 'Want another?'

'Aye, why not.'

They had another drink together and then the young man was back again, struggling with two cups of wine and a tankard of beer for himself.

'Mind if I join you again, ladies?' he asked.

His own crew of little fuckwits seemed to have left for the day by then and Eline *did* mind a bit, but Nama showed him a welcoming smile. At least she got a free drink out of it, so she supposed that was something.

'What do you want?' she demanded.

'Nothing from you,' he said, and turned to Nama before she could react.

'So, you. Shining girl. What can you do?'

'What?' Nama asked, obviously nonplussed by the question. 'I can read, which is more than a lot of people can, and even write a bit. I . . . I'm a whore, truth be told.'

'Seems a waste,' the man said.

'Fuck off, there's no shame in it. I'm licensed, we both are. We work out of the House of Silver Bells.'

Eline winced to hear that, as she had no desire whatsoever for this man to know where she lived or how she made her way in the world, but Nama and her mouth had just well and truly thrown that into the shithouse.

'I don't see no knots,' he said.

'Our day off, innit?' Nama said.

'Aye, that's as maybe,' he said. 'But what can you *do?*'

'Fuck,' Nama said bluntly, and again there was no shame in her voice. 'That's my job, and I'm good at it.'

'I'm sure you are,' he said. 'What else?'

'I don't follow,' Nama confessed.

'The mending of hurts, do you have that? The setting of fires, or the calling of them? The drawing of glyphs, perhaps?'

Nama blinked at him, and Eline shook her head. She was the older woman and it was her place to take charge of the situation, so she did.

'Neither of us have the faintest fucking idea what you're talking about,' she said after a moment, 'so thanks for the drinks and all that but maybe fuck off now, aye?'

Kurt ignored her and gave Nama a long look.

'How much do you charge an hour?' he asked her.

Nama named a figure, adding an extra mark onto it for good measure, but he just nodded.

'Might be I'll be seeing you, then,' he said.

*

They barely made it back to the House of Silver Bells in time for supper, and by then both were quite the worse for wear. Madame was not pleased, to put it mildly.

'Thank the Maiden we are closed tonight,' she told them both in the hall when they came stumbling in, giggling together. 'I do *not* put drunken whores in front of my clients. It's bad for business, and it's bad for the reputation of the house. You are an absolute disgrace, the pair of you.'

'It's our day off,' Nama protested, slurring slightly as she spoke.

Madame sighed, but Nama had the right of it and Eline couldn't see how Madame had the authority to control *every* aspect of their lives, much as she would no doubt have liked to.

'Go and eat,' Madame said at last. 'It might sober you both up a bit, if nothing else.'

They *were* both quite drunk by then, to be fair.

'Yes, ma'am,' Eline managed, and dragged Nama down the corridor to the common room before the younger woman collapsed into a fit of giggles.

'She ain't happy with us,' she said at last, when her shoulders stopped shaking.

'No,' Eline allowed, 'I don't think she is. Ah well, we've broken no rules. Godsday is ours to do with as we will, after temple. Supper it is, then.'

Supper was served in the common room the same as the Godsday lunch had been, and it was well enough. Cold meats mostly, the offcuts of the lunchtime roast, and bread and roast onions and pottage. They retired early that night, and both of them had heavy heads the next morning.

That was all very well apart from having to stand their turn at cleaning that morning, pushing their brooms listlessly about the common room while their heads throbbed and they both tried not to throw up. Nothing of great note happened until the house opened for business that evening.

Nama was already working but Eline was in the boudoir with Madame and two of the household guard, taking another lesson in the use of the fan. Fans were ubiquitous amongst women of society, and she had learned that there was a whole silent language to their usage. She had also learned that some of the other girls took extremely ill to her having one when they didn't. Elsie, who worked on the third floor, had openly sneered at her over breakfast that morning, and Eline could feel the sullen resentment in the other woman's glare. Madame's pet, they no doubt thought her. Eline was still trying to remember the movements of the fan and their meanings, and Madame was ruthlessly drilling elocution into her at the same time. Today it seemed that was her focus, that and manners.

'No!' Madame snapped at her. 'You will never "'ave one", whatever you think that means. For the Goddess's sake, Eline! One will gracefully accept an offered drink and drop your host or hostess a curtsey in respect if they offer it themselves, although they probably won't. How deep a curtsey you should offer is a world of traps and poisonous subtlety, so best if they don't. If a footman offers it you will do no such thing, accepting it as the simple duty of a servant. Curtsey to a footman and you'll make yourself a laughing-stock. Servants are to be treated as below your notice, whoever they belong to.'

'So I'm not to thank servants at all?' Eline asked, displaying her naivety.

'Gods, no,' Madame said. 'Servants are not people, Eline, they are *things*. They are the things that fill your glass. They are the things that bring your dinner. No one you acknowledge. Just things that are there. Things a courtesan would expect. You have to understand, my dear, a courtesan does not lead a normal life. For what *I* charge you out at, I expect you to live like a princess. And you will, believe me.

These were things a courtesan needed to know, apparently: the way to regard servants, the gestures of the fan that signalled approval or invitation and those that were mortal insults.

There was a tap at the door, and then Marcoss entered without waiting for a reply.

'Customer to see you, ma'am,' he said, and Eline blinked back surprise as she saw him usher that Kurt into the room.

Customers were usually dealt with in the hall, and shown up to the room of whichever girl they had picked, or often whoever there was if anyone was even available. The house lacked the number of girls it needed, as Eline had already noticed. It was rare indeed for a customer to be shown into Madame's presence, and that meant he had money to spend.

Serious money.

'May I help you, m'lord?' Madame asked, dropping Kurt a short curtsey.

He was even more richly dressed tonight, and really did look like he could have had a 'Lan' in his name, although from having heard him speak in the Rat Eline thought that was extremely unlikely. There was nothing lordly about this one, but there was definitely something sly.

Something she didn't trust, even if she couldn't have entirely said why.

It wasn't just his overly slick hair, although she had to admit that was definitely a part of it. Ugh. She could imagine the oily feel of it in her hands, and the thought made her feel a bit sick. What Nama saw in him was an absolute mystery to Eline.

'I want to see Nama,' he said, 'but your man says she's not available.'

Madame's brow furrowed as she thought for a moment, obviously figuring advance bookings and timetables in her head.

'Nama is otherwise engaged with another client,' she said, and gestured vaguely at Eline. 'Eline, however, is currently available.'

'I'm not surprised, at her age,' Kurt said, and Eline could honestly have thrown herself at his throat for that remark in front of Madame. 'I reckon I'll wait for Nama.'

'It . . . may be some time,' Madame said. 'She's booked for the next hour.'

'I'll wait,' Kurt said again, and fixed her with a look that said he wasn't taking no for an answer.

'Very well,' Madame said. 'Marcoss, dear, please show this gentleman to the salon and see that he is provided for.'

There was a substantial door fee to so much as set foot in the House of Silver Bells, of course, before you'd even met a girl, and any gentleman who had to wait for his girl of choice was hosted in the salon with free wine and brandy for as long as it took. At least it got rid of Kurt, and Eline was glad of that if nothing else.

His presence there, though, that she was anything *but* glad of. She couldn't put her finger on what it was, but there was just something about him that made her skin crawl. Nama might like him but Eline very much did not.

'Now, dear,' Madame said, 'until somebody finally wants you, shall we work on your dance? You're shit at it.'

Eline sighed, and resigned herself to the lesson.

She hated dance, but she had to allow that Madame was right. The complicated moves of the courtly dances of society were nothing at all like what she was used to and she felt awkward even attempting them.

It was all so unnatural, with leaps and twists and constant changes of partner, nothing at all like the fast, flowing grace of her mother's dance that she had so eagerly embraced as a child among the wagons. Still, she knew that was something that would have to change if she was ever to show her face at a society ball. A courtesan had to be a woman of many skills, after all.

And killing was only one of them.

Chapter 7

Of course somebody wanted her in the end that night, and that meant she had to put up with it. She couldn't command the high prices of the courtesans, of course, not yet at least, and given her age she suspected Madame was selling her cheaper than she was Nama, but even so the house was expensive, whichever girl a man picked. Why would anyone pay silver to lie with *her*? She had thirty-five years to her and had borne two children, and had the stretch-marks to prove it. The cheekbones of a duchess aside, she really couldn't understand the attraction. Still, it kept a roof over her head and food in her belly, so no matter, she supposed. It could have been a lot worse. Even if the fat man hadn't hanged her, she'd have been on the streets and starving once the rent money ran out.

Whatever it takes.

What *was* of matter was that she was supposed to be murdering Madame, and so far she had still seen no possible way to do it. The woman was always guarded, *always*. In all her time in the house, Eline had never seen Madame alone. Not once. She even walked across the yard to the shithouse with a guard at her side.

She was mulling the idea over breakfast in the common room when Nama came and joined her, a plate of black bread and bacon in one hand and a mug of small beer in the other.

'Mind if I join you?'

Eline gestured at the vacant chair opposite her.

Apart from Nama none of the other women at the house had seemed remotely interested in extending friendship to her. They had their own circles, their own little bitchy cliques, and she thought all of them had judged her too old to be either a threat or of any interest and so they largely ignored her.

'Please do,' she said, and smiled as Nama sat and took a mouthful of her breakfast beer. 'How was last night with your sweetheart?'

She was teasing, of course she was, but Nama just gave her a look.

'Ain't like that,' she said. 'He didn't even want to fuck.'

'Oh gods,' Eline said, remembering some of her stranger customers. 'What *did* he want then, if you want to talk about it? No bother if you don't.'

'Nah, nothing like that,' Nama said. 'He just wanted to talk. Paid me my hourly rate but just to talk. Ain't going to complain about that.'

Eline paused for a moment as the Alarian girl started attacking her breakfast with an unusual hunger.

'I've got one like that,' she said. 'Becoming a regular, he is. Poor old fucker, he just misses having a conversation with his wife I think, now she's died. Some of them are sad like that, but a bit sweet too in their way. He don't mean no harm, just wants a woman to talk to, you know what I mean? Strange though, your Kurt didn't strike me as the type.'

'He ain't,' Nama said. 'I dunno how to explain it, really. Oh, he'd have fucked if he wanted to, I'm sure, but he didn't. Probably gets it somewhere else for free anyway, looking like that. Handsome bastard. That wasn't what he was here for. He went on about people who shine, and what it means. Asked me who else I've seen shine in the city, but I couldn't give him any names or that. He . . . showed me things.'

Eline snorted into her own beer. 'I bet he did.'

'Not like that, you dirty cow,' Nama said, and laughed. 'Fuck me, I thought you were supposed to be the prim one who don't belong here. Starting to wonder about that, to be honest.'

'Got to blend in, haven't I?' Eline said, and winked at her.

Perhaps, she thought then, she was a better actress than she had thought she was. Or perhaps Madame's lessons were starting to sink in.

A courtesan is a person,' Madame had told her a few days ago, *'but she is the person that her patron has bought and paid for. An artificial person, I suppose. She is not herself, ever. She has no self. Forget that, right now. She is a fabrication, an act. An art form, if you will. The courtesan's personality, demeanour, appearance, behaviour, are all entirely financially negotiable. Everything is, in this life. The house will take care of that side of things for you, of course.*

Of course they would.

For their fucking ninety percent.

The courtesan's trade was basically all acting. Playing a part, whichever part had been bought and paid for by her patron. Madame was slowly teaching her an arsenal of acts, she realised. Weapons that the courtesan could use to deliver the outcome that she wanted.

'Nah, it's like this,' Nama said.

She had a quick look over her shoulder to make sure none of the others were looking in their direction, then held her hand out, palm up, and screwed her face up in intense concentration like she badly needed to crap.

'Do you need the shithouse?' Eline asked. 'You know where it is; I won't mind waiting.'

'Shut *up*,' Nama whispered.

A moment later a tiny flame kindled in the palm of her hand, dancing and flickering in the draughts and morning sunlight of the common room of the House of Silver Bells. She exhaled hard and it grew larger, reaching almost three inches in height from her hand before she clenched her fist and extinguished it.

'That's—' Eline started, but Nama gave her a fierce look.

'You can't tell *anyone*,' she said. 'I mean it, Eline.'

Witchcraft, that had been the word on the tip of Eline's tongue.

People had been hanged for less, once the Church got wind of it.

'Fucking *blood*, Nama,' she said. 'You . . . you ought not to be able to do that. No cunt should be able to do that.'

'Kurt can, and way more besides,' she said. 'He reckons that anyone who shines can, with a bit of teaching. The cunning, he calls that, and he spent silver last night for my time to *teach* me, not to fuck me.'

'More fool him,' said Eline. 'So now what? You're a whore *and* a fucking witch?'

'You're a whore too,' Nama shot back at her, 'and I ain't a fucking witch. But apparently I'm a cunning woman, and that's different. According to Kurt, anyway. That's a fine thing, apparently, and it's more than *you* can do.'

It was, Eline had to allow, but it was far too close to witchcraft for her liking. Oh, there were magicians, of course there were. There was a whole house of magicians in Dannsburg, so she had heard anyway, and perhaps another in Ellinburg away to the east, depending on who you asked. She supposed they were all well and good, and they were certainly respected. They'd had a fight with the house of law in Dannsburg a year or two before, so she'd heard it, and got the worst of the exchange because of course they fucking had. No one got the better of the house of law, that was known the length and breadth of the country, but by all accounts the magicians were still there.

She thought of the fat man then, and the house of law and what she'd heard of Dannsburg, and found that she wasn't at all surprised the magicians had got the worst of it. Even so, magicians were very respectable indeed, whereas witches were to be hated and feared. The cunning folk were somewhere in between, and no one really knew what to do with them.

And now apparently Nama was one of them, and Eline really didn't know what to do with *that*.

Well, the first thing to do with that was to tell the fat man, obviously. She worked for him after all, and if she didn't and he found out anyway she'd be in trouble. Besides, she knew he'd be pleased. Having a cunning woman on his payroll had obvious benefits for him, and she needed his good favour above all else. Perhaps *he* would know what to do with it. It was Tradesday, the second day after Godsday, and after she had finished her morning chores she had the afternoon to herself until they opened that evening. She slipped out of the house alone and went to see him.

She found herself once more in the back room of the nondescript house, facing the fat man. He had been idly playing the lute when she walked in, but now he put his instrument down and looked at her. He wasn't bad at it, to be fair, but she found the fact that a dread and terrible Queen's Man obviously enjoyed music somewhat disquieting. It . . . she wasn't sure how to express it. Humanised him, she supposed. This boggart that had come calling liked to play the lute? That couldn't be right, could it? This went against all her expectations of what a Queen's Man was, but she supposed that at the end of the day they were still just people like everyone else, with their own lives and tastes and even hobbies, after a fashion. The thought of that made her more uncomfortable than she could have reasonably expressed.

The Queen's Men were supposed to be cold, merciless monsters, not musicians.

She cleared her throat, and dipped him a small curtsey.

'Eline,' he greeted her, if not warmly. 'What can I do for you this fine morning? Is the job done?'

She cleared her throat again, and looked away.

'Not . . . not as yet,' she said. 'Madame is training me as a courtesan, but she is forever under guard. Not once have I seen her alone, not even for a moment.'

'A courtesan?' he said, and for a moment he looked thoughtful. 'Actually, that might not be a bad outcome, in the great scheme of things. Courtesans are fucking useful. So what are you here for, if you've no success to report to me?'

'One of the other girls, one I have formed the beginnings of a friendship with, is apparently a cunning woman,' Eline admitted. 'Or she has the makings of one, anyway. I thought you should know. It's your Nama, the one you sent to me to make my introduction to the House of Silver Bells. On Godsday morning she had no idea, and by breakfast today she could conjure a flame in the palm of her hand.'

The fat man frowned at her.

'And how's that then?' he asked.

'We went out drinking together after Godsday lunch,' Eline confessed, 'and we met this bloke in the Rat. Nama said he shined. Oily fucker, to my mind, but Nama seemed to like him. Then . . . Oh I don't know, we ended up talking to him. He bought us a drink, two drinks, whatever, and he told Nama what it meant when folk shine and he told her that she did too. Then last night he came to the house and hired her, paid her hourly rate but didn't want to bed her. She said he wanted to teach her, for whatever reason, and this morning she's showing me *witchcraft* over breakfast. I thought you should know, is all.'

'Hmmm,' said the fat man. 'And does he have a name, this oily fucker?'

'Called himself Kurt,' Eline said, then paused to think about it. 'Actually he was trying to tell folk to call him the Rat King, but no one was taking *that* seriously as I'm sure you can imagine.'

'The Rat King . . . Kurt, aye?' the fat man said, and she thought he went a little pale as he said it. 'Well, it's a common enough name, I suppose.'

'Someone you know?' Eline asked.

'Mind your fucking own,' the fat man snapped at her. 'Anyway, I've news for you, as you're here. Your daughter has found a position in service, in Dannsburg. I thought you would want to know.'

'Yes, of course,' Eline said, waiting for the blow to land.

There always was one, with the Queen's Men. She had learned that much already.

'Indeed, she has found employment with the house of Lady Lan Yetrova, one of the richest society widows in the country.'

'That . . . that sounds wonderful,' Eline said, almost visibly cringing for what she knew must be to come. 'Is she a good employer?'

'Actually, yes,' he said. 'Unlike most of the capital's nobility, she is known to be very fair, even kind to her staff, in her way. Unless you steal from her. No, you don't do that.'

Eline felt her heart crash into the pit of her stomach. She knew where this was going as plainly as if the man had been holding up a board with the answer painted on it.

'Her Ladyship has a great deal of jewellery,' he went on. 'A very great deal, yet she seems to be able to know exactly where every piece is at any given time. If one were to go missing, even a simple diamond ring, and be found in a maid's garret . . . Oh dear. That wouldn't end well for the maid, now would it?'

'No,' Eline had to say. 'I dare say it wouldn't.'

'I'm just saying, that's all,' he said. 'I like to keep your mind focused on the job at hand. You've had a week already and nothing's happened. I'm sure you understand me in this.'

'Of course, sir,' Eline said.

Even a simpleton could not have failed to understand the veiled threat in the man's words, after all.

'Good,' he said. 'I think we're beginning to build a trust between us, Eline. You can call me Luka, by the way. Now fuck off and figure out a way to kill that woman, I've a letter I need to write to Dannsburg.'

Chapter 8

Eline returned to the House of Silver Bells in time for supper, and found herself once more sitting with Nama.

'I've been practising,' the younger woman whispered to her as they pulled a capon apart between them. 'I managed to light the fire in the grate in my room this afternoon.'

'I've been able to do that since I had four years to me,' Eline said, around a mouthful of meat. 'Any halfwit can do that, so pardon me if I'm not impressed.'

'Not with flint and steel and kindling, you idiot,' Nama said, and lowered her voice even further. 'Any fool or child can do that, I agree. I mean with the cunning. Just by looking at it, and *willing* it.'

'Horseshit,' Eline said shortly, but she wondered if it really was.

She remembered seeing the flame dancing in the other woman's palm that morning, and wondered if it was really such a leap for her to be able to conjure it in her fireplace instead.

'Not horseshit,' Nama said. 'I can do this, Eline. I can really do this!'

'Well keep it to your fucking self, if you can,' Eline advised her quietly. 'I can't see Madame approving, and whatever you want to call it I can see a lot of folk naming it witchcraft. I know we've only known each other just over a week but I'd be grieved to see you hang, and you fucking well will if the temple gets wind of this.'

'I know,' Nama said. 'Kurt said to keep it quiet, but I had to tell you. I had to tell *someone*, and you're really the only person I've got to tell.'

Eline blinked at her. 'You've worked here ages, haven't you? Don't you have any friends amongst the other girls?'

'No,' Nama confessed. 'Not really. Look around you, Eline. I'm the only brown face in here. They call me "tea monkey" behind my back, I

53

know they do, and don't none of them want to be friends with the likes of me.'

'I . . .' started Eline, who had honestly never even given a thought to it.

There were no shortage of Alarians on the streets where she had lived with Caromir, and people were just people, so far as she was concerned; all poor in their own ways and making the best they could out of life, but of course Nama was right. She *was* the only Alarian girl at the Bells, and maybe that made some of the others take against her. She had no idea why, but such was life. People could be such cunts about that sort of thing, and for no reason that she could see.

'Fuck,' she said at last.

'Don't you pity me,' Nama warned her. 'Don't you *fucking* dare, Eline. I mean it.'

'Wouldn't dream of it,' she assured her new friend, as she finally realised that was what Nama was. A friend, and the first one she had truly had since before she had married Caromir. 'Just saying, is all.'

'It's fucking shit,' Nama muttered, but Eline's words had been enough to let her busy herself with her supper.

'Aye,' Eline allowed, and did the same.

'He's coming back tonight,' Nama said, once she had picked the bones clean on her plate. 'Paying again, and again I doubt he wants to fuck. Don't strike me as the type, you know? I mean, I would if he wanted to, wouldn't even mind to be honest, but I don't think it's that. Reckon he wants to teach me some more.'

'Why would he pay to do that, when it sounds like something you should be paying *him* for?'

Nama shrugged. 'Don't know,' she said, and winked at Eline, 'but I won't have to get down on my knees in the ashes to light my own fire tomorrow morning, will I? Ain't complaining.'

Eline gave her a long look.

'You don't think,' she said after a moment, 'there's the tiniest chance he might want something in return?'

'Who doesn't?' Nama said. 'Ain't nothing free in this fucking world.'

'Aye, perhaps not,' Eline had to admit. 'So long as you remember that.'

'Course I will,' Nama said, but Eline wasn't so sure that she would.

'Aye, well,' she said again, for want of anything else.

'Fuck it,' Nama said. 'Life is what it is.'

Eline looked at this Alarian girl, who had probably been whoring since she was a child. She supposed life *was* what it was, for her at least, but then had her life as a respectable married woman really been any better? Married to a decorated veteran, at that.

No. No, it had fucking well not.

'I went to see *him* this afternoon,' she confessed. 'I had to tell him some things.'

'About me,' Nama said at once.

'Aye,' Eline said, seeing no reason to lie about it. 'I'm sorry but I did.'

'Don't be sorry,' Nama said, 'and in truth I thank you for it. If he can find me a place at the house of magicians . . . Do they even take in women, there? I don't fucking know. And Alarian women at that? I doubt it, but you never know, do you? I've got to try, now I know what I can do. Anything to make a better life for myself.'

Eline took a long draught of her supper wine and looked at her friend.

Of course they probably didn't, although she supposed there was always the chance that they might. She had no idea, although she assumed the fat man, the man who had told her to call him Luka, probably did. If not he could find out, she was sure. He had someone he wrote to in Dannsburg, anyway, and she had absolutely no doubt that *they* would know.

Dannsburg.

The name of the capital city raised the fine hairs on the back of her forearms, even if she had absolutely no idea why. There was just something about it . . . all the stories she had heard of Dannsburg, some of them obviously grown very tall in the telling, but even so the very name conjured visions of huge dark walls topped with heads on spikes.

She didn't know it then, but she wasn't far wrong.

'There's just no way,' Eline said to the fat man – Luka, she reminded herself – one morning a week later, once she had finished her chores at the house. 'She's never alone, night or day. Never. I've tried *everything*, even following her to the shithouse but there is *always* a guard!'

'I don't want to hear that,' Luka said. 'Trust me, *Dannsburg* doesn't want to hear that. Not one little bit. You don't say "it can't be done" to the Provost Marshal, believe you me. Not if you want to keep the fucking head on your shoulders you don't.'

'I'm sure you don't, but that doesn't change the facts of the matter,' Eline snapped at him. 'Yes, I killed my husband but I am not a soldier and I never have been, and I'm not an assassin either. I don't know how to do this.'

'All right,' Luka conceded after a moment. 'You're not a soldier or an assassin. So what are you?'

'A wife and a mother,' Eline said, 'although I'm not even a wife anymore. A widow now, and that still sounds strange to say. I was a herbalist once, I suppose. Sort of, anyway. When I was a girl, that is. Before I married.'

A slow smile spread across Luka's face.

'Then fucking poison her,' he said. 'You must know how.'

'I . . .' Eline had to admit she hadn't even thought of that. 'I could try I suppose, although precious little grows in Drathburg. I'll need some things.'

'There's nothing the house of law can't get for you,' Luka said. 'Give me a list.'

'Aconite, hemlock, foxglove,' she said at once, reciting all the poisons she could remember her mother warning her of when she'd been a little girl, all the perils of the hedgerows and the roadside ditches.

Of course, she hadn't been a herbalist before she'd been married, not at fifteen she hadn't. Barely an apprentice, and that unofficial. She had a little knowledge, no more than that, but she'd had to tell him *something*. Something to stop her hanging, something to protect her children.

Whatever it took.

That, Eline thought, was all that mattered. Whatever she told this man, whatever she had to do or pretend to be able to do, that was all that mattered. Aconite, hemlock, foxglove. All poisonous, she knew that. Her mother had said so enough times. What did you do with them, to kill a person?

She had no idea.

Still, nothing much happened for the next three weeks save the relentless grind of work and Madame's lessons, and Nama's continuing trysts with her mysterious cunning man. The girl had a way about her now, something furtive that Eline wasn't sure she liked. They still got on well enough, and had made a habit of their afternoons drinking together after temple on Godsdays, but Nama had stopped talking to her about her progress with the cunning.

The less I know about that the better, Eline told herself, but she wasn't entirely sure if that was true. She felt an obligation to the younger woman, stupid though that may be, something motherly that made her feel that she should be looking out for her.

That's the last thing she wants.

Aye, it probably was, but she couldn't shake the feeling all the same.

Either way it was Queensday, the day before Coinsday, and Madame had Eline summoned to her study when she had been just about to head up to her room to start working for the night. That was if anyone wanted her, she supposed. She wasn't exactly the woman in highest demand at the Silver Bells, as Madame never tired of reminding her.

Marcoss himself ushered her in, and the feel of his hard hand on her arm through the sleeve of her kirtle made her quiver with revulsion. There really was something about Marcoss that made her stomach turn, but still she couldn't have articulated exactly what it was.

Who was he in his war, and what did he do there?

Nothing good, she was sure. His war would have been Krathzgrad, she supposed, with the age of him. That had been a siege, she knew that from what Caromir had told her, and an ugly one at that.

Not that there was any other sort. Starving civilians to death to make an enemy army surrender wasn't any sort of noble, to her mind, but such was the world they lived in.

'Ma'am?' she asked, as she was shown into Madame's presence.

As always the woman was guarded, three of the bastards in there that night, and again Eline wondered how in the gods' names she was ever supposed to get the chance to kill this horrible bitch. Luka's patience wouldn't last for ever, she knew, but the job was beginning to look simply impossible for one of her meagre skills. The knife just couldn't be done, as she had explained to Luka, and even when her poisons arrived from Dannsburg she had to admit she had no real idea what to do with them.

'Ah, Eline,' Madame said as she looked up at her. 'I have good news for you.'

'Ma'am?'

'I have an assignation for you, your first proper one as a courtesan. Tomorrow night, in fact. The Baron Lan Elenkov.'

Eline gaped. They had spent all afternoon on her fan lessons and she was starting to feel *slightly* more confident in her role, but she still couldn't dance for shit and her deportment, so Madame had informed her, left a lot to be desired.

'I'm not trained!' Eline exclaimed, mortified at the thought of being sent to someone with a 'Lan' in his name when she still had practically no idea what she was doing. 'I'll fuck it up!'

'No you won't,' Madame assured her. 'It's only a reception, not a ball; the gods only know I wouldn't send you to one of those, not with the lamentable state of your dancing. All you have to do is hang off his arm and look vaguely aristocratic, and I'm confident you can do that. Just try not to speak too much, your elocution still isn't quite there – although it's getting considerably better, which is *far* more than can be said for your dance. Truth be told, Lan Elenkov is an old friend of mine, from . . . times before. When we both did different things than we do now, but that's of no matter. He knows you're only half trained. In fact, through a series of catastrophic business investments he can't really afford a fully trained courtesan these days, and he has long been happy to give my new trainees a first outing for a competitive price.'

'I'm being tested?' Eline asked.

'In a way, I suppose,' Madame said. 'What you're really doing is gaining experience, and more than that you will be being seen in society. Seen by more important gentlemen with deeper pockets, we can but hope. You will have to look splendid, naturally, and I doubt you own any splendour. The house will, of course, loan you a magnificent gown and suitable jewellery for the evening for an additional five percent of your fee.'

On top of their existing ninety percent commission? That only leaves me five percent of the fucking fee for myself!

Eline clutched her hands together in front of her to keep from screaming at the unfairness of it all, and managed a short nod. It was vital, she knew. If she was to ever to have the chance to kill Madame she would have to become more established as a courtesan, get closer to her, and that meant she would need to catch the eye of a more worthwhile patron than this Lan Elenkov seemed to be. She would need to look the part to have any chance of doing that, she knew. Looks were everything for a woman in society, after all.

'Very well,' Madame said, and showed her a small smile. 'Don't look so pinched, dear, that's still fifty marks for you.'

Eline almost fainted as she figured the numbers in her head.

Fifty?

She stood to make *fifty* for one night's work? Fifty marks would have clothed her children for ten years and more. That was the moment that she realised she knew absolutely nothing about the aristocracy, even its lower and supposedly more impoverished branches like this Baron Lan Elenkov seemed to be. It was a different world, utterly beyond her comprehension.

That a man could pay an entire gold crown for one night's company seemed absolutely otherworldly, to her. She had never even seen a single gold crown in her entire life.

And she wasn't even really trained yet? What the fuck did a fully qualified courtesan make?

There had to be a catch, and she dreaded to think what it was.

'What . . . what will he want?' she finally asked. She honestly couldn't imagine what depravities a man would pay a whole gold crown for.

'Company,' Madame said. 'Oh gods, I can't imagine you'll have to attempt to fuck him, if that's what you're worried about. He has the best part of eighty years to him, my dear. I suppose if he wants to, you'll have to *try* to raise the beast, but I can't see you having much luck, especially not once he's been drinking. Which he will have been, by the way. A great deal, I daresay. He just likes to look the part, and in society a big part of "looking the part" is an attractive companion. Hold onto his arm, speak as little as possible, don't swear, and try not to get in a fight with any of the other women and you'll be fine.'

'A fight?'

'Ah,' Madame said.

Oh gods, here it comes.

There was always *something,* be it with Madame or Luka the Queen's Man, some fucking catch waiting to bite you in the arse when you thought for once something might actually be going your way. No such luck, not in Drathburg.

'Courtesans are fiercely competitive,' Madame explained to her. 'Most of the men there will be with their actual wives, and I assure you *they* will know at a glance what you are and hate you on sight lest their husbands' heads be turned. The other courtesans will of course *also* know what you are, and hate you as potential competition. It won't be like it is here at the Silver Bells, the friendship you have built with Nama and the accord of indifference you seem to have established with the other girls. Well done, by the way; that was probably the best way to handle it. But no, in the world of the courtesan the competition for the most desirable patron can quite literally come down to the knife. There are no friendships to be found there, I assure you. Do try to come home alive, dear.'

Chapter 9

Coinsday evening rolled around, and Baron Lan Elenkov's carriage drew up at the gates of the House of Silver Bells to collect Eline.

He wasn't in it, of course. Barons didn't wait on whores, however expensive they may have suddenly become, but two footmen came to the door of the bawdy house where Loran admitted them. He bade them wait in the hall until Marcoss could escort Eline down the stairs to her assignation. She was magnificently dressed in a beautiful gown of sea-green silk that offset her hair perfectly, and obviously she wore no knot that night. Society receptions were occasions for subtlety, after all. A rope of the Madame's diamonds glittered at her throat, and if those were perhaps less subtle, they certainly made a statement.

For an additional five percent.

Truth be told she was a little surprised that Madame trusted her to come back at all and not just do a runner with the jewellery, but deep down she knew that would have been more than her life was worth. There was something about Madame, and there was *definitely* something about Marcoss, that told her she wouldn't have made it five miles if she ran. She had to speak to Luka about this, she knew, but not that night. That night she was going to a society reception on the arm of a baron, insane as the thought sounded in her head.

An old baron, aye, and one no longer as rich as he had been, but still one who was in a position to spend an entire gold crown for the privilege of her company for the evening. The idea made her head spin. She had her fan tucked through her sash at the angle that Madame had taught her was fashionable that month, and five silver marks in her purse in the extremely unlikely eventuality that she had to spend any of her own money that night.

Something would have gone horribly wrong if she did, Madame had explained to her, but she had also taught her that a lady should *never* be in a position where she couldn't afford to get home to safety at her own expense.

Never place yourself entirely at a man's mercy, however wealthy he may be, Madame had instructed her. *As I said, I have known the Baron Lan Elenkov for a very long time and I know you will be safe with him, but things can happen. Robbers on the streets, for one. Gods forbid, but he's old enough to have an attack of the heart and drop dead at your feet in the middle of the reception. You always have to at least have the funds about you to hire a carriage home and a man or two for protection, if the worst happens. Never, never, let yourself be defenceless. A woman cannot afford to be defenceless in this world.*

Eline had shown her a grim smile. No shit.

I know that.

I murdered my husband.

'Yes, ma'am,' she had said, and then Madame had truly surprised her.

'Take this as well,' she said, and pressed something into Eline's hand.

It was a slender stiletto in a thin leather sheath, just about small enough to conceal in her pouch.

'Ma'am, I—'

'Take it,' Madame interrupted her. 'You are a junior, half-trained courtesan on the arm of an aged and faded baron and I doubt you will attract the ire of any of the others, but this is a society reception and should you draw the attention of a duke or earl patronising one of the other girls, do not be surprised if they try to kill you. Competition is *very* stiff, as I have said. Should that happen, and I doubt it will, don't be afraid to defend yourself. I will worry about the consequences with whoever they work for later. This is what I have people like Marcoss for, or at least partly anyway. I have invested too much in you now to want to have to pay to bury you as well, girl.'

Eline gaped at her. Had she? She'd had lessons, yes, but had Madame really invested that much compared to how much commission she took from Eline's bedroom fees? A few hours here and there on elocution, deportment, dance, the language of fans. Did that really amount to so much? She doubted it, somehow. She dropped the stiletto into her pouch, not really knowing what else to do with it.

She hadn't really, until that moment, grasped what a vipers' nest she was stepping into. Still, there was something in Madame's face, something that made her think that perhaps she *did* actually care. About her investment, of course, about her *merchandise*, but . . . perhaps there was something more?

Could Madame actually care about *her*, now she had begun to shape Eline into the creature she had no doubt once been herself?

She wanted to doubt it, but . . .

Oh, what was she thinking? She was still supposed to be murdering this awful woman, if she could ever work out a way to do it. She couldn't afford to start fucking *liking* her; no good would come of that, she knew.

'Move, woman,' Marcoss hissed in her ear, and gave her a shove in the small of her back that propelled her towards the two waiting footmen.

She took a slightly ungainly step forwards, then remembered Madame's deportment lessons and pulled herself together. She regarded the two footmen and gave them a small smile, although she knew all too well that they understood what she was.

'My carriage?' she enquired, with all the studied arrogance that Madame had taught her.

'Awaits without, ma'am,' one of the footmen assured her before he opened the front door for her. Loran gave him a look for touching the door that was obviously his, but the baron's footman ignored him. 'Allow me.'

Eline swept past with the carefully practiced demeanour of a duchess, and waited for another footman to open the carriage door and hand her up into the conveyance.

'And where are we meeting my lord baron?' she asked.

'At his home, ma'am,' the footman assured her. 'We're going there first to pick him up. You'll arrive at the reception together.'

'I should think so,' Eline said, and settled back against the opulent velvet cushions of the bench with a haughty sniff as she again remembered what Madame had taught her. 'A lady can hardly arrive at a society function alone. That would not be seemly.'

I'm no lady, but what matter? I don't have to be, I just have to look and sound like one.

Oh yes, she thought, she could do this. For fifty silver marks in her purse she could do anything.

Could she, though? Oh, she could hang on to the arm of the almost eighty-year-old Baron Lan Elenkov as they slowly circulated through the crowds of the Earl Lan Klasskoff's reception at his palatial house in the north quarter, that was no hardship. She had been surprised to discover that the baron lived in a five-story terraced townhouse that for an aristocrat would be described as quite modest, but here in the earl's palace surrounded by its formal gardens she could sip wine from a tall goblet and exchange empty pleasantries with the other women she met; Madame had taught her well enough how to do that. She had a glass in one hand and her fan in the other, but already all her fan lessons were starting to desert her.

'My dear,' the baron quavered weakly in her ear, 'I do much look forward to making your closer acquaintance later this evening.'

He already had his sixth glass of brandy of the evening in his hand, and Eline thought that even without his age taken into consideration the possibility of *that* was limited, to say the least.

A courtesan is a person, Madame had told her, *but she is the person that her patron has bought and paid for.*

The Baron Lan Elenkov had paid for a playful young girl, and although Eline was neither of those things she played the part as best as she was able.

She giggled on cue. Oh yes, Madame had taught her a few things over the last several weeks and no mistake. She could feel herself slipping into character, the way Madame had taught her to.

Leave yourself, my dear, Madame had said. *Forget you have a self. Become the character. Become the courtesan. Believe me, it's easier that way.*

'Oh, Baron, you are naughty,' she said, and remembered to fan herself in the way that said she was flattered by his attention.

She wasn't, of course. Revolted would have been the more accurate word, but the language of fans was what it was and her reaction told the whole room she had accepted his advance. That was what he wanted, and she understood that. She doubted there was a soul there who thought he would actually be fucking her later, not at his age, but her message said he was welcome to if he wanted and that was what he needed, that reinforcement, that boost to his social standing.

It was honestly quite sad, to Eline's mind, but fifty marks.

Fifty marks!

She knew she had to hang on to that thought, and ignore the looks of scorn she was getting from some of the senior courtesans in the room. Far from Madame's fears of jealousy, they looked on her with something approaching pity. To be reduced to pandering to this decrepit old baron while they hung off the arms of counts and earls? Pathetic.

Eline knew it, and her face flushed with the realisation. To the actual wives she was a joke, she knew. Not the threat Madame had thought she might appear as. Who the fuck would want *her*?

She couldn't, in that moment, think why in the world Madame had thought anyone *would* be jealous.

The baron is paying a whole gold crown for my company, insane as that sounds.

She knew she had to remember that, and not let such thoughts of doubt dent her confidence.

You can show no weakness, Madame had told her. *The others will see it, and seize on it. You swim with the sharks now, my dear.*

That was the absolute truth, and she knew it. She understood cliques and bitchiness from the few years she had spent in the city's free school, and to her mind this was little different. She tucked her fan back into her sash and smiled, and took the baron's arm.

'Shall we circulate?' she asked him, loud enough to be heard.

Circulate they did, and she found herself introduced to the sort of people she had never for a moment thought she would have ever had the opportunity to meet. She was even briefly presented to their host himself, the Earl Lan Klasskoff. Eline had dipped him a very low curtsey indeed, and been intrigued when he enquired which house she belonged to.

Belonged to stung somewhat, she had to admit, but he smiled when she named the Silver Bells. That, at least, seemed it conveyed some level of legitimacy to her position.

'Ah, Madame still does not disappoint,' the earl had said before turning away to ignore her completely as he engaged in some conversation about the international shipping trade with the finely dressed gentleman standing beside him.

'Come,' the baron murmured in her ear, and just then he sounded a lot less drunk than he had looked. 'You've caught the earl's eye, that's the night's work done.'

'What do you mean?' Eline asked as he steered her through the crowd to a less-packed corner of the hall where they found vacant seats in a nook beneath the sweeping stair.

'Gods, my knee hurts,' the baron admitted as he allowed himself to sink onto a low settle under the stairs. 'Oh, girl, surely you know how this works. I'm no one really, not these days anyway. Once . . . yes. Perhaps I was. When my ships sailed the Poppy Winds and Madame and I were . . . closer than we are now, shall we say. But now? No. Now I am an old man, and almost bankrupt.'

Almost bankrupt, but still able to spend a gold crown on a single night's company?

It came to Eline then, Eline who had lived in rat-infested poverty with Caromir, that some people's definition of 'bankrupt' was perhaps not quite the same as hers.

'My lord,' Eline said, slipping into character with less difficulty than she had expected, 'is there anything I can do to ease your discomfort?'

She gave the baron a flirtatious smile, but he just waved a dismissive hand at her.

'I play a part, as do you,' he said quietly. 'For the love of the gods, what do you take me for? I've a granddaughter older than you, and I know you're not the youth you pretend to be. Always Madame trains her girls this way, and yes perhaps it is good for my public standing to be seen with them, but do you seriously think I'm interested?'

'I don't seriously think you're capable,' Eline snapped back, and to her surprise the baron laughed.

'Honestly, probably not,' he said. 'I wouldn't know. I haven't tried in twenty years, not since the death of my beloved wife. She was my world, you understand? I play the part of the debauched old lech, because such are the ways of society and it gives me an easy role to slip into. An expected character, you might say, like the stock roles from the plays at the theatre. People know what to *do* with certain characters, how to react to them, and that means they don't pay them too much attention. A bit like the courtesan, you see? It is entirely a false face. Between us, my dear, I drink so very much I can't get drunk even if I try to, and I have no interest whatsoever in the physical enjoyment of courtesans. None of them are my Leandra, so what's the bloody point?'

'I . . .' Eline started, completely nonplussed by the baron's words.

'I loved her,' he went on. 'I *still* love her, even after all these years. She gave me three beautiful children. Sadly my daughter was widowed some twenty-five years ago before her husband could give her children, and has never really recovered from that, but I still have two strong sons and they have sons and daughters of their own now. Good men, both of them. They're away at sea, trying to resuscitate my dire finances. I am still faithful to her memory, you understand? Madame was a business associate in the poppy trade, in case you were wondering, not my mistress. I was never unfaithful to my late wife, not even with her. I entertain Madame's trainee courtesans as a favour to her, to help repay an old debt from . . . long ago. I never lie with them, as I will not lie with you tonight. So if you were trying to steel yourself to lie down with this decrepit, brandy-sodden old man later tonight, take solace from the fact that you will not be asked to do so.'

'My lord, I never thought—' Eline started again, before he cut her off with a sharp laugh.

'Oh yes you bloody well did,' he said. 'There's a footman over there, get up and go and get us both another drink. My knee is killing me. I might not want to bed you but I *am* paying for you, so make yourself useful. I'll have another brandy.'

Eline rose to her feet as gracefully as she could manage and slipped through the crowd to the footman bearing his silver tray, and returned a moment later with a tall glass of wine for herself in one hand and a generously filled cut-glass tumbler of brandy in the other.

She passed the tumbler to the baron, and he smiled briefly as he took it.

'Good girl,' he said.

'Please don't talk to me like a pet dog,' Eline said. 'I really don't care for it.'

The baron had let his mask slip, had for some reason showed her what she could only assume was his true self, so she felt that she could do the same to him. Perhaps that was a mistake and it was another false face, and no doubt Madame would have been very firm that it was, but all the same he smiled at her.

'Yes,' he said. 'I suppose here, out of the hearing of others, there is perhaps an opportunity to actually be ourselves and not have to play our parts. You have to understand, Eline, just how rare a chance that is in society circles.'

Eline took a long drink of wine and looked at the baron over the top of her glass as she made a decision.

'Why are you being civil to me, all of a sudden?' she asked at last.

The baron smiled, his teeth glinting in the candlelight.

'I think we may have an acquaintance in common,' he said, after he had swallowed most of his brandy.

'Oh? And who's that, beyond Madame?'

'Do you perhaps know a fat man called Luka?'

67

Chapter 10

Eline almost choked on her wine, which she supposed really told him all he needed to know.

'It's not an uncommon name,' she managed at last, 'and a lot of wealthy men are on the generously built side.'

'And play the lute?' the baron pressed, and then lowered his voice so that no one but her could possibly have heard him, 'and carry the Queen's Warrant?'

'Oh gods,' Eline said, and put her wine glass down on a side table before her shaking hand betrayed her. 'I . . . might have an idea who you speak of.'

'Of course you have,' the baron said quietly. 'You work for him, don't you?'

Eline covered her shock with a cough, but the baron rescued her by putting a hand on her knee and leaning in as though he meant to kiss her, for appearances' sake.

'It wasn't her,' he said in a low voice. 'Tell Luka it can't be done, and stop trying. If you kill her for this crime that she didn't commit, I swear I will have you exterminated myself.'

The baron leaned forward toward her as he said it, a fire burning in his old eyes and a taut intensity in his jaw that in that moment made him look absolutely murderous.

Who were *you?* Eline thought.

Eline jerked away from him with a very un-courtesan-like look of horror on her face.

Put another hundred marks on the bill, you stupid girl.

Madame had told her that for a slap, yes, but not for a direct threat of death! Who *was* this horrible old man, and what on earth had she got herself into?

Yes, she feared Luka and what he could do, but she was beginning to fear the aged Baron Lan Elenkov every bit as much.

Perhaps more, in that moment.

My ships sailed the Poppy Winds, he had said, and those words made him both a smuggler and almost certainly a pirate as well. How many men had he murdered, on the high seas? How many ships had he taken?

'My lord, I don't understand,' she started, but the baron cut her off with a glare that belied both his age and the amount he'd had to drink.

There was nothing drunken in his sharp eyes in that moment, and she could see the man he had once been. A man both fierce in his younger years and, she thought then, still utterly ruthless when the occasion demanded it.

'This thing your Luka accused Madame of, the death of the duke, I swear before Our Lady of Eternal Sorrows that she had no hand in,' the baron said. 'It happened in the Silver Bells, that I cannot deny, but Madame had no part of it.'

'Then who—'

'Seek a girl called Elizaveta,' he said. 'She was whoring out of the Bells at the time the duke died, and my spies tell me she was the last person to see him alive. There, I think you may find your killer.'

'Your spies?' Eline whispered. 'Who even *are* you?'

'An old friend of Madame's, as I told you,' the baron said. 'A retired merchant seaman who may have certain connections abroad. You really don't need to know any more than that.'

'Why was the duke killed, tell me that at least?'

'Ours is not the only country to have had ... complications, shall we say, with its royal succession. The duke was of the house of Marodieva, and next in line for the Immalian throne.'

'Who?' Eline asked, looking at him in bewilderment. 'Where? Is that a place?'

'Immalia? Oh yes, of course it is. It's in the mountains to the north and east of Kastavia, which you *must* have heard of, surely?'

'Um,' said Eline, who in that moment wasn't sure if she had or not. It sounded vaguely familiar, at least. 'Yes, yes of course.'

'Liar,' the baron said, but he tempered the word with a smile. 'Foreign climes, foreign politics. Not much of our concern, is it, save where it interferes with business.'

'Which I assume this did?'

'Oh yes, very much so I'm afraid. Someone had the duke removed, and I think that person was Immalian but it definitely wasn't their hand who held the knife. Find Elizaveta, and you will have either found your killer or at the very least someone who knows who they were.'

Eline swallowed.

She couldn't personally have given a flying fuck who had killed this duke whose name she didn't even know, but she knew that Luka very much did, and Luka held power of life and death over not only her but her children, too.

Whatever it takes.

'How do I broach this with Luka?' she asked after a moment. 'May I mention your name?'

'In the god's names, no,' the baron snapped at her. 'I don't think he even knows I exist, and I like it very well that way. Even if he does he *certainly* doesn't know who I actually am, and marks me only for the drunken old lech I pretend to be. Make something up, girl. You're a courtesan, or almost anyway. You're effectively an actress; lying is supposed to be what you're best at. Now get in my lap and look coy, the earl is approaching.'

It seemed the time for candid speech and honesty was well and truly over, and a moment later Eline was making herself settle onto the baron's thin, bony thighs and giggle excessively. It made her feel a little bit ill, in all honesty, but she found that she could do it.

Fifty marks.

At least it sounded like she wasn't going to have to go to bed with him and on the surface of it that made the evening easy money, but she wondered if it really was. Foreign politics was a new battleground to her, and one far wider and potentially more dangerous than the rivalries of her fellow courtesans. She wasn't really going to get dragged into that shit, was she?

The Earl Lan Klasskoff swept past with his stunningly beautiful if absolutely icy-looking wife on his arm, and she paused to give Eline and the baron a scathing look.

'For the love of the gods, Lan Elenkov,' she said, 'have you no shame at all?'

'I assure you, ma'am, none whatsoever,' the baron said.

Now that Eline was listening for it, she could tell that he was affecting a drunken slur that hadn't been there a moment before when he had been speaking to her. It was all a lie, of course, like everything else. Like her coquettish behaviour, her sitting in his lap as the Countess Lan Klasskoff sneered down at them both. The life of a courtesan *was* a lie, of course she knew that, but it seemed that the life of a baron involved in intrigue might not be so very much different.

'Your *granddaughter* is older than she is!'

'I know,' Lan Elenkov said, and leered at the earl with an exaggerated wink. 'Good, isn't it?'

The countess made a disgusted noise and tugged on her husband's arm, and they vanished into the crowd.

'You're quite the actor yourself,' Eline acknowledged.

'One has to be, in the circles I move in,' he said.

Again she found herself wondering exactly what circles those might be.

I swear I will have you exterminated myself.

That was, to speak lightly of it, not a comforting thought.

The baron's coach returned Eline to the House of Silver Bells some time after the second hour of the morning. It was Godsday by then of course and she knew she would have to be up for temple in a few hours, but all the same she found Nama waiting up for her in the common room.

'How did it go?' the younger woman asked, eyes bright with excitement. 'A society ball!'

'Not a ball, only a reception,' Eline said, and yawned. 'In truth it was quite dull.'

Nama frowned at her.

'How can anything at the house of the Earl Lan Klasskoff possibly be *dull*?'

'When your assignation is with a man approaching his eightieth year, very easily,' Eline lied.

If Nama was going to keep secrets from her about the cunning, then that made it all the easier to keep what the baron had told her secret from Nama.

'Oh gods, you didn't have to, did you?' Nama asked.

'Thankfully not,' Eline said. 'I really think we should turn in, we've temple in the morning.'

'It *is* the morning,' Nama said, 'and so what? I usually catch an hour or so in my pew. You don't snore, do you?'

Eline, who had no idea if she did or not, blinked at her.

'I . . . don't think so,' she said at last. 'Look, sorry, Nama, but I really think I'd rather just go to bed.'

'Spoilsport,' Nama said. 'Oh, come *on*, tell me. Did you have to at least attempt to fuck him, little wrinkly cock and all?'

'No, thank the gods,' Eline said. 'He didn't even want to, truth be told. He just wanted a companion for the evening. That's what courtesans are *for*, by and large.'

'Horseshit,' Nama said bluntly. 'No cunt is stupid enough to pay that much just for some tart to drape off his arm as a decoration for a few hours. If he didn't want a leg over then he wanted *something*, didn't he? A political thing, maybe? *That* is mostly what courtesans are for, as you should bloody well know by now if Madame's been teaching you right.'

Eline blinked and looked at Nama's narrowed eyes, and wondered if perhaps they were working their way around the edges of something here.

She shrugged and rubbed her temples.

'I really am going to bed,' she said.

'Oh no you ain't,' Nama said, and suddenly she had Eline by both arms and was pushing her forcefully back into one of the armchairs in the common room. 'I want to hear about this.'

'What the fuck for?' Eline protested. 'A grotty old drunken baron paid a lot of money to be seen in society with me sitting in his lap tonight. It's pathetic, if you ask me. Ain't no more to it than that, but if it makes him happy then who gives a fuck? Payday for me, innit?'

'And there ain't any more to it?' Nama challenged her, and the hard look on the girl's face made Eline feel cold. 'Are you sure about that?'

Again, Eline wondered if they might be working their way around the edges of something. Whether they were or not, there was definitely something Nama wasn't telling her.

'For the love of the gods,' she started, but Nama wasn't having it and she quite clearly wasn't going to leave it there.

'We both work for *him*,' she said, and now her voice was hushed. 'For the fucking Queen's Men, unless I've missed my guess.'

Eline realised then that Nama knew even less than she did, and in that moment she caved. Perhaps that was unwise, but it was the choice she made then when it was approaching the third hour after midnight and she had far too much wine inside her to make sensible decisions.

'You don't miss your guess at all,' she said quietly.

'Thought so,' Nama said, easing up. 'You know what they say about the Queen's Men, don't you? "Always someone watching, and always someone to watch the watchers." Probably explains why he's got me watching *you*.

I don't know who the fuck watches me, but I'd bet gold that someone does.'

'I do,' Eline said, and in that moment her voice was iron. The younger woman had started trying to push her around, and she suddenly realised that she absolutely wasn't having that.

Not even a little bit she wasn't.

Not anymore. Not after Caromir. Never again.

'What?'

Eline glared at her. 'I told him about your cunning,' she said. 'He never asked me to, but I thought he ought to know. That's how they *work*, Nama. I don't know what he's got over you and if you don't want to tell me then I respect that but as you said he has very much got things over me, and I'll do whatever I have to that keeps him sweet. I have children and he holds their lives in the palm of his hand, as he has made *very* clear to me.'

'Fucking hell,' Nama said, after a long pause.

'Aye,' Eline had to agree. 'I'll talk to him. About tonight, I mean. Last night, whenever the fuck it was. About the baron. I'm *tired*, Nama. Please just let me go to bed. We have to be up for temple in less than four hours and I'm fucked.'

'Hah, be grateful you ain't,' Nama joked, but she stepped back and let Eline get to her feet. 'You got off light there, I reckon. Go on then, but be sure that you see him after temple tomorrow. We can meet in the Rat afterwards.'

'For what, a fucking debriefing?' Eline snapped, remembering some of Caromir's army phrases from his endless bloody stories about the supposed glory of serving garrison duty during peace time. She had never really been entirely sure what he had got his medal *for*, exactly, but it certainly hadn't been won in combat as he'd never seen a day of it in all his twenty years of service. 'I don't work for you, Nama, and don't ever make the mistake of thinking that I do. Now shut up, I'm going to bed.'

Chapter 11

By the next morning Eline had a thick head and a sour feeling of regret for talking to Nama like that. The girl was young, she had to remind herself, and probably every bit as scared of the Queen's Men as she was herself. She meant well, Eline could only tell herself, although of course Nama still had no idea why she was in the house at Luka's direction or what he wanted her to do. She honestly had no idea what Nama would have thought of that if she *had* known, but it was definitely best that she didn't. She wasn't even sure Nama knew his name.

Madame was hard to like, it was true, but over the weeks of her training Eline had at least come to respect her. Her employer had quite obviously been a courtesan herself in her younger years, and perhaps even still was to a certain set of the older gentlemen of society, and she was incredibly skilled in the associated arts of her trade. Her subtlety with the fan was nothing short of artistry, and she still danced like she was floating on air. Eline could not imagine she would ever dance like that, although she was slowly getting better.

Slowly, slowly, everything was so fucking slow. She whored away her nights and spent most of her days on Madame's lessons, and yes she was gradually improving but it chafed at her how slow she was to learn.

Still, that morning, after they'd all had their medicine, she took her sore head to temple with Nama and Madame and the other girls, and managed to doze a little in her pew while the priest droned on and on. Nama was silently sound-out beside her, but Eline *didn't* know if she snored or not and honestly didn't dare let herself go all the way to sleep in case it turned out that she did. She dreaded to think what Madame would have made of a full snore in the middle of the priest's seemingly endless sermon. Nothing good, she was sure.

Eventually it was over, and they returned to the House of Silver Bells for lunch. The Godsday roast was done by then, and filling the house with a mouth-watering smell, and Eline was happy to sit down to table with Nama and the other girls in the common room. Nama was to her left but there was a blonde woman she had never spoken to before called Katherine at her right, and she felt no extension of friendship from her.

'You're the old one,' Katherine said to her, without introduction or explanation. It seemed she meant to be rude, on purpose. 'Why the bloody hell are you here?'

'I used to work out of the Petal,' Eline said, remembering her cover story, 'but you know what happened there. We've all got to work, ain't we?'

'At your fucking age?' Katherine said. She had all of twenty-five years to her, if that, from the look of her. Probably less, with how the whoring lifestyle aged a woman. 'You ought to have found better by now. A steady man. A marriage.'

'I had both of those,' Eline said, and gave the blonde woman a blunt look. 'It was shit, and then he died. So here I fucking am.'

'Again,' Katherine said. 'Lying on your back again, legs in the air for strangers. At your age. It's pathetic. I won't be doing that, you mark me. I'll make more of myself than that, you sad old tart.'

'Do you,' Eline whispered quietly, 'want a knife in the ribs? Because you're going to fucking get one in a minute, you bitch. Madame is training me as a courtesan.'

She still had the stiletto Madame had given her in her pouch, after all, and she had no intention of giving it back unless someone asked, which they hadn't. She had a feeling Madame had wanted her to keep it but hadn't wanted to say so, and again that caused her feelings about the woman to become even more confused. *Did* she care about her?

Eline had no idea, but she was starting to think that the idea wasn't completely impossible.

'A courtesan, is it?' the other woman spat, and turned to address the rest of the table. 'Oh get her, all jumped the fuck up. Better than us, she is, girls. A fucking courtesan, this one. Not just a whore like us.'

'Shut the fuck up, Kat,' Nama growled from the other side of her. 'She's all right.'

'She's a fucking prig,' Katherine said, and she seemed determined to pick a fight for no reason that Eline could see. 'Stuck-up bitch, with her husband and his house and—'

Eline lost her shit all at once.

Everything, all the shock and the trauma of it, came down on her like a thunderbolt in that single moment.

I killed a man.

I took a life.

I murdered my husband.

Oh no, she was not over what she had done at *all*.

You want a fight, you're getting one!

Once moment she was forking slabs of the Godsday roast into her mouth and the next she was launching herself at Katherine's throat, and she had no idea when the transition had happened.

It was instinct, *rage*.

Red mist, pure and simple.

She dived onto the other woman and sent her chair crashing to the floor as she landed on top of her with her hands around her neck and *fuck* whether she was still sane or not. She had her house? She had her *husband*?

Oh no, bitch, no I have not.

'His fucking *house*?' Eline all but shrieked in her face. 'Do you know what he did to me, in his *fucking* house?'

She was aware of hands on her shoulders, Nama pulling her back as she flailed at Katherine's face. At least, she supposed later, she hadn't drawn the stiletto. It could have been worse.

It could always be worse.

That was a thing you had to learn in this world, she supposed: however bad things were, it could always be worse. The world has an endless capacity to make things worse and that was the simple truth of the matter.

'Eline, no!' Nama shouted as she dragged her off the other woman. 'Stop it!'

If they're on the floor, you're done, she remembered her mother telling her. *Time to leave it there, Eline.* Marcoss was there a moment later, looming in the doorway.

'What the fuck,' he said slowly, 'is going on in here?'

'Nothing,' Nama and Katherine said almost simultaneously, and a moment later Eline echoed them.

Matters between the girls were nothing the household guard needed to know about, that was very obvious, and Marcoss himself needed to know even less so. She knew that the worst thing in the world she could have done right then was to say anything to him.

Snitches get stitches, after all, even Eline knew that, and in all honesty she supposed she *had* started it herself. The violent part, anyway. Either way this was between them, and no business of Marcoss's.

He gave them a short nod.

'See that it fucking stays that way,' he said. 'You tarts sort your own hierarchy out, that's fine by me, but if anyone hurts anyone else in the way a punter will notice then I *will* have a problem with it. Then I'll have to do something to you that *doesn't* show but will hurt very fucking badly indeed, do you understand me?'

'Yes Marcoss,' they all muttered, and Eline could tell that none of them liked it any better than she did.

There was something about him that went beyond the normal pimp, something that made her think he was far more dangerous than that. For one thing he worked for Madame and she was obviously *someone*, even if Eline hadn't quite worked out who yet.

Madame was a business associate in the poppy trade.

That alone made her a gangster of some sort, but Marcoss was more than that. She remembered Caromir's tales of the Quiet Men who had been in great demand in the siege lines.

'Quiet Men' was army slang for the throat-slitters and sentry killers, she knew that much, and she could well imagine Marcoss had been one of those back in his war. Caromir had been forever going on about the Quiet Men, like he worshipped them or something. Caromir from the garrison, who had never seen a day's battle in his life.

There was something about Marcoss, some cloud of dark menace that seemed to hang over his head that left her in no doubt at all of what he had once been. Crawling through the wire in the dead of night, opening throats and slipping away into the silence undetected, aye, she could well imagine Marcoss had done those things on the blasted and poisoned battlefields below the walls of Krathzgrad. Those things had to change a man as far as she was concerned, and probably not for the better in her opinion. She thought then that she was looking at the end product of those experiences standing right there in front of her, and the thought made her feel cold. No man could come back from that and still be truly human, surely?

'Right, fucking behave yourselves then,' he said, and stalked back out of the room to leave them to their Godsday lunch.

Eline realised Katherine was staring at her.

'All right,' the blonde said after a moment, as though extending a truce. 'Maybe I was being a bitch.'

'You were,' Eline assured her, before Nama jabbed her in the ribs and brought her back to her senses. 'Maybe I shouldn't have gone for you like that.'

To her surprise Katherine smiled.

'Fuck it,' she said, 'one bitch has got to stand up to another, ain't she, and I can respect you for that. Least you didn't say nothing to Marcoss.'

'I'm not a snitch,' Eline said, and Katherine nodded.

'Good,' she said. 'Now how about you and your pet tea monkey eat your lunch and I'll eat mine, and we say no more about it?'

Eline stiffened at the slur, but she felt Nama's hand tighten on her arm to tell her to shut up.

'Aye,' she said instead, and they sat back down at table to eat.

'Kat's a Skanian,' Nama whispered in Eline's ear. 'She gets a pass.'

'How the fuck is that?'

'You don't know what happened in the capital a couple of years ago? Skanians were persecuted to the point of extinction. Queenkillers, people called them, and they lynched them in the streets and drove them out of the city to starve on the roads. We nearly had a fucking war over it. It was a genocide, just about. If she calls me 'tea monkey' then it's in solidarity. She can get away with it, but she's the only fucking one who can.'

Eline had absolutely no idea what the younger woman was talking about. Caromir had read the news sheets, aye, and raged about the things that gave him an excuse to drink instead of work, but he had always tossed them into the fire when he was done with them and never told her what else they had said other than the parts that he wanted to shout about. He had never spoken to her about these Skanians, or whatever had happened to them. Perhaps he hadn't understood, or more likely simply hadn't cared, but that was beside the point. She had just been a *wife*, after all, a glorified domestic servant who had to entertain his sexual advances and endless boasting as well, not anyone you *talked* to. Gods, no.

No, he wouldn't have done that. Wives were for skivvying, fucking and beating, at least in Caromir's book anyway. He had treated her like a *thing*, not a person, and she supposed that was probably how she had adapted to the whoring life so easily. It really wasn't much different, although it came with fewer domestic chores and at least no one hit her anymore. It was, on balance, probably better when you thought about it.

Do you know what he did to me, in his fucking house?

She felt her hands trying to shake, and gripped her cutlery hard as she tried to force down the rest of her lunch.

I murdered my husband.

'I should go and see *him* when we're done here,' Eline whispered to Nama after she had choked down another mouthful. 'See you in the Rat after?'

'What for, a fucking debriefing?' Nama mocked, and Eline flushed.

'Sorry about that,' she said. 'It was late and I was drunk.'

'I should think you fucking were,' Nama said. 'All right, the Rat it is, and let's get drunk again.'

Eline had to laugh at that.

'Aye, let's do that,' she said.

After all, they were whores with money in their purses and an afternoon off. What else were they going to do?

Chapter 12

Appealing though getting drunk in the Rat with Nama sounded, Eline knew she had to see Luka first. He wasn't there when she arrived at the house, but a big man had the door and he seemed affable enough.

'All right?' he said. 'I'm Sam, and I keep the boss's door when he ain't here. Who the fuck are you?'

He had maybe forty years to him and that probably made him a veteran of Messia and Abingon the same as Luka, and Eline gave him a nod of respect. She wasn't wearing the knot as it was Godsday and she was off work, and he obviously had no idea who she was.

'I'm Eline,' she said. 'I work for him too.'

'Aye, well, lot of people in the city do,' this Sam said, and she wondered how much she could believe that.

Truth be told he seemed a bit simple to her but there was a *lot* of him, and his frame almost filled the doorway.

'Can I come in? I've things I need to tell him, when he comes home.'

Sam's brow crinkled as he made an exaggerated show of thinking about it.

'Reckon so,' he said eventually. 'If you're lying he'll fucking kill you, or more likely have me do it. You might as well have a sit while you're waiting. Shame to do it, you're pretty, but there we are.'

He didn't sound like he much cared one way or the other, and that made Eline shiver right down to her bones. The Queen's Men and their operatives seemed to care not one jot about individual lives, and human rights simply didn't exist to them. They barely existed in the Crown constitution, in all honesty, but on the streets?

Not at all.

'My thanks,' she said, and the huge man let her into the house and showed her the way she already knew to the back room.

There was a bottle of brandy and a number of glasses standing on the cupboard so she helped herself to a drink while she waited.

She hadn't had *that* many by the time Luka came home, she told herself, but it was definitely more than it should have been.

'Eline,' he greeted her as he walked into the room and fixed her glass of his brandy with a hard stare. 'How good of you to turn up pissed and with no progress to report to me. Again. Your poisons have arrived from Dannsburg, by the way.'

'Thanks, but I'm not sure I need them now,' Eline said.

Luka gave her a long look. 'Then she's already dead?'

'Ah, no,' Eline confessed. 'Not as such. I had an assignation, as a courtesan you understand, with a gentleman of connections. He, ah, never told me his true name but he was adamant Madame had no hand in—'

'Oh gods, that's Lan Elenkov,' Luka said at once.

I don't think he even knows I exist, Lan Elenkov had told her.

It seemed the baron had been wrong about that. The Queen's Men knew *everything*.

Assume I know everything, and you'll never be caught in a lie.

'Good,' Luka continued. 'The whole point of your assignment was to draw him out of hiding. I know fucking well your Madame didn't kill the duke, but poking *that* was always going to bring him out of the woodwork. What did he tell you?'

'A woman,' Eline ventured, her head spinning with this new information. How easily he had played her, set her an impossible objective he quite obviously hadn't needed or even *wanted* her to achieve. 'Elizaveta, the baron called her. Apparently she used to work at the Bells. She's the one he suspects of the murder.'

'Mmmm,' Luka said. 'Possibly. *Possibly.* All right, find her. Get the truth out of her.'

'How?' Eline asked.

'I don't fucking care,' Luka snapped at her. 'Kick the shit out of her. Break her fingers, I really do not give one single ounce of shit. Just find out who killed that duke, because if it was Kastavia then we have got a *very* big problem.'

'What the fuck,' Eline asked then, 'was the point of telling me to kill Madame?'

Luka smirked.

'I just wanted to see if you would be prepared to try. I knew you probably couldn't actually do it, but you at least tried. Following her to the shithouse, asking me for poisons. Killing your abuser in the heat of the moment and killing a stranger in cold blood are very different things, after all. I was getting the measure of you, Eline, and now I think I have it. Now I think I know what you're prepared to do, and that is important to me.'

Eline didn't want to think about that. She cleared her throat and returned to the original subject at hand.

'My assignation thought the killer was someone in Immalia,' she ventured again.

'I hope so, girl,' Luka said. 'I fucking well hope so.'

Eline met up with Nama in the Rat as they had agreed, and Kurt was already there at her table because of course he fucking was.

'What news?' Nama said, when she joined them with a cup of cheap wine in her hand.

'I'm looking for a woman,' Eline said.

'Ain't we all?' Kurt said, and leered at Nama in a way that made Eline want to punch him in the throat.

Nama ignored him. 'What woman?'

'Elizaveta,' she said. 'She used to work out of the Bells, apparently. You remember her?'

'Oh,' Nama said, and she looked a bit evasive then. 'She left after . . . Well. Some shit happened, then no one saw her again.'

Eline looked sideways at Kurt. 'Don't you need a piss by now?' she asked, rather pointedly even by her standards.

'No, but I can take a hint,' he said, and got up and headed to the door that led out to the courtyard where the shithouse was.

Eline watched him leave, then leaned over the table to talk quietly to her friend. 'When you say "some shit happened" you mean a duke died in the house, yes?'

'Aye, well maybe,' Nama admitted. 'I don't know anything about that.'

'No, apparently no one does,' Eline said. 'Fuck's sake, who *was* this Elizaveta?'

'Just some whore,' Nama said. 'No one special. The thing happened, and the next morning she wasn't there. There was just a dead duke in her room, and all the shit that came with it. That's when *he* turned up, obviously.'

'And he thinks you know something about it,' Eline said. '*That's* what he's got over you, isn't it?'

'But I *don't*,' Nama protested. 'I'll do doubles with another girl sometimes if they're paying enough but I never did with Elizaveta. I weren't there, Eline. I honest to the gods don't know what happened. I've been on my fucking *knees* pleading to him that I don't know what happened, and I think even he at least sort of believes me now. I was fucking this scabby merchant at the time and I even gave up his name to the fat man, and he found him and got him to back up my story. I wasn't *there!*'

Luka, Eline thought. *His name is Luka, and apparently you don't know that.*

She wondered whether to tell her or not, and decided against it. Maintaining Luka's trust was paramount.

'Who's likely to know where she went?' she asked.

Nama shrugged.

'Where do whores go?' she said. 'Some other stew, if she was lucky. The street, otherwise. I don't fucking know. Truth be told she was on her last warning at the Bells as it was. Losing her looks, she was, too fond of a bit of the poppy. Not making Madame enough money anymore. I reckon she'd have been out on her ear in another month or two even if . . . you know . . . nothing had happened.'

'And you don't know how to find her?'

Eline realised she was leaning over the table, almost nose to nose with the other woman like she wanted to start a fight and she *didn't*, but . . . Aye, *but.* Ever since she had killed Caromir she had felt a violence bubbling up within her, some fury of Our Lady of Eternal Sorrows welling up from the core of her being telling her that perhaps this was the way to make her way in the world. The way of the Lady of Death.

She took a long breath, and sat back in her seat. Caromir had boasted to her of battle shock and the men who suffered from it, and obviously she had never been in a battle in her life any more than he had, but she *had* killed a man. She had killed Caromir himself, for the Lady's sake.

I took a life.

I killed a man.

That was more than he had ever done.

Her hands trembled on the table, and she thought in that moment that perhaps she understood battle shock better than Caromir ever had. Kurt came back then, and took his seat at the table whether he was welcome or not. Eline was pretty sure he knew he wasn't, and simply didn't care.

'That's as long as I can pretend to take a piss without people thinking there's something wrong with me,' he said, 'and I wouldn't ever want that. Now, may I buy you lovely ladies another drink?'

Eline didn't want his company one little bit but she knew she was getting it whether she did or not so she figured she might as well get a drink out of him as go without. Free drink was free drink, after all, and she wouldn't feel like she owed him anything for it.

'Aye,' she said. 'Wine.'

He nodded and headed to the bar, and Eline was aware of Nama looking at her.

'I thought you were going to go for me then,' the Alarian girl said. 'The same way you went for Kat.'

'Nearly did,' Eline confessed, and looked down at her hands. 'Don't mean nothing by it. Ever since . . . Well, I told you what happened. With my husband, I mean. I haven't . . . I haven't been quite right since, Nama.'

'No, I can see that,' Nama said. 'Fuck's sake, Eline.'

'I know.'

She swallowed, and said nothing. What else, really, could she have said? What could excuse it? Nothing that she could think of. It was like there was a pressure in her head, something that needed an outlet she hadn't found. Something that only wanted to manifest in violence, but surely there had to be a better way than that?

If there was, Eline was yet to find it.

Kurt came back then with their cups of wine and a tankard for himself.

'Now, my lovelies,' he said, in a way that put Eline's back up at once, 'what's the word in the world of whores?'

'The word is "cunt" if it's applied to you,' Eline snapped. 'Now here's one for you, as you seem so sure you know everything: where the fuck is Elizaveta?'

Kurt snorted laughter and beer in equal measure, and wiped his nose on the back of his sleeve in a truly revolting manner.

'Her from the Bells? The one what may or may not have done for a duke?' he asked.

Eline glared at him. 'You know fucking well who I mean.'

'I last heard tell of her down by the river,' Kurt said. 'No other house would have her after what happened, the way I heard it. Wouldn't know, of course. Just what I heard, you understand me?'

'Oh no, you wouldn't know, would you?' Eline sneered, and Nama kicked her under the table to tell her to shut up.

'Me?' Kurt said. 'What do I know of the business of whores?'

'You know everything that goes on in this city,' Nama said, and the fawning tone in her voice made Eline's hackles rise even more. 'Come on, tell my mate what she wants to know.'

Kurt snorted and took a long drink of his beer.

'If a man wanted to fuck Elizaveta, and the gods only know why he would these days,' he said, 'he'd seek out Black Nose Bob down by the river. He runs her, and some equally grotty scrubs alongside. She's fallen a long way from her days at the Silver Bells, believe you me.'

'Black Nose Bob?' Eline asked. 'Why do they call him that?'

'Had his nose bit off in a fight, or so he says. More than likely it rotted off from the Maiden's Pox,' Kurt said. 'Either way he wears a fake wooden nose and it's gone black from wear. Grotty bastard, either way, but he runs the riverside girls.'

'And she's one of those now?'

'So I heard. Not that I'd know, like.'

Eline looked at him and thought that he would know very well indeed.

Chapter 13

The next day was Maidensday, the first day of the week, and Eline was supposed to be doing chores around the house in the morning but she gladly paid Marcoss the customary forfeit of coin to get out of it and slipped out of the house alone.

After her night with the baron she could well afford it, after all. Loran on the door tried to stop her, of course, but she managed to convince him she was only going to market to spend her new-found windfall on clothes and frippery, so he let her go with a grumbling admonishment not to go any further from the house than that.

'Take care in the city,' Marcoss said, which rather surprised her.

Once she was around the corner and out of sight Eline untied her bawd's knot and stuffed the thick yellow cord into her pouch with her stiletto and her purse and handkerchief and bag of pins. Without it she could pass for any city goodwife, in her demure grey kirtle and good green cloak.

She had no interest in the market, and instead made her way through the crowded streets in the direction of the towering spire of Drathburg's Great Temple of All Gods, half the city away. Loran would have pitched a fit, but she knew she had to do it before she lost her mind altogether.

There was no dedicated temple of Our Lady of Eternal Sorrows in Drathburg, and she doubted there was anywhere else either. Few worshipped the Lady of Death before their time came to stand before Her, as all did in the end, but once that time came *all* sought Her favour. Every Great Temple had a chapel dedicated to Her name though, and that was where Eline was headed. She had to get herself under control, she knew that all too well. She had so, *so* nearly attacked Nama the night before, and that was the last thing she wanted to do. That and the fight with Katherine were so out of character for her that she knew . . . No. No, she *didn't* know, and that was the whole problem. What the fuck was *wrong* with her?

Killing Caromir had done something to her, something that had fucked her up good and proper, but she was struggling to understand exactly what. Who else would know, but a priest of Death?

She reached the Great Temple at last, and its wide doors were standing open in the morning sun, welcoming all who wished to worship any of the Faith's wide pantheon of gods and goddesses. Eline knew little of religion beyond what she had learned as a girl and heard at the temple of the Harvest Maiden that Madame made them attend, and even there she seldom listened. All the same she remembered Caromir's dark mutterings about Our Lady when he had oh so frequently been in his cups. She was, it seemed, widely revered amongst soldiers, which Eline supposed made sense.

Don't ask Her for nothing, she remembered him slurring. *She don't help, not never. Best you can hope for is She knows your name and She don't take your life today.*

Eline swallowed as she stepped into the vast knave of the Great Temple, searching the carved stone effigies of the gods for the one she wanted. There was the Storm Lord clutching His great carved lightning bolt, there the Forge Father with hammer in hand, the Harvest Maiden with Her sheaves of wheat and then there, *there*, the shrouded woman with the sword in Her hands. Eline made her way towards the statue of Our Lady and knelt briefly in front of it before she reached for the door that led to Her chapel.

The room was small, with maybe a dozen pews and a graven altar on which two lamps burned. Lamps were traditionally for funerals, to light the deceased's way into the grey lands. Even Eline knew that, remembering it from her mother's own sad, modest funeral. What they could afford, which had been little enough. At least she had been able to scrape together enough to see her buried properly, not just thrown into the pauper's mass grave outside the city walls that she knew would have been Caromir's preference. She lingered on that thought for a moment, and found her feelings about having killed Caromir diminishing. She paused for a moment, taking it in, then slowly walked down the narrow transept to kneel once more before the altar.

She stayed there for a long time, trying to pray and realising she had no idea how. Instead she found herself wondering what she was truly doing there.

I'm not even really a religious woman, she thought but she knew she needed ... *something*, even if she didn't really know what. Who did you turn to at a time like that, if not a priest?

What do I want? What can kneeling on a stone floor in a temple possibly teach me?

A moment later she became aware of a tall man standing in front of her. She looked up and saw that he was bearded and wore a long black priest's robe over the same sort of coat and doublet and shirt that any man who wasn't a pauper wore, and around his waist he wore a belt that supported a long sword.

It seemed incongruous to see a priest wearing a sword, but she had heard that the servants of the Lady of Death seldom went unarmed and she supposed that made sense.

'My name is Father Shepherd,' he said. 'Do you seek the Lady's blessing, Daughter?'

His voice was deep and solemn, but there was something welcoming in his eyes as he looked down at her, something that made her want to trust him.

'I ...' Eline started, and the memories came back to her. Killing Caromir, fighting Katherine in the Bells, almost attacking Nama the night before. She wasn't sure about a blessing as such, but she knew she needed help of some sort, at least. 'Yes, Father.'

He frowned at her for a moment, then smiled.

'You're new to the faith of Our Lady, aren't you?'

'Um, yes, Father,' she confessed.

'The form of it is simple,' he explained. 'You ask for my blessing and you state your name and your trade, and I bless you so that Our Lady might know you and stay Her hand this day. Our faith and our doctrine is a simple one designed to be understood by everyone, be they beggar or king, as all face Her in their last moments.'

Eline supposed that made sense, but all the same she felt ashamed to admit it in front of this priest. Nonetheless, she bowed her head. She *needed* this, she knew she did, even if she didn't really know why.

'Blessing, Father?' she said. 'My name is Eline and ... and I'm a whore.'

The last words came out in a panicked rush, but all the same she felt the priest's cool, dry hand alight briefly on her forehead.

'Our Lady go with you, Daughter,' he said.

'You ... you don't mind?' Eline said, looking up at him in open astonishment.

He was a *priest*, after all.

He snorted.

'Don't you know your scripture? Don't you know what Our Lady has to say on the subject of sexual relations?' he demanded, then relented and smiled. 'No, of course you don't. "Lie with whom thou wilt, so long as both be willing." That's it. That's the entirety of it. Our Lady simply does not care who we lie with, so long as no one is harmed by it.'

'Thank you, Father,' Eline whispered.

'Why are you here?' the priest asked her. 'I see very few but the aged and the dying, and you appear to be neither of those things.'

'I . . .' Eline started, and faltered to a stop.

'You are recently bereaved?' the priest said. 'A parent, perhaps? Lady forbid, a child?'

'No,' Eline whispered.

The priest looked at her for a long moment, then the corner of his mouth turned up in the beginnings of a wry smile.

'Who did you kill?' he asked softly.

'My husband,' Eline confessed.

The priest nodded slowly.

'And did he deserve it?'

'I think so,' Eline said.

'Why?'

'He *beat* me,' Eline almost shouted, and before she could get herself under any semblance of control she was howling tears. Now that she was kneeling before this priest she found she was pouring her heart out in a tidal wave of grief and sorrow and long-buried hurt. 'For *years*, he beat me, he raped me, he . . . he would have killed my *children* if I hadn't put myself between him and them time after time after time!'

Again the priest reached out and put his hand on her sweat-slick forehead as the salt streamed down her cheeks.

'Our Lady forgives you,' he said. 'In Her eyes you have done no wrong. Praise be to Our Lady of Eternal Sorrows, and blessed be the Ascended Martyr.'

'Blessed be,' Eline sobbed, and she felt a weight lift from her heart as she spoke.

She had, she realised in that moment, finally found a faith she could believe in. Her heart belonged to Our Lady now, she knew.

*

That night found Eline down beside the river. She wasn't working that night, having paid the forfeit for a night off. That was something she would never normally have been able to afford to do, but after her night with the baron she had the coin for it.

Drathburg wasn't a heavily industrial city like she'd heard Ellinburg was, but all the same the riverside and its trade docks were probably the worst part of town, and she had her wits about her and her stiletto in her pouch for all the good that was. Just the weight of it gave her a probably misplaced sense of confidence, but she was acutely aware that she had no real idea how to use it.

There were warehouses and inns and taverns, some of them burning the red lantern over their front doors that said they were stews as well. That wasn't what she was looking for. From what she had heard from Kurt in the Rat last night she was looking for Elizaveta among the street girls, and there were plenty of those around the docks. They had their skirts hitched to the hip on one side, some of them, bodices tight around the waist and loose at the chest, so obvious it was laughable. Even so, it seemed Eline had the look of a whore herself now, demurely dressed even though she was.

'What's your hourly?' a man shouted at her from across the street.

'Fuck off, I'm not working,' Eline replied, before one of the street girls could stab her for trying to take her territory. 'I'm looking for a pimp, actually. You know Black Nose Bob?'

'Never heard of him,' the bloke said, and turned his back to continue his endless pursuit of carnal pleasure.

'You want Bob?' a voice said.

Eline turned and looked down at her. The poor girl couldn't have had more than fourteen years to her and that was probably being generous with the truth. Technically old enough to be working, in the eyes of the law at least, but only fucking just and Eline didn't like it one little bit. It made her think too much of her own daughter, and how she would have felt if it had been *her* out there on those unforgiving streets.

'Aye,' she said.

'He'll be in the Lobster,' the girl said. 'Gizza penny?'

Eline sighed and fished a small silver coin out of her purse, but held it tight in her hand.

'He run a girl called Elizaveta?'

'Stuck-up name,' the street scrub said. 'He runs a lot of girls, I dunno. My name's Molly. That's a good enough name for anyone.'

'It is,' Eline agreed, and gave the girl the penny. 'Where's this Lobster?'

The girl gave her directions, and Eline followed them to a run-down tavern near the water's edge. It was called The Lobster Pot, but close enough.

She pushed through the door and into the familiar smell of a cheap tavern. It smelled of eggs and vomit and tallow, stale beer and piss. She looked around her and saw her man at once. That had to be Black Nose Bob, sitting at a table, wearing a badly discoloured wooden prosthetic nose and drinking cheap brandy from a chipped glass. Whether he'd really lost his nose in a fight or to the pox was anyone's guess, but the deep scars on his cheeks told her it was probably the latter. He was an older man, wearing a stained red doublet over a grubby white shirt, and he had two ugly, lumpen thugs beside him that were presumably his low-rent bodyguards. He was surrounded by a few grotty scrubs that she could only assume had the misfortune to work for him.

There really was no good way to do this.

Eline strode straight up to Black Nose Bob's table and asked him straight out where she could find Elizaveta.

'Elizaveta, is it?' he asked. 'And what do you want her for?'

'My old mate, ain't she?' Eline said. 'We both worked at the Bells.'

She supposed that was close enough to true to at least sort of sound it, and that was good enough for her. Black Nose Bob looked up at her.

'One of Madame's, are you?'

'Something like that,' Eline said. 'She sees me all right.'

'Well, you won't find that slag with me,' Black Nose Bob said. 'I kicked her out a month ago. Fucking poppy-head. I ain't having it.'

'She told me she'd got off it,' Eline said, making it up as she went along now that she had his attention.

'She was fucking lying, wasn't she?' Bob said, and turned to spit into the fireplace. 'Take a lesson, girlie. Addicts talk shit. They lie to their friends, to their families if they still have one, anyone. If someone's a fucking poppy-head you sack them right off, you hear me? That's a lesson for life and no mistake. Now get out. You want Elizaveta you'll find her selling her tail on the fucking docks where she belongs.'

Eline nodded and left the tavern before he felt the need to have her thrown out, which he looked like he was considering. She headed back out onto the street and made her way down toward the docks themselves.

She was almost there when a patrol of the City Guard rounded a corner and almost walked into her.

'Oh, for fuck's sake,' said the Guard sergeant as she saw Eline. She was a big woman, clearly burly under her leather and mail, and she had a short sword at one hip and a long wooden club at the other that her fingers kept brushing as she spoke, like she really wanted to hit someone with it. 'Another scrub, and not even a pretty one this time. We've been scraping you whores off the streets all night, but you keep coming back.'

Eline looked her in the eyes.

'Whoring ain't illegal,' she said.

'*Licensed* whoring ain't,' the sergeant agreed. 'Scrubs fucking are.'

'I'm licensed, and not even working tonight so I'm not your problem. Anyway, there's a man in that tavern,' she said, pointing back up the hill. 'The Lobster. He's called Black Nose Bob, and you'll leave me alone and arrest *him* if you're wise.'

The Guard sergeant laughed.

'And I'll listen to you because why?'

Eline flushed, and never before had she so envied Luka's ability to show the Warrant and immediately shut down conversations like this.

'I work for a man,' she said. 'A fat man who you probably know. A man who carries something you *definitely* know. You might know his name.'

'You mean Luka?' the sergeant said, which in itself told Eline she wasn't very bright.

She nodded.

'Aye,' she said. 'Go arrest that prick. Take him to our mutual friend, tell him Eline sent you. He'll know who I am.'

The Guard sergeant looked at her for a long moment with a frown on her face, clearly wondering whether she could believe her and weighing up the risk of not if Eline was actually telling her the truth. Eventually she nodded to her.

'Reckon we can do that,' she said.

She led her troop of guardsmen off towards the Lobster, and Eline continued her stroll through the streets of the docks.

There was no shortage of working girls on the corners and in the alleys, and she didn't even really know what Elizaveta looked like. Nama had described her, of course, but that was then and who knew what she looked like by now. She wandered the streets at random, listening to the girls' talk and hoping to hear names while fending off the occasional challenge about territory with protestations of innocence, until she found herself in an alley behind a warehouse and a closed workshop. It was very dark there, and the reek of old piss was almost overpowering.

The sudden shove sent Eline stumbling forward into the wall beside her, cracking her head on the rough stone. She gasped and saw stars for a moment, heard footsteps behind her. She turned groggily, and there she was. This woman, this Elizaveta she had been hunting, had found her first. She had a long rusty knife in her hand and a hard, flinty look on her face. As Kurt had implied, the time between her flight from the Bells and now had not been kind to Elizaveta. Now she was thin and dirty, and two of her front teeth were missing.

'Gonna cut you up, bitch,' she promised. 'You getting in my business. Bad idea. Very bad.'

One of the scrubs at Bob's table had obviously warned her Eline was asking questions about her.

The knife was too dull to reflect the moonlight, but its point looked sharp enough. Eline felt a moment of sheer terror, but her right hand was in her pouch and a moment later fumbled out with Madame's stiletto in it, the same way she had taken up her kitchen knife when Caromir had reared up over her for the very last time. She realised in that moment that her pouch was probably the worst place to keep it.

Too awkward, and I don't even know how to use it! Eline thought in a panic.

But she did.

I killed a man. I murdered my husband.

Elizaveta took another step, slightly to her right this time, as though she wanted to dance.

Dance!

Like the folk dances from the caravans, the ones her mother had taught her on long nights on the road. Dance, yes! *Real* dancing, not all that courtly shit Madame was trying to teach her now. The sort of dancing done beside campfires within the circle of the wagons, the spinning, whirling dance of joyful abandon. Even the menfolk of the caravans had danced, Eline remembered, after the women had taken their turns, but the men had danced with knives in their hands.

The memories came crashing back. Elizaveta lunged and Eline turned and stepped back, and through the veil of time into a world of long-buried memory and instinct. Her arms crossed gracefully in front of her and the stiletto caressed Elizaveta's forearm without thought, bringing blood dark in the dim light.

Eline continued her spin and flashed her arm out the other way, slashing her blade across Elizaveta's face. The woman stumbled backwards with a cry, dropping her own blade to the cobbles. Eline stamped and flung her arms out with the traditional shout of joy, and felt her blade punch deep into the other woman's side. Hot wetness sprayed across her hand but she was still moving, feeling the familiar grace of the dance adapt perfectly to knife fighting. What it was for, what it was really and truly *for* and always had been, she realised in that moment. Gods it was so *easy*, now she finally saw it.

Another whirling spin, a twist to bring her closer, and her elbow crashed into Elizaveta's temple and dropped her to the ground like a sack of turnips. Eline's dance slowed until it stopped altogether. She looked down at the other woman lying on the filthy cobbles in a spreading pool of blood and, again in the traditional gesture of the caravans, she spat on her.

Victorious.

Chapter 14

'A knife fight?' Nama gaped at her. 'How did you win a *knife fight* of all things? Have you ever been in one before?'

'No,' Eline confessed.

'I'd bet a crown to a copper that a street scrub had,' Nama said. 'How the fuck . . .?'

'I used to dance,' Eline said shyly.

'Dance? I thought you said you were shit at dancing.'

'Oh, I am,' Eline said. 'The courtly sort that Madame is teaching me, I meant when I said that. When I was a girl I danced the dance of the wagons, and I was good at it. It . . . sort of came back to me.'

Nama looked nonplussed. 'What? What wagons?'

Eline sighed and looked at her friend, deciding how much she could really trust her. She had never told anyone this, not even Caromir. Travelling people weren't exactly looked on fondly by the settled population, to put it mildly.

'When I was a baby girl,' she began, 'I was born in a wagon. My mother was one of the travelling people, and so was I until I was almost thirteen and we had to settle in a city for Ma to be able to make enough for us to live on. We settled here in Drathburg, and then I met and married Caromir and Ma caught the plague and died, and . . . Well, you know the rest of it.'

'Travelling people,' Nama said quietly, and Eline wasn't quite sure how to take that.

'Aye, travelling people,' she snapped. 'Oh yes, Nama, it was wild and exciting and free and all that *utter shit* from the stories, but we were always moving, always on the road, keeping one step ahead of the fucking vagrancy laws. Hounded and persecuted across the country and back again, scratching a living wherever we could. Precious little romance in that, I assure you.'

Nama showed her a sad smile, and stepped forward to embrace her.

'Do you think an orphan immigrant girl doesn't know what that feels like?' she said, and stroked Eline's hair for a moment. 'Anyway, your people won't need to worry about the vagrancy laws any more. The new Prince Regent repealed them months ago, the way I heard it in the market square.'

'Really?' Eline asked. 'That's good, at least, and about fucking time, too. Maybe this one will turn out to be better than the last.'

'Aye,' Nama said. 'Would you . . . would you show me some of your dance?'

Eline shuffled her feet nervously. She had danced her dance not an hour ago, and she had killed a woman with it.

I killed a man. I killed a woman.

You obviously are.

Aye, the woman had been trying to kill *her*, but . . . Fuck it. Just *fuck* it. If she was truly to turn her face to Our Lady of Eternal Sorrows then what matter? Father Shepherd himself had forgiven her, after all. They had entered the Lady's embrace now, Caromir and Elizaveta both, and what fault was that of hers? It had been Her plan for them, or so she told herself.

Our Lady forgives you. In Her eyes you have done no wrong.

She would take that, the words of a priest, and take solace from it.

She took a deep breath and nodded, then slowly stepped backwards and folded her hands in front of her, falling into the First Posture as she had been taught it as a girl. She let out a sudden wild cry and raised her hands, clapping and stamping on the bare wooden boards of the room. Then she was spinning without warning, arms crossing and whirling as her feet took her in a complicated pattern of steps, facing one direction then another and her hands always moving in endless circles and figure-of-eights. She ended her dance with the stamp and outflung arms that had also ended Elizaveta, and let out her cry once more.

'That,' she said, once she had got her breath back. 'But with a knife in my hand.'

She looked at Nama, and saw the girl's mouth was gaping open.

'We . . .' she started. 'We have something similar in Alarian culture. Less wild perhaps, more fluid, but the intent is the same. Under the oppressive rule of some cruel emperor or other hundreds of years ago we were forbidden to bear arms or learn martial skills, or so the story goes. They hid them instead, hid their fighting arts in folk dances and disguised their weapons as farm tools. It seems your people may have done much the same thing.'

Eline frowned at that, having never given much thought before to the menfolk of the wagons performing their dances with knives in their hands. It was just how it was done, just some old tradition, or so she had thought at the time.

'Fuck, that makes sense now you say it,' she said. 'I think—'

'You need another knife,' Nama interrupted her. 'You're a blade dancer, Eline, and your dance is for two.'

Eline swallowed, but she immediately saw the sense of the girl's words. The moves were for both hands equally, of course they were. She saw that now, and nodded slowly.

'Aye,' she said. 'I think I do.'

The next day's dance lesson was hopeless. Now that Eline had remembered how to *truly* dance, she found Madame's lessons even more insufferable than before.

'Gods, girl, I swear you're getting worse, not better,' Madame lamented. 'You need a partner, to practice properly. A man who can truly dance.'

She snapped her fingers, and one of her attendant thugs stepped forward and offered a short bow.

'Ma'am?'

'Find Marcoss, and tell him what I need.'

'Ma'am,' the man said again, and left the room.

Eline sighed and wondered what sort of oily foreign dancing master Marcoss was likely to bring her. Kastavians, in her opinion, were particularly unpleasant for all that their nation was inexplicably regarded as more cultured than her own. She remembered pissing on a Kastavian merchant's face and frowned to herself. Culture, indeed. Horrible people. She blinked in surprise when, not twenty minutes later, Marcoss himself stepped into the room wearing tight hose and soft shoes obviously designed for dancing. They had spent the intervening time working on her elocution, and in that at least Eline was improving rapidly. She could truly sound like an aristocrat now, when she wanted to anyway, and that was good at least. Ma would have been proud, she knew, to hear her speak like that.

'Marcoss is a wonderful dancer,' Madame said, as she looked up when he entered. 'If he can't teach you, no one can.'

He was? Eline looked at the heavily built, stern-faced older man, and she wondered. Oh, how she wondered. A Quiet Man, she had thought him, from the trenches of Krathzgrad, but perhaps the two things weren't so far apart as all that after all. Dancing and killing went well together, as she had so recently discovered herself.

'Begin,' Madame said, and they bowed to each other and took up the opening postures of one of the courtly dances Madame had been trying to teach her for weeks.

It was completely different with Marcoss. Before he had terrified her, but now she found in movement he completed her. The leaps turned into lifts, which she had never understood they were supposed to be. He swirled her through the air with a grace that frankly astonished her, then they spun and whirled to join again, but . . . But no.

Eline was in her own world by then, a world of dance, and she was dancing *her* dance, her mother's dance, and Marcoss was forgotten.

'Stop!' Madame snapped. 'What in the names of the gods are you doing, girl?'

'I know what she's doing,' Marcoss said quietly. 'Do it again, gypsy girl.'

Eline's jaw clenched at the slur, but she made herself push the resentment away. If Nama could bear 'tea monkey' then she could bear 'gypsy', she supposed. She wasn't even sure he meant anything by it. It was simply how most of the settled thought of the travelling people, and nothing to be done about it.

She took up the First Posture once more, and began again.

After a few minutes Marcoss held up a hand to tell her to stop. He gave her a nod of respect that she thought was actually sincere.

'You're good,' he said while she was still struggling to get her breath back. 'Not fit enough for it, but we can work on your conditioning. You've a blade, I know that, but you need another. It's a two-handed reel you dance.'

'I . . . yes,' Eline said, wondering how the fuck he knew that.

'Don't look so surprised,' he said. 'We had a couple of your lads in my company back in the war. Both Quiet Men, like me. I know you've guessed that, and now you know why. Marie, give her another of your little presents.'

Madame unlocked the bottom drawer of her desk and produced another stiletto as fine and perfectly balanced as the first one.

'I have these specially made,' she said, 'and I give one to each of my precious courtesans before their first assignation. One is usually enough, and they are *not* cheap.'

'Not enough for her,' Marcoss said firmly enough that it shut down the conversation. 'A blade dancer deserves two.'

Eline took the offered weapon and nodded to Madame in respectful gratitude, but all the same something was bothering her.

Who was really in charge here, Madame or Marcoss?

Later that night Marcoss summoned Eline to his sparsely furnished rooms above the floor where the girls worked and had her dance for him again, this time with her twin blades in her hands.

He watched with pursed lips until she got to her final move, the stamp and shout and outflung arms, then held up a hand to stop her.

'Hold position,' he said, so she did. 'Look at your wrists.'

She frowned but did so, her wrists and palms turned up to drive her blades out to either side in the killing strokes.

'You see what's wrong with that?'

Eline frowned.

'No,' she admitted, and he laughed.

'Nah, nor did we until the gypsy lads, *your* lads, put us right. You have to understand how it was at Krathzgrad, Eline. These days Quiet Men are an established military discipline, just another part of the army. One or two specialists attached to each company to do what's necessary when the time comes. Before Krathzgrad we didn't exist. That was the first war our country had ever fought that needed people like us. Trenches, you see, subterfuge and murder. Not open battlefields and cavalry charges, and no one really knew what to do with that. Our general, I reckon, got his colonels together and had them round up the hardest, maddest bastards they could find and throw us all together into one single special operations regiment. We were making shit up as we went along, you understand me?'

'Aye, I suppose so,' Eline said, wondering what this little history lesson had to do with anything.

'Like I say, we were making it up as we went along, each man teaching his own skills to the others until we figured out what worked best. Me, I knew how to break necks. Taught them that, I did, and they still do it my way even now.'

He sounded proud of that, and Eline had to grudgingly admit she didn't blame him. Quiet Men were revered in military circles, she had learned that much from Caromir, and if ever a man was built for breaking necks it was Marcoss. Also, she was starting to get the feeling that he didn't get to have an actual conversation very often and was enjoying having this one, so she nodded encouragingly.

'Some of the lads knew explosives and demolition, and that was good, and some knew throws and others garottes, but the gypsy lads? They knew knife fighting like no others, and they taught us well. They danced much like you do, but that that they'd never teach us. Not much of it, anyway. They taught us some of the postures, and how to spin with our cuts, but that was about it. They said the whole dance was a private thing, a family thing, and we could respect that. They did teach us one very important thing though: reverse your blades.'

Eline blinked at him.

'I don't follow.'

Marcoss took a step towards her.

'I'll show you, just don't fucking stab me,' he said, and there was even a ghost of a smile on his granite face.

'I won't,' Eline said, and to her surprise she found she didn't even want to any more.

Marcoss was a cruel, ruthless bastard, and he may or may not have actually been pulling Madame's strings all along, but she was becoming increasingly sure he was . . . if not exactly on her side, at least not an enemy. For now, anyway.

He reached out and took her right hand, removed the stiletto and flipped it over before pressing the hilt back into her palm. Now the blade protruded downwards from her grip, between her little finger and the meatiest part of her hand. He folded her thumb over the pommel.

'Hold it lightly until you strike,' he said. 'Use finger pressure and most of all your thumb to vary the angle of the blade for cuts, and only grip it tight at the moment of contact when you stab. You do the other one.'

Eline smoothly pivoted the blade in her left hand, covered the pommel with her thumb and looked a question at him. He repositioned her thumb slightly, and nodded.

'These are double-edged and those are the best type of fighting knives, so it doesn't matter,' he said, 'but if you're ever stuck with a single-bladed knife the cutting edge goes forward not back, you understand? Bend your wrists back and hold the blades against the insides of your forearms.'

Again Eline did as he said, and he nodded towards the glass over his shaving stand. She looked at her slightly silvered reflection, and realised she couldn't see the blades concealed in her hands at all. The advantages of that were obvious, but it still felt like a fucking awkward way to hold a knife, never mind two.

'But how do I fight like this?' she asked.

'You don't,' Marcoss said, and this time there was *definitely* respect in his tone. 'You're better than brawling. You *dance*. First posture!'

Eline flowed into it more gracefully than she thought she had ever done before, the knives trailing from her hands like streamers.

'Remember, thumb and finger pressure to vary the angle of the blades,' Marcoss said. 'Now dance for me, gypsy girl.'

Perhaps he did it on purpose, but the sting of that hateful word had Eline moving at once and he was right, she *could* move the blades in her hands almost without thought and it was as though her body just knew how to move with them, her arms following the knives not the other way around. Her parries became savage attacks to her imaginary opponent's arms as she whirled and circled, ignoring his weapon altogether and going straight for the limb that held it. Her cuts looped and sliced where before they had flicked and nicked, and when she finished with her shout and stamp she wasn't so much thrusting her blades out as hammering them in, palms down this time. Instead of her shoulders doing the work now it was her hips and all the good, strong muscles of her back.

That last strike, she thought as she fought to get her breath back, would have punched through mail.

'Not bad,' Marcoss said, 'although your parry-cut on the third spin exposed your left. You might have got away with it in a street fight, but a skilled opponent would have killed you right there. Again, and keep your left up this time.'

Eline danced three more times until she was too exhausted to continue, and Marcoss was almost satisfied. Almost.

'Your right cross heel turn is weak,' he said as she clung to the sides of his washbasin and tried hard not to puke. 'And your fitness is woeful.'

'My . . .' Eline gulped and choked and gulped again, but just about managed to hold it down. 'My right heel what? I don't even know what that is!'

'Another thing,' he said. 'Your pouch is just about the worst possible place to keep your weapons. Tomorrow morning you're excused chores. Get yourself to the market, find a leather worker and get them to sew some straps to your sheaths. Wear them on the inside of your forearms, under your sleeves where you can get at them fast.'

'Under my sleeves?' Eline repeated, still struggling to hold in vomit.

'Well I've known courtesans to keep their blade down their bodice, but I reckon that'd be bastard uncomfortable with two of the things.'

'Aye,' Eline said, and nodded weakly.

Marcoss grinned at her, an expression she would never have thought to see on his face.

'Trust me,' he said, and the hand he put on her shoulder then was almost fatherly. She felt no threat from it, at least, no male lust now. 'I'm a dancing master. And your dance is steel.'

Chapter 15

After well over a month in the house the inevitable finally happened, and Madame put Eline on light duties for a week to see out her moon blood. That meant only having to suck cocks, apparently, and while it meant less money as fewer customers simply wanted that she supposed it left her more time for her lessons. She was still flush from her night with the baron so she could bear the loss. Whether she could bear to dance for much longer with near-crippling cramps was another matter.

'You must become used to it,' Madame scolded her as she almost doubled over in pain after a particularly difficult leap and turn. It was Godsday and Marcoss had been away from the house since Temple that morning, off in the city on some business or another, so once more she danced the hated courtly dance alone. 'Would you turn down an assignation with an earl for the sake of your bloods and a stomachache? You had better not, girl. Besides, you will find now that such things occur less frequently as the years pass, and the medicine will help. Mine have long since stopped altogether, and I don't miss them one bit.'

Eline supposed she could take some comfort from that. She took far greater comfort that they had come at all, as after six weeks with nothing she had been on the verge of panic. To conceive again now, unlikely though it was at her age, would have been a catastrophe. Oh, the customers were *supposed* to wear a Maiden's Glove on their cocks of course, but many flat refused and paid extra not to have to. Every girl in the house took the money and suffered it. That was the very definition of their job, after all: take the money, and suffer it. That was, in essence, what a whore did.

Suffer it, for money.

There was also the noxious and supposedly alchemical concoction Madame made the girls force down every Godsday before Temple, of course. It was supposed to keep the girls infertile and safe from the various Diseases of the Maiden that so afflicted common street scrubs, but Eline wasn't prepared to bet on either of those things being remotely true.

Even so, it was Godsday again and after temple and a detour to kneel before the altar of Our Lady in her chapel at the great temple and her lessons with Madame, Eline headed to the Rat to meet Nama as was their custom by then. Godsday lessons were a recent and somewhat unwelcome new innovation that cut into her prayer time in the chapel, but it seemed Madame wanted to step up her training hours now that she was spending time learning fighting from Marcoss as well. That at least was going well, far better than her formal dance lessons were anyway. She sparred with him now, using carved wooden blades, and although she seldom won it had happened, which had seemed to please him enormously.

She walked to the Rat and found that as usual Kurt had joined them uninvited at their table and inserted himself into the conversation. He had at least bought them both a drink, that was something, so Eline suffered that too and did her level best to ignore him. Horrible young man as far as she was concerned.

'Where have you been?' Nama asked. 'Off praying to your creepy death goddess again?'

Eline shrugged. 'It brings me comfort,' she said. 'That and Madame wanted me. More bloody dance lessons.'

Kurt just snorted scornfully.

'Death goddess, is it?' he sneered. 'I knew one like you before.'

Eline ignored him.

After a while Nama excused herself to visit the shithouse in the yard and relieve herself of several more cups of wine than she should have had by that hour. Kurt turned his ratty little eyes on Eline.

'So you're a whore too, then, like my Nama.'

He already knew that of course, but still Eline bristled all the same.

'She's not *your* anything,' she said, and that wasn't the first time she'd had to tell him that. 'She's my friend, and you'll leave her alone if you're wise.'

'I don't believe that I will,' Kurt said. 'I ain't taking my orders from you, oldest profession or not.'

'No, it's not that,' Eline said. 'The oldest profession is midwifery.'

Kurt blinked at that, then scoffed. 'That's just—'

Eline cut him off dead.

'No,' she snapped. 'You don't get to sneer at midwives, *cunning man* or not. It was the midwife saved my life with my daughter, and probably my baby's too. Makes you uncomfortable, doesn't it? That a woman can be powerful and use that power to help other women, and no man needed. You don't like that, do you?'

'Needed a man to get in the family way in the first place though, didn't you?' Kurt said, with a look of smug satisfaction that said he thought he'd won the argument.

'Wasn't my choice,' Eline shot back. 'The woman often doesn't get a choice, but I got my beautiful daughter out of it and no thanks to *him*. That was down to the midwife and her skills, to undo the harm that cunt did to me and make something good come of it. In that way we overpowered him in the end. All the strength and the violence and the *man* of him, but we beat him, her and me. We beat him in that place where women have *always* fought, the battle of the bloody bed. And you don't like that.'

'I don't like *you*,' Kurt snarled at her.

Eline held his fierce glare, and she didn't blink.

'Good,' she said. 'I don't want you to.'

Nama came back shortly after, but by then Kurt had stormed off and out of the tavern.

'Where's Kurt?' the girl asked, looking around in dismay.

'Gone,' Eline snapped, then made herself smile at her friend. 'He's got the right arse with me, and I can't say I'm sorry about that.'

'Oh gods, you haven't gone and upset him, have you? He's supposed to be teaching me again tomorrow night. Two full hours with me he's bought, and paid Madame in advance to be sure he gets them on time.'

'Don't care if I have,' Eline said. 'Why, Nama? Why are you letting him do this?'

'Told you,' Nama said. 'To learn, to test what I can do. Maybe to find a way out of this life and make something of myself, if I can get good enough.'

'But he's got so much over you already, and every hour you let him teach you is more and more you give him. He's using you, Nama, can't you see that?'

'No more than I'm using him,' Nama said. 'Ain't nothing free in this world, is there?'

No, there wasn't. Eline knew that well enough, from the times she had minded Jottie's children when the old tart had been off with some fancy man or other. Jottie had been a widow, but a very merry one as the saying went. She had been notorious on their streets. Still, she had taken Eline's children in a time or two but then as soon as there was a bit of coin in it for her she had ratted Eline out to the *fucking* Guard.

No, you couldn't trust anyone in this life and that was the Lady's own truth. Everyone wanted *something*, be it coin or favours or sex or information. How could Nama not see that?

'Exactly!' Eline said in exasperation. 'He wants something, Nama, I just don't know what it is yet. He, oh gods, he doesn't know who you work for, does he? Who we both work for, that is, and I don't mean Madame.'

'No, of course not,' Nama said, but she didn't sound quite as confident as Eline would have liked.

Eline narrowed her eyes and frowned. She supposed now she would have to tell Luka about this as well, that Nama might well have let slip to Kurt that they worked for him as well as Madame, and wasn't he going to be just delighted?

No, she thought, no he fucking well wasn't.

She needed to see him anyway, to see what he'd got out of Black Nose Bob, so she bade Nama a fairly brusque goodbye and took her leave of the Rat while the sun was beginning to sink over the rooftops.

That big lad, Sam, was on the door again when she got to the house and this time he showed her in with no hesitation. Luka hadn't seemed to mind her being let in last time and that was obviously good enough for him. Sam definitely struck her as a bit simple but he was pleasant enough in his way, and he ushered her into the hall without any fuss.

'You'll know the way,' he said, and Eline nodded to him. 'To the boss's drinks cupboard, I mean.'

He showed her an exaggerated wink, and Eline couldn't help but smile.

'That I do, Sam,' she said, and patted him briefly on his massive arm as she passed. 'That I definitely do.'

She went into the house and down the hall as he closed the door again behind her, and she let herself into Luka's parlour. To her surprise he was there, sitting in an armchair and leafing through a sheaf of papers with a frown of concentration on his face. She had assumed he only had Sam mind the house when he was out in and about the city, and said as much.

'Got a fucking prisoner to mind now, haven't I?' Luka snapped at her. 'He's chained up in the cellar since the Guard brought him here but I don't know what the fuck you thought I was going to do with him.'

'I thought . . .' Eline started. 'I mean, interrogate him. Elizaveta wasn't anyone, just some dirty poppy addict. He was the one who–'

'He was briefly her pimp after the fact of the event, you stupid bitch,' Luka snapped at her, and Eline had to admit he had a point. Perhaps she might have fucked up a little bit there, but the circumstances had been what they had been and she had needed to improvise on the spot. 'It was Elizaveta I wanted, but you had to go and fucking kill her, didn't you?'

'She was trying to kill *me*!' Eline protested. 'What was I supposed to do?'

Luka grunted and threw the papers down on the side table beside his chair. She suspected he didn't read very well, or at least found it hard work.

'Aye, suppose you didn't have a lot of choice,' he grumbled. 'Although I thought you said you weren't a killer. Lied about that, didn't you? And stop looking at my brandy bottle like that. Just pour yourself one or sit down and shut up.'

Eline poured herself one, then took the chair he had waved at.

'So he's no use?' she said.

'There's plenty of things I can have him hanged for,' Luka said, 'but in this? No. No, I don't think so. He's just a dockside pimp with a side-line in burglary to order and fencing stolen goods. Oh, he'll swing, don't you worry on that score, but it doesn't get us any closer to the matter in hand.'

'How well did he know Elizaveta?' Eline asked.

'How the fuck do I know?'

I rather thought you might have asked him, Eline thought, but managed not to say it. Queen's Man he might have been, but she was honestly starting to think she could have run an investigation better than him.

'I just wondered,' she said carefully, letting Madame's expertly tutored elocution lessons slowly take over her natural accent until she was speaking with the aristocratic authority required of a real courtesan, 'if, while she was working for him, he might have asked her why she left the Bells. If, you know, she might have told him something about what happened.'

She took a slow sip of her brandy and tried not to look superior while he slowly thought it over.

'I suppose she might,' he said at last. 'Fucking doubt it though.'

'But you haven't actually asked him?'

'Martyr's *blood*, Eline!' he shouted at her, 'I'm a busy man. You go and ask him, if you're so keen on his fucking opinion! Take Sam with you if you do, though. He's dangerous.'

Eline looked at Luka for a long moment, and slowly came to the realisation that perhaps she was cleverer than he was. That last had obviously been intended to be a veiled threat, but he had already told her the man was chained up and therefore no threat at all. The Queen's Men were monstrously powerful, but from what she had seen so far they definitely didn't seem to be terribly efficient.

'All right,' she said after a moment.

She swallowed her brandy and put the glass down on the table beside her.

Luka stared at her like a man at the card table whose bluff has just been called.

'I mean . . .' he started.

'No, it's all right,' Eline said. 'And I'll take Sam, like you said.'

She swept out of the room before Luka could think of anything else to say, and smiled at Sam where he stood in the hallway picking his nails ostentatiously with the point of a dagger. He had cut himself twice, she noticed.

'Can I borrow you?' Eline asked sweetly. 'Boss wants me to talk to the prisoner, but I don't really want to do it on my own.'

'Aye, 'course,' Sam said, and a sucked a bleeding fingertip with a wince. 'My old boss used to do this,' he went on. 'Pick her nails with a dagger, I mean. Fuck knows why, it hurts.'

Eline smiled and shrugged, and let him lead her to the door that led to the cellar steps. He picked up a taper from a shelf and lit it from a nearby oil lamp before opening the door.

'What was she like, your old boss?' she asked, if only to make conversation as they picked their way down the steps into the increasing gloom.

'Brilliant,' Sam said. 'She was the proper boss's second until he went into government and that and she took over. Right hard, Bloody Anne was, but she was fair and you knew where you stood with her. She was my sergeant at Abingon, *and* I was at her wedding too. Proud to know her, I am.'

'What sort of man did she marry?'

'Man?' Sam said, and laughed. 'Nah, she married her woman, in the Great Temple in Ellinburg at that, and fuck what anyone thought of it. I can respect that.'

Lie with whom thou wilt, so long as both be willing.

'Aye, that's fair,' Eline said. 'So can I.'

She thought of her own marriage, and what a disaster it had been and

110

thought then that perhaps this Bloody Anne might have had the right of it after all whoever she was or had been. There was no saying she was even still alive after all, a lot of veterans weren't, but Sam had obviously thought a lot of her. Eline herself didn't like women in that way, but she had no problem with those who did and she could see how perhaps it might be less awful, in a way. Perhaps, but then of course she wouldn't have her children. No, that wasn't for her, she knew.

They had reached the bottom of the steps by then, and she stepped down onto a hard-packed earthen floor. Sam took a lamp off a shelf and lit it with the taper, and when he held it up she saw Black Nose Bob sitting on the floor in manacles that were chained to a great eye bolt set into the rough stone wall behind him.

He glared at her, but she just smiled.

'Remember me?' she asked.

'Fuck off, bitch,' Bob said.

Eline tutted and shook her head slowly. She leaned harder into Madame's elocution lessons until she was addressing him like she was a duchess.

A particularly angry one.

You're effectively an actress.

The Baron Lan Elenkov had said that to her and she realised now just how true those words were, and not only in matters of seduction. The skills of the courtesan had many applications, after all.

'That's not very polite, is it? My employer wants to have you hanged, by the way. I assure you he *will* hang you, unless I can change his mind.'

'Well, he can shiv me, I suppose,' Bob said, and rattled his chains. 'Not much I can fucking do about it from here, is there?'

'No, he can have you publicly executed as a criminal, at the city gallows,' Eline said in her heavily practiced cut-glass accent. 'He's government, you idiot. All your assets, such as they are, will be forfeit to the Crown. Your family, if you have any, will starve in the gutter. Now, shall we talk?'

'About what?'

'About Elizaveta.'

'Fuck off.'

'Sam, hurt him please,' Eline said.

She thought she had the measure of the big man by then, and he proved her right. Getting the measure of people had always been something Eline had been good at. She'd had to be, dirt-poor as she was in those days and trading more on favours than actual money. She certainly hadn't been buying much with the pittance Caromir had given her to keep their house, but the slum economy largely ran on the basis of favours exchanged. A bit of sewing here, taking in some laundry there, children watched when someone wanted them off their hands for a few hours, it all added up. People returned the favours in their own way, each with what they had or knew how to do. The butcher, for example, whose children she took in every Queensday afternoon when the woman was at market and busy with her stall, gave her ham offcuts for cheap. Goodwife Ellis down the street kept chickens, and paid her in eggs for mending her husband's tired old work clothes when a thin patch wore through. Oh yes, Eline knew what people wanted and what they knew how to do, and in that moment she knew *exactly* what Sam could do.

She wasn't wrong.

He showed no hesitation whatsoever before kicking Black Nose Bob in the face. The man's head snapped to the side and his prosthetic nose flew off as the cord broke, and blood dribbled from his split lips.

'That do?' Sam asked.

'I don't know,' Eline said. '*Will* that do, Bob, or do I need to ask him to do it again?'

Bob was predictably even uglier without his nose, the ragged hole in his face dribbling green snot. He hawked and spat a gob of it at her feet, but missed. Which was probably for the best for everyone, all things considered. If he had spoiled her good shoes she might have taken that *extremely* ill.

'Sam and I will be leaving this cellar shortly,' Eline informed him. 'Whether we leave you alive or dead behind us isn't really going to trouble my employer. He's already upset with me for bringing you here at all. If I just leave, you'll hang when he gets around to making it happen. If you piss me off any further I will have Sam kill you right here. He won't mind, will you Sam?'

'Nope,' the big man said, and there was no emotion in his tone.

Veterans, in Eline's experience, especially veterans of Abingon, didn't really have a lot of that. Veterans of Krathzgrad, like Marcoss, seemed to have none whatsoever. The thought made her feel a little cold. Her only experience of veterans until very recently had been Caromir and some of the other slum men. These men who had fought and killed in battle were made of a different stuff indeed, and she had to admit there was a part of her that feared them. Respected them too, yes, for what they had been prepared to risk and to do for their country, but she feared them nonetheless. These ones who had come home, the ones with blood on their hands who never spoke of it, those she did not take lightly.

'On the other hand,' she went on, 'if you wanted to answer some questions, questions about Elizaveta and what happened, I may be able to talk my employer around. Perhaps. I make no promises. But face facts, Bob, it's the best offer you're going to get.'

'Martyr's fucking blood,' the man muttered. 'You mad bitch. You can't just go around murdering people in cellars.'

'I work for a man who carries the Queen's Warrant,' Eline said. 'I assure you that I absolutely can.'

'Then I ain't got a lot of fucking choice, have I?'

'No,' she said. 'That is my entire point. Shall we start again? Elizaveta. Who the *fuck* was she working for?'

'I don't know,' Bob said, and it was so transparently a lie that Eline lost her patience all at once.

'Sam,' she said, and that was all it took.

Sam kicked him again, and again, and again, his massive boot slamming into the man's ribs until there must have been more of them broken than not.

Eline held up a hand to tell him to stop.

'That will do,' she said. 'For now, anyway. Shall we try again, Bob? Who was she working for?'

'This bloke,' Bob said, and there was bloody froth on his lips that said one of those broken ribs had at least grazed a lung, if not punctured it altogether. 'Smarmy cunt. He came around the Bells a few times. I remember her telling me, boasting about how much he'd paid her. Just trying to get her own rate up from me, I reckoned, but . . .' He paused to cough and spit blood, and Eline fleetingly wondered if perhaps Sam had been a bit too thorough. Oh well, no use worrying about it now. 'But he had serious money. Gold to spend, you know, and she weren't worth gold even then. Elizaveta was pretty, but she was already a poppy-head, even if she could still just about hide it. Reckon he was her supplier, you know? Foreign geezer.'

'What *type* of foreign?' Eline pressed him. 'Alarian? Kastavian? Immalian?'

'Fuck does it matter?' Bob said, and spat blood again although there was less of it this time, and she figured his lung probably wasn't punctured after all. Not that she much cared one way or the other by that point. 'White bloke so not Alarian, but whatever. They're all greasy fuckers.'

'My employer says it matters a great deal,' Eline said.

'Then your boss is out of fucking luck,' Bob said. 'She never told me. Doubt she knew herself. Foreign is foreign, innit?'

'No,' Eline said. 'I'm afraid it really isn't. Sam, would you be a love and pop upstairs and see what the boss want us to do with this specimen who hasn't told us anything remotely useful? I expect you'll want to bring a knife with you when you come back.'

Sam nodded and turned to the stairs.

'Wait, wait!' Bob shouted. 'I remember now!'

'Oh, really?' Eline said, and affected a look of scornful surprise. 'Do tell.'

Chapter 16

'You are *fucking* joking,' Luka shouted at her when she told him. 'This is a fucking catastrophe!'

'Forgive my ignorance, but I don't really understand why,' Eline said.

'Kastavia?' Luke echoed at her. 'A Kastavian agent assassinated the heir to the Immalian throne on *our* soil, and in a fucking whorehouse at that?'

'Apparently,' Eline said, which was evidently not what you might have called the right thing to say.

'Do you think,' Luka said slowly, 'our country can afford another war, within a decade of Abingon? Because if you do, Eline, you are *fucking* delusional!'

'No, probably not,' she said, although in truth she had no idea, 'but I don't see why we'd need to. This was Kastavian aggression against Immalia, surely? Not our problem.'

'Aye, but in *our country!*' he all but screamed at her. 'Do you know anything about Immalian culture? No, of course you fucking don't, you up-jumped whore. You don't know anything about fucking anything, do you? Put-on posh accent or not, you're just a barely literate commoner. Immalia will never, and I mean *never*, believe we weren't complicit in this.'

Eline swallowed the insult and met the Queen's Man's eyes.

A barely literate commoner, was she? Aye, that was fair, and the truth if she was honest with herself about it, but from what she had seen so was he. It wasn't schooling that made a Queen's Man, that much was already obvious. He quite clearly had no more of it than she did, if even that much.

'And were we?' she asked.

Luka reached for his brandy glass and drained it, then coughed for a long moment as though deliberately delaying his response.

'Not that I know of,' he said.

'But it's not impossible?'

'No of course it isn't fucking impossible,' he snapped, 'and that's the main thing I'm worried about. The Provost Marshal doesn't tell me everything, or probably even most things. If . . . Oh gods, if he helped arrange this for whatever reason he had *better* not have forgotten what plausible deniability looks like.'

Eline frowned.

'This Provost Marshal,' she said. 'I assume he's your boss?'

Everyone answered to someone, after all, even a great and terrible Queen's Man like Luka.

'Aye,' Luka muttered, and got up to pour himself another brandy.

He didn't offer her one.

Eline looked at him for a long moment, then refilled her own glass without asking. He gave her a look but said nothing, and Eline began to feel more confident in her position with him right then. Oh yes, he had the Queen's Warrant and she didn't, but she could already feel the balance of power starting to tilt in her favour. If she was beginning to suspect she was cleverer than Luka then she was pretty sure he was as well, and she knew she could capitalise on that.

'Can't you write and ask him?' she said, arching an eyebrow over the raised crystal glass in her hand.

Luka snorted. 'You haven't met him,' he said.

'No,' she said. 'I haven't.'

She sat back in her chair and looked at him, letting the question stand.

'Look,' Luka said, 'it's like this. If I ask him he'll either deny it, lie to me, laugh at me, or tell me to fuck off. Or any combination of the above, to be honest. You have to understand, Eline, I've known the Provost Marshal since we were *children*. We were at school together back in Ellinburg, for fuck's sake, and we've gone through a fuck of a lot together since then. A war, for one, and everything that came after. Our relationship has . . . shall we say changed somewhat over the years. Our lives have gone in what you might call completely different directions, but the past is the past and it's still there whatever happens. But one thing that has most definitely changed is that he is now very much my boss, more so than he has ever been before. Back in the days when . . . before I took the Warrant, I mean. Well, I could have just left, if I'd wanted to. I didn't, but now I can't. If he has secrets that he doesn't want to share, and I'm sure he has, then that's just how it is and nothing to be done about it.'

Eline made a noncommittal noise and looked at Luka over her glass.

'Perhaps you're *too* close to him,' she said.

'Fuck does that mean?'

'I mean, if I went to Dannsburg and—'

'No,' Luka snapped to cut her off, his voice flat and brooking no argument. 'You get an audience with the Provost Marshal over my dead fucking body, Eline. It's not going to happen, believe you me.'

'All right, not that then,' Eline said, but his words told her just how scared of this Provost Marshal who was allegedly an old school friend he really was.

She wondered about that. It seemed strange to her in itself, but then of course she had no idea who the Provost Marshal actually was or what he and Luka had done together in their war, which she was still assuming must have been Abingon. Or whatever 'everything that came after' might have been. The war where Sam had said he had served under his Bloody Anne, she remembered. She wondered then if he remembered whoever this man was, and what if anything of use he could tell her.

Not much, probably, but you never knew.

'Fuck it all,' Luka said after a moment, 'I'm just going to hang the cunt and have done with him. Then we need to find whoever this bloody Kastavian was.'

'Don't you think that would be easier with Bob's help?' Eline said.

'What's he going to tell us that's true?' Luka asked. 'That prick would sell his mother for a penny.'

'I don't think he would, actually,' Eline said. 'I had to get Sam to hurt him really quite badly to make him give up even what we've got so far.'

Luka frowned at her.

'You've got a bit of a talent for this, haven't you?' he asked after a moment.

'I have been hurt all my adult life,' Eline said. 'I know how it feels to be hurt, and therefore I know how to hurt other people.'

Luka thought about that for a moment before he nodded.

'Aye, that's fair I suppose,' he said.

'Let Bob live,' she said. 'For now, at least. I think we can still make use of him.'

'Cunt costs me money,' Luka grumbled. 'Needs feeding and that.'

'Oh, for pity's sake,' Eline snapped, 'are you seriously trying to tell me the house of law can't afford to keep a prisoner alive?'

'Not the point,' Luka muttered. 'What's he for, really?'

'Information, hopefully,' Eline said. 'If we can find this Kastavian agent, Bob will probably at least recognise him.'

'And how the fuck do we do that?'

Eline rubbed the bridge of her nose between finger and thumb and tried not to look too exasperated. Admittedly, she didn't try very hard.

'The City Guard keep a log of foreigners coming into the city, don't they?' she asked. 'Everyone has to pay the gate tax, after all.'

'Everyone except the bloody nobility,' Luka agreed, 'but aye. You've got a point there.'

'Then get the captain of the Guard to pull the logs and have someone go through them,' Eline said, and by now she was *sure* she could run an investigation better than Luka could. After the long years of abuse and constant belittling and scorn from Caromir, Eline thought she had never really realised that she was an intelligent woman. He had spent long enough telling her she was stupid, after all, and only now was she realising he had been wrong. She had been a girl of only fifteen when she had married him, after all. She found now that she was, and she knew she could use that to her advantage. 'Have them look for ports of origin, Kastavian names. They're different enough from ours that something ought to flag up.'

'Aye, and he'll probably be a fucking wool or wine merchant,' Luka said. Eline shrugged.

'Most of them probably will be,' she said. 'They're our main exports, after all. But at least we'll know who they are. Then we, and by that I mean you and your spy network, can find out who went where once they were inside the city. Once we know who went to the Silver Bells we've got our man. Then we just have to find him. I'm sure the Bells keeps some sort of record too, but Madame's hardly likely to let me see it. I'm afraid you'll have to do this the hard way.'

Luka looked at her for a long moment, and she drained her glass.

'Aye,' he said at last. 'That sounds like it would work.'

Eline got up and crossed to the cupboard. She refilled her glass with another generous slosh of his brandy.

'Want another?' she asked him.

'Fucking hell,' Nama said when they met up back at the House of Silver Bells that evening. 'Sounds like you put him in his place good and proper.'

It was late and they had the common room to themselves, but even so she made herself keep her voice down.

'Oh, I wouldn't presume to say that,' Eline said. 'I made some suggestions, that's all. Helpful ones, I hope.'

'What's this even about?' Nama asked her, and Eline went quiet all at once.

She liked the Alarian girl and counted her as a friend, but she knew she couldn't share what had happened with Black Nose Bob. Even confirming her suspicion that Luka was a Queen's Man had been a mistake, she knew, and now Nama was so deep in Kurt's pocket she felt she could trust her with her secrets even less than before.

'Just stuff,' she said. 'Work, you know?'

'Work that ain't whoring?'

'Exactly.'

'Government work?'

Eline pulled a face.

'Perhaps,' she said at last.

'I could do with some of that,' Nama said hopefully. 'I've had enough of this life.'

'Ain't we all?' Eline said, throwing her elocution lessons to the wind now that she was home.

Home, she realised, was how she had come to think of the Silver Bells. How easily one could adjust to the present, when the past had been so, so much worse. Yes, she missed her children, of course she did, but they had grown and gone anyway, so what matter? Yes the life of a whore wasn't one she would have chosen for herself, but it was still better than what she had known before. That said a lot in itself.

'Fuck's sake,' Nama snapped, 'you ain't even been working tonight. We've been rammed! I've done six punters tonight, Eline. Six. I am done in, and I mean that.'

'I'm a courtesan now,' Eline said. 'That makes so much fucking money Madame doesn't need me whoring when I could be training and learning how to make her even *more* money. And besides, if you can bed a courtesan for the price of a whore why would you hire her as a courtesan? Exclusivity is everything. For gentlemen of society it's the cachet, the bragging rights as much as anything else, or so Madame says anyway. I've been meaning to ask you, though: why ain't there enough girls here? I mean, the place is nice enough as stews go. Madame feeds us well and Marcoss and his lads look after us to see no one gets hurt, and it pays well. It's a better life than I had before, that's for sure. With the number of scrubs out on the streets you'd think there'd be a fucking *queue* to work here.'

'Aye, well,' Nama said. 'There are rumours, is all. What the street scrubs have heard about this place puts them off even asking.'

'What rumours?'

'Just . . .' Nama said, and hesitated. 'Well, sometimes a girl just isn't here anymore, and no one knows where she went. "Oh, she left," we get told, and that's the end of the matter.'

'So?' Eline asked. 'This is a job not a prison; we can leave any time we want.'

'Can we? Tried that, have you? How long do you think it would take Marcoss to track you down and bring you back, if Madame didn't want to lose you?'

Eline shrugged. 'Maybe,' she admitted. 'But these girls still leave?'

'The rumours say,' Nama said, lowering her voice, 'well, sometimes Madame sells them.'

'We sell ourselves every night,' Eline argued. 'That's the fucking job, Nama.'

'No,' Nama said, 'we don't. We rent ourselves out for an hour or two, that's all. When I say "sell" that's exactly what I mean. Permanently, like.'

'That's not–' Eline started, but Nama cut her off.

'Slavery might not be legal, but that doesn't mean it don't exist,' she said. 'Fuck's sake, Eline, poppy resin is illegal but the city is still riddled with it. If it ain't robbery, rape or murder then "illegal" means "punishable with a fine", and *that* means "legal for rich people". It always bloody has done and that's the simple fact of the matter, and even rape is fucking negotiable.'

Eline swallowed. 'Exactly when were you planning on telling me this?' she demanded.

'When you noticed something was wrong,' Nama said, 'which was about five minutes ago.'

'Do you think it's actually true?'

'I dunno, do I?' Nama said. 'That's why it's a rumour not a fact, you idiot. I doubt anyone but Madame and your boyfriend Marcoss know for sure either way.'

'Oh, stop it,' Eline snapped. 'He's my dancing master, and that's *all* he is.'

Nama sniggered. 'More rumours,' she said. 'No one gossips like soldiers and whores, after all.'

'Well, they can pack it in right now,' Eline said. 'There's *nothing* between me and Marcoss. Not like you and your Kurt.'

Nama blinked at her like she'd been slapped.

'Nah,' she said. 'That ain't like that either.'

'Then what *is* it like, Nama?'

'It's like . . .' Nama started, and fell silent for a moment.

She got up to poke the fire and toss another stick in before she started again.

'It's weird,' she admitted at last. 'I mean he's young and he's handsome, or at least I think he is anyway, but when he drops the street face and the swagger it's like talking to your grandpa. It's like he's young to look at but he's old inside, do you know what I mean?'

'No,' Eline had to say. 'I never knew a grandfather, after all, nor my father neither really. He died when I was little, before we settled. He was a carpenter, but that's about all I really know. That was part of why we had to, you understand?'

'I suppose,' Nama said, although Eline could see that she didn't.

Settling was a big decision for one of the travelling people, and one she knew her mother wouldn't have taken lightly.

'I don't even know what he died of,' Eline said, and she could feel the tears burning at the backs of her eyes. 'Ma would never say. A fight, maybe. I don't know.'

Nama showed her a sad smile. 'My da,' she said, 'well, when he realised we couldn't make it here he fucked off back to Alaria by himself. Never heard from him again. Bastard left Ma to fend for herself with me and my brothers. She took up whoring, as she didn't know how to do anything else and she had three children to feed. I suppose I sort of followed her into the life.'

'What happened to your brothers?' Eline asked.

'Army,' Nama said, although that would have been Eline's first guess anyway. 'It's the only way out of the slums for most lads, you know? Fuck knows where they are now.'

Eline thought of her own son, and squeezed her eyes tight shut to keep from weeping.

Chapter 17

After she took her leave of Nama, Eline went up to her room and sat quietly on the edge of her bed. She opened the small chest where she kept her clothes and rummaged under her spare cloak to find the little wooden carving of a cat that her father had made for her when she had been a girl. She took it out, and she hugged it and she sobbed. Apart from her necessities it had been the only thing in Caromir's house that she had cared enough about to take with her. It was quite crude really, but she had loved it for as long as she could remember and it was all she had of him left. All she had of either of her parents, in truth. Her mother had given her love, and probably most of their meagre supplies of food, but nothing tangible that she could hold and cry over. They had been too poor for that, for physical things. But love was priceless.

She was still crying when someone rapped on the door.

Eline scrambled to hide the cat again, frantically wiping her eyes on her sleeve as she did so.

Don't be Marcoss, she thought as she dropped the lid of the chest just in time. *Oh Lady*, please *don't be Marcoss.*

The door opened, and to her utter astonishment Madame walked in.

'Are you all right?' the older woman asked. 'I heard you crying.'

'I . . .' Eline started, utterly nonplussed by what seemed to be Madame's genuine concern for her.

'I was just going to bed myself,' Madame said. 'I passed your room, and I heard you.'

'I had a . . . difficult conversation, that's all,' Eline said.

'Is someone picking on you?' Madame demanded. 'Because if they are –'

'No!' Eline interrupted urgently, thinking back to her fight with

Katherine in the common room over Godsday lunch, the one Marcoss had put a swift stop to. 'Nothing like that. With a friend, in truth. We were talking about our pasts, that's all. Bad memories.'

'Ah,' Madame said, and took a step into the room. She was wearing a gown of ruffled green silk that night, low-cut as was her style, but elegant enough for all that. 'We all have those, my dear. I doubt there's a woman in this house who had a happy childhood.'

'No,' Eline allowed, 'I daresay not. We wouldn't be here otherwise, would we?'

Madame looked at her for a long moment.

'I am trying,' she said. 'Trying to make the best for you that I can. As a courtesan you will at least make good money, *very* good money in truth. Good connections, too. In time, you might even find yourself a patron and your way out of this life.'

'I'm making most of that money for *you*, though, aren't I?' she couldn't help saying, the bitterness welling up in the back of her throat as she thought of the house's fucking ninety percent.

Madame smiled.

'Of course,' she said. 'I am not a charity, Eline, but I *do* have your best interests at heart.'

'Do you?' Eline shot back at her, and all at once she felt her grip on rationality start to fall apart once more.

Is it battle shock? Or a version of it, anyway?

What else could it be?

I killed a man. I killed a woman.

You obviously are.

'You're not planning to *sell* me, once I'm trained?'

Madame threw her head back and laughed.

'For the love of the gods, this again?' she said. 'Which stupid girl have you been listening to tonight? Don't tell me. It's Nama, isn't it?'

Eline said nothing.

'*Think* about it, Eline. You know full well how much I charge for my girls, and how much commission I take from that. You're not a fool. How much would I have to sell a girl for to make back that investment in training and that great a loss of revenue? You think *anyone* would pay that much? No. No one is being sold from the House of Silver Bells.'

'Then where do they go?' Eline demanded. 'And why aren't there enough of us?'

'The lucky ones leave because they find a patron prepared to keep them as a full-time mistress,' Madame said. 'Whatever you may have heard, you *can* leave if you wish, although I do hope you don't. I think you have a bright future here. And there aren't enough of you because I am *picky*. Very picky indeed. I will not hire a woman who isn't licensed, trained, clean, and, above all, beautiful, and that excludes almost every scrub out there on those filthy streets. I am not a slaver, Eline.'

Eline nodded slowly, and for some reason found that she believed her. Madame had leaned into the economics of it rather than the morality, and that made it infinitely more believable. If the numbers didn't work then no, no she wouldn't, would she?

If they had done then it might have been a different matter, Eline knew, but she could see that they simply didn't and that was a relief in itself.

'I understand,' she said eventually.

'Now,' Madame said, 'I suggest you try to sleep. I need you working tomorrow night, and right now you look like shit.'

Eline sighed. Wet-cheeked and puffy-eyed, she supposed she probably did.

'Yes, ma'am,' she said, and Madame turned on her heel and stalked out of the room, closing the door behind her.

Eline prepared herself for bed and slipped under the covers in the plain linen night dress she wore when she wasn't working, but not before she had fished the carved cat back out of the chest again.

She held it close to her as she slept, and cried silently into her pillow.

The next morning she and Nama were on chores together, much to their irritation. The working girls didn't have to do too much around the house as Madame retained a couple of serving maids for domestic tasks, but there was still a rota for dusting and sweeping and other shit that none of them wanted to do. It kept them in their place, Eline supposed was the rationale, but that didn't mean they didn't all hate it.

'I don't think you need to worry about girls being sold,' Eline muttered to Nama as they pushed their brooms half-heartedly around the kitchen. 'Madame spoke to me last night.'

'And you believe her, do you?'

'Aye, I do actually,' Eline said. 'Thing she pointed out is, the numbers don't work. She makes more money keeping us than she ever could from selling us, and I can see how that's true.'

'I ain't good with numbers,' Nama admitted.

'I am,' Eline said, and it was true. 'I worked it out and she's right. They must really just leave, when they find some geezer prepared to put them up in a place and let them live as a kept woman. That's as close to winning as you're going to get, I reckon. A retained mistress, almost her own woman and being paid for doing nothing except when he wants it. She just doesn't tell us because she doesn't want us getting ideas and *all* fucking leaving, you know what I mean?'

'I suppose,' Nama said, but she looked strangely disappointed.

She wanted there to be something, Eline realised. *Some great and terrible secret conspiracy. Something in her life that wasn't mundane and depressing.*

Eline hated to be the bearer of bad news, but there simply wasn't. Their life was what it was, drudgery and whoring. Except for one thing that she had and Nama didn't.

She still had a Kastavian agent to find.

The seamstress greatly resembled a shrew, or perhaps a ferret. Eline could never remember which was which. She had already tried the market, on Queensday afternoon with Nama and a few of the other girls, but of course the stalls there only sold second-hand clothes. They probably wouldn't fit properly and most of them were shabby anyway. No good, not for her new station. No, new clothes had to be made to order and that was simply how it worked.

She had made a point of wearing the knot to visit the seamstress's shop, to ensure everyone knew where they stood and what was what.

'So, you're licensed then?' the woman said, peering at her over her counter.

A weasel, possibly.

'Yes,' Eline said.

The seamstress sniffed and nodded.

'I know the sort of thing you'll be after, then.'

'No,' Eline said. 'I'm training as a courtesan. I want aristocratic, you understand me? Nothing too, you know, whorish.'

'Hah!' the seamstress spat.

Eline regarded the small woman and frowned at her. A stoat, perhaps. She wasn't too sure of the difference there, either. Something like that, anyway. Something that looked like it would bite you, and probably had fleas.

She had spent enough time mending clothes for friends and neighbours to understand how sewing worked. Making clothes up from scratch was perhaps a bit beyond her talents but she knew how to patch them up, what mother didn't? She'd had to keep her children, if not exactly well dressed, then at least presentable. In the alleys and side-streets of the slums where she had lived with Caromir, 'presentable' had been as good at as it got, and that had been the children's Godsday best. Their day-to-day clothes had been as tatty and worn as her own, and those no different from anyone else's on those streets.

This bitch looking down on her made Eline want to punch her throat out. She would *fucking* show her.

She made herself remember Father Shepherd's words in that moment, and she took a deep breath and she calmed herself.

Rise above it, she told herself.

Her mother had taught her when to walk away from a fight, and she knew she had had the right of that. All the same, so far life had taught her that money had two main purposes. One was to make things easier for yourself.

The other was to humiliate other people.

'Make me,' she said quietly, 'some nice clothes. That's all I'm asking you to do.'

'Cost you,' the seamstress shot back at her.

Eline figured the numbers in her head, factoring in the cost of the sort of fabrics she wanted, the costs of the cutting table and the amount of needlework it would take, and came up with what was to her mind a very generous offer.

'I daresay it will,' she said. 'How does ten marks sound?'

The other woman blanched. Eline's father, she remembered, had been lucky to bring home four marks a month. She hadn't been able to spend four marks a *year* to clothe her children, or herself for that matter. Ten was a considerable amount of money she was putting on the table, but she had it and she knew what she wanted.

And she was going to get it.

People who had money, she had long since realised, got what they wanted. She was someone who had money now, and she found that she liked it. She liked it a great deal, in fact, compared to how she had lived with Caromir.

'I reckon we can make that work,' the seamstress said at last.

Eline showed her a small smile. She rested her forearms against the counter and felt the solidity of her stilettoes against the inside of her wrists.

'I'm sure we can,' she said. 'Loose sleeves, please.'

For enough money, she was beginning to realise, you could probably make *anything* work.

Of course you could, and that suited her well enough. She laid the coins down on the counter one after another, and with each coin the stoat became more friendly until Eline was worried she was going to invite her to stay for a cup of tea. Still, with that done she returned to the House of Silver Bells and realised she still had several hours free until she needed to start working.

Whoring, she told herself, but it was still a job and work was work. Yes she was a courtesan now and she didn't have to work *every* night anymore, but so far she'd had only a single assignation and she still needed to bring in a certain level of income for the house. Everyone who wasn't a wealthy noble had to work one way or another, and at least her trade paid well enough. It *was* a trade, as legitimate as any other, and she had long since made her peace with that fact. Not one she would have chosen perhaps, no, but a legitimate trade nonetheless. It was perfectly legal so long as you were licensed and there was no shame in it, not really. She drew herself a mug of small beer from the barrel in the kitchen and took it out into the yard behind the house with her to take the afternoon air, and there she found Nama.

The younger woman was crouched down in the dirt between the back door and the small wooden shithouse, and she was surrounded by rats. She had her hands stretched out in front of her and was obviously feeding them. Eline stared in horrified fascination as the ghastly things took food from her hands, their disgusting naked tails twitching in the air as they snuffled at Nama's palms.

'Nama, what in the names of the gods are you doing?' she demanded.

'Feeding the rats,' Nama said, and there was a far-away, dreamlike tone to her voice. 'Beautiful things, rats.'

'Are you out of your fucking mind?' Eline demanded. 'They're disgusting vermin and they carry disease.'

'So do most people,' Nama said. 'I like the rats. They talk to me, sometimes.'

'I . . .' Eline started, and realised she didn't even know what to do with that. 'Is this some more bollocks your Kurt has put in your head?'

'Look at them,' Nama said, and she reached out and stroked one the length of its back. It didn't even flinch. 'Lovely.'

Eline turned on her heel and went back into the house and left the girl to it. Perhaps she was mad, who knew, but she wasn't hurting herself or anyone else, so Eline figured it was none of her affair. Leaving other people to their business and keeping your own nose out was, she had long since discovered, probably for the best.

That was just how the world was.

Chapter 18

About a week or so later a barefoot urchin boy came to the house in the afternoon, carrying a message. It was just a folded and sealed piece of paper, but the seal was still intact and no doubt the boy couldn't read anyway, so what matter? It was addressed to 'Miss Eline', which Loran on the door found insultingly funny. He called her down to receive it anyway, and she thanked the lad and tipped him a silver penny from her own purse for his trouble.

The red wax seal was something fanciful and meaningless, not the crown and rose of the house of law, but she already knew who it must be from. Who else would write to the likes of her? Of course Luka wasn't stupid enough to use the official seal and therefore tell whoever received the message who she worked for, but all the same she wondered whose arms those truly were. Anyone's, in fact? Eline thought probably not.

It was the middle of the afternoon on Queensday and most of the girls were at market, so she retired to the deserted common room to read her letter in peace. She settled down beside the crackling fire in the grate and split the seal with her thumbnail.

Luka's handwriting hadn't improved. His childish scrawl simply said:

Found a likely one, Eline.
Come by the house when you can. I want your opinion.
L.

That was progress in itself, she supposed. He wanted her opinion, which was almost asking her what to do next. And she wasn't summoned on a deadline, but at her pleasure. Oh yes, she thought, the balance of power was *definitely* tipping in her direction even if Luka didn't know it himself.

Truth be told, she suspected he didn't. Some men, in her experience, naturally deferred to a woman's judgement. Something about their mothers perhaps, she wouldn't know; but it was definitely a thing she had seen. Not with cunts like Caromir; no, they always thought they knew best. But some, certainly.

She re-read the note once more, then tossed it into the fire.

Queensday was the principal market day in Drathburg, but also usually the quietest night in the house. A working man might give two-thirds of his pay to his wife to keep their house and she supposed, what with market, most men's wives had spent all their money by that night, and it was usually the next day, Coinsday, before they came flocking back again with their week's wage heavy in their purses.

Yes, she supposed she could probably slip away that evening if no one was looking, which they probably wouldn't be. Loran tended to visit the theatre on a Queensday evening, or so he said, and most of his underlings would have taken advantage of his absence by then and been drinking. Rumour had it that Loran was more likely to be visiting a molly house, where men dressed as women could meet other men for more than just friendship, but that was no business of hers.

Lie with whom thou wilt, so long as both be willing.

Our Lady had no quarrel with the molly houses, and that was good enough for her. Whatever made you happy, she supposed. It wasn't hurting her, was it? If it was good enough for a goddess it was good enough for anyone, so far as she could see.

She knew the workings of the house by then, its strengths and its weaknesses, and getting in and out was nowhere near as hard as Nama had originally led her to believe. If she went out the back door and across the yard past the shithouse and into the alley then Gorath on the gate wouldn't even know she'd gone, and honestly what business was it of his anyway?

None at all, as far as she was concerned. This was, as she had said to Nama, a job not a prison.

She waited through supper then slipped away as she had planned, and was at Luka's house by the seventh hour after noon in the evening twilight. Sam let her in as usual, and she made her way to the back room Luka obviously used as his office.

'You wrote to me,' she said, by way of introduction.

'Aye,' Luka said, and looked up at her from the sheaf of badly printed news sheets in his hand. 'Have you seen all this shit?'

Eline shook her head. 'I don't read the sheets,' she said.

'You should,' he said. 'You *can* read, can't you?'

'Yes of course I can fucking read,' Eline snapped back at him, although in truth it was work for her. 'I just don't want to read that shit. My husband read them and that was half the problem.'

'It's useful,' Luka told her. 'This is what most of the general public read, and what they believe. Of course *what* they believe depends greatly on which sheet they read, and the sheets publish what they think their readership want to hear so who knows what you can actually trust, but there we are. It's a good gauge of public opinion, either way.'

Eline made a noncommittal noise and helped herself to a glass of his brandy.

'Perhaps I'll start,' she said. 'You wanted me.'

She didn't even phrase it as a question.

'Aye,' Luka said. 'Like I wrote, I've found a likely one.'

'A Kastavian?'

'No, a fucking earthworm!' Luka snapped at her. 'Yes, of course a fucking Kastavian. Do you, Eline, think I'm fucking stupid?'

Eline looked at him for a long moment. No, no of course she didn't think he was stupid. He was a Queen's Man after all, and he would never have earned the warrant if he had been. He was, though, clearly not as clever as he thought he was.

'Of course not,' she said, trying to be as diplomatic as possible. 'I do think, however, that perhaps we have different skillsets.'

'Of course we fucking have,' Luka said, 'and that's why I wanted you here. You're a woman, for one thing.'

'What in Our Lady's name does that have to do with anything?' Eline demanded.

'I dunno, nothing maybe,' Luka said, and he looked defensive then. 'It's just . . . I threatened this bloke, and nothing. I had Sam hurt him, and nothing. I just thought maybe . . . I dunno.'

Eline sighed. He really didn't have the faintest idea what he was saying, did he? All the same, he might have been right. Some people, Eline had noticed over the years, sometimes spoke wisdom by complete accident. Perhaps he was right, perhaps her being a woman *might* make a difference. Nonsense to do with his mother, probably, but it was definitely worth a try. That, and he had obviously realised, albeit not consciously, that she was perhaps better at interrogation than he was.

Then an idea came to her. A particularly nasty one.

Lady, what is wrong with me?

Battle shock, it must be.

'What do we know about him?'

'Kastavian, obviously,' Luka said. 'Came into the city three weeks before the murder. Wine merchant looking to buy, or so he told the gate guards. Couple of lads with him but they were obviously just muscle for the road, no one who matters. He went to –'

'Who says they don't matter?' Eline interrupted him. 'One of those could just as easily have been behind this as him.'

Luka blinked at her.

'Well, I suppose,' he said, 'but they were local blokes. Probably hired off the Varnburg docks he landed at. Not Kastavian, anyway.'

'So he says,' Eline said. 'Have you interviewed them?'

Luka shrugged helplessly.

'Long gone,' he said. 'They were just his escort for the road.'

Eline rubbed the bridge of her nose and swallowed a sigh.

This wasn't going to get any easier, was it?

'And why is he still here, with the deed long done?'

'Well I asked, obviously,' Luka said, 'but he spun me some yarn about the best time to buy wine and all that shit. I reckon he was planning something else, but buggered if I can get him to tell me what.'

'I see,' she said at last. 'All right, I'll see him.'

Luka gave her a look that made her realise she was talking like she was his boss and not the other way around, and she swallowed nervously.

Bad plan, Eline, she told herself.

'Aye, you will,' Luka said. 'So put down that glass of my fucking brandy and come with me.'

'I thought Sam would –'

'Sam's got the fucking door,' he said. 'You're doing this with me.'

Eline nodded and followed Luka the way she had followed Sam before. Luka paused to light a taper just like Sam had the last time she had visited the cellar, and she put a hand on his arm to stay him.

'Let me lead,' she said. 'A courtesan is basically an actress, after all. Let me act. I know how to do this.'

'Aye,' Luka said after a moment. 'Whatever gets it done.'

He led the way down into the cellar, took down the lamp from its shelf at the bottom of the steps and lit it. The Kastavian stranger was there alone, and she looked a question at Luka.

'Where's Bob?' she asked, switching to her carefully practiced aristocratic accent now they were within earshot of the prisoner.

'In the city gaol,' Luka said. 'He can rot in there until he hangs or I need him again, which I doubt I will. Fuck him, either way.'

Eline resisted the urge to scream. 'I see,' she forced out through clenched teeth.

Lady's sake, she thought. If Black Nose Bob really knew anything useful he would be unlikely to survive a night in the city gaol. Ah well, it was what it was, she supposed, and nothing to be done about it now.

She turned to the prisoner, secured with chains to the wall as Bob had been, and turned an equally well-trained withering glare on him. Madame knew what she was doing, after all, and she was a *very* good teacher.

'Name?' she demanded.

'Bogdan Milev,' he said. 'Who the fuck are you?'

'An associate of this gentleman, whom I believe you have already met.'

The man scowled, but said nothing.

'I also believe,' Eline continued, 'you have been asked some questions. As I understand it, you have not been terribly forthcoming with answers so far.'

'Fuck off,' this Bogdan Milev said, his voice heavy with his Kastavian accent. 'I ain't saying anything to you, woman.'

She smiled at him, and turned to Luka.

'My dear,' she said, 'would to be kind enough to pull this gentleman's britches and smallclothes down for me? I'd really rather not, myself.'

To his credit Luka didn't blink, but just did as she said while Milev struggled fruitlessly against his manacles. His legs flailed and kicked but the strength of Luka's bulk easily overcame him, and he soon had the man's clothes pooled around his ankles.

Eline's hands slid up her sleeves and she produced her two stilettoes. She smoothly reversed the blades in her hands the way Marcoss had taught her. Milev's eyes followed every movement of the knives, alive with mounting terror.

'Lift his shirt tails up, please,' she said, and Luka did as she asked to expose the man's genitals.

There were, it had occurred to Eline while they had still been upstairs, things that one man wouldn't dream of doing to another. Probably wouldn't even think of, in all honesty. But she had, and that worried her in itself.

'Now, Master Milev,' she said, leaning once more into her elocution lessons until her voice was as sharp as broken glass. 'Something here is abundantly obvious. I have two stilettoes, and you have two testicles. Which one would you like me to nail to the floor first?'

'Wait, wait!' Milev said, and she could hear the rising panic in his voice now. 'You can't do that! You ain't a Queen's Man too, are you? You can't be, you're only a *woman*!'

'No, I'm not a Queen's Man,' Eline said. 'I am more of an adviser. A specialist, you might say. And I assure you, I very much can.'

'She's not joking,' Luka said. 'Give it up, Milev. Who hired you to kill that duke, and why are you still here? What was coming next?'

'I *can't*!' the man said, ignoring her completely now as he spoke to Luka. 'This goes too high. I . . . I just can't.'

'Oh dear,' Eline said. 'I am so very sad to hear that.'

Milev spat at her. He had obviously realised that she was bluffing.

I'm just an actress, a courtesan, she told herself. *I'm not really going to do this. Am I?*

I am also a spy, and apparently a killer. Is torturer too great a leap to make, to keep my children safe from the ruthless power of the Crown?

She thought about it for a moment, and remembered her promise to herself, and to her beloved children.

Whatever it takes.

Even so, she couldn't do *this*. She just couldn't.

No one humane could.

'You won't do it, bitch,' Milev said, and he sounded defiant now. 'You haven't got the fucking nerve. You're only a woman, anyway. Back in Kastavia your husband would already have beaten you bloody for even suggesting—'

Eline's left blade came down like a hammer.

They were back upstairs, and Luka was shakily drinking a very large brandy.

'Fucking *blood*, Eline,' he said once he had drained half of it. 'I never thought you'd really . . . Fucking *fuck*, woman!'

'Neither did I,' Eline confessed, taking a sip of her own drink. 'But he touched a nerve.'

'I should think he fucking well did,' Luka said.

Milev's testicle had all but exploded when her stiletto went though it. The man had shrieked, puked, and passed out in the space of barely a heartbeat. Even now her blade was still embedded through what was left of his right ball, pinning it tight to the packed earthen floor of Luka's cellar. That probably, it occurred to her then, hurt a hideous amount.

Oh, well.

'He'll live,' she said. 'For a while, anyway, even without treatment. We'll have another go when he comes round. I honestly don't think he's going to refuse me a second time, do you?'

'You seriously want to go back down there?' Luka asked, and he looked a bit pale at the prospect.

'Of course I do,' Eline said. 'I want my blade back, for one thing. They're expensive, and Madame will go up the wall if I ask her for yet another one. Some answers would be nice, too.'

Luka finished his drink and poured them both another, and shook his head slowly.

'You are one mad bitch,' he said.

'I've already made more progress than you and Sam managed between you,' she pointed out. 'He'll be terrified of me now. Whatever gets it done, remember?'

Luka sighed. 'I met a woman like you once before, back in Dannsburg. She *was* a Queen's Man, but ... by Our Lady, Eline, I was *not* expecting that!'

'No, neither was he,' Eline said. 'That's why it's going to work.'

Chapter 19

After a while the wailing started, the distant howls of a wounded animal floating up from the cellar. Sam opened the door of the room and nodded at Luka.

'Reckon your bloke's awake,' he said, and frowned slowly. 'The fuck did you do to him, boss?'

'Not me,' Luka said, and shot Eline a look. 'This one. You'll be polite to her, Sam, if you're wise.'

'Always have been,' the big man said, and Eline showed him a smile.

He had been, to be fair.

'Yes, you have,' she agreed. 'Thank you, Sam.'

He blushed a bit and left the room, returning to his post at the front door. Eline looked the question at Luka.

'Aye, all right,' he said, and put his drink down. 'This is going to be fucking ugly, though.'

'I know,' Eline said, lapsing back into her courtesan's voice. 'But ugly gets results.'

He sighed and led the way back down to the cellar, although Eline knew the way well enough herself by then.

Let the man lead, she told herself. *They like that.*

Luka re-lit the lamp, and Milev screamed when he saw Eline.

'No!' he begged. 'For the love of the gods, man, don't let her anywhere near me!'

'You're not overly fond of my friend, then?' Luka asked.

Milev was actually in tears, and his voice was thick with unspeakable agony.

'Anything,' he blubbered. 'Just don't let that monster near me!'

'How do you feel?' Luka asked him.

139

'You're a man, how the fuck do you think I feel? Please, for the love of the gods take it out. Take it *out!*'

'Hmmm,' Luka said. 'Who hired you to kill that duke, and why are you still here? What was coming next?'

Milev said something incomprehensible, and vomited down his shirt again.

'Please!' he wailed.

After another moment of staring at him Luka obviously took pity and reached down to wrench Eline's stiletto out of his testicle. Milev shrieked again and passed out once more.

'This might be a slow process,' Luka observed as he passed the blade back to Eline.

She took it carefully and cleaned it on the bottom of Milev's britches before she slid it back into its concealed sheath.

'No, I'm out of patience,' she said, still using her courtesan's voice even though she was only speaking to Luka now. 'Throw a bucket of water over him. By the smell in here he's soiled himself anyway. A wash will do him good.'

She was right about that, too. There was a distinctive brown stain on the earthen floor underneath the man's bared backside, and he stank to high heaven. Luka shook his head but whistled for Sam, who stuck his head around the top of the cellar steps a moment later.

'Everything all right down there, boss?' he asked.

He couldn't have failed to hear the screaming and obviously knew it *wasn't* all right for Milev, but by then Eline knew Sam simply wouldn't care about that. She really was warming to the big man, she had to admit to herself. Not in *that* way, gods no, but it was clear to her that he was faithful and he was loyal, and those were traits she could value in a man.

In a retainer, perhaps.

'Fetch us a bucket of water, would you, lad?' Luka asked.

'Aye, boss,' Sam said, and Eline heard him clumping off towards the pump in the kitchen.

'You really are quite something,' Luka observed to Eline while they waited.

'You're the Queen's Man,' she said.

'Aye, maybe, but I'm a spy and the propaganda man,' he said. 'I'm the one who makes people see things the way the Provost Marshal wants them seen, and roots out anyone who don't. This . . . this sort of thing has never been my bag.'

'But it's mine?'

'Apparently,' he said, and shifted his feet in a way that almost made her think he was nervous. 'Never gone in for that, myself.'

'I never thought I would either,' Eline said, 'but Our Lady moves in mysterious ways.'

'Never went in for *that*, either,' Luka said. 'Religion, that's the boss's bag.'

She was about to ask what he meant but just then Sam came down the stairs with a wooden pail of water and dumped the lot over Milev's head without needing to be asked.

The man awoke spluttering and sobbing, and Sam nodded in satisfaction at a job well done before he returned to his watch on the door.

'Now then,' Luka said, 'I believe I asked you some questions. Namely, who hired you to kill that duke, and why are you still here? What was coming next?'

'Nothing was coming next,' Milev confessed, dripping wet and still choking on what even Eline could imagine must have been truly sickening pain. 'I'm still here because I don't fucking dare go home.'

'And why is that then?' Eline asked, and the man visibly cringed at the sound of her voice.

'Don't let the bitch *near* me,' he begged Luka again.

'She's here in the room with us too,' Luka observed, 'so I'd suggest you try not to ignore her. I don't think you want to upset her again, do you, Master Milev?'

'Please,' Milev sobbed. 'All right, all right, I was hired by a man in Kastavia. A high-ranking general, name of Vachkov. He obviously wants to fuck with the Immalian succession but I swear to all the gods I don't know why. I just know that if I go back home after having done what he wanted I'd be lucky to see another dawn. I'm *hiding*, you understand? He knows the job is done but I've had it put about I got killed doing it, and I'm praying he believes that.'

'Hmmm,' Luka said again. 'He's a scary man, then. Is he as scary as us?'

'Please, I don't know anything else,' Milev said. 'You have to believe me!'

'Why?' Eline said. 'Why do we have to believe anything you say?'

'Leave me alone, you ghastly *woman*!' Milev screamed at her.

141

Eline frowned, and treated him to a glare. 'If you denigrate me for being a woman one more time, I swear to Our Lady I'll stab the other one as well,' she said.

'Easy, Eline,' Luka said, and she winced to hear him use her name in front of the prisoner. That was *never* a good idea, even she knew that. He turned back to Milev and continued. 'You were hired by a Kastavian general called Vachkov to kill the duke and fuck up the Immalian succession, but you don't know why. You contracted a poppy addict whore called Elizaveta to actually do the deed, which she did, and now you don't dare go home for fear of being murdered to hide the trail of evidence, is that about the size of it?'

'Y-yes,' Milev stammered.

'And there's nothing else of use you can tell us?'

'No, I swear, that really is all of it!'

Luka paused for a moment, then nodded.

He took Eline's elbow and led her back up the stairs.

They reached the hall, and he looked towards the door.

'Sam,' he said, 'get down there and kill that cunt, there's a good lad.'

'Aye, boss,' Sam said.

It was late when Eline made it back to the Bells and thankfully she managed to evade Nama for once and make it back to her room in peace without having to endure the other woman's endless questions. She felt drained, numb, curiously unfeeling considering what she had done that night.

Battle shock, it's a form of battle shock. It must be.

You didn't have to have literally been in battle to experience shock, she of all people knew that. Two decades of marriage to Caromir had taught her that well enough. She told herself that over and over again, but still she couldn't shake the memory of her blade slamming down through Bogdan Milev's right testicle and how she had felt *nothing*.

That ain't right, Eline, she told herself, but that didn't change the facts of the matter.

Another man dead, and not before she'd tortured him to the edge of sanity. She, Eline, she had done that. She sat down on the edge of her bed and looked down at her hands, and they weren't shaking at *all*.

In Our Lady's name.

In Her eyes you have done no wrong.

She undressed and washed and pissed into the pot, and eventually she slept a deep, uninterrupted sleep. She felt no disturbance at all, in fact, until the next morning when a messenger brought a letter to the house for her.

They had finished breakfast by then and she didn't have chores that morning, so she took the sealed note back up to her room to read it in peace. It wasn't from Luka this time.

My dearest Eline,

I do hope this note finds you well. I think I owe you my gratitude, and perhaps something approaching an explanation. I would be grateful if you could call upon me at my house this evening to renew our acquaintance.

Your most respectful admirer,

Baron Lan Elenkov

Eline blinked and read the note again. What in the names of the gods was going on?

Still, this was effectively an assignation and she knew she had to broker it through the house or risk breaking the terms of her agreement with Madame, and she certainly wasn't ready to do that yet. Fifty marks was still fifty marks, after all, and with the amount of money she had spent on forfeits and new clothes she could well do with it.

She folded the letter and tucked it into her pouch, then took a deep breath and made her way back downstairs to Madame's study. She rapped nervously on the door.

'Come,' the older woman's imperious voice called, and Eline opened the door.

Madame was seated behind her desk surrounded by papers and open ledgers and flanked by two of the house thugs. She looked a question at Eline as she entered.

'Ma'am,' Eline said.

'Eline,' Madame replied. 'I have barely digested my breakfast and I have a great deal of work to do. What can you possibly want at this ungodly hour of the morning?'

'I received this, ma'am,' Eline said, and thrust the letter out at her. 'A request for an assignation. I thought I should bring it to you. It's for tonight.'

'*Tonight?*' Madame echoed in obvious shock. 'Who thinks he has you at his bloody beck and call, exactly? And on Coinsday at that? It's our busiest night of the week, everyone who matters knows that. A courtesan is usually booked weeks, if not *months*, in advance.'

'The baron again,' Eline said as Madame spread open the letter and quickly scanned it.

'Hmmm,' Madame said. 'He's the best-paying client you've got so far, the *only* client in fact, so yes I suppose we can arrange this but it is *most* irregular. Well done for bringing this to me, by the way. I would have been very upset if you hadn't.'

I'd have been out on the streets tomorrow if I hadn't and I know it, Eline thought bitterly.

'Ma'am,' she said, and nodded respectfully.

'It's strange, though,' Madame said. 'There is no significant social event this evening that I'm aware of, and I *would* be aware of it if there was. The note reads as though the baron simply desires your company. And what's all this about an explanation?'

'I have no idea, ma'am,' Eline lied.

Madame frowned for a moment, then she shrugged.

'He's very old,' she said. 'Perhaps his mind is wandering. Still, at least you know you probably won't have to attempt to bed him so it's easy money if nothing else. And it's not a society occasion so you won't need to hire jewellery or a ballgown from me this time, having already bought yourself some perfectly tasteful clothes, so you stand to make a full hundred marks this time. Here, write back to him and tell him you'll be there. Be sure to cite your fee, won't you? One crown, as before.'

A hundred marks, all for her!

Madame pushed paper and pen, the inkwell and the sifter of sand across the desk and waved Eline into one of the two visitors' chairs that faced her.

Eline hurriedly did as she was told, feeling slightly ashamed of her poor handwriting, but Madame nodded in approval. It was still better than Luka's, she supposed.

'At least you can write,' Madame said, and took the freshly sanded letter from Eline. 'I wasn't sure.'

Always tests, always. Was the woman never satisfied?

Madame folded the letter and melted wax over her desk lamp then closed it with the seal of the house, and passed it to the scarred young thug who stood beside her.

'Give that to Loran, and have him send it with a runner to the Baron Lan Elenkov's house,' she said.

The man nodded and did as she said, and Madame turned back to Eline.

'I do hope you haven't got yourself involved in some sort of intrigue, dear,' she said.

Eline met her eyes.

The Immalian succession.

Kastavian assassins right there in Drathburg.

The Queen's Men.

Her blade, punching through a spy's testicle.

'No, ma'am,' she said, and she didn't blink.

Chapter 20

'A crown?' the baron slurred when she was shown into his presence in his opulent drawing room. 'For a blasted conversation? Madame has a bloody cheek.'

'At less than a day's notice?' Eline said. 'You're lucky she didn't double it.'

'She knows I'm all but bankrupt,' the baron grumbled, and took a healthy sip from the glass of brandy in his hand.

Eline looked pointedly at the extravagant paintings on his walls, the polished silver on the cupboard, the fine Alarian carpet underfoot and the three footmen who attended them.

'Indeed,' she said dryly. 'Your poverty cannot fail to inspire sympathy, my lord baron.'

'Bugger off,' he grumbled, then looked around at the servants. 'You three bugger off too. If my guest wants a drink I'm sure she can see where the cupboard is.'

He had a half-full glass in his own hand already of course, although he was rapidly draining that.

The footmen duly took their leave of their performatively dissolute master, and Eline did indeed help herself to a glass before turning to face him.

'Now, what's this about?' she asked.

The baron's drunken façade disappeared at once, the same as it had at the Earl Lan Klasskoff's reception.

'I wanted to thank you,' he said. 'You have successfully turned the eyes of the Queen's Men away from my old friend, Madame, who is entirely innocent in this matter, and for that you have my gratitude.'

'Yes, and for which I have avoided being, as I believe you put it, *exterminated*.'

'My apologies,' the baron said. 'The point needed to be made at the time, that's all.'

Eline sipped her drink and remained standing, regarding the baron over the rim of the glass.

'This is a very strange game we play,' she said at last.

The baron laughed. 'Yes,' he said. 'It's called politics.'

'I don't think I care for it.'

'I don't think anyone does,' he confessed. 'All the same, the game needs to be played.'

'Does it?' Eline challenged him. 'You, *all but bankrupt* in the midst of your conspicuous wealth, need to involve yourself in it why, exactly?'

The baron laughed, and held his glass out for her to refill.

'My knee hurts,' he said. 'You wouldn't make an old man get up to pour his own drink, would you? Not when he's paying Madame a blasted gold crown for a couple of hours of your time?'

Eline smiled.

'Of course not, my lord,' she said, and dutifully refilled the baron's glass from the bottle in her other hand.

She might only get ten percent of that crown, but that was still a hundred marks. She wondered what her mother would have thought of that.

It wasn't even work, really, as she knew the baron didn't actually want to bed her anyway. He wanted . . . She didn't know what.

A *political thing*, as Nama had put it. That was, she already knew by then, probably going to be much, much worse in the long run.

No, no, on balance she supposed her mother would probably have been appalled, but she was long dead so what did that matter?

'For the gods' sake sit down, woman,' the baron said, once he'd sipped his drink. 'That's better. Now that you know Madame *didn't* kill the Immalian duke, who did?'

Eline blinked at him.

'What in the world makes you think I know the answer to that?' she asked.

Her heart was skipping in her chest. The baron and Luka obviously weren't entirely on the same side here, but she had totally lost track of who knew what. The baron hadn't thought Luka even knew who he was and he had been completely wrong about that. Luka had set her to kill Madame purely as a ruse to draw Lan Elenkov onto the game board, but why?

What did this semi-retired smuggler and pirate have to do with anything? The prime smuggling routes from their country were to Alaria and back, so what in the Lady's name did Kastavia and Immalia have to do with anything?

'If you don't know by now then your man Luka isn't very good at his job,' the baron observed.

No, he isn't particularly, Eline couldn't help but think. *But I am, and that, my dear lord baron, is* not *something I want you to know.*

'Since you so enjoy the game of politics,' she said, 'what do you know about the way it is played in Immalia and Kastavia?'

The baron snorted into his brandy.

'She charges me a gold crown for your company and yet wants you to interrogate *me*, for the privilege? Madame truly has no shame these days. Or is that *you* asking, or your master?'

'Does it matter?'

The baron emptied his glass and held it out for another refill.

'It really rather depends what you want to know.'

'You said you may have certain connections abroad,' Eline reminded him. 'Where, exactly?'

'I may have been lying about that.'

She looked once more at the conspicuous wealth of the drawing room in the modest house of this supposedly almost bankrupt man.

'I really don't think you were.'

'Perhaps not,' the baron admitted. 'Still, at least you have managed to turn Luka away from Madame and put him on the right scent.'

He was never on Madame's scent, he was on yours for some reason I haven't worked out yet, Eline thought. *I don't think you need to know that, either.*

'Which is what?' Eline demanded. 'Your foreign connections lie *where*, exactly?'

The baron took another sip of his drink and looked at her.

'You're a surprisingly intelligent woman, Eline,' he said. 'Where do you think?'

'Immalia,' she said immediately, 'or somewhere else altogether. You asked who really had the duke killed, and if you were working for Kastavia you'd fucking well know the answer to that.'

'Ahhh,' the baron said, and Eline could have kicked herself. She had fallen straight into that trap like a blindfolded schoolgirl. 'Perhaps not as intelligent as all that, then. Or perhaps still just a little naïve. Finding your way, perhaps, in this world of ours.'

Apparently I still have an awful lot to learn about this world of politics, she chided herself. *Never admit to knowing anything, ever.*

The baron looked at the pinched expression on her face and laughed.

'Oh, I shouldn't tease,' he said. 'I'm just still getting the measure of you, my dear.'

'I don't care for it,' Eline said.

'No, I dare say you don't,' the baron said, and held out his glass for yet another refill in a way that said he didn't give a fuck whether she cared for it or not. His capacity for drink seemed to know no limit, and yet still he seemed sober as a priest. *How much does a man have to drink*, she wondered, *to have this level of tolerance?* She obliged, and he sipped from his glass. 'So, Kastavia, then. Do you have a name?'

Eline swallowed. Luka would kill her if he even knew she'd had this conversation, or more likely have Sam do it for him, but she couldn't think of a better way to move the investigation forwards. The baron obviously knew more than Luka did, and it seemed to her that the Queen's Man was doing little more than grope in the dark anyway. He really *didn't* give her the impression that he knew what he was doing. If she could use the Baron Lan Elenkov for information then why not? Yes, it meant giving him information in return, but as Nama had so rightly said there was nothing free in this world so what matter?

'Does the name General Vachkov mean anything to you?'

The baron kept his expression completely neutral.

'Now where would you have heard a name like that?' he asked.

'From a man I interrogated,' Eline admitted. 'A man who said he had been hired by this general to arrange the duke's assassination.'

'And you believed him, did you?'

Eline's temper snapped. 'Considering I had recently nailed his right testicle to the floor, yes I did, actually. I think his chances of lying to me after that were vanishingly small, don't you?'

Perhaps she *hadn't* wanted the baron to know how good she really was, but this was a direct challenge to her intelligence and her interrogation skills and she wasn't having that. Perhaps that was naïve of her, new to this world as she was, but she wanted to make her mark. She saw possibilities in this future, however remote they might be.

The baron winced, then laughed.

'I suppose that would do it,' he said. 'Eline, my dear, could I interest you in a job?'

That threw her completely. Of all the things she thought he might have been about to say, that wasn't one of them.

'I already have a job,' she said. 'Two jobs in fact, as you are plainly aware.'

'Obviously, we would have to replace one with the other,' he said. 'I would never seek to steal you away from my friend Madame, but this Luka . . . Shall we say he is no friend of yours.'

'And are *you*?' Eline challenged him.

The baron coughed and took a sip of his drink.

'It seems to me,' he said after a moment, 'that you have a certain set of skills that I would find very valuable.'

'And nothing over me that I care about,' Eline said. 'The same cannot be said for my current employer.'

The baron looked at her for a long moment.

'And exactly what *has* he got over you?'

'I don't think you need to know that,' Eline said.

'I am paying a good deal for your company tonight,' the baron reminded her. 'Although you're obviously not *that* naïve, then.'

'This isn't that sort of business arrangement,' Eline shot back. 'You have paid for my company and my cunt. You have the one, and I know you don't want the other. If you've changed your mind on the second then come and take it, but there are no trades. Those are the things you have paid Madame for. For my secrets, no.'

The baron roared with laugher.

'Oh, you are Madame's creature in truth, aren't you?' he snorted. 'Gods, you're a find. I wish I had swept you up from the gutter before Luka did.'

'But you didn't,' Eline pointed out. 'And with nothing to hold over me, I'd have told you to fuck off anyway.'

Lan Elenkov snorted again and drained his glass. It occurred to Eline then that a courtesan probably seldom had a conversation like this with a client.

If ever. This was not a normal life she lived, even by the courtesan's standards.

'Would you?' he said. 'With enough money waved in front of the new-made widow with no income, I really don't think you would have done, you know.'

'We'll never know, will we?'

Eline held his gaze, but a part of her wished he *had* found her first. At least he had no way to threaten her children, at least that she knew of, and if it could have been purely a business arrangement then . . . It didn't matter. It was what it was, and Luka and the Queen's Men held the power of life and death over her precious son and daughter. She was painfully aware of that fact, and whatever temptations the baron dangled in front of her could never make her forget it.

'So no, you *can't* interest me in a job,' she said at last, to bring the conversation back to where she wanted it. 'What can you tell me about this Vachkov?'

'Nothing whatsoever,' Lan Elenkov said, and she saw his wrinkled old face close up like a clam. 'That's the sort of information I could only possibly share with a . . . All right, not an employee then. I see your difficulty there and I can appreciate it. Someone I had a business arrangement with, perhaps.'

Eline frowned for a moment.

'Outline this proposed business arrangement,' she said.

'Very well,' Lan Elenkov said, and sat back in his seat to look at her over the rim of his glass. 'Condition one: Luka does not know about this, ever. Condition two: if I need someone interrogated, you will do it every bit as ruthlessly as you interrogated your Kastavian spy. You obviously have a talent for that, and that's something I could use. Condition three: if Luka wishes to move against any agent of the Immalian throne you do *nothing* until you have told me of it, and waited for my instructions.'

'And what's in it for me?'

'Well primarily an answer to the question you asked,' he said. 'And a hundred marks a month as a retainer.'

I'm all but bankrupt.

Oh, was he *fuck!*

Once again Eline was late back to the House of Silver Bells, and this time she *didn't* manage to evade Nama on her way back into the house.

'Do you even still work here?' the younger woman challenged her when they bumped into each other in the otherwise deserted common room.

It was late and most of the girls were in bed by then, and Eline knew damn well Nama must have been waiting up for her.

'Not as such, no,' she said. 'I'm a courtesan now, Nama, not just a common whore. I had an assignation tonight, a noble gentleman. Madame brokered it, of course. I would never go outside the House. That's me off whoring for *weeks*, if I want to be.'

'So that leaves me doing five punters back to back,' Nama grumbled. 'I'm knackered and I'm *sore*, Eline.'

Eline could only shrug. 'It's the job,' she said. 'Madame agreed to it, as I said. She knows how many girls she's got.'

'And she doesn't *care*,' Nama countered. 'You didn't mention it yesterday.'

'I didn't *know* about it yesterday,' Eline snapped back at her. 'Or the day before, whenever it was. What time is it, anyway?'

'I don't know,' Nama said. 'Late. Early. Whatever. We're a night-time economy, Eline. Who knows whether it's still today, last night or tomorrow? It could be next year, I don't know. Who cares? It's *now*, and I'm sore and you're drunk and one of us obviously had a *fucking* better night than the other one did.'

'Not me,' Eline said. 'My night was not pleasant at all.'

'Well, there you are then,' Nama said, although quite where Eline was supposed to find herself after that rather nonsensical exchange was a mystery to her. 'Time is different for rats.'

Nama didn't seem entirely rational to her, right then. She could sort of see what the younger woman was getting at, but her phrasing was all over the place and she sounded like she was drunk out of her mind, although if she had been working Eline knew she couldn't be. Madame would never have allowed that. And *rats*? *What*? She frowned at Nama.

'Nama,' she said slowly, 'don't take this the wrong way, but have you been at the poppy resin?'

'Fuck that, no,' Nama said. 'I hate that shit as much as you do. It's . . . I dunno know how to explain it. It's the cunning, Eline. It does something to my head. Kurt came by earlier, only a half hour booking but he showed me a new thing and . . . I don't feel very well now.'

'Aye, right you are,' Eline said, and even she didn't quite know what she meant by that. She knew the younger woman wasn't making sense, but that was about it. She just wanted to go to *bed*.

She wanted her bed and that was the whole truth of it in that moment, and she really didn't want to talk about any of this old shit. As long as Nama hadn't been smoking fucking poppy resin she could put it from her mind, she supposed. She was much more concerned with what the baron had said to her.

A hundred marks a month for probably doing nothing at all was a windfall indeed, but the main thing on her mind was that she would be going behind the backs of the Queen's Men.

This was a very dangerous game she played indeed and she knew it, in Our Lady's name.

Chapter 21

The next day everyone's head was a bit sore, but at least there were no bad feelings between Eline and Nama. The Alarian girl didn't even seem to remember their previous conversation, which Eline had to admit worried her some, for all that she hadn't wanted to have a falling out about it.

That morning was Godsday, of course, and that meant medicine and temple and all that shit, and after temple was mercifully done Eline slipped away from the others to head to *her* temple.

'Keep me some Godsday lunch, I'll be back soon,' she said to Nama, and hurried off up the road to the Great Temple to kneel before the alter of Our Lady in Her chapel.

The priest was there in front of her again a few moments later, this Father Shepherd who had greeted her before. This time Eline just bowed her head before him, remembering his lessons from her previous visit.

'Blessing, Father,' she said. 'My name's Eline, and I'm a whore.'

He reached down and put his hand on her forehead.

'Our Lady go with you, Daughter,' he said.

'What?' she said, and stumbled to a stop.

Could she really confide in this priest, she asked herself. Oh, she had given her heart to Our Lady of Eternal Sorrows, but . . . Aye, *but*. She didn't know this man, not really.

'Daughter?'

'What if I'm more than that?'

'The more that you tell Our Lady the better She will know you, and the more likely She will be to stay Her hand today,' the priest said. 'Each to their talents, in Her service.'

She remembered confessing the sin of murder to this priest before, and how he had forgiven her for it.

'Perhaps . . . Father, how much can I trust you?'

'You can trust a priest with anything,' Father Shepherd assured her. 'Anything at all. What you tell me is between you and Our Lady, and nobody else.'

'Not even the Queen's Men?' Eline almost whispered.

Father Shepherd looked down at her then with an unreadable expression on his face.

'No loyal daughter would have anything to tell me that she would fear the Queen's Men to hear, surely?' he said eventually. 'The Queen's Men punish only the guilty. If you have nothing to hide then you have nothing to fear.'

'Of course, Father,' Eline said, and bent to kiss his hand.

She was, she realised then, in completely the wrong place.

The Church and the state were far too close for comfort in those days, and even more so since the new Prince Regent had taken the throne. There had used to be at least a theoretical distance between the two, but now since the Martyr's Ascendance that gap had become vanishingly small.

Eline kissed the priest's hand once again all the same, but as she took her leave of his chapel she was reasonably sure she wouldn't be back, or at least any time soon. She had given her heart to the Lady and nothing was going to change that, but the Church, it seemed to her, were in the pocket of the Queen's Men.

Why wasn't that a surprise?

Eventually, after a late, cold lunch she met up with Nama in the Rat as was their Godsday afternoon tradition and, oh joy, there was Kurt waiting for them at their table.

Every fucking week that arsehole was there, grinning at her like an overgrown rat. Nama was at the bar ordering a fresh round when Eline walked in, and it seemed Kurt wasn't buying all Nama's drinks anymore, but honestly Eline had expected that to happen weeks ago. She just shrugged and joined her friend while the tapman poured their wine and drew a fresh mug of beer for that horrible wanker who seemed to have so ingratiated himself into their lives.

'He's here again, then,' Eline observed as she took her cup of wine.

She paid for the round, suddenly conscious of how much more she was making than her friend was. Especially since she had taken the baron's deal.

A hundred marks a month for basically nothing but the rare chance of information; how could she possibly not have done?

Yes, yes; if Luka ever found out he'd quite likely have her skinned alive, or at best murdered or hanged, but she really couldn't see how he would. So long as no one snitched on her, and in Our Lady's name she was *not* telling Nama about what had happened, she couldn't really see how anyone would ever know. So she reckoned she was safe enough, and if not, well, she couldn't see that her children would ever even know she had died. Not from Dannsburg or wherever her boy was in the army, they wouldn't.

'On me,' she said.

Nama frowned. 'Generous of you,' she said.

'I saw the baron again the other night so I'm flush right now,' she said. 'Look, you've been good to me, Nama. Really good to me. You got me the job when I needed it. *Really* needed it, I mean. It wasn't just the fat man's orders; I'd have been destitute on the streets without it. And you made it not too unbearable with Kat and the other girls. The least I can do is buy you a fucking drink.'

'Aye, that's fair,' Nama said after a moment, and lifted her cup of wine to her friend.

Eline tapped hers against it, and they both drank.

'Shall we see what your sweetheart wants?' Eline asked after a moment.

'You know it ain't like that, you cow,' Nama said, but she was smiling when she said it. 'Aye, come on then. He'll want his beer if nothing else.'

'If only I thought it would be nothing else,' Eline said. 'Ah well, I'm sure you know what you're doing.'

Nama put a hand on her arm to stay her as she turned away.

'I *don't* know what I'm doing, Eline,' she confessed. 'Last night I . . . I don't know where last night went. I was done working and I was waiting up for you, and then I woke up in my bed this morning, and I have absolutely no idea if you even came home, never mind whether we spoke or not, and I swear I hadn't been drinking. I lost, I don't know, maybe four hours, if not more. Tell me you didn't find me on the floor and put me to bed yourself?'

'No,' Eline said. 'We spoke, but you honestly weren't making a lot of sense. You put yourself to bed.'

'Then why can't I remember any of it?' Nama demanded.

Eline could only shrug. 'You said Kurt had shown you something new, and . . . I forget exactly how you phrased it, but it confused you for sure. You really weren't yourself last night, Nama.'

'He told me something as well,' Nama confessed. 'He said I'm already far stronger than I've got any right to be this soon after discovering my cunning, and learning too fast for my own good. He thought maybe it's something to do with the medicine Madame feeds us. It's alchemy, after all, or so she says anyway, and he thought maybe it wasn't mixing well with the cunning. And the cunning, well, it only works sometimes. Sometimes it's easy, sometimes nothing happens. The thing Kurt showed me is what to do when it doesn't want to work, how to steal someone else's strength to *make* it work, and . . . and I don't think that did me any good.'

Eline frowned. 'Is that possible?' she asked. 'The medicine, I mean?'

'I don't—' Nama started, but Kurt interrupted her.

'Oi!' he shouted across the room. 'A man could die of thirst in this fucking tavern.'

Nama hurried to their table with his beer in one hand and her cup of wine in the other, and Eline reluctantly followed.

'Sorry,' Nama said as she put the tankard down in front of him. 'Got talking.'

'To *her* again,' Kurt observed, giving Eline something of a look.

'She's my mate,' Nama said, but Eline couldn't help but think she sounded overly defensive about it.

'I bet she is,' Kurt sneered. 'Great and mighty courtesan now, ain't she? Mixed up in politics and all that shit. Coining it in, she is. But in return for what?'

Eline shot him a look.

'I have no idea what you're talking about,' she said.

'Oh of course you fucking haven't,' Kurt sneered, and he laughed at her. 'I knew one like you before, last time. A bloke, but all the same it comes to the same thing. Some fucking little oik who ended up city governor, and more. Oh no, nothing corrupts people as fast as money does, except fucking *politics*.'

He almost spat the last word, and Eline held his stare.

'What makes you think I know anything about that?'

'I hear things,' Kurt said. 'You know, they say you're never more than six feet away from a rat in a city. They listen, the rats do.'

'You are fucking mad, mate,' Eline said.

Kurt laughed in her face.

'Am I? Perhaps I am, what the fuck does it matter? I know where you were last night.'

'No you don't,' Eline said.

'But I do,' Kurt said. 'You can't trust that cunt, however much he's paying you. He's worse than the other one.'

'I have no idea what you're−' she started, but Kurt cut her off.

'You're playing a dangerous game, girlie,' he growled, and Eline blinked at him.

To look at he was at least ten, maybe fifteen, years younger than she, but in that moment she realised what Nama had meant about how talking to him was like talking to your grandpa. That really *was* what it felt like, or so she could only assume. She'd never known a grandpa of her own, but he certainly seemed a great deal older than he looked, in that moment. It was almost as if . . . No, the thought was mad, but for a brief moment Eline had the feeling that Kurt had lived before and been reborn, with all the wisdom and cynicism of the old man he had perhaps once been.

'You're playing both ends against the middle,' he went on, disrupting her ridiculous train of thought, 'and that's going to bite you in the arse sooner or later. I mean yes, points for business acumen, but I'm taking them away again for survival instinct, you know what I mean?'

'I, personally, have no clue whatsoever,' Nama said.

Kurt turned his charming, somehow fake smile on her.

'I know you haven't, love,' he said, and then shot Eline a look. 'But *she* has. Haven't you?'

'I do what needs doing,' Eline said. 'That's all you need to know about that.'

'Oh, don't we all?' Kurt said. 'Don't we all indeed do that? But consider this, pretty girl. When something looks too good to be true, it probably fucking is.'

She looked at Kurt then, and wondered what his angle was. She knew he didn't think she was pretty and was honestly quite glad about that, so what had *that* been about? Making Nama jealous, perhaps? But then he had just been so staggeringly condescending to Nama that even that didn't make any sense. And calling her 'girlie' when Eline was almost − not quite, mind but almost − old enough to be his mother?

'You ain't right, are you?' Eline said bluntly. 'I don't mean just that you're a social shithead, anyone can see that. I mean you're not *right*. Are you? Something about you is not fucking normal.'

Kurt laughed and drained his beer before thumping the empty tankard down on the table.

'Must be off,' he said.

He fucked off out of the tavern after that, which Eline wasn't remotely sorry about, but she could see that Nama was.

'Mate,' Eline said, and took a sip of her wine. 'I know we didn't want this coming between us but what the *fuck* is he doing to you? You were out of your mind last night, after he visited, and how many punters did you say you'd seen?'

'Five,' Eline said.

'After him?'

'Aye.'

'And do you remember any of them?'

'No, Eline, I don't, and as far as I'm concerned that's a *good* thing. Why the fuck would I want to remember that if I didn't have to? Why would I want to remember what we do? What you *used* to do.'

'Don't be like that. It was Madame's decision to make me a courtesan, not mine,' Eline said, but she had to wonder.

Eline thought for a moment.

With the money she had made from her previous two assignations she was under no pressure to work again any time soon, and now the baron was paying her a hundred marks a month? That, she had already resolved, was *not* going through Madame or the house. The baron, she was sure, wouldn't want anyone knowing about it and, to be honest, she was buggered if she was giving up that much money she had earned herself with no help from anyone else.

She would still have to work enough to cover her board, lodging and training if nothing else, she knew that well enough. Madame was, as she had made very clear, not a charity. In fact, now that she thought about it, her new off-the-books income might be harder to hide than she had expected.

She needed to make a given percentage for the house to pay her way, but an extra hundred marks a month would be hard to hide, unless . . . A very successful courtesan made so much more than that it would never be noticed.

Eline sat forward. She knew what she had to do. One night with a duke could bury her illicit income from the baron for a year or more. She had only to embrace her new life: *fully* embrace it.

Chapter 22

The next invitation really *was* a surprise when it came, a few uneventful days later. It was from the baron again, of course, but this time it was for Nama too. This one, she knew at once, *did* have to go through the house.

Just a minor reception at some other baron's house, of course, nothing like as grand as the Earl Lan Klasskoff's had been. Eline and Nama both wondered how he knew the Alarian girl even existed.

'You've never mentioned me to him?' Nama asked, for at least the third time.

'I don't think so,' Eline said. 'Lady's sake, Nama, no offence but I can't see why on earth I would have done.'

Nama spat into the hearth to show what she thought of that, but eventually even she had to admit that she thought that was fair.

'I suppose not,' she said. 'How do we do this? I mean, I've never been a courtesan before. What's the form of it?'

'First,' Eline said, 'and most important, we take it to Madame.'

'She'll take all our money,' Nama protested.

'No,' Eline said. 'She'll take *most* of our money. Different thing. Do you know what she charges for a courtesan for a night?'

'No idea,' Nama admitted, and Eline smiled at her.

'How would you like to make a hundred marks for a night's work when you don't even have to fuck anyone?'

Nama gaped at her.

'A hundred marks? You are *fucking* shitting me,' she said. 'No wonder you bought the drinks the other night.'

'Welcome to the world of just how fucking rich the aristocracy are compared to the rest of us,' Eline said. 'You have to understand, Nama, this is *not* the same world we live in. Not even a little bit it isn't.'

'But I'm not a courtesan,' Nama protested. 'I mean, I've always wanted to be but Madame's been training you for months. Talking posh, dancing, singing, fans, all of that. I don't know how to do *any* of that shit!'

'No,' Eline allowed, and wiped a hand over her lips to hide her sudden nervousness. There was just no good way to approach this, was there? 'I think that's the point.'

'Oh, for fuck's sake,' Nama snapped. 'Because I'm Alarian? Because I'm *exotic*? I'm supposed to be the clumsy savage, am I? Oh, fuck that *right* off, Eline, I'm not playing.'

Eline leaned close and put her hand on Nama's arm.

'Listen,' she said. 'The baron's not like that. I think he's up to something. I don't know what, but I get the feeling he's trying to draw out people who *would* think like that. But I don't think he's one of them.'

'And you think that why?'

Eline realised she had absolutely no idea. It was just gut instinct.

'How would he even know your name?' she asked instead.

'I think . . .' Nama said, and hesitated. 'I wouldn't be surprised if Kurt knew *him*. Kurt could have said something. Kurt seems to know just about fucking everyone in Drathburg, for all that he shouldn't. It's the rats.'

'What? What the fuck have rats got to do with anything?'

'They see everything,' Nama said dreamily, and again Eline shook her head.

She was honestly starting to wonder if Nama might be going insane, and found herself wondering once again if Nama might be taking the poppy.

'Right you are,' she said instead, if only to put the conversation aside. 'Come on, let's go and get it brokered.'

Madame was surprised, to say the least. Eline at least was a mostly trained courtesan and had entertained the baron before, but Nama? Nama was just a whore and there was no dressing that up. A licensed one, aye, but she was a world away from being a courtesan.

'Why,' Madame asked, 'and I mean no disrespect here, dear, in the world does he want you as well?'

Eline got the impression she meant as much disrespect as she could possibly muster without flat-out saying it, but Nama met Madame blade for blade, and she resolved to stay out of it, at least for now.

'Because I'm brown,' Nama said bluntly. 'I'm pretty, I know I am, but I'm also an uncouth, barely literate *tea monkey*. That's what he's showing off alongside his posh new courtesan. An exotic. A fucking *pet*! No, ma'am, please don't try to dress it up as anything else, I know what it is. All I ask is I get the same rate and percentage that Eline does. That's only fair.'

'Eline is a trained courtesan and you're not,' Madame said.

Eline's resolve to stay out of it collapsed at once.

'He doesn't *want* trained, that's the whole point,' she said. 'She gets what I do or I'm not doing it either.'

'Oh, very well,' Madame sighed, after a moment. 'I'll have to bill him two whole crowns for the pair of you then, and the gods only know if he can actually afford it, but that's a hundred marks each for you so think yourselves lucky. You, especially, think yourself *very* lucky.'

That last was aimed at Nama, obviously, and the Alarian girl at least flushed.

Eline could sort of see both sides of it. Nama *wasn't* trained in the courtesan's arts so technically wasn't worth anything like that much, but for the baron to want to hire her at that rate just because she was different was so staggeringly insulting that she deserved every penny of it, to Eline's mind. She wasn't sure what the baron was after, and a small part of her couldn't help wonder if perhaps in some way Kurt *did* have something to do with it. All that nonsense about rats was obviously bollocks, but that didn't mean Kurt didn't have influence in the city, and if so she had no idea what he thought he was doing with it. All the same, the baron was no fool, and he must have *some* reason.

'Ma'am,' Eline said at last, and she led Nama back out of Madame's study by the elbow before she had the chance to say something they would all have regretted.

A few hours later Madame had obviously done whatever was needed to secure the engagement and the baron's household had sent word that his carriage would be there to collect them both at the seventh hour of the afternoon. That left them time for a hasty cold supper and to change into their best frocks and apply their paints and powders, and then Loran was banging on their doors to tell them to stir themselves. Eline strapped on her stilettoes and picked up her purse of emergency money, which had considerably increased in size and weight since the night of her first assignation. She met Nama in the hall.

'Got your emergency fund?' she asked her quietly.

Nama showed her a blank look.

'What?'

'Never place yourself entirely at a man's mercy, however wealthy he may be,' Eline said, repeating one of Madame's first lessons to her. 'Things can happen. You always have to have at least the funds about you to hire a carriage home and some protection, if the worst happens.'

'I don't—' Nama started.

Eline's fingers dipped into her pouch and she took out five marks.

'Here, have this,' she said, and pressed the coins into Nama's hand. 'All being well, you won't need it and can give it back to me tomorrow. The main thing is never, *never*, let yourself be defenceless. A woman cannot afford to be defenceless in this world.'

'No fucking shit,' Nama said.

'Oh, one other thing,' Eline said, and she realised she was using her courtesan's voice now without even realising she had switched, 'do try not to say "fuck" too often. In fact, say as little as you can possibly get away with. I'll do the talking, if need be.'

The baron's carriage was there to collect them a few minutes later, and to Eline's surprise he was already in it. It seemed that nobles sometimes *did* call on courtesans after all. A footman handed them both up to sit on the padded velvet bench, Eline beside the baron and Nama opposite, and Eline nodded him a greeting.

'My lord baron,' she said. 'Allow me to present my associate, Nama of the Silver Bells. I believe you have already heard her name?'

True to type the baron was sitting there with a glass of brandy in his hand, and Eline noticed there was a bottle standing in a specially worked holder in the lining of the door by his elbow.

'Of course I have, or I wouldn't have asked for her, would I?' he said.

'And why did you?' Eline asked.

'Hmm,' the baron said. 'I hear things. I hear a great deal of things, Eline, and I dare say many of them are not true. Many of the others that probably *are* true are not to my liking in the short term. In the long term . . . We shall see. Anyway, an associate of mine knows a gentleman who knows . . . Oh, it doesn't matter, does it? Street people, and the night economy. Everyone knows everyone in this city, at the end of the day. I have heard Nama's name, and I very much wanted to meet her. Tonight, especially.'

'What's special about tonight?' Eline asked, latching on to it immediately. 'I thought we were just going for a few drinks at some minor baron's house?'

'We were,' Lan Elenkov assured her, although he had already quite obviously had more than a few drinks before they even got there. Or was pretending he had, anyway. In fact that night he was pretending to be even more drunk than usual. 'This is something rather different . . . Are you familiar with the concept of cat and mouse, Eline?'

'We had a cat when I was a child,' she said. 'Back on the wagon, I mean. Ferocious thing, he was. Big stripey monster with claws like knives. There were never any mice or rats wherever *we* made camp.'

'Oh, gods, yes, travelling people,' he said. 'I think you told me about that. If not, someone else did. I forget, I forget . . . Someone always tells me. Someone always . . . That's rather what I mean I suppose, yes, but not really. Cat and mouse, you see.'

'You mean a trap set?'

The baron laughed and drained his glass.

'Oh, you're *good*,' he said, but Eline was aware of Nama giving them both a bewildered look. 'Did I ever tell you that I àm a gambling man?'

He hadn't, but Eline found the fact didn't surprise her one little bit. Most merchants essentially were, after all. If you boiled it down to the gristle, that was what they *did*. All mercantile ventures were basically gambles, at the end of the day. That the baron was a gambling man was no surprise at all, she supposed, although at that moment she found herself wondering what exactly he was gambling *on*.

The bomb went off a few seconds later.

A great section of the narrow street the carriage had been traversing collapsed in a huge cloud of smoke and stone dust and the stench of burned blasting powder as falling rubble blocked the road, and a moment later there were five mounted men moving up to surround the baron's carriage.

'Well bugger,' the baron said, in a way that suggested that he hadn't been surprised in the slightest.

'Stand and deliver!' one of them shouted, then paused to cough through the clouds of choking dust.

Eline looked out of the window to see loaded crossbows pointed at them from horseback.

'Deliver you what?' the baron shouted. 'I am all but bankrupt, man!'

'Yourself, you old cunt,' the man who was obviously their leader demanded. 'We're taking you with us.'

Lan Elenkov looked pointedly at Eline and Nama. 'Well?' he said.

'Not a chance,' Nama said. 'I'm not having this.'

Eline was the verge of despair now. 'What are we going to *do*?'

'Kill them, of course,' Nama said.

'There are five of them, and ahorse at that,' Eline said. 'I can't work fucking miracles!'

'Well apparently I can,' Nama said. 'Watch this.'

She raised her hands.

The first firebolt flew from her hand and smashed through the carriage window in an explosion of broken glass and took the lead highwayman or whatever he was full in the face. He fell screaming from his horse as crossbows started to thump and bolts slam into the wooden coachwork. The baron cheered, then gasped as Eline smashed him in the chest with her forearm to slam him back against the bench as another bolt blew through the opposite window and missed him by a matter of inches.

Nama shot another blast out of that window, and by the shrieks, Eline knew she had found a second mark.

'Can't you do anything bigger?' the baron demanded. 'Rolling ring of fire, something like that?'

'I don't even know what that is, and I'm not hurting the horses,' Nama shouted. 'It's not their fault.'

'I knew magicians who could—' the baron started.

'I am *not* hurting the horses,' Nama snarled, and a moment later she had thrown herself out of the door and down to the street.

'Get on the floor and stay down. I'm going after her,' Eline yelled, and a moment later she was on the cobbles with her blades in her hands.

There were three highwaymen left, looking desperate now as their horses reared and bucked under them in a state of obvious panic in the firelit street. One of the men was thrown from the back of his rearing mount to crash to the ground and Eline was on him a moment later, blades flashing in her hands as she ended him with a whirl and a stamp and a cry of triumph.

Got to keep that left up, Eline chastised herself. *What would Marcoss say?*

Oh well, it seemed Nama was so powerful now she was sure the girl could heal any wound she might take with her cunning, and that at least was reassuring.

Firelight flared in her peripheral vision as Nama shot another man off his horse to die screaming in the gutter. The riderless horses were stampeding now, fleeing in a wild dash to get away from the flames and the screams. The last one threw its rider as it jumped a pile of smoking rubble and Nama threw her head back and let out something between a squeal and a howl. A moment later a great tide of rats burst out of an alley and fell on the man, chittering and biting as they buried him under an undulating mass of fur and spreading blood.

Eline swallowed her disgust and threw herself into the onslaught, and her blades rose and fell, rose and fell.

And it was done.

Chapter 23

They never made it to the reception. In truth, Eline doubted they had ever been intended to. From what she had pieced together, the Baron Lan Elenkov had sprung a trap he knew had been waiting for him, and had been counting on the two women to get him out of it. He knew Eline, of course, but how the fuck he knew about Nama and what she could do was anyone's guess. Even Eline would never have imagined that she could do *that*.

Once the terrified coachman had calmed down, Lan Elenkov had instructed the man to drive them back to his own house, and now the three of them were in his drawing room with glasses of brandy in their hands. The coachman had been given a bottle and sent back to his lodgings above the stable to drink himself to sleep and hopefully forget all about it. Even Nama had brandy, for all that Eline had never seen her drink anything stronger than wine before. She supposed after *that* the girl probably needed one. The were both sooty and dishevelled, and Eline's dress was absolutely ruined, of course, after rolling with the highwaymen and rats, but the less she thought about that the better.

She supposed she could always buy another one. The stoat-faced seamstress had been fast enough, with enough money put in front of her, and for the first time in her life Eline found that money wasn't something she really needed to worry about. That was a relief, even if nothing else was.

'I don't suppose,' Eline said after a long moment had passed, 'you feel like explaining exactly what the fuck just happened?'

'You saved my life, my dears,' the baron said, 'and that makes you money extremely well spent. I had been rather banking on that, in all honesty.'

'Evidently,' Eline said, and gave him a long look. 'I've never heard of a man hiring courtesans as bodyguards before.'

'Haven't you?' the baron asked. 'Then you should read more history. It is *far* from unprecedented.'

Madame's training hadn't included that much history, she had to allow.

'Consider,' the baron went on. 'If I had been travelling with five visibly armed thugs riding with my carriage, would they still have attacked? I doubt it somehow, which means they would still be alive now and planning another attempt on my life at a time when perhaps I might *not* have been expecting it. But alone, with only two beautiful women for company? Well, I mean you don't *look* dangerous, do you? The best way to spring a trap is to walk straight into it, with defences the enemy don't realise you have. That was you two, and you both did a *marvellous* job.'

'But how did you know we would?' Eline pressed him. 'You're right, we *don't* look dangerous and I didn't even know Nama *was*, at least not to that extent.'

'People tell me things,' the baron said again. 'I know Marcoss is honing your, ah, shall we say, dancing skills; and I know very well what Marcoss is capable of. You were a given, at close combat, at least. Nama, well . . . That was the part that was a gamble.'

'You didn't believe in me?' Nama asked.

'I didn't *know* you, dear,' he said. 'I wasn't sure whether I believed in the man who told me about you.'

'Was he, perchance,' Eline started, 'a greasy young man called Kurt?'

The baron laughed.

'You're a natural at this, aren't you?' he said, and she realised that what she had said was exactly how he had first asked her if she knew a fat man called Luka.

'I don't know what you—' she started, but he interrupted her by reaching for the brandy bottle and sloshing more into her glass without asking.

He looked the question at Nama and she too held her glass out for a refill.

'Good,' the baron said, once he had refreshed his own drink.

'What is?' Nama asked. 'I mean thanks for the money and that, but this has been a fucking shit night so far. I've killed three men and *I never fucking did that before!*'

Nama's glass hit the thick Alarian carpet beneath her with a dull thud as she dropped it and spilled brandy everywhere and, a moment later, she was on the floor beside it, sobbing.

Oh gods, Eline supposed that Nama hadn't at that. She remembered how she had felt after the first life she had taken, and the second. After

Milev and then the other two tonight, it was almost becoming business as usual. But of course Nama didn't feel like that.

Eline dropped to her knees on the wet carpet and took the howling girl in her arms, holding her as best she could. Her dress was fucked anyway, so what did a bit of brandy matter? She was aware of the baron, watching them soundlessly.

'We were defending our patron,' she murmured. 'It was the right thing to do. You said yourself that you weren't having it from those men.'

'It was just talk,' Nama sniffled. 'I was *scared*, Eline. I didn't even know if . . . if I could . . .'

'Well, you could,' Eline said, 'and you did. And we're alive because of it. I couldn't have taken them on my own; probably not even one of them, not on horseback. And you didn't hurt the horses; they all got away safely.'

She knew that mattered to the girl, and she was making a point of it to try and calm her down.

Nama nodded slowly, and wiped the back of her sleeve across her streaming eyes.

'That's good,' she managed at last. 'He said . . . he said only if you have to, but I had to, didn't I?'

'Yes,' Eline said, and she said it in her courtesan's voice and made it sound as authoritative and decisive as possible. 'You *did* have to, and you stepped up and did what was necessary. You did well, Nama, and you have my sincere thanks as well as the baron's.'

'I killed three men,' Nama said, and started crying again.

'We would all be dead if you hadn't,' Eline said, injecting chill authority into her voice. 'Now pull yourself together, girl. You wanted to see the life of a courtesan, and *this is part of it.*'

'Fucking hell, Eline,' Nama managed after a moment, but at least she had stopped crying. 'This ain't like just being a whore, is it?'

'No,' Eline said. 'It isn't.'

The baron got up then and left the room.

He returned from the hall a few moments later.

'I have asked a footman to go out and hire Nama a carriage home,' he said to Eline. 'I would be grateful if you would stay for a while, my dear.'

Nama shot Eline a look that was both amused, and horrified.

Not that, Eline mouthed at her.

No, never that. The baron wanted something, a *political* thing, she was sure, and that was clearly not for Nama's ears.

'Of course, my lord baron,' she said.

It was late and Eline was still riding the shakes from having killed another two men that night, but this was work and it needed doing. If she could make her peace with doing the work of a whore, and she realised that she had, then she supposed she could make her peace with doing the work of whatever the fuck she was now.

I don't even know what I am now, Eline thought to herself. *Courtesan? Spy? Killer? Government agent? I have absolutely no idea.*

They were, she realised, quite possibly all the same thing.

A footman eventually came in to tell Nama that the hired carriage had arrived, and he quite firmly herded her out of the baron's presence.

Eline got up and refilled her glass without asking, then did the baron's for him too before he started on about how much his knee hurt yet again. Perhaps it did, she wouldn't know, but she was already tired of hearing about it. That done, she sat down opposite him and fixed him with a look.

'What is going on?' she asked him, and if that was perhaps somewhat blunt then she found she didn't really care anymore.

'An attempt on my life,' the baron said. 'Hardly the first one I've ever experienced, but the first one for a long time. At least I knew this one was coming.'

'How?'

'People tell me things,' the baron said again, and smiled.

'Oh, maybe,' Eline said, giving up on getting a straight answer to that question. 'So you have a good network of spies and listeners. Well done. It seems that being a noble in this city is a dangerous occupation.'

'Isn't it everywhere?' the baron countered. 'Safer than Dannsburg, that's for certain. The aristocracy is, to put it in the language of whores, absolutely fucking ruthless.'

Eline ignored the pointless insult that she knew wasn't even meant as one. This was just how people like the baron thought, and how they thought of people like her.

Time to change the subject, she told herself.

'I keep turning the duke's murder over in my mind, but I can't make it make sense,' she said. 'Why would Kastavia even want to ruin the Immalian king's succession?'

'Because he isn't the legitimate King of Immalia,' the baron said.

Eline blinked at him in surprise.

'Then who is?'

'I am.'

'Excuse me, fucking *what*?' Eline said. '*How*? You're only a baron!'

'Of course I'm bloody not, I'm technically the Grand Duke of Immia and by right of birth King of Immalia,' he said. 'And how does a royal dynasty ever change? A bad succession, two claimants to the throne. The inevitable civil war. My claim was far the stronger, but alas my army was not. This was, oh gods, sixty or so years ago now. My rival slaughtered us on the battlefield and I fled the country with what money I had left. I was young then, very young, little more than a boy in truth. I went to sea, and turned to commerce and smuggling to rebuild my fortune. Mostly smuggling, truth be told. I have always been good at business, and the poppy trade is *very* lucrative. It's not so difficult, if you have a brain on you. Thirty years at sea, and I retired here a wealthy man everyone had forgotten about. I took a minor title and a false name to place myself beneath notice, and have remained here ever since.'

Eline boggled. This man, this supposed baron, was a *king*?

'I am, as you have clearly worked out, fairly wealthy and not without political influence back home, where my House still has many supporters who would welcome my return to the throne,' the baron continued. 'Just, sadly, not quite enough to turn the tide to revolution. I have worked hard to hide both of those things, and even Madame thinks I lost all my money in bad business ventures. I would be *very* pleased if you keep that little fact to yourself, by the way. And it may surprise you to learn that I live very simply for a noble of my means. Any noble, even a minor one like a baron, living in a house this small would consider themselves impoverished. That is what the aristocracy is like, Eline.'

Eline just gaped at him, at this deposed foreign king, and wondered how the living fuck murdering her husband had brought her here.

Eline woke up the next morning and realised that, no, she hadn't dreamed it. Oh gods, this put her in a *very* difficult position.

You're playing both ends against the middle, Kurt had said, and much as it pained her, she had to admit he was right about that.

Surely she *had* to tell Luka about this, but . . . But fucking *how*? The Baron Lan Elenkov, elderly minor noble widely regarded as a drunken lech was really the rightful King of Immalia? Or so he said he was, anyway. How the *fuck* was she supposed to broach that with Luka in a way that wouldn't result in him laughing in her face? Of course she had no way of knowing if the baron had remotely been telling her the truth, but surely no one would tell so outrageous a lie. There had definitely been a serious attempt on his life last night, and that seemed a lot more than a supposedly impoverished minor baron of no consequence would have warranted.

'Oh gods,' Eline muttered to herself as she hauled herself out of bed.

How the actual *fuck* had she got herself entangled in this mess of foreign politics?

I don't need this, she told herself, and made herself have a wash and a piss and get dressed before she went down for breakfast. Nama was there waiting for her.

'What did he want?' the Alarian girl demanded, before Eline even had a mug of small beer in her hand.

'To talk,' Eline said, and went to make that right at the barrel. No one started their day without small beer, after all. 'No more than that.'

'About *what*?'

'Political things,' Eline said. 'You'd the right of that, at least.'

'Like what?'

Eline looked at her friend for a long moment.

'It's best if you don't know the answer to that,' she said.

'Oh aye, best for *who*?'

'You,' Eline assured her in a way that brooked no argument. 'Trust me, Nama, you don't want to be anywhere near this. And you want your Kurt anywhere near it even less.'

Eline liked Nama and she counted her as a friend but she *didn't* like Kurt and she didn't trust him, and while Nama was still so close to him it was becoming difficult to trust her either.

They were difficult days indeed, in a time when the world wouldn't sit still.

Chapter 24

Eline made herself go to the fat man's house a few days later. Luka had received a letter from Dannsburg.

'There's word,' he said. 'From the Provost Marshal.'

'Oh, aye?'

'Aye,' Luka said, and if anything he looked something approaching shamefaced about it. 'It seems we *did* know about this, or at least the house of law did. No cunt told me, but it's only my city they did it in. That's got Iagin written all over it, the evil old bastard. The bloke we killed the other night, that Milev arsehole, was smuggled into the country through Varnburg with the full cooperation of a colleague of mine. A woman who works in Varnburg the same way I do here. And that means the Provost Marshal fucking signed off on it. No way would Sabine have agreed to this otherwise.'

'Who?' Eline asked, bewildered by the new names.

'Doesn't matter,' Luka said, and flushed in a way that implied he had said too much already. 'Oh, fuck all that shit, it just doesn't matter. What *does* matter is that whatever is going on, our government is perfectly happy, even keen, to help the Kastavians fuck up the Immalian succession, and I don't know *why*.'

'I think I do,' Eline said, and tried to hide her smile as she watched Luka's expression change.

'What do you mean?'

'Immalia had a civil war sixty or so years ago. The House of Marodieva won, and deposed the existing dynasty. I have a feeling Kastavia want to reverse that and bring back the old regime.'

He goggled at her. 'You're not even supposed to *know* about that,' he said.

'Luka,' she said, 'I am not a fool. I heard a few things, and I pieced the rest together for myself.'

'Well, the first I bloody heard about it was when the Provost Marshal's letter came,' Luka grumbled, 'but you're right. Kastavia and Immalia used to be allies, but they've been at each other's throats ever since the new dynasty conquered Immalia, and it's come close to war between them on several occasions, apparently.'

'So why do we care?'

'That's the bit I don't know,' Luka admitted, 'but apparently we do. Fucking politics, I don't know. I know we have no quarrel with Kastavia. They're a major trade partner, but this? Even the Provost Marshal is unlikely to risk us getting drawn into another war for the sake of trade revenue.'

'Is he?' Eline said. 'Obviously you know him a lot better than I do, which is to say not at all, but are you absolutely sure about that? Money is behind almost everything, in my experience.'

I am still fairly wealthy and not without political influence back home.

When the baron said 'fairly' wealthy he meant 'enormously', Eline knew that well enough. Thirty years a poppy smuggler almost guaranteed it, in fact. She couldn't help wondering if that influence might well extend to his former allies in Kastavia. All the same, it still didn't quite work.

'I remember you said you had to care about the duke's death, because Dannsburg said so,' she said. 'Why would they, if they already knew exactly what had happened and why?'

'Plausible deniability, like I said,' Luka said. 'That's why I wasn't told, I suppose. I had to investigate, and be *seen* to be investigating, by whatever Immalian spies are watching me. And they will be, and they will know who I am and who I work for. It's fucking inevitable in this business.'

'But they won't know who *I* am, I assume?'

Luka snorted. 'They'll know I frequently have a whore call at my house these days. Hardly anything remarkable about that.'

'I suppose not,' she said.

That meant that as long as she stayed beneath the Immalians' notice, it was safe to continue working for the baron, and that was good. She took a sip of the brandy she had helped herself to on her arrival and looked at Luka.

'You do know who the Baron Lan Elenkov actually is, I also assume?'

'Yes of course I do,' Luka said. 'As of about six months ago, anyway. I think the house of law has always known, but they had rather lost track of him. Then someone who knew what they were looking for spotted him here in Drathburg. This is why I set you on your wild goose chase to assassinate Madame, to flush him out of hiding. I knew he'd find out about it, and I knew he wouldn't want his old friend and business partner being accidentally killed by an incompetent would-be assassin. There was always a chance you might have actually managed it, after all. He acted fast to get to speak to you, as I'd hoped. He only knew about you because of his spy network. It's not like Madame was advertising you before you were trained, so why would anyone else have requested you when they didn't know you existed? At least now we have eyes on him again.'

'Well, that worked well enough, I suppose,' Eline said, 'but if you know who he is, why in the gods' names can't you just speak to him?'

'No,' Luka said at once. 'Plausible deniability, remember? If Kastavia wishes to act to destabilise the Immalian throne then, well, that's between them and just shit that happened. If we helped a little bit, well, who's to know? If we acknowledge that, in our view at least, the rightful King of Immalia is living in our country and we acted in his favour, we'll be at war with Immalia next fucking week. The country simply *cannot* afford it, Eline.'

'But with Kastavia on our side, surely?' Eline said.

Luka pursed his lips.

'Perhaps,' he said. 'Wars are *expensive*, and alliances are cheap and easily discarded. Would they stand beside us on the battlefield? Perhaps. Perhaps not. The Provost Marshal is not prepared to place a bet on that.'

'Why is this all about your precious Provost Marshal?' Eline demanded. 'What does the Prince Regent have to say about it?'

Luka said nothing for a long moment.

'The power of government,' he said eventually, 'lies in obscurity. What makes you think they couldn't be the same man?'

'Are they?' Eline asked, a shocked look on her face.

'I didn't say that,' Luka said. 'I just asked you a question.'

'Perhaps,' Eline said, 'but even so. Surely that's not possible.'

'I don't see how either,' Luka muttered. 'I can only assume, if it is true, he doesn't sleep.'

Eline was still thinking about that when she went to bed that night. The Provost Marshal of the Queen's Men and Prince Regent couldn't be the same man, surely? There simply weren't enough hours in the day to make that possible. No, surely no one could hold both positions at once. Luka had obviously just been trying to point out to her how little she really knew about the workings of government, and she supposed he was right about that.

She sighed and turned over in her blankets, and tried to think of the political problem instead, but it was no good. She still couldn't really make it make sense. Her government wanted to help the government of Kastavia, which she had barely heard of, fuck up the royal succession of Immalia, which she had *never* heard of until a few weeks ago. Kastavia didn't even *have* royalty, she remembered someone telling her, but something else instead that she found she couldn't remember the name of. Luka seemed to think everything was all a perfectly normal thing that might be happening, even though he quite obviously didn't really understand why any more than she did.

And the Baron Lan Elenkov was really the rightful King of Immalia, or as rightful any king was, at least? That she was still struggling with as well, although she supposed it was no more implausible than any other royal claim.

It was no good. She was in over her head and she knew it.

She reached out in the darkness, opened her chest of possessions and groped inside it until she found the small carved wooden cat her father had made for her. She hugged it to her chest, and, after a while, finally managed a fitful, uneasy sleep.

There was a letter for her the next morning, an invitation to the baron's house. In all honesty she had nothing better to do that morning, so she went, and she didn't even feel the need to mention it to Madame this time. Since she had taken the baron's generous retainer it would have felt wrong to try to charge him the house's rate for every meeting, and she supposed what Madame didn't know wouldn't hurt her. She was received at the door by a footman who stared long and hard at the bawd's knot tied brazenly on her left shoulder, a very disapproving look on his thin, pinched face.

'My name is Eline,' she said, using the full force of her courtesan's accent. 'I'm here to see the lord baron, at his invitation.'

You are a mere servant, and beneath my notice, that tone said. If she had had her fan on her she would even have made the gesture for it to reinforce the message, that was how annoyed she was by the disdainful expression on his face.

The footman turned away without a word and walked into the hall, and Eline took the liberty of following him without waiting to be asked. Under normal social circumstances that would have been unforgivably rude, but these were not normal circumstances and she knew it. The man was deliberately being a cunt to her, and she wasn't having it.

The footman tapped on the baron's study door and waited a moment for a muffled response, then opened the door and stepped forward.

'A whore to see you, my lord,' he said, which was even ruder.

Eline found her hand was up her sleeve before she'd even finished forming the thought. She resisted the urge to stab the man, although in all truth only just.

'Where are your manners, Jenkin?' she heard the baron snap, and in that moment he didn't sound drunk at all. 'Show the lady in, and bugger off. In fact, you can bugger off completely. I've had more than enough of your sneers and your judgement, thank you very much. Consider your employment here at an end, and get out of my house. If you are still here when the lady leaves, I will have the other men beat you with their cudgels and throw you in the canal.'

The footman went white as a sheet and glanced at Eline, obviously in that moment finally wondering who she might in fact *really* be. Eline couldn't resist it; she stuck her tongue out at him. He turned and fled.

The man had obviously made the mistake, in her view the very grave and quite possibly fatal mistake, of falling for the baron's act. Of seeing him as the drunken, slightly comedic, harmless figure of fun he presented himself as. He was, she had long since realised, none of those things at *all*.

She entered the room and met the flinty glare in the baron's eyes and yes, she could see the king in him there, this deposed but still ferocious foreign monarch who it appeared she now served.

'Thank you, my lord,' she said. She closed the door behind her, and having checked that they were now alone she dropped him a low curtsey. 'Your Majesty,' she said.

'No,' the baron said. 'No, Eline, never do that. Not even in private. Make a habit of *that* and sooner or later you'll do it in front of the wrong person, and then where shall I be? "My lord" is good enough for me. For now, at least.'

'Very well,' Eline said, and looked down at the baron where he sat sprawled indolently in a low armchair. 'What can I do for you, my lord?'

'Take a brandy, if you want one,' he said, raising his own glass to her.

'Bit early for me,' Eline said. 'What else?'

'Sit down, for one thing,' the baron said. 'I'll get a crick in my poor old neck looking up at you all the time. Why do you seem to so dislike chairs?'

'I ...' Eline said, then she took a seat and for some mad reason she couldn't even have explained to herself she told him the truth. 'My husband disliked it. He always said, "Why are you sitting? A wife should be on her feet working, or on her back fucking", and then he usually hit me after he had said it.'

'Gods,' said the baron. 'He sounds like a complete cunt.'

'He was,' Eline said. 'That's why I murdered him.'

The baron nodded, apparently not remotely concerned by her confession.

'Don't blame you,' he said, and it seemed that was to be the end of that. 'You're good at that sort of thing, after all. Actually, that's what I wanted you for.'

'What, murder?' Eline asked, and she was only half joking.

'Probably, yes,' the baron said, and she could see he wasn't joking at all. 'I have a great-nephew, in Dannsburg. A bright young military officer, only in his thirties but already a colonel. He makes good money, but can't hold onto it to save his life. Terrible gambler, you see. He's got himself into a spot of bother in the city, with some rather unpleasant people. I need you to go and sort it out for him. Remove the problem, shall we say. Take your little witch girl, I think you might need her. Actually it probably wouldn't be a bad idea to take Luka as well; he knows the city and you don't.'

'I can't *take* Luka,' Eline protested. 'I work for *him*, not the other way around.'

'Do you?' Lan Elenkov asked, and he smirked at her over the rim of his glass. 'Are you sure that's still absolutely the shape of things, Eline?'

Eline, who wasn't, kept her face very still.

He wanted her to go to Dannsburg, and probably murder his great-nephew's creditors, and for what?

For a hundred marks a month, she reminded herself, and wondered then if she was really still working on a political thing at all.

But if she could work for one government couldn't she work for another, even one in exile? And, it had to be said, the baron paid her *considerably* more than Luka did. Besides, her daughter was in Dannsburg. If she played this right she might even get a chance to see her.

'Who is this great-nephew of yours, exactly?'

'My late sister's grandson. Good lad really, war hero and all that. Bit of a *strange* one, if you know what I mean. Likes men in the way I very much don't, but I suppose he can't help that. Calls himself Bakrylov, no idea where he got that from, and doesn't even claim a 'Lan' in his name. He's keeping his head even further down than I do, since his grandparents were both killed in our little civil war. I don't think anyone in Dannsburg even knows he's Immalian.'

'But the House of Marodieva do, don't they?' Eline said. 'Or at least, so you suspect.'

The baron smiled.

'You're good,' he said, and it wasn't the first time he had told her that. 'Perhaps, perhaps not. Either way, I want the matter resolved.'

'He's an army colonel and a war hero,' Eline said, pressing the point. 'That's a fairly senior position in society even without a 'Lan' in his name. Has he no contacts in the capital who could make this go away?'

The baron considered his glass of brandy.

'I hear,' he said, 'and remember people do tell me things, my dear, that he has certain connections to the house of law. But this, no, this is not something he would want them to learn of, I don't think.'

'But you want me to take Luka with me, if I can talk him around? He's a Queen's Man.'

'Make something up,' the baron told her. 'You're a courtesan; acting and lying are your main functions. Well, lying and spying and killing, I suppose. Occasionally bedding, too, I dare say, but in all honesty probably not all that often from what I know of courtesans. Lie to him, Eline. He is, as I can't imagine you have failed to notice, not actually all that clever.'

No, Eline had to admit to herself, she hadn't failed to notice that at all.

Chapter 25

Eline called on Luka after supper that evening, and by then it most definitely was not too early for a brandy, so she helped herself to one without waiting to be asked.

'What exactly do you think you're doing?' Luka asked her.

'Having a drink,' Eline said, and she turned and looked at him. 'And preparing to go to Dannsburg.'

Luka spluttered on his own drink, and coughed hard for a moment. 'I told you, no,' he said. 'You get an audience with the Provost Marshal over—'

'Your dead body, yes I remember,' Eline said. 'I have no desire to meet your precious Provost Marshal; he sounds like an extremely unpleasant man. I have a colonel to speak to, and some matters of personal finance to resolve for him, that's all.'

'What the fuck are you talking about?'

'A favour for a patron,' Eline said.

'This is fucking Lan Elenkov again, isn't it?' he demanded.

'Perhaps,' Eline said. 'I *did* ask you if you know who he really is.'

'Aye, and as I said, of course I fucking do. Well, I do *now*, anyway. That's no reason to be running his fucking errands.'

'I'd quite like you to come with me actually,' Eline said, ignoring him completely. 'You know Dannsburg and I don't. You'd be useful.'

However hard she worked the courtesan's aristocratic accent he wasn't having that, not one little bit he wasn't.

'You fucking work for me, not the other way around,' he said, his voice falling into a low tone of menace.

'Well,' Eline said. 'You pay me, that's all. You pay me a very small amount, in fact.'

'Five marks a month is more than a master craftsman makes,' Luka said, 'and that's on top of what you get out of Madame. You're well enough paid.'

'For a minor civil servant of our impoverished nation, perhaps,' Eline said, and she met Luka's eyes and held his stare ruthlessly until he finally worked it out.

'Oh gods,' he said at last. 'How much is the baron paying you?'

'A great deal more than you,' Eline said.

Luka gulped brandy and coughed again. 'I can double it,' he said at last.

Eline smiled, and she saw Luka's face fall with the realisation that he had been defeated. He thought about it for a moment, then his defeated look transformed into fury.

'I can have Sam in here in two heartbeats flat,' he said, and as the big man was on the door just at the end of the hall, she supposed that was true. 'You're not indispensable, Eline.'

'You'd have him kill me?' Eline asked with an innocent smile.

'If I have to,' Luka said.

'Do you think he could?'

'What? You're vicious, I'll give you that, but Sam is fucking huge and strong as three men.'

'He's a large target, yes,' Eline said, 'and I don't doubt that he's strong. But fast? That I *do* doubt. And trained in close combat by a former Quiet Man and veteran of Krathzgrad? No. He's not that.'

'You think you could take him?' Luka asked, and now the threat sounded like it had turned into a genuine question.

'On my own?' Eline asked. 'Perhaps. Possibly. I like to think probably, but it's by no means a sure thing. Few things are, when it comes down to blades. With Nama beside me? Oh yes.'

'Nama?' Luka asked, blinking at her.

'Yes, *your* Nama,' Eline said. 'We come as one piece on the game board these days, as the baron has obviously worked out. Her wants her on this job as well, you see.'

'Nama's just a low-rent spy and whore,' Luka said.

'I told you about her seeing this Kurt,' Eline said. 'She's a cunning woman.'

'Well, you did, at that,' Luka said, 'but how much can she possibly have learned already?'

Eline smiled at him, and Luka went pale.

'Nah,' he said after a moment. 'It can't be *that* Kurt. He's dead.'

184

'I have absolutely no idea which Kurt it is,' Eline said, having no idea what he meant. 'It's hardly an uncommon name, as you said yourself, but she can fight with the cunning like nothing I've ever seen. She's *dangerous*, Luka, and that makes her an asset. She's also little more than a child and has tied herself so closely to me. I mean to make use of her, whether she likes it or not.'

If that sounded ruthless then so be it. A ruthless woman was, she realised, what she was fast becoming. You had to if you wanted to survive in those days, and she understood that all too well.

Luka looked at her for a long moment, then nodded slowly.

'You get this,' he said, and that sounded a lot like what the baron had said to her earlier in the day. 'You get how this fucking works, don't you?'

'Yes,' Eline said, and in that moment she realised for perhaps the first time that it was true. 'I do.'

'You haven't forgotten the important thing though, have you?' Luka said quietly. 'Your children.'

Eline stiffened.

'No, Luka, I very much have not,' she said in a voice like ice. 'I will never forget my children. I hold them close to my heart, always. But here's something for you to also bear in mind: if I can take Sam, I can most definitely take *you*.'

'It is very unwise,' Luka said softly, 'to threaten a Queen's Man.'

'It is equally unwise,' Eline replied, and held his gaze with a look of daggers, 'to threaten a mother's children.'

'Hah, I supposed I deserved that,' Luka said. 'It's not something I enjoyed doing, you understand. Now, do I need to keep doing it?'

'No,' Eline said.

Luka smiled. 'I knew I liked you,' he said. 'Very well, your children are off the table. This is now a business arrangement, just like the one you seem to have with Lan Elenkov.'

'Good,' Eline said, and sipped her brandy. 'So, fancy coming to Dannsburg with me?'

'I'm afraid not,' Luka said. 'I am needed here. This is my city, Eline. Each of the Queen's Men have one, and Drathburg is mine to mind until such time as the Provost Marshal summons me back to the capital. I can't just go swanning off because you feel like it.'

'Bugger,' said Eline, in a very un-courtesan-like way. 'I suppose Nama and I shall have to fend for ourselves in the big bad city, then.'

'Looks that way,' Luka said. 'Talk to your patron. Tell him you'll do it; I'm all right with that so long as you don't take forever about it. I only really hired you to flush him out so I could keep eyes on him and you've done that, so I don't actually need you at the moment. But I *will* want you back at some point. Just understand that the Immalian spies – I suppose I should say the Marodievan spies, if we don't want this to become any more confusing than it already is – are out there. Two factions of fucking Immalians, it's enough to tie a man's head in knots. Civil wars are a fucking nightmare. Anyway, those who have been watching me will almost certainly have noticed you now, too. Be careful on the road.'

'Understood,' Eline said.

'Oh,' he added, 'when you get there, stay at the Bountiful Harvest, if you can afford it. It's nice. Pricey, but nice.'

She nodded.

That done she left Luka's house and flagged down and hired yet another carriage to take her back to the baron's residence, and as she dropped a couple of silver pennies into the coachman's hand she found herself grateful that these bastards paid her as much as they did. Being a spy, it seemed, was an expensive business.

A new footman admitted her at the baron's door, and ushered her into to Lan Elenkov's presence in his drawing room.

He looked up at her, and showed her a slow, lazy smile that was obviously for the footman's benefit.

'Not too early for a drink now, surely?' he enquired, with a heavy slur in his voice.

'Definitely not,' Eline said, and waved vaguely at the footman. 'Brandy please, then you may leave us.'

The footman gave her a slight bow and poured for her, then discreetly left the room. As the door closed behind him the baron looked up at her where she stood beside the crackling fireplace.

'For the love of the gods, will you sit down?' he snapped. 'I am not your husband, and I very much doubt any man will ever hit you again.'

'I sincerely hope not,' Eline said. 'For their sake.'

'Yes, quite,' said the baron. 'Now, will you go to Dannsburg for me? You and Nama, I mean. More to the point, will Luka go with you?'

'Nama, yes,' Eline said, although she hadn't so much as mentioned it to the girl yet. 'Luka, no.'

'Bugger,' the baron said. 'Is this still about your children? I might be able to do something to help, there. I don't know who or where they are, but I dare say I could find out if I threw enough gold at the question.'

'No,' Eline said. 'I have pointed out a few facts of life to Luka, and that threat at least has been withdrawn. For now, anyway.'

'You think you can trust the word of a Queen's Man?' the baron barked at her.

'Gods, no,' Eline said. 'I can fucking threaten one, though.'

Lan Elenkov laughed.

'I'm sure you can, my dear. I have seen you fight. I dare say you could threaten almost anyone, and be taken seriously.'

Eline remembered her last dancing lesson with Marcoss, and how he had finally seemed genuinely impressed. She had beaten him, that time.

'I think so too, now,' Eline said.

'Good,' the baron said. 'Just you and Nama then, but that should be enough. A hundred marks above your standing retainer, and the same for her. I know how you feel about that, so I'll pay her equal. Having seen her cunning, I have come to realise she probably deserves it, lack of social graces notwithstanding. Now, a few things: Dannsburg is a long way. I will arrange a carriage and a coachman who is a veteran and absolutely trustworthy. You will have additional money for the road, for expenses and inns and such. I would advise you not to travel with *too* much coin, as the roads can be hazardous, but take this.'

He reached into the pocket of his coat and held out a small silver object with an ornately carved base of red onyx.

'A copy of my house seal,' he said. 'With that, and a few signatures, you can draw on an, if not unlimited, certainly substantial amount of money from the bank in Dannsburg if you need it. I have already sent letters of introduction ahead. I will want it *all* accounted for, naturally, but operating expenses are only to be expected.'

'If you've that much money, why don't you simply pay your great-nephew's debts for him and be done with it?' she asked.

The baron snorted. 'Gods, no,' he said. 'If I do that once the little snot will only be back a month or two later wanting *more* debts paid off. He doesn't need to know how wealthy I really am any more than anyone else does. What he needs is some sense scared into him. You're going to do that, Eline. You and the witch.'

'Please don't call her that,' Eline said.

'Nama, then,' the baron conceded.

'How do I find him?' Eline asked.

'I wouldn't recommend asking at the castle,' he said, and laughed. 'I doubt the army high command approve of strange women knocking on the door enquiring of the whereabouts of senior officers, and especially not one of Bakrylov's . . . reputation, shall we say. Find a gaming house called the Jolly Joker, that's where most of his markers are held. If he's not there you can be sure they'll know how to contact him. Oh, and one other thing . . .'

The baron tailed off, and Eline felt her heart sink as she looked at him and sipped her brandy. There was always fucking something, wasn't there? With him or the Queen's Men, or anything to do with fucking politics, there was always *something* to piss in the beer and turn a simple job into a hard one.

'What's that then?'

'My great-nephew is, as I may have mentioned, a decorated war hero. From a certain point of view, anyway. He has also received, ah, shall we say "notoriety", for a subsequent action on home soil. He is, to be perfectly blunt, loathed by the general population. So I would be careful who you mention his name to.'

Eline's heart sank even further. This job had just got a lot harder.

'I see,' said Eline.

She had to tell Madame, of course. That went about as well as might be expected.

'Dannsburg?' Madame said. 'You're going to Dannsburg, and without so much as a by-your-leave? It's easily a week's journey each way if not more if the weather is bad, and never mind how long you'll be there. How am I supposed to do without you?'

'You said I was free to leave anytime I wished,' Eline said. 'So I'm leaving. For a few weeks, at least. All being well, I'll come back, in time.'

'*And* you want to take Nama?' Madame demanded, although Eline hadn't even mentioned that little fact yet. 'Oh yes, I know all about that for all that I dare say even she doesn't yet. You are lucky, Eline, very lucky indeed, that my good friend the baron Lan Elenkov has already written to me about this, *and* agreed to pay the house a generous stipend to cover your lost earnings while you're about whatever mad errand he has set you on. The gods only know how he can afford it, but there we are.'

'So . . . you don't mind?'

'*Mind*? I mind a very great deal, but I am prepared to chalk this one up on the board of favours the baron owes me,' Madame said. 'At least I won't be losing any money, but don't expect the other girls to take this kindly. This is extra work they will have to do, to make up for your and Nama's absence.'

'We'll be gone before they know about it,' Eline assured her.

'That,' Madame said, 'would probably be best.'

Her audience over, Eline went up the stairs to Nama's room and knocked on her door.

'Are you working?' she called through the thick wood. 'It's Eline.'

There was a muffled sound from within.

'Gimmie a few moments.'

Eline could hear thumping noises from within, the unmistakeable sound of the back of a bedstead hitting the wall.

She sighed and went down to the salon to help herself to a glass of wine. It was meant for the punters but no one was looking, so fuck it. She sipped and went back up the stairs again, and settled in a chair in the hall until she heard a loud and unpleasant grunt, followed by a very unconvincing moan of feigned female pleasure. Nama was certainly no actress, that was for sure.

Eline closed her eyes and sipped wine while she waited for a large, nondescript and slightly smelly man to excuse himself from Nama's room and clump off down the stairs, still buttoning his britches as he went.

'Can I come in now?' she asked.

'Aye,' Nama said.

Eline entered the room and found her friend cleaning herself at the washstand. She turned away to give Nama her privacy and waited until the other girl had finished her necessary acts of hygiene, sitting on the side of the bed that faced the other way.

'Gods,' Nama muttered to herself. 'Why do we have to do this?'

'How would you like to not, for a while at least?' Eline asked her.

'What do you think?' Nama demanded. 'Do you seriously think I fucking *enjoy* this?'

'No, of course not. Come to Dannsburg with me.'

'What? Dannsburg? Fucking *Dannsburg*?' The younger woman seemed completely nonplussed. 'As in the capital city? *That* Dannsburg?'

'It's the only Dannsburg I've ever heard of,' Eline said. 'A job for my patron.'

'Does it pay?' Nama asked eagerly.

'Oh yes,' Eline said.

'And what sort of job? The last time I worked for him I killed three men, and I haven't fucking forgotten that,' Nama said. 'Will I have to do that again?'

'I don't know,' Eline answered honestly. 'Quite possibly.'

'How much?'

'A hundred marks.'

'Fuck yes,' said Nama.

Chapter 26

Selling your skills, that was basically what a whore did. That was what a carpenter did too, when you came down to it, or a smith or a quarryman or a seamstress. All work is whoring, at the end of the day, so far as Eline could see. Selling skills, for money. Was murder any different?

She couldn't see how it was.

The baron's hired coach was there for them at first light, with the coachman who she had been assured could be trusted sitting on the box and the single footman, not liveried, who came and banged on the door for them. The coach bore no livery either, nothing to say it came from the house of Lan Elenkov. In fact it was quite plain, unornamented and even a bit scruffy. That, Eline realised, was probably for the best on the largely lawless roads of the countryside. Nothing to draw attention.

There was a note waiting for her on the scuffed red leather of the padded bench inside. She picked it up and read.

My dear Eline,

I'd advise you both not to wear the bawd's knot while away. Such may attract unwanted attention, especially in the country towns and villages where you will be forced to sleep. Travel as a minor noble lady in reduced circumstances with her Alarian maid and two remaining retainers, and nothing more than that.

I do wish you the very best of luck.

It wasn't signed, but was quite obviously from the baron. Eline read it twice then passed it to Nama, and started untying the knot on her shoulder.

'Wait, I'm your fucking *servant* now?' Nama said, after she had struggled through reading the note. She *could* read, but it was obviously work for her, and, to be fair, the baron's handwriting wasn't the easiest to decipher.

'No of course not,' Eline said. 'It's just pretend. But please, take your knot off.'

'I . . .' Nama said. 'I never take it off, except on Godsday. I don't even know who I am, without it.'

'You're a *spy*,' Eline hissed at her. 'For the love of the gods, Nama, you have to be able to wear more than one face if you're to play this game.'

Nama reluctantly untied the thick yellow cord and tucked it protectively into her pouch.

'I feel naked without it,' she admitted.

'Don't think of yourself as naked,' Eline said. 'Think of yourself as free.'

Nama thought about that for a moment, then stared out of the carriage window for a very long time. They were out of the city now, into the farming country where men and their sons toiled endlessly up and down their fields behind their horses and their ploughs, turning the soil while their wives worked their hands raw in the dairies and the butteries and the brewhouse, swarms of children around their feet and often pregnant yet again. Farming life was brutal, even Eline knew that, and she felt for them as they rode past in their well-sprung carriage with silver in their purses. The life of the courtesan, of the whore, was far from perfect but perhaps, she thought, it could have been worse.

One thing life had taught her was that it could *always* be worse.

'How long to Dannsburg?' Nama asked her, breaking her train of thought. Eline shrugged.

'Depends on the weather,' she said. 'Maybe nine days, maybe twelve. If it rains hard the roads will turn to shit, and we'll be slowed to a crawl. If it stays fair and dry, we might make it in eight like Madame said.'

'How do you *know*?' Nama asked her. 'I've never been out of Drathburg in my life.'

'Nor have I, not since I was a little girl on the wagons,' Eline said. 'But in those days we went all over the country. Always moving, as I think I told you. Staying ahead of the vagrancy laws. I've never been into Dannsburg itself, but we camped not far from it once, before we were driven off by the Guard. That wasn't a good time. That close to the capital, the travelling people were most definitely not welcome. Vermin, they called us, thieves, and they ran us out of the county with dogs and fucking cavalry.'

'Gods, what pricks,' Nama said.

'Yes.'

Eline found she had no more to say about that, and she let her head relax back onto the padded leather bench behind her and allowed the steady rocking motion of the carriage to lull her to sleep. She dozed fitfully, drifting up and down through layers of sleep and wakefulness until eventually Nama put a hand on her arm to wake her.

'We're . . . somewhere,' she said.

'Hmmm?'

Eline shook herself awake and looked out of the window. It was twilight and it seemed she had dozed most of the day away. That didn't bode well for her chances of sleeping that night, she thought, with a sigh.

They seemed to be beside a village green with a coaching inn overlooking it, and she could see their footman engaged in conversation with one of the inn's stable boys. The inn was old and precarious-looking, the bottom story built of stone but each of the uppers made of wood and daub and each leaning out a bit further than the one below.

'I think I'd rather sleep in the coach,' Eline muttered.

'Nonsense,' Nama said. 'It'll be fine. Even the newest bit has to be a hundred years old. If it's stood this long it will stand another night.'

'It had better.'

All the same she clambered down from the coach with a sigh of relief and followed her friend and her footman into the inn as the coachman worked with the stable boys to see the coach stowed for the night and the horses cared for.

Eline stood at the desk and realised she was so tired she was almost swaying on her heels for all that she had been asleep most of the day.

'Rooms, please,' she said to the small, rat-faced innkeeper.

She was sounding aristocratic but not too much so, modulating her tone to adopt the role the baron had given her. A minor lady in reduced circumstances, with her servant and two retainers. The men would sleep above the stables, of course, with the stable boys and the pot washer, but she secured a room for herself with a trundle cot for Nama, and that was perfect.

Obviously Nama didn't think it was perfect. Not one little bit she didn't.

'A trundle?' she demanded once the maid had shown them to their room and left them alone.

'You're supposed to be my servant, and I'm supposed to be poor,' Eline reminded her.

'All the same,' Nama said, and Eline saw what she meant.

The bed was a double, at least, but the cot was a sad little thing that a child would have been uncomfortable in.

'Let's have a drink, and get some food,' Eline said. 'You can always sleep in the bed with me.'

'Aye, that's fair,' Nama said. 'Thank you, then.'

Eline supposed they had gone down to eat after that, and probably both drunk far too much for two women who had to spend the whole next day in a slowly swaying carriage. Either way the next morning they had woken up back to back in the big bed. At least it was warm, with her friend in the bed beside her.

All was well enough until halfway through breakfast when Nama had to run out the back door to be violently sick in the yard behind the inn where the shithouse was, and five minutes later Eline had to do the same.

'Perhaps,' Eline said when she staggered back to their table, wiping a hand across the back of her mouth, 'tonight we shouldn't drink so much.'

'You fucking think?' Nama said, and the girl's normally rich brown complexion was looking positively grey that morning. 'Gods, Eline, how much did we put away last night?'

'Too much,' their coachman said, and fixed them both with a stern look that told her he had worked for the baron for more than a few days. 'You've a job to do, both of you. Yes we're on the road and what happens on the road stays on the road, everyone knows that, but when we get there our employer will expect results.'

'Of course,' Eline said. 'He'll get them, don't worry.'

'Hmmm,' the coachman said.

He was a bulky older man, pushing fifty, and he certainly had the stern look of a veteran about him. He also wore a sword, Eline had noticed, which wasn't exactly usual for a coachman. Still, if he stopped people bothering them that was good, as far as she was concerned.

His name was Gregori, apparently, and the much younger footman was Pavel. They were all at breakfast together, although obviously as the supposed lady it was Eline who was paying for it. Still, at least the baron had given her expense money for the road and that was good too, as it turned out coaching inns cost a lot more than she had thought they would. That was another thing she had learned in life: *everything* cost more than she had thought it would.

They were back on the road an hour later, and the women's heads at least were still heavy from drink. They dozed together for most of the day, and when they stopped again at another village that evening they were both considerably more restrained. The journey continued in this way, in day after day of grinding tedium, but at least the weather was as kind as could be expected for that time of year. Six days passed uneventfully, until on the seventh day they were attacked.

They were deep in farming country, the crops recently harvested and the endless fields of wheat cut down to stubble, when Pavel spotted three men on horseback galloping towards them across the fields.

'Ma'am!' he shouted. 'Danger abroad!'

Eline woke with a start and looked out of the carriage window, and she knew. These weren't just brigands or highwaymen; there was nothing about their shabby carriage that implied enough wealth to make it worth the risk. These had to be the Marodievan agents Luka had warned her of. She rammed an elbow into Nama's side to rouse her.

'We're under attack,' she said, as the first crossbow bolt slammed into the side of the speeding carriage and narrowly missed the window.

'The fuck?' Nama said groggily. 'Who by?'

She had been properly asleep, Eline realised.

'Marodievans,' she said.

Nama showed her a blank look.

'Who?'

'*Enemies!* Does it matter who, when they're fucking shooting at us?'

Nama woke up all at once then and released the catch that dropped the carriage window down into the cavity of the door. She raised a hand and, as Eline would later have testified on her knees before a judge or a god, she *growled*.

Fire erupted from her fingers and consumed the rider utterly, sending him flying from his terrified mount as the animal fled, unharmed, down the road and away. The dry stubble started to burn, and it caught *fast*. Nama shot another rider off his horse into the fire as the third made it to the road and bore down on them. Eline piled out of the door of the still-moving carriage with her blades in her hands but Gregori had handed the reins to Pavel by then and he leaped from his coachman's box with his short sword in his hand. He fell on the rider, knocking him to the gritty dust of the road. They rolled and tumbled, and Gregori's sword went flying from his hand as the rider slammed him under the chin with his elbow. The rider had a long knife in his hand now and he raised it with a grin of triumph.

Eline was there a moment later, and her blades reaped the courtesan's harvest as Gregori looked on in open-mouthed surprise and the man's horse ran for its life.

Such was life on the lawless roads of the countryside, as Eline told herself once she had cleaned her blades, dusted herself down and shaken hands with a clearly impressed Gregori.

'Who the fuck taught you to fight?' Gregori asked.

Eline smiled.

'Do you perchance know a man called Marcoss?' she asked, and the expression on Gregori's face told her very well that he did.

She thought she had probably had her last telling off from Gregori.

That done, she climbed back into the carriage and thumped on the roof to get them going again. There was thick sandy dust on the hem of her dress, but she wasn't hurt and if that was all she had to show for the altercation then that was good. She supposed she could live with a bit of grit, all things considered, and at least she had Nama right there with her to heal her if it had all gone wrong.

'Well done,' she told Nama, once she was again seated beside her.

'Fucking hell,' Nama said in a shaky voice, but they left the burning corpses behind them in the field of fire, and they didn't look back.

Chapter 27

At last, one afternoon some nine days after setting off from Drathburg, they sighted the distant walls of Dannsburg.

Huge dark walls topped with heads on spikes, that was how Eline had imagined Dannsburg, and she saw now that she wasn't far wrong. The walls were huge indeed, if not dark, and for some reason inexplicably covered with scaffolding, but there were definitely heads on spikes atop them.

'We're here at last, then,' Nama said, rousing herself from her fitful doze beside her on the bench.

'Looks that way,' Eline said.

There was a long queue of traffic waiting to enter the city, and Gregori skilfully slotted their carriage into the line with only one shout of abuse from a farmer driving a haywain behind two oxen. Pavel shouted back at him from his place beside the coachman on his box, citing the name of the entirely fictitious Lady Eline, and the farmer lapsed into a sullen silence.

It seemed to take forever but eventually they reached the gates, and a surly-looking sergeant of the City Guard presented himself at the window. He wore polished half-armour and a red surcoat bearing the white rose of the royal arms. There was a gate tax to enter the city, of course, but it seemed not to apply to the nobility.

'You are?' he asked brusquely.

'The Lady Eline of Drathburg,' Eline said in her carefully modulated voice. 'My maid, and two retainers of no consequence.'

'No guards? No outriders?'

'No, sergeant,' Eline admitted, and lowered her eyes bashfully. 'I fear my fortunes fare less well than once they did.'

'Then you've been fucking lucky to have made it here in one piece,' the sergeant said. 'Pardon my Kastavian. Aye, in you go. No toll for you, m'lady.'

Aye, she had been lucky she supposed. From a certain point of view. A lot of things, Eline thought then, depended on a certain point of view.

She treated him to a delightful smile, and thumped on the roof to tell Gregori to get them moving before the man changed his mind.

'My fortunes fare less well than once they did?' Nama echoed in a very poor imitation of Eline's accent, and snorted laughter. 'You can be *so* full of shit sometimes, Eline.'

'It's called acting,' Eline snapped at her, then relented. 'It's the stock in trade of the courtesan, Nama. The false face. You have to make yourself truly believe it, to be convincing.'

'So you have to be full of shit,' Nama said.

Eline met her eyes.

'Yes,' she said. 'That is the essence of it, I suppose.'

Nama snorted laughter, and Pavel leaned down from the driver's box to speak to her.

'Where to, ma'am?' he asked.

The streets were absolutely teeming, foot traffic and wagons and carriages, lines of livestock being herded along between the sedan chairs and dray carts. The city was a sea of red banners, and across each danced the white rose of the royal house. The chaos and noise was overwhelming, even compared to the slums of Drathburg. The surge of commerce, the staggering weight of massed humanity that made a capital city what it was. She remembered Luka's words to her.

'An inn called the Bountiful Harvest,' she said. 'I'm told it's nice, there.'

'As you say, ma'am. Cost you, though.'

Pavel, at least, had obviously been to Dannsburg before.

It'll cost the baron, Eline thought, and fingered the shape of his house seal through her pouch. If she had to do this, and it appeared that she did, there was no way on the gods' green earth she was doing it on the cheap. The man was a *king*, for the Lady's sake, albeit a king without a country. That notwithstanding, he was clearly staggeringly wealthy and she intended to make the most of *that* that she possibly could. Yes, expenses had to be accounted for, but would a man like him even think that the Bountiful Harvest *was* expensive? She doubted it, somehow.

They eventually made their way through the churning Dannsburg traffic, and Gregori steered their carriage into the stable yard against the protesting shouts of other coachmen and wagon drivers as he cut across them.

Eline disembarked while he was greeting the inn's stable boys, and Pavel carried most of their luggage around to the main door while Gregori made arrangements with the stable hands. Eline found the innkeeper waiting for them, a pleasant expression on his face. He would have seen the carriage arrive, of course, and if he didn't know exactly who she was then she was obviously *someone*, and in Dannsburg of course that mattered a great deal.

'How can I help you, Lady . . .' he trailed off, the question obviously a leading one.

'Eline of Drathburg,' she said, giving him a little more of the cut-glass accent than she had offered the Guard sergeant at the city walls. 'There are four of us; me, my maid and two retainers.'

The inn was nearly full, apparently, but adjoining rooms were found for Nama and herself. Pavel and Gregori would have to share, apparently. Pavel seemed perfectly happy with that, but she supposed that was between them and none of her business.

She nodded and reached for the offered quill and inkwell to sign the book of admittance.

The Bountiful Harvest wasn't simply expensive; it was *eye-wateringly* expensive. She suspected everything in Dannsburg would be.

She passed coins to the innkeeper, and asked directions to the bank. It seemed she would be needing to visit it even sooner than she had expected. That done, she told Pavel to take their luggage up to their rooms, and turned to Nama.

'A drink, to wash the dust of the road from our throats?' she suggested.

Nama nodded in agreement, although for the last day of solid rain the roads had been more mud than dust, and they made their way to the common room and ordered wine. Truth be told, Eline was starting to rather prefer brandy these days, but it was only the fifth hour of the afternoon and apparently it wasn't seemly for a lady to drink spirits before sunset. If at all, depending who you asked. She wondered how much she still cared about that, and realised the answer was not one bit.

A lean young footman brought their drinks, and Eline appreciated his figure as he poured for them. First her miserable marriage and then whoring had probably put her off sex for life, but that didn't mean she couldn't still appreciate a well-turned calf and a nice arse. She was only human, after all.

'Tell me,' she said, as he started to turn away, 'do you perhaps know a gambling house called the Jolly Joker?'

'Yes, ma'am,' he said.

He gave her directions, and Eline smiled her gratitude and tipped him a silver penny.

'You don't fancy *him*, do you?' Nama asked in disbelief once the man was out of earshot.

'What if I do? You fancy your Kurt, and he's fucking horrible.'

'No he ain't.'

'Yes,' Eline said, 'he is. Anyway, it's not like I'm going to do anything about it. A woman can look, can't she?'

'Suppose,' Nama said, and then she laughed. 'Gods, Eline, I thought you were dead inside.'

'I am,' Eline said, and she realised she meant it. 'He's just pretty, that's all. Like a painting. I can look at a pretty painting and not want to go to bed with it.'

'Suppose,' Nama said again, and took a long swallow of wine. 'Look, what are we going to find at this Jolly Joker?'

'I have no idea,' Eline said. 'Best case, Colonel Bakrylov. Worst case, his creditors, with knives in their hands. In between . . . I have absolutely no idea. Be prepared to fight, if we have to.'

'And all this, to settle your baron's nephew's debts?'

'Great-nephew,' Eline corrected her, and lowered her voice, 'and no. That in part, I suppose, but the baron suspects these are no ordinary creditors. The men who attacked us on the road, the Marodievans, he thinks these blokes are them too. Trying to apply pressure to the baron through threats to his great-nephew. We're here to put a stop to that.'

'And again he sends two tarts instead of a mercenary company, which I'm sure he could easily afford,' Nama complained. 'It makes no sense, Eline.'

'It makes perfect sense,' Eline assured her. 'We blend in. A mercenary company clumping around would probably not even have been let into the city, but *us*? A country lady and her maid, where's the harm in that? Getting through the gate was no trouble, was it? And now we're in the city and free to do as we like. When it comes right down to it, Nama, between us we are an assassin and a cunning woman. We are *more* dangerous than a mercenary company, and a fuck of a lot harder to see coming.'

Nama sighed, apparently appeased. 'So what's the plan?'

'We go to the Jolly Joker after dinner,' Eline said. 'A hand or two of cards, lose a bit of money, I don't care, and see who's there. If the colonel is, then well and good. Assuming he probably isn't, because luck is never that much on our side, I make a few discreet, and I mean *very* discreet enquiries, and try to find out when he will be. Then we go back when he is, and we talk to him. Find out who the problem is. We'll take the rest of it from there.'

'You make it sound so bloody easy,' Nama grumbled.

'That's because it *is*,' Eline assured her. 'If your false face is secure enough, it is honestly a piece of piss.'

'It can't be,' Nama said, 'or everyone would be doing it.'

'The extremely high risk of death puts most people off,' Eline pointed out, and Nama had no answer to that.

They reached the Jolly Joker by the eighth hour after noon, and by then it was dark and Eline had decided it was definitely not too early for a brandy. They had hired a street carriage as their own horses would probably benefit from the rest after their long journey. Eline had to admit she knew precious little about horses, as she had been very young when she and her mother were still travelling, but it struck her as sensible.

'You reckon those two are at it?' Nama asked as the carriage rolled away from the Bountiful Harvest, jolting over the cobbles. 'Gregori and Pavel?'

'Probably,' Eline said. 'So what?'

'Nothing,' Nama said. 'Quite liked Pavel, that's all. He's got nice eyes.'

'Reckon you're out of luck, there,' Eline said, and Nama laughed.

'Ah well,' she said. 'Can't have everything.'

'That you can't,' Eline agreed.

She had thought Caromir had nice eyes once, too. And his muscles, and his corporal's stripes, an impressive moustache and a medal on his chest. Hadn't stopped him being a cunt though, had it? *A man isn't how he looks*, she wanted to say to Nama. *A man is how he acts.*

She wanted to say that, but she didn't. The girl was young, and her mistakes were hers and hers alone to make, as Eline had made her own in her day. Should she have told her? Perhaps, but Nama would only have told her to mind her business as she herself would have told any interfering older woman when she had been that age, too. She had been marrying her sweetheart, her brave soldier, who was going to be so good to her, and keep her safe, and . . . And look how that had turned out.

She jolted out of her bitter reverie as the carriage drew up outside the Jolly Joker and Nama nudged her arm to bring her back to the present.

'We're here,' she said, and Eline forced her wandering mind to focus.

'Right,' she said. 'Scrap being my maid, they'll never buy a maid playing cards in a place like this. You're my . . . distant cousin, that'll do for tonight.'

'I hate all this play-acting, it's so confusing,' Nama grumbled.

'I know,' Eline said. 'I'm not keen on it either but the rest of it . . . Truth be told, that I *don't* hate.'

'The spying, you mean?' Nama asked her. 'Or the killing?'

Eline swallowed. She had meant the spying, and the intrigue that came with it, the puzzles to solve and the people she had met and . . . But all truth be told, no, she found she no longer hated the killing either. The people she had fought had either attacked her first or they had simply *needed* killing, and she realised she was all right with either of those scenarios. It was Our Lady's plan for them, after all.

'Yes,' she said eventually.

'What the fuck does "yes" mean?'

'It means shut up, and let's get a drink and go and lose some of the baron's money until we learn something useful.'

Nama sighed.

'If you say so,' she said.

They alighted from the carriage and Eline told the driver to wait for them. She cordially greeted the two footmen who awaited them at the door and found herself wondering who this place actually belonged to.

'The Lady Eline of Drathburg,' she announced herself, 'and my cousin Nama. I would play your tables, if it please you.'

'Of course, my lady,' one of them said, and held the door open to usher them into the gaming house's warm embrace.

'My thanks,' Eline said, and dropped a silver penny into the man's hand without even looking.

'You are getting too good at this shit,' Nama whispered as she followed Eline into the main room, but Eline ignored her.

She *was* getting good at it, and to her mind that was a good thing. This was a big part of her job, playing the aristocrat. That was what courtesans *did*, and she knew she needed to be very good at it indeed.

Their first port of call was the bar, where they ordered drinks and enquired about games that could be joined. Eline opted for cards, of course, as that was favoured by the nobility and Madame had taught her at least the rudiments of it, whereas Nama wanted dice which apparently she was already quite familiar with.

Dice was widely regarded as common, a game for soldiers and servants and criminals, Eline knew that well enough, but she let it go. In truth Nama *was* common, of course, but she didn't want to think about that purely because she knew she was as well, and that night she had to forget that fact if her false face as a lady was going to bear scrutiny.

You must believe in it, she remembered Madame telling her. *Become the courtesan's persona. There can be no self-doubt, Eline, or others will sense it and that will be your undoing.*

Sadly, it didn't look like the colonel was there that night, or at least not anyone who looked like she imagined he would, but she found a likely-looking card game and bought in. She was welcomed well enough once she had put silver down on the table, anyway.

To Eline's surprise it didn't take too long to learn something, although she *did* have to lose some money to get there. She really wasn't very good at cards, she had to admit, but somehow she won the first hand anyway. She suspected Nama might have had something to do with that. A *lot* to do with it, probably. There didn't seem to be *anything* the girl couldn't do with her cunning. She also noticed Nama was drinking brandy, despite not being used to it. A *lot* of brandy, from what she could see. She doubled up on the next hand and lost the lot. Oh well, it wasn't her money, she supposed.

She learned that the colonel was usually in there on a Knightsday evening, which was tomorrow, and would probably play straight through to Queensday. She also learned that he was every bit as unpopular as the baron had told her.

'The Butcher?' the man at her table had asked in astonishment. 'The fuck do you want that cunt for?'

Eline had made something up and had already forgotten what it was, but all the same the man's face had spoken volumes. Volumes of violence, if truth be told. Colonel Bakrylov, it seemed, was not what you would call a popular man. Eline found herself wondering what on earth the man could have done to have earned this much hatred. All the same, apparently he would play from Knightsday evening through to Queensday?

That's nearly three fucking days, Eline thought to herself. *No wonder the fool is in debt.*

She pulled Nama away from the dice table where the girl seemed to have won herself almost half a crown, and hauled her outside and up into the carriage.

'You idiot,' Eline hissed as she thumped the roof to get the hired carriage moving. 'What do you think would have happened when they realised you were cheating?'

'Wasn't cheating,' Nama said, with a distinct slur in her voice. 'Not really, an' that. They were good dice. Something Kurt taught me about probability, that's all. Which is why they fell my way, y'know?'

She giggled and hiccupped.

'You're drunk,' Eline said.

'Aye,' Nama admitted. 'Drunk and fuckin' minted, now. I like Dannsburg. S'good here, innit?'

Eline put a hand to her head in exasperation.

'I'm putting you to bed,' she said. 'We'll discuss the rest of it in the morning.'

Chapter 28

The next morning Nama was looking quite sorry for herself, and Eline was not feeling merciful.

'You and I need to *fucking* talk,' she said when she met Nama in the common room for breakfast.

'Oh don't,' Nama said, and she already had one hand pressed against her left eye socket as though it was causing her excruciating pain.

Perhaps it was, Eline wouldn't know. A mean part of her *hoped* it was. She bloody deserved it.

'Look,' she said, and she lowered her voice below the background murmur of the common room, 'you can't do shit like that. Cunning woman or not, someone will fucking *notice*.'

'I suppose so,' Nama admitted. 'Maybe I'll have to lose a bit tonight to make up for it. Buggered if I'm showing a loss overall though.'

'Tonight?'

'Aye, it's Knightsday innit? He should be in tonight.'

Eline sighed.

'I suppose it is.'

'It is,' Nama said again, and then put a hand to her head with a look on her face that said she was about to puke from the pain.

'Right,' Eline said after a moment. 'We're getting something to eat whether you like it or not. Then I'm rounding up Gregori and going for a walk in the city and you, my girl, are going back to bed. You are absolutely fucked and there's no other word for it.'

'At least I haven't been for a week, but I suppose that's fair,' Nama said, but Eline was past caring whether it was fair or not.

Eline sighed again. She really didn't want to end up becoming a mother figure to Nama, but it looked like it was happening whether she liked *that* or not, either.

'Mother figure' only made her think of her own daughter, of course, and how badly she wanted to see her again. She was somewhere here in Dannsburg as well, of course, in service at the house of the Lady Lan Yetrova or so Luka had told her, but of course she didn't have the faintest idea where that was.

They choked down breakfast, and Eline sent Nama back up to her room to feel sorry for herself and sleep it off while she went to rouse Gregori out of the room he shared with Pavel. She found them sitting together at the table, sharing a breakfast of bacon and black bread with mugs of small beer.

'Fancy showing me around the city?' she asked Gregori.

'Aye, why not?' the man said.

He finished his last mouthful of breakfast, drained his tankard, and looked at Pavel.

'You keep the other one safe, right?'

'Aye.'

'Her name is Nama, and she's gone back to bed anyway,' Eline said. 'State of her this morning, it's the best place for her.'

'Right you are,' Pavel said, and he didn't look like he cared much one way or the other about that. He looked up at Gregori though as the older man stood and buckled his sword belt around his waist, and right then he *did* look like he cared. 'Be careful,' he said.

'Always am,' Gregori said. 'That's why I'm still alive.'

He followed Eline down the stairs to the stable yard.

'Carriage or walk?' he asked her.

'Walk, I think,' she said. 'It's a nice morning, and we can't talk if you're driving a carriage. Beside, the horses probably need to rest.'

She honestly had no idea whether they did or not, but it sounded to her like something a coachman would appreciate hearing.

And it *was* nice, at that. The late autumn sun was bright if low in the sky, and the day looked like it was going to be dry and fair.

'Yes, ma'am,' Gregori said.

He was deferential enough, in the way of servants, but she couldn't have said she found the man exactly engaging.

'I'd like to see the city,' she said. 'Understand what I'm working with. You've been here before?'

'Aye,' Gregori said. 'His lordship always sends me and Pavel when he needs something taking to or from Dannsburg.'

'That happen often, does it?'

'Don't think that's any of your business,' Gregori said, and on reflection she supposed it probably wasn't at that.

'You and Pavel,' she ventured. 'Close, are you?'

'Not your business either, but aye. You could say that.'

'Lovers? Not that I mind, of course, I just like to understand the dynamic.'

'Aye,' Gregori said again, and looked at her out of the corner of his eye. 'And you and Nama?'

'No,' she said.

He shrugged.

'Ain't no one's business anyway, is it?'

'No,' she said again.

'Doesn't matter,' Gregori said. 'It's not like I'm ashamed of it.'

'Good,' she said. 'You shouldn't be. Lie with whom thou wilt, so long as both be willing.'

'What's that, scripture?'

'Yes,' Eline said. 'The word of Our Lady of Eternal Sorrows.'

Gregori grunted at that, and led her to the end of the avenue. There were huge buildings in the distance, a castle on a high hill and behind that to the north the rearing spire of a grand temple.

'That there is the castle,' he said, as though that wasn't obvious. 'That's where the army top brass live, and half their soldiers. Beyond that, the Grand High Temple of All Gods. Holiest place in the land, that is, or so they say. Don't go in for that sort of thing much, myself. Beyond *that* is Cannon Hill, but that's outside the walls and there's nothing up there now but dead grass. Over there, where all the scaffolding is, that's where they're building the first Temple of the Martyr. Over there, you see where there's a blue flag not a red one? Only one in the city, that is. That's the house of magicians. Fucking lucky that's even still standing after what happened.'

Eline squinted and she *could* see the blue flag, adorned with what appeared to be a many-pointed star picked out on it in white.

'And the house of law?' Eline asked.

'Oh, that's miles away behind us,' Gregori said. 'Can't see it from here. It's down near the river, close to the palace. Fucking huge, it is, and the palace even bigger. They're both fixed up now, but half the Royal Mall is still covered in scaffolding and stone masons who should be working on the walls and aren't. Government priorities, apparently.'

'What *happened* here?' Eline asked. 'The whole city looks like it's been bombed.'

'That's because it was,' Gregori said, and she realised he wasn't joking. 'A regime change, my lady, is seldom achieved peacefully.'

A bad succession, two claimants to the throne. The inevitable civil war.

That was how the baron had explained it to her, but had that really happened *here*? She thought that if there had been civil war in her own country, even *she* would have heard of it. No, this must have been something else, something faster, more localised and perhaps more drastic than that. The further they walked into the city the more scaffolding they saw, some buildings in various stages of being rebuilt, and some that were still rubble.

'Were you here when it happened?' she asked Gregori.

'No, thank the gods,' the man said. 'It was fucking awful, from what I hear. Explosions and blood and fire, and a few days later there was a new arse on the throne. No fucking about. The gods only know how many people dead, and half the city destroyed in the process. Fuck's sake, *royalty!* Bunch of cunts, the lot of them. Pardon my language, ma'am.'

He paused for a moment to spit in the gutter, and right then Eline couldn't even find it in herself to hold that against him.

'But there's stability now?'

'Aye,' Gregori admitted after a moment. 'To be fair this cunt's better than the last cunt, but that's like saying dysentery is better than the cock-rot.'

'I know what you mean,' Eline said.

Working for Luka, for the baron, was better than living with Caromir had been, but that still didn't mean it would have been her choice. A quiet life with a loving husband and children who hadn't had to leave to find work, to service or the army. *That* would have been her choice, but who got to make their own choices in this life? Well, everyone she supposed, but how often did the choices you made deliver the outcome you wanted? Very fucking seldom, in her experience.

'Are you coming?' Gregori asked, and Eline realised she had drifted off for a moment on a tide of her own bleak, bitter thoughts.

'Yes, yes,' she said, and hurried to catch up with him.

He led her into a street lined with shops.

'This is Trade Street,' he said. 'Anything you can't buy here or at the market, you probably can't get in Dannsburg. Except poppy resin, but there's other places you can buy that if you want it.'

'I really don't,' Eline said, and she meant it. 'Dreadful stuff. Shouldn't be allowed.'

'It isn't, but what difference does that make?' Gregori said. '"Illegal" and "can't get it" are not the same thing, especially in Dannsburg. But aye, I'm with you on that. I like a drink as much as the next man or woman, but fuck if I am going anywhere near that shit.'

'Good,' Eline said. 'Keep it that way.'

Gregori rounded on her.

'I am probably twenty fucking years older than you,' he said, although he probably wasn't. 'Don't speak to me like my fucking mother.'

'I am not your mother,' Eline said, ratcheting up the aristocratic accent to its absolute height, 'but I *am* your employer.'

'No,' Gregori said, 'you ain't. The baron is. You, I'm afraid, *my lady*, are just an up-jumped tart in his employ, and we're all dressed up and pretending otherwise.'

'Just a tart?' Eline asked mildly. 'You saw me dance, on the road. You even asked me who my teacher was.'

'There was that,' Gregori had to admit. 'You're good, I'll give you that, but how the fuck do you know Marcoss?'

Eline smiled.

'Buy me a bowl of tea and I'll tell you,' she said.

Tea in those days was rare and very, very expensive, imported all the way from Alaria, and tea rooms were exclusive places where only people with at least a reasonable amount of money ever went. Eline sat across the table from Gregori as the serving boy brought them each a steaming bowl, and sat back in her chair to look at him.

'You work for the baron,' she said.

'Yes, obviously,' Gregori said.

'It wasn't a question, I know you do,' Eline said. 'What has he told you about me?'

'You're a whore, and you work for him,' Gregori said. 'In fact *you're* almost a courtesan, apparently. The other one, she's just a whore.'

'Her name is Nama,' Eline snapped. 'Is that all?'

'Pretty much, aye,' Gregori said. 'But then his nibs is full of shit and secrets, isn't he? Her shooting fire out of her fucking hands, you fighting like a war goddess on a dusty road . . . he never mentioned none of *that*, did he?'

'Apparently not,' Eline said. 'Did it ever occur to you, Gregori, what *else* he might not have mentioned to you?'

'Look, Eline,' he said, and he sipped his tea then rubbed his hand over his face, 'I'm not one of you lot. Not a plotter or a schemer. Give me a job to do and I'll do it. Expect me to figure out what the job is three moves ahead and I'm sorry but you've probably hired the wrong bloke. That just ain't how my head works, you know what I mean? I'm a grunt, not an officer. I'll work for you if you pay me, but I can't fucking think for you.'

'No shame in that, either,' Eline said. 'Each to their talents, in Her service.'

'Is that more of your sodding scripture?'

'Does it matter if it is? It's just common sense, as most of Our Lady's doctrine is.'

'If you say so,' Gregori muttered. 'Look, do you want to see a bit more of the city?'

'Actually I'd like to see the bank,' said Eline.

Gregori blinked.

'The fuck for?'

'For money, of course,' Eline said. 'The fuck does anyone ever want to see a bank for otherwise? The charming staff, the wonderful cosy atmosphere? I don't think so somehow.'

'Do you *have* money, in the bank?'

'No, but the boss has. And the prices that bastard inn is charging us, I need it.'

'Aye, that's fair,' Gregori said, and he drained his bowl of tea. 'Come on then. I know the way.'

Eline set hers down half full, but then she hadn't really wanted it anyway. She had just wanted to see if he would buy it for her if she asked, and he had.

Always measure the weight of the scales of power, she thought, and she wondered where that thought had come from. Temple, perhaps, but if it had then she didn't remember it. Perhaps it was just a thought she had had, all by herself.

They were halfway down Trade Street when Gregori suddenly pointed at a jeweller's shop.

'You'll want to go in there, ma'am,' he said.

'The baron isn't likely to approve of buying me jewellery,' Eline said.

'No,' he growled, 'you'll *want* to go in there, right now.'

Eline suddenly realised they were being followed by three cloaked men.

The jewellers had a lot of security, of course it had, and as soon as she and Gregori stepped into to the shop she saw him exchange a look with one of the guards. Two of them were on the door with crossbows in their hands a moment later.

'This is not good,' Gregori said, and then a pane of the front window shattered as a crossbow bolt flew through it.

Broken glass exploded across the interior of the shop like flying razor blades, and the shopkeeper screamed.

'*Down!*' Gregori shouted, and all but threw himself on Eline to bear her to the thankfully carpeted floor.

'Fuck's sake!' Eline shouted.

The shop's security were shooting now, and the first brought down one of the attackers but the second missed and started to frantically reload with the ratchet span for his crossbow.

Gregori rolled off her and drew his sword as he got to his feet.

'I can't fight crossbowmen with stilettoes,' Eline said, arming herself.

'Agreed,' he said. 'Get behind the counter.'

Another bolt smashed through the window, then, as the shooter was reloading, Gregori charged out into the street with the shop's two security men behind him. Between them they brought down the second would-be assassin with their blades, but the third slipped around them and sprinted into the shop.

'Gods have mercy!' wailed the shopkeeper, hands at her cheeks and a look of sheer terror on her ashen face.

Eline was up and blades reversed in her hands in less than a heartbeat, and she spun around the cut of the man's sword and hammered a blade through the side of his neck without a moment's hesitation. She twisted her hips savagely and ripped her blade out sideways to tear his throat open in a crimson spray that decorated the displayed jewellery like rubies.

'My god has no mercy,' she snarled.

Gregori crashed back into the shop a moment later, but the thing was done. The last attacker was dead at Eline's feet.

He gaped at her.

'You ain't fucking normal,' he said.

'I had nothing to do with it. It was Our Lady's plan for him.'

'But he's twice your fuckin' size!'

'Perhaps,' Eline said as she cleaned her blades on the corpse's coat before she spat on him in the traditional gesture of the caravans, 'but when it's a matter of blades, speed beats strength nine times out of ten. Had we both been unarmed, he'd have murdered me. With blades, no.'

'Evidently not,' Gregori said. He looked around the room, at the blood-splattered jewellery displays and the shopkeeper who was clearly still in shock. 'Is this a matter for the Guard?'

'Fuck no,' Eline said. 'Nothing I do is, unless I need someone arrested.'

'And is that likely to happen?'

'In this city? I very much doubt it,' Eline said.

'Good.'

She looked at the shopkeeper, who seemed catatonic, and snapped her fingers in front of the woman's face to bring her out of it.

'Do you know someone who can make this go away?' she asked.

'Wh–what?' the woman asked, and blinked as though once again seeing the corpse on her floor and the blood-splattered necklaces for the first time. 'I . . . Probably. There's a man, Leonov, who works for Mr Iagin, who . . .'

'Doesn't matter,' Eline said. 'Just get rid of it. This didn't happen. We weren't here, you understand?'

Iagin, she thought. She was sure she had heard that name somewhere before, but she was buggered if she could remember where. Oh well, she'd think about it later.

'Robbers, in my shop!' the woman exclaimed suddenly, and reached to her throat as though to clutch the pearls she wasn't wearing.

'Aye,' Gregori said. 'Not any more.'

'Thank you, thank you!' the woman said, and hurried out from behind her counter to present Eline with a delicate gold bracelet.

'With my deepest gratitude,' she said. 'They could have taken every-thing. I could have been bankrupt without you!'

Eline, who had brought the assassins down on the woman's shop in the first place, if unwittingly, accepted the gift with a smile.

'My thanks,' she said, and slipped the bracelet around her left wrist.

It looked well there, she had to admit. A trophy of the morning's work, perhaps, or a gift born out of respect and gratitude.

Either seemed fitting, under the circumstances, but it was a gift well given with good intentions and Eline had no qualms about taking it.

She had done what had needed doing, that was all, and as far as she was concerned this was fair recompense for a job well done.

In Our Lady's name.

Chapter 29

By the time they returned to the Bountiful Harvest, Eline's purse now heavier to the tune of several gold crowns of the baron's money since her trip to the bank, Nama had finally surfaced and was just about in a fit state to eat lunch.

'How was the city?' she asked as Eline joined her at their shared table.

'Interesting,' Eline said. 'Busy, and violent.'

'Violent?' Nama blinked at her for a moment. 'With the amount of City Guard on the streets here I would have expected it to be anything but.'

'Yes,' Eline said, 'but they can't be everywhere. This was a targeted attack.'

'Wait, what? An attack? On *you*?'

'Yes, I think so,' she said. 'Marodievans, I can only assume. Didn't really get the chance to ask.'

She reached for her glass of wine, and the light made her new gold bracelet gleam as her sleeve rode up.

'You didn't have that this morning,' Nama said.

'No,' Eline agreed. 'I didn't. A ... gift, shall we say, from a grateful shopkeeper.'

'Eline,' Nama said, lowering her voice to little more than a whisper, 'what the fuck did you do this morning?'

'Went for a walk, saw the sights. Drank tea. Killed a man. Went to the bank. Nothing unusual.'

She held Nama's gaze, and she didn't blink.

Nama swallowed.

'I think,' she said after a long pause, 'I'm starting to be a bit scared of you.'

Eline smiled.

'A hundred marks to go on holiday and not even have to fuck anyone for a few weeks,' Eline said. 'You didn't honestly think this was going to be easy, did you?'

'Perhaps not,' Nama said, but Eline thought she might have been lying about that.

She liked Nama but the girl was still staggeringly naïve about some things.

'So, tonight,' she said. 'We're going back to the Jolly Joker, and you are *not* drinking that much again and you are *not* cheating at dice, is that absolutely understood?'

'Yes, Mother,' Nama said, and Eline came dangerously close to punching her.

'Nama,' she said.

'Sorry,' the girl said, and she did at least have the good grace to look a bit bashful about it. 'I just . . . I'm *sorry*, all right? This is the first time I've been out of Drathburg in my life, since I was too young to remember anyway. You can't blame me for trying to have a bit of fun.'

'No,' Eline admitted, 'but I *will* blame you if you fuck this up. So see that you don't.'

'Aye, that's fair,' Nama had to allow.

Eline just nodded at that, and finished her lunch.

They idled the afternoon away, Eline reading a book from the inn's surprisingly well-stocked shelves while she sipped wine in the common room and Nama away up in her room doing the gods only knew what to practice her cunning.

Talking to rats, probably.

They met again for dinner, and when it was time to go out she had the innkeeper arrange a hired carriage to take them back to the Jolly Joker around the ninth hour.

'Remember,' Eline said, 'no cheating at dice tonight.'

'I know, I know,' Nama muttered. 'It's just so *easy*, you know?'

'So is getting stabbed,' Eline said, and she didn't think she could have made that any clearer if she had tried. 'Lady's sake, Nama, the Joker might seem respectable but whoever owns it almost certainly *isn't*, don't you grasp that?'

'I suppose so,' Nama muttered.

'I *know* so,' Eline said. 'Places like that never are.'

'Never are what?'

'Owned by anyone respectable, I mean,' she said. 'Never. Those foot-men are anything bloody but, and if that place isn't owned by a gangster I'll eat my petticoat.'

She rubbed a hand across her temples. Gods but she was tired.

The fight that morning was to blame, she could only suppose, although she'd had all afternoon sitting on her arse with her nose in a book to recover.

Aecharias and Meledia, that was what she had been reading, one of the great classical plays that was still regularly performed at the theatre. A tragedy, of course, of fated lovers and the tale of the war their love had spawned. Madame had told her that much, and it had sounded intriguing at the time. She found she didn't really care for it in truth, and much pre-ferred the bawdy tales of the theatre of the previous century, but it seemed to her that a courtesan should read such things, or at least be seen to. It was all part of the false face, after all. She tried not to smile at the obvious symbolism of Aecharias's 'magic sword', but perhaps that was just her dirty mind at work. The rest of it was humourless enough, it had to be said. Perhaps the playwright, whose name she had already forgotten, had meant it unironically. That made it even funnier, as far as she was concerned.

'Anyway, we're nearly there,' she said as the carriage rattled down the street to the Jolly Joker. 'Behave yourself, you understand me?'

'Can I at least play, or do I need to attend milady's side lest she wish for her fan or finds herself in need of her smelling salts in case a man does something scandalous in her presence?'

'Oh, fuck off,' Eline said, but she meant it in a good-natured way. 'Play all you want, just don't fucking cheat this time. Anyway, I've got my fan in my sash and I find precious little scandalous. And don't come crying to me if you lose all the money you won last night.'

'How about if I just cheat a little bit?'

Eline shot the girl a look, but the mischievous look on her young face made her laugh despite herself.

She is so like my own daughter.

Eline desperately wanted to see her daughter now she was in Danns-burg herself, but she knew it was out of the question even if she could find her. This business was far too dangerous to risk bringing her beloved girl to the attention of the Marodievans.

'Just don't get fucking caught,' she said, and then they were there.

Don't get caught, she thought, was the essence of it. *Don't get caught* was always more important than actually being innocent. Innocence could be lied about, could be re-framed, could be twisted against you. Not getting caught made whatever it was not an issue in the first place. A courtesan, she thought then, should never be caught.

Nor a spy.

The wordplay made her smile, but then the carriage pulled up outside the Jolly Joker. Eline paid the coachman, and they disembarked into the warm, welcoming glow of lanterns.

The proprietor of the Jolly Joker obviously recognised them from the previous night, and he welcomed them with a wide smile.

'Lady Eline, how good to see you again,' he said, although he gave Nama something of a sideways glance, one that told Eline he had his eye on the girl and almost certainly suspected her of having been cheating last night.

Still, she had lost a double pot herself at the card table, so she supposed they at least had – what had Luka called it? – plausible deniability, that was it. She was beginning to understand exactly what he had meant by that, and how important it was.

She approached the bar, and the man behind it greeted her.

'How may I serve you?'

'I was hoping to meet a . . . an acquaintance,' she said.

She had been about to say *friend*, until she remembered that the baron had told her almost everyone in Dannsburg appeared to hate his great-nephew.

'And who is that, ma'am?'

'One Colonel Bakrylov,' she said, and noticed how his expression darkened. 'I don't know him well, or even really what he looks like. Truth be told we're more correspondents than even acquaintances.'

'Bakrylov the Butcher,' the man growled. In truth he looked like he wanted to spit, but didn't quite dare do it in front of her. 'He's at table three, playing a man you would be *very* well advised not to annoy.'

He indicated subtly across the room, and Eline saw a handsome man who wore a dark-red coat of military cut and sported the customary bristling side whiskers of a cavalry officer. He was sat across the table from a darker-skinned man, who was scowling murderously. Each had a glass in front of him, and there was a half-empty bottle of brandy on the table.

One of his creditors, Eline had no doubt, and that almost certainly made him a Marodievan. The colonel had a good stack of coins in front of him.

'And why is that, then?' Eline asked.

'Some men,' the proprietor said in a stage-whisper that half the house probably heard, 'are well connected, and want everyone to know it. Others are considerably better connected than they want people to know.'

'I see,' she said.

Eline smiled slightly as an idea birthed itself in the back of her head.

'Brandies, please,' she told the man, in her sharpest cut-glass accent. 'I believe we will both join the colonel. Nama, attend me.'

'I thought I could play dice?' Nama whispered as she followed Eline across the gaming floor.

'Change of plan,' she said. 'We, by which I mean you, need to make us win. A lot.'

'Ah,' Nama said. 'I . . . Well, I can try. The cunning doesn't always work, remember? The probability thing is particularly difficult.'

'Try *hard*,' Eline said, and then they were at Bakrylov's table.

'Colonel,' Eline said, and offered him a curtsey. 'May we join you and your partner?'

Bakrylov looked up at her and frowned, then took in Nama beside her and made the obvious assumption. Two ladies, approaching two gentlemen in public? Who could blame him, she supposed.

'My dear lady,' he said, mouth twisting into a smirk, 'I think you may have rather missed your mark with me.'

'No, no,' Eline said. 'Just fancied a game, that's all, and who wouldn't want to say they'd taken a dozen crowns from the decorated war hero Colonel Bakrylov?'

He laughed at that, and kicked a chair out from under the table for her as a footman brought brandies for her and Nama.

'You needn't have bothered,' he said, 'we have a bottle for the table. I can always buy another when we run out.'

'You're very confident, Bakrylov,' said the other man, who still hadn't introduced himself.

'I'm very winning,' Bakrylov said, and grinned. 'Madam, allow me to introduce my associate, Mihail Antoniev. And forgive me, I'm sure we must have met, but . . .'

'Perhaps at a ball? The Earl Lan Klasskoff's? The Lady Eline of Drathburg,' she said. 'My distant cousin, Nama.'

'Your cousin, yes,' Bakrylov said, and winked at her in a way that would have been staggeringly rude if she hadn't realised he was making fun. 'You want to buy in?'

'How much?'

'Only a crown a head,' Bakrylov said. 'It's just a friendly few hands.'

Only a crown? She wondered then just how fucking in debt he truly was, if he thought a buy-in of a whole gold crown was 'just a friendly few hands'.

'Very well,' she said, fishing two of the baron's gold crowns out of her pouch. She didn't blink and she kept her hand from shaking for all that it very much wanted to as she set them on the table. She prayed to Our Lady that Nama could cheat at cards as well as she did at dice. If she lost this much of the baron's money gambling of all things, he would fucking kill her. She had absolutely no doubt about that at all.

They played the hand, and, to her enormous relief, Eline won.

'Again?' Bakrylov asked, and tossed back his brandy before pouring another round for them all.

Eline's glass was already empty, so she was grateful for the refill.

'Why not?' she said.

They played another round and this time Bakrylov won, and the bastard raised.

'Another crown,' he said.

Eline reluctantly reached into her purse once more, feeling it getting lighter by the moment.

Antoniev glared at the colonel but met his raise and they played again, and Eline won again. That was more like it.

She met Nama's eyes over the table, and the girl gave her a tiny nod.

'Again,' she said, and dealt the cards.

This time Antoniev won, much to Eline's horror, and raked in a pot that by now had to be enough that even an aristocrat would have missed it. Eline felt her stomach twist as a slow, evil smile spread across the foreign man's face as he watched Bakrylov. Eline couldn't afford to lose this much of the baron's money, she just *couldn't*.

Nama reached for the brandy bottle and poured for the table again, emptying it.

'Double up and go again,' she announced. 'One last hoorah before we call it a night. My cousin will cover my stake, won't you, dearest?'

Eline almost choked on her brandy. That would be all the gold she had left, and she wasn't sure quite how deep the baron's pockets really were. If she lost it all and the bank turned her away in the morning, they would be on the streets, and she would probably end up with a knife through her ribs when he found out about it.

'Oh, why not?' Bakrylov said, and lazily threw gold coins into the pot as though it was nothing at all.

Perhaps it wasn't, to him, although if his debts were really as bad as the baron had said Eline couldn't really see how. He must have been borrowing from somewhere else, she supposed, to cover the creditors he already had at the Jolly Joker. From where, exactly, she dreaded to think.

She met Nama's eyes, and once more the girl gave her a tiny nod. She had no choice really; it was this or walk away empty-handed, and look a fool in the process. She bought in once again, all the gold she had left, and Antoniev dealt the cards.

Eline looked down at her hand and forced herself not to smile. Three kings and a knight. They went round the table a few times, and each time she pitched another handful of silver marks into the now-towering pot, raising and raising again.

At the last draw, she got the king of swords. She placed the knight face down on the table in front of her and tucked the king smugly into her fan of cards with the other three. That hand was almost unbeatable.

Almost, but not quite.

She swallowed, and felt cold sweat on the palms of her hands.

I have to trust her, she thought. *I have to, or I am fucking done.*

'Call,' she said.

Bakrylov, who it seemed had been bluffing, threw his hand down in disgust and picked up the fresh brandy bottle that a footman had brought them not five minutes before.

Antoniev showed her three queens and the eight of cups, and sneered at her. Eline showed him her four kings and her middle finger, and swept the by then enormous pot into her hands.

'Mine, I think,' she said.

'Fuck you!' Antoniev shouted, loud enough to make the proprietor turn a look on their table.

'No, I don't think so,' Eline said, and she slipped her fan from her sash and made the gesture that said 'you can't afford me'.

And that was done.

Chapter 30

'I am absolutely fucked,' Eline said in the back of the hired carriage that was slowly jolting them over the cobbles back to the Bountiful Harvest. 'I don't think I've ever been this tired but still awake in my life before.'

'Sorry,' Nama said. 'The trick didn't want to work, and it had to come from *somewhere*.'

'What did?'

'The . . . I don't know. Strength, I suppose. Whatever the cunning runs off. I don't fucking know how it works, Eline, I just know how to *make* it work. Sort of, anyway. And when it doesn't, I have to steal the strength to force it. That was the thing Kurt taught me. I told you about this, remember? After the night I wasn't myself. Kurt is great at showing me how to do something but shit at explaining *how* it works, you know? Maybe even he doesn't know. Doesn't fucking matter, does it, long as it works?'

'Did you *know* I was going to win that last hand? Because it would have been my death sentence if I hadn't.'

'Still trusted me though, didn't you?' Nama said. 'And yes, I did know although again I don't know how. Have to admit I was draining you pretty hard by then so I'm not fucking surprised you're tired. Surprised you're even still awake, to be honest. But aye, I knew. Had to let Antoniev win one, didn't I, or he'd never have agreed to double up.'

'I nearly fucking died of fright when you said that,' Eline slurred, but by then her chin was on her chest and she was in that strange floating place between asleep and awake.

'Don't worry about it,' Nama said. 'Nearly home. My turn to put *you* to bed tonight, innit?'

Eline supposed that it probably was, at that.

'I just . . . I can't believe that just happened.'

'Well, it did,' Nama said. 'Sorry about stealing from you like that but if I hadn't I wouldn't have been able to do it, and that's the simple truth. Fire is easy, that trick really isn't.'

'You couldn't have taken it from some stranger?'

'I . . . I don't think so. I don't think it works like that, from what Kurt said. I *know* you, and I think that matters. I don't think trying to drain some random bloke at the bar would have worked, or at least nowhere near as well. How much did we win, anyway?'

'Loads,' Eline whispered, 'and keep your voice down. This is a hired carriage, after all, so fuck knows how much we can trust the driver. Should have brought Gregori and Pavel.'

'Well, we didn't,' Nama pointed out. 'Lesson learned, perhaps.'

'Aye,' Eline said, and yawned hugely. 'Are we nearly home?'

'Not far, I don't think,' Nama said. 'Look, Eline, money is nice and everything but how has this actually helped? What are we supposed to do now?'

'Invite him to dinner,' Eline said, and then she *did* fall asleep.

True to her word, Nama must have put her to bed, and she woke up sometime around the tenth hour of the next morning wearing only her smallclothes under her blankets. She had missed breakfast, of course, but her body had obviously needed sleep much more than food and she found she was glad of it.

Once she was up and washed and dressed, she made her way downstairs, still feeling a little weak, and found Nama waiting for her in the common room.

'Morning,' Nama said.

'Aye,' Eline muttered, and smiled as the girl put a mug of small beer in her hand.

'Get that down you,' Nama said. 'It'll do you good.'

It would, Eline knew. She drank, and settled gratefully into a chair opposite her friend.

'Where's the money?' she asked.

'In your chest,' Nama said. 'You won it fair and square, after all.'

She smirked though, and Eline had to laugh.

'Did I fuck,' she said, and laughed. 'Half of that is yours, the way I see it.'

'Good of you,' Nama said. 'Like I said last night though, although I doubt you remember it, how does this help the colonel? You were so out of it you were on about inviting him for dinner.'

'Wasn't out of it,' Eline said. 'Not then, anyway. Fuck knows what I said after that, but I meant that bit. Find me a pen and paper, will you?'

Nama shook her head in obvious bewilderment and went away into the inn, and came back a few minutes later with paper and ink and wax, a freshly sharpened quill and a sifter of sand.

'Dinner here, you mean?' she said, handing them over.

'Don't see why not,' Eline said. 'I want a quiet word with him, away from prying eyes and flapping ears, and the inn has a private dining room.'

'Why, though?'

'I've made more than enough to pay off his debts now, I must have done even if I *did* take some of it off him last night, and may that teach him a lesson. The baron said he wanted some sense frightened into him. I reckon we can do that, you and me.'

'You think so?' Nama asked. 'Do you know just how in debt he actually is?'

'Well, no,' Eline admitted, and then she thought about it.

Really *thought* about it, through the new lens of what she had seen and learned in Dannsburg since they had been there. She must have won at least twenty crowns last night if not more, a truly prodigious sum as far as she was concerned, and the gods only knew how much silver on top, but the colonel's words kept coming back to her.

Only a crown. It's just a friendly few hands. Raise. Double up.

Like it was pocket change.

What did a high-stakes game run to among the aristocracy, truly? She dreaded to think. He could be *hundreds* of crowns in debt for all she knew.

'Perhaps not,' she confessed at last. 'All right then, change of plan. We frighten him, then we find out who his creditors are and we frighten *them*. At the very least.'

Nama looked at her, and sighed.

'We're going to have to kill them, aren't we?'

'Yes,' Eline said. 'Almost certainly. That, I think, is what the baron is really paying us for.'

Nama fell silent and Eline carefully penned a letter to Colonel Bakrylov care of the castle, and most cordially invited him to dine with her at her lodgings at the Bountiful Harvest that evening. At least the Harvest was one of the most expensive inns in the capital, so that carried a certain cachet in its own right. That done, she sealed it with his great-uncle's house seal, which should be enough to almost guarantee his acceptance if only through curiosity, and gave it and a silver penny to the innkeeper to have a boy deliver it.

'Also,' she said to the man, 'I would plead the use of the inn's private dining room this evening, a decent menu and suitable footmen. I am entertaining a guest. Put it on my bill, of course.'

The innkeeper looked dubiously at her, and Eline placed a gold crown on the counter to put an end to *that*.

Yes, I can afford it, thank you very much, she thought, in her courtesan's voice.

A crown would keep her and her party at the inn treated like royalty for at least another month, and she could well afford it now, indeed.

'Ma'am,' the innkeeper said respectfully, and rang a bell to summon a houseman to go out and find a suitable runner.

So inefficient, Eline couldn't help but think, when he could simply have retained a messenger on the house staff for next to nothing compared to what the place charged a night. So many of the workings of monied society, she had noticed, were monstrously inefficient.

When you had enough, she supposed, in fact that staggeringly much *more* than enough, it didn't really matter, but it still annoyed her for no reason she could have clearly expressed. Having been dirt-poor herself, she felt every copper spent should be spent *efficiently*, and on the right things. Those who had been born to wealth and privilege obviously felt differently.

She felt the germ of an idea begin to form at the back of her mind then, although at that hour of the morning she wasn't able to coax it out to full fruition.

She sighed and went back to the common room to finish her small beer with Nama.

'How do you feel, anyway?' Nama asked her as she regained her seat. 'I never . . . Well, never actually did that before.'

Eline looked at her. 'Never did *what* before, exactly?'

'Stole someone else's strength, like I did to you last night.'

'Then how did you know what would happen?'

'I don't rightly know,' Nama confessed. 'I know if I did it too often or for too long you'd sicken and die. Didn't know . . . Well, I didn't know exactly how long that was.'

'And Kurt didn't fucking explain that rather important point to you?'

'Kurt didn't explain *any* of it to me, other than that's how to make the cunning work when it doesn't want to,' Nama said, and she lowered her eyes. 'Don't know how I know, but it ain't from him. The rats told me, maybe.'

Eline drained her beer and sighed.

'Rats don't talk, Nama.'

'They do to me,' the girl said. 'Lovely things, rats are. They tell me things. Sometimes, anyway. They say in a city you're never more than six feet away from a rat.'

'Yes, I've heard that before and might be it's true but listen to yourself, woman. You sound absolutely insane.'

Nama shrugged, and again Eline felt the beginning of an idea.

'That thing you did before, with the rats,' she said. 'Calling them. When we fought those highwaymen back in Drathburg, you remember. Reckon you could do that again?'

'Oh yes,' Nama said. 'Easy, now. They'll come when I call.'

Eline looked at the dreamy expression on her friend's face, and swallowed.

'Perhaps it's my turn to be a bit scared of *you*, now,' she said. 'Nama, are they real rats? Like, from the alleys and the sewers or whatever? Or, you know, *not*?'

'Don't know,' Nama confessed. 'Look, Eline, I've said this before. I can do it, but that doesn't mean I know *how* I do it, does that make sense? I call the rats and the rats come. Where they come *from* exactly, well. That's a deeper question than I can answer. One for your priest, perhaps.'

Oh aye, Eline could just imagine herself on her knees in the chapel of Our Lady, kneeling before Father Shepherd and asking him where the magic rats came from. He'd have had her reported to the Church authorities for witchcraft and carted off to the city madhouse before she could even ask for the Lady's blessing.

'I don't think so, somehow,' she said. 'Anyway, we'll have the colonel for dinner tonight and get some information out of him, put the fear into him one way or another, then we'll see about these creditors of his.'

'Have him for dinner?' Nama said, and laughed. 'Don't think he'd like that.'

'Oh, you know what I bloody mean,' Eline said, but she had to laugh too. She had a sudden mental image of the colonel's butchered corpse

227

spread out on a huge platter on a vast dinner table, roasted and ready to eat with an apple in his mouth, and she didn't find that funny at *all*.

Where *that* thought had come from she didn't know, but she saw the sudden sparkle of mirth in Nama's eyes and she wondered.

Oh, how she wondered what that girl could do.

Chapter 31

Of course it was a fucking disaster.

She was sitting at the head of the table in the private dining room with Nama seated subserviently at her left hand, a fresh white linen cloth spread on the table and all the good plate and silverware set out, when a footman knocked discreetly on the door.

'Your guests, ma'am,' he announced.

'Show him in,' Eline said, and perhaps she was still a bit sleepy and hadn't been listening as well as she should have been, but Nama wasn't.

'*Guests*?' she hissed at Eline. 'We only invited the—'

Two men pushed passed the footman into the room and shut the door in his face, and one quickly reached down to bolt it behind him.

Neither of them was Bakrylov.

This, Eline realised suddenly, had gone horribly wrong.

'Who in the world—' she started, but the one who seemed to be in charge laughed to cut her off.

He wore a rich red brocade coat like a lord and a ruffled white shirt under his doublet, and he had a long, wickedly curved knife at his belt. The other, the one who had bolted the door, was dressed in black and could have been anyone, plain-faced and placid.

'I think,' Red Coat said, 'the emissaries of Baron Lan Elenkov are about to find their evening has well and truly gone to the whores. Unfortunate expression I know, given your professions. Life can be so cruel, sometimes.'

'Where's the colonel?' Eline demanded.

'On his way to Messia, at the head of a fresh garrison,' the man said. 'Urgent orders from the Crown. I fear the peace has not held. Don't feel snubbed; your invitation never reached him, and there is one less messenger

229

boy on the streets of Dannsburg than there was this morning. That, *my lady*, is not your problem. We are.'

Eline's heart sank as she realised she'd got that poor boy killed, but she forced herself to swallow the hurt.

'Are you?' Eline asked him. 'And why's that then?'

'Because we are here, and because your nose and the nose of your illegitimate employer have been poking into places where we do not wish them poked. The throne of Immalia has no tolerance for sedition, or false claimants.'

Oh gods, Eline thought, *using the baron's seal had been a fucking terrible idea.*

'You're Marodievans, then?'

'We are loyal servants of the Immalian throne. The two are the same thing these days, can't you get that through your thick whore head?'

Eline's blades were in her hands a heartbeat later.

'Oh dear,' the man said, and drew his knife. 'I thought you might do that.'

'Nama!' Eline shouted, just as Nama shouted, 'He shines!'

'No,' said the man in black, and he gave Nama a savage look.

She flew backwards across the room and crashed into the wall, seemingly pinned there by invisible nails.

Eline flipped her blades over in her hands and adopted the first posture. The man in red immediately dropped into a fighting stance of his own.

'Ah,' he said as he saw how she held her stilettoes. 'Like that, is it?'

'It might be,' Eline said, and went for him with no warning at all.

He deflected one of her blades with his knife and swayed out of the way of the other, then he struck back with almost blinding speed. Eline dodged but in truth only just, and she felt the very tip of his hooked blade slice through the sleeve of her dress as she spun away.

Fuck, he's fast! she thought with mounting horror. She had never fought a truly skilled opponent before, and this bloke was obviously every bit as good as she was. Quite possibly better, in fact. She chanced a glance across the room as she spun again, and saw Nama was still pinned to the wall, and the other man was still staring at her. It seemed holding her with his own cunning was taking his full concentration, thus the two of them had effectively cancelled each other out.

You and me, then, Eline thought.

She whirled and caught the man a glancing cut across the cheek, enough to bring blood but not enough to do serious damage. He remained silent, not a cry or a curse, and almost took Eline's throat out with a strike she barely saw coming. She hurled herself backwards in the very nick of time, and in that moment realised she was eventually going to lose. She was tiring already, and he quite obviously was not.

'Think about rats!' Nama screamed at her.

Eline, breathless now, kicked a chair over in her opponent's path and thought about rats as hard as she possibly could. Rats, hordes of them, black and brown and grey with naked pink tails, chittering and squealing and . . . A wave of sudden exhaustion hit her like a hammer, and she staggered against the side of the table.

They came down the chimney, boiling out into the room in a great furry tide of teeth and claws and furious animal hatred.

'The fuck?' the man shouted, and moment later he was covered in rats.

He screamed and flailed about with his blade to no avail, howling as he was gradually overcome. The other man whipped around and raised his hands as more rats bore down on him.

Nama, suddenly released by his broken concentration, grinned savagely.

'Oh no you don't,' she said, and put an explosive bolt of fire through the back of the man's head.

Eline collapsed, and everything went black.

When she came round she was sitting propped up against the wall, and the girl was crouched down beside her with a concerned look on her face. The rats were gone.

The corpses very much were not.

'Oh, thank the gods,' Nama said. 'I thought I'd killed you, for a moment there.'

'How long was I out?'

'Maybe ten minutes. A footman knocked to ask if everything was all right, what with the shouting and that, but I lied and said your guests were just drunk, and nothing to worry about. Gods, I really did think you were dead. I couldn't feel a pulse.'

Eline smiled weakly.

'Do you know how to check a pulse?'

'No, not really,' Nama confessed. 'Want a brandy?'

'Gods, yes. What the fuck *happened*?'

Nama poured for them both from one of the bottles on the cupboard then helped Eline to her feet and into a chair. She put her drink down on the table in front of her.

Eline just clutched the glass for a moment, then swallowed the contents in a single burning draught. Nama, who had had the sense to bring the bottle to the table with her, refilled it at once.

'That little shit had me completely pinned,' she said. 'I couldn't really do *anything*, but I remembered what you said about the rats, and could I call them again. I mean yes, but I had hardly any strength at all with how hard he was holding me. I had to steal the lot, from you I mean, all in one go. Oh fuck, Eline, I really truly thought I'd killed you!'

'Well, you didn't,' Eline said, and put her hand on the back of Nama's for a moment and gave it a reassuring squeeze. 'That cunt nearly did, though. I'd never have taken him, Nama. He was just too good.'

'We're a team,' Nama reminded her. 'Between us, I don't reckon there's much we can't do.'

'Aye, I hope so,' Eline said. 'We need to get back to Drathburg, sharpish. I well and truly fucked up by using the baron's seal on that thrice-damned invitation. I've probably gone and put him in danger, Nama.'

Nama let out a shaky laugh.

'Small problem,' she pointed out. 'We are sitting in the private dining room of one of the poshest inns in the entire capital city, with two ruined corpses for company. I don't think there's any amount of money will make the innkeeper overlook that little fact.'

'Fuck,' Eline said. 'I'm so groggy I hadn't even thought of that.'

She looked at the bodies. The one Nama had shot was virtually headless. The other one . . . She looked away, and tried not to think about it. She put her head in her hands and shuddered violently for a moment.

Bodies burning in a field of fire. Body torn to bloody rags by spectral rats. I killed my husband.

'Can't you burn them away to ash?' Eline asked at last.

'Afraid not,' Nama said. 'That takes a ridiculous amount of heat, and I just can't do it. Best I could manage is hideously burned meat, and that doesn't help us. Besides, even if I could it would burn the fucking inn down, and we don't want that.'

'Fucking *fuck!*' Eline shouted, and slammed down another brandy. 'Think, Eline. Fucking *think*, woman!'

She racked her brains for names, people she had heard of, people she knew about, searching for someone who could help. She couldn't go to the house of law, that was obvious, as she had absolutely no way to prove that she worked for Luka. That would be signing her own death warrant and no mistake. There must be *someone* though, someone who . . . What had that jeweller said about the bodies she and Gregori had left in her shop? *There's a man, Leonov, who works for Mr Iagin*, that was it. She gasped as she suddenly remembered where she had heard the name Iagin before, and a slow smile spread across her face.

'I think I have an idea,' she said.

'I fucking hope so,' Nama said.

'Give me a moment.'

Eline got carefully to her feet and paused to put a hand to her head for a moment. Once she had steadied herself she slipped out of the room, closing the door swiftly behind her. She located the innkeeper in the common room and took him discreetly to one side to speak to him in a low voice.

'Tell me,' she said, 'do you perhaps know a man called Leonov?'

'I . . . might have heard the name,' the innkeeper said, going a little pale.

'Know how to get a message to him? An urgent one, I mean.'

The man sighed, obviously remembering the whole gold crown she had so recently given him.

'Yes,' he admitted.

'Good,' Eline said. 'Please invite him here as my guest with the utmost speed. Mention Mr Iagin's name.'

The man went white, and gaped at her like a freshly landed fish.

'At once, Lady Eline,' he said. 'I assure you, at once.'

'Thank you,' Eline said quietly, and returned to the private dining room to join Nama for another brandy.

'And?' Nama asked.

'Help is on its way, or so I very much hope,' she said, 'although I think I've just put the fox in the henhouse using *that* name.'

Nama frowned. 'What?'

'Names can be magic words, in their way,' Eline said. 'Mentioning the right name to the right person can work miracles.'

The miracle worked itself in a little over an hour, and three men walked into the room. One, obviously the leader, wore a very rich, dark coat of the sort favoured by businessmen, which Eline knew was a friendly euphemism for gangsters. The other two were huge and obviously his muscle.

The man in the coat, this Leonov, took in the scene at a glance and didn't seem at all bothered by it.

'You appear to have a problem, Lady Eline,' he said. 'Two problems, in fact.'

'Yes,' Eline said.

'I have a problem too,' said Leonov. 'That problem is how you know my name, and far more to the point how the *fuck* do you know Iagin?'

'I don't,' Eline admitted, 'but I work for a man who does.'

'And who's that then?'

'Luka, in Drathburg.'

Leonov laughed then, and reached out to shake her hand.

'Ah, I know Luka,' he said. 'So, you're not a Queen's Man but you work for one and can't prove it, yes? There, my lady, we have a great deal in common.'

'Thank the gods,' Nama said.

Leonov blinked at her. 'And you are?'

'Nama,' she said. 'I work for Luka as well.'

'Good,' Leonov said. 'Now, I assume you want this to go away?'

'No, I thought I'd parade the bodies through the fucking common room,' Eline snapped at him. 'Yes, of course I want this to go away.'

Leonov sighed. 'All I ever seem to do these days is lose bodies for people. I'll have the fattest pigs south of the river in no time, at this rate.'

'I should make a confession,' Eline said. 'The jeweller's shop . . . That was me, as well.'

'Thanks,' Leonov said, 'I can stop bloody looking now, then. What are you, a one-woman invasion?'

'Well, not *just* me,' Eline explained. 'My coachman as well.'

'Famously dangerous, coachmen are,' he said, and laughed again. 'If I needed any more convincing that you work for the Service that would have done it. All right, I'll send a dray cart and some lads who know how to be quiet. We'll get this cleaned up for you and say no more about it.'

'Thank you,' Eline said, and she meant it.

'Well,' Nama said, once the men had left, 'it seems working for the Queen's Men does have certain advantages.'

'Too right,' Eline said. 'The innkeeper would have fed us to the City Guard otherwise. We just need to keep him out of here until Leonov's quiet lads have been and gone, and taken our problems away with them.'

She swayed on her feet then, and had to grab at the back of a chair to keep from falling.

'Mate, you are fucked,' Nama said. 'Go to bed, I'll take care of it.'

Eline blinked at her. 'You sure?' she asked, but in truth she could hardly keep her eyes open.

'Certain,' Nama said. 'All I've got to do is let them in. Go on, bed.'

'Aye,' Eline said. 'Thank you.'

She left her friend to it and hauled herself up the stairs to her room. She barely had time to get undressed before she collapsed into bed, and was asleep in seconds.

Gods, that was close, she remembered thinking as she drifted off, and then nothing more.

Chapter 32

The next morning found Eline in the common room with Nama, having lunch together although in truth she had only just dragged herself out of bed.

'How did it go?' she asked quietly.

'Fine,' Nama said. 'Leonov's lads parked their cart in the yard and came in the back way through the kitchens. I let them into the dining room through the serving door, and they wrapped our problems up in sacking and took them out the same way. Never said a word. I was up half the night cleaning, mind, but I found a bucket and a scrubbing brush in the kitchens. Reckon we've got away with it, for as close as the innkeeper is likely to want to look anyway. I just spread it around that we got a bit rowdy last night, to explain the noise.'

'Well, our friend said they knew how to be quiet,' Eline said. 'Perhaps he meant it literally. I can see how mute servants could be useful, for work like that.'

'I suppose so, although I can't say I'd ever have thought of that,' Nama said. 'You really have taken to being a spy or agent or whatever you are, haven't you?'

Eline just snorted, and tucked into her food.

'What are we doing this afternoon?' Nama asked.

'Bugger all if I can help it,' Eline said. 'Twelve straight hours' sleep and I'm still shattered. I'll have to try to get one of the maids to take my good dress to a seamstress and have that torn sleeve mended, though. It's the best dress I've got. I'd do it myself if I wasn't so bloody tired. Still, at least I can afford to have plenty more made up now, once we get back to Drathburg.'

'I'll do it,' Nama said. 'You rest. I'm sorry, Eline, truly I am.'

'Well don't be,' Eline said in surprise. 'For the gods' sakes don't feel guilty about this, Nama. I'd have been dead in a minute or two more if you hadn't done what you did.'

'Do you really think so?'

'I fucking *know* so,' Eline assured her. 'He was better than me, simple as that, not to mention faster and stronger. However good you are there is always someone better, you remember that. I sure as fuck couldn't take Marcoss in a real fight, for example; I know that much.'

'Aye, I suppose not,' Nama said. 'Look, if anything like that ever happens again, kill the cunning man first next time, aye? Leave the rest to me.'

Eline nodded. 'Good plan,' she said.

She gave Nama her dress to have seen to, then curled up on her bed with the inn's copy of *Aecharias and Meledia*. She was asleep again before she knew it.

She was awoken some two hours later by a rap on her door. She sat up and blinked herself to awareness, and found she did seem to be starting to feel better now she'd had yet more sleep.

She opened the door to find Gregori in the hallway outside.

'What is it?' she asked.

'Miss Nama said you were wanting to go back to Drathburg,' he said.

'Yes,' she said. 'First thing tomorrow, if that's all right with you.'

'Fine,' he said. 'I'll get and see to the coach and harness then, so we can get a good early start in the morning.'

'Thank you,' she said, and yawned again.

Perhaps she wasn't quite there yet after all, but it seemed she wasn't getting any more rest.

'Oh, and there are two gentlemen downstairs asking for you,' Gregori added, as though that hadn't been his main reason for waking her. 'I wouldn't keep them waiting, if I were you.'

It was never going to be that easy, was it? Nothing ever fucking was. Eline sighed and nodded, and went to the mirror over her washstand to tidy her hair. That done, she headed down to the common room.

She spotted Leonov at once, and he had another man with him.

This man was a lot older, in his sixties at least, with thinning grey hair and a great white moustache that all but covered his mouth. He wore a sombre black coat and a thick black leather doublet worked with a pattern of vines and thorns, and he had a mug of beer in his hand.

Leonov saw her as soon as she came down the stairs and waved her over to their table.

'Leonov,' she said, as she took a seat at their table and accepted a welcome glass of wine from an unusually attentive footman. 'I thank you for your assistance last night, but I hadn't thought to see you again.'

'My employer wanted to meet you,' Leonov explained. 'May I present—'

'You'll be Iagin, then,' Eline interrupted.

'Aye,' the older man said. 'I am indeed. I run every inn, stew, bathhouse, gaming house and protection racket in this fucking city. I am *Mr* Iagin, to the many and various low-lifes of Dannsburg, and absolutely no one fucks with me.'

'I'm sure they don't,' Eline said as she met the gangster's steely glare. 'But that's not all you are, is it?'

'No,' Iagin conceded. 'I carry something that you would recognise, something I'm sure I don't need to cause a scene by showing you here.'

'I know what the Warrant looks like,' Eline assured him quietly. 'You're a Queen's Man, aren't you?'

Iagin snorted.

'I was there when we swore Luka into the Service, and he almost shat himself at the initiation,' he said. 'I've been a Queen's Man for fucking decades.'

'I thought so,' she said. 'I remembered Luka mentioning your name, in some matter of disinformation.'

'That's what I'm best at,' Iagin admitted, 'but it's far from all I know how to do. Leonov told me what happened last night, Eline, at least as best as he could describe it. It sounded like one of those problems of yours had been fucking half-eaten, and that ain't usual.'

'That's because it had been,' Eline said, holding his gaze steadily. 'I have a cunning woman. She's very good with rats.'

'Thought so,' Iagin said. 'You seem like a resourceful woman, Eline.'

'Perhaps I am,' she said, and held her peace.

You don't scare me, she told herself, for all that he really should have done.

Show any fear, any weakness at all to a man like that and you were done, she knew. Caromir had taught her that much.

No.

No, she was absolutely not fucking having it.

This man, this gangster and Queen's Man, even on his home turf, was *not* putting the fear into her and that was all there was to it. She simply was not having it. Never again.

'What do you actually want?' she asked after a long silent moment had passed.

'You,' Iagin said bluntly. 'If you ever get fed up with working for Luka you come back here and present yourself at the house of law and you ask for me. I'll leave your name and description with the door guards, and they keep records of referrals for *years*, Eline. A referral from a Queen's Man is *very* rare, and not a thing to be forgotten. You ever want a job in Dannsburg, you've got one with me.'

'Thank you,' Eline said, 'but I already have more than enough work as it is.'

'Just bear it in mind,' Iagin said, and he drained his beer and got to his feet with Leonov at his heels like a faithful hound. 'See you again, perhaps,' he said, and the two of them left the inn.

They were on the road shortly after breakfast. Nama had collected Eline's good dress from the seamstress, and they had been all packed and ready to go before they ate. The journey home was as slow and dull as the last time. At least no one attacked them this time, she supposed that was something, but Eline found that the supposed pleasure of travel was entirely lost on her.

Still, she got plenty of opportunity to rest, and by the time they finally reached the gates of Drathburg she was feeling as good as she ever did.

The Guard sergeant heard her say 'The Lady Eline' in her cut-glass accent, and waved them through with no charge and no questions asked.

The power of the aristocracy never ceased to amaze Eline, or to repulse her. She still wasn't sure which it was. Either way she wasn't asked to pay the gate toll. It wasn't much longer before Gregori pulled their carriage up in the stable yard of the House of Silver Bells.

'Thank you,' she said to him as Pavel started to unload their luggage. 'Stay a while, if you can. I think I'll have want of you shortly.'

Gregori just shrugged. 'His nibs won't even know we're back yet, so no bother to me.'

He sat back on his coachman's box and started to doze. The weather on the way home had been foul, and Eline supposed that after the best part of a dozen days' driving he was exhausted. The poor horses weren't faring any better, she was sure, but at her words he kept them hitched and just waited while the stable boys brought them water and bags of grain.

She and Nama went into the house through the back way, and they met Loran in the hall.

'You're back at last, then,' he said.

'Aye,' Eline said. 'Madame said we could go, you know that.'

He just grunted at that.

'She wants you,' he said to Eline. 'She said as soon as you showed your face. That means now, girlie.'

'Gods,' Eline muttered, but she supposed she had little enough choice. 'Bags to our rooms, please,' she told Pavel, then followed Loran to Madame's study.

He knocked brusquely on the door. 'She's back,' he called out.

'Come,' Madame called from within, and he opened the door and ushered her into her mistress's presence.

'Ma'am,' Eline said, and dipped Madame a small curtsey in an obeisance that she really didn't feel any more.

She and Nama had killed how many men since she had been away? Four, five? More than that, she thought. She had quite honestly lost count, and that in itself told her a lot about how much she had changed in service to the Rose Throne. Nama had been right though, they *had* become a team.

'How was Dannsburg?' Madame asked her through gritted teeth, in a way that told Eline she already knew exactly how it had been.

A lone messenger on horseback travelled a lot faster than a laden carriage did, of course, so in all honesty she probably did.

'We made it back,' Eline said. 'So could have been worse.'

'Could have been a *fucking* sight better though, couldn't it?' Madame shouted at her.

'Yes, ma'am,' Eline admitted.

The older woman snorted in irritation. 'Oh, for the love of the gods, go and speak to the baron,' she said. 'He's expecting you.'

If the messenger, whoever they had been, had reached Drathburg before she had then Eline supposed he would be, at that. And he was *not* going to be pleased with her. Not one little bit he wasn't.

'Yes, ma'am,' she said again. 'I will.'

'Now,' Madame said. 'Not tomorrow, not after supper, fucking *now*.'

Eline curtseyed again and left.

Nama was upstairs supervising Pavel and their unpacking, so Eline left her to it and hurried back to the stable yard and Gregori. She gave him an address that wasn't the baron's, and climbed back into the carriage.

'We'll just have to do without Pavel,' she said. 'This won't wait.'

'As you say, ma'am,' Gregori said, and flicked the reins to get his team moving.

They drew up outside Luka's house not long after, and Eline bade Gregori wait as she climbed down from the carriage.

'Wait here,' she said.

'Well don't be too long, ma'am, I'm half blocking the road,' he said. 'If the Guard come by I'll get moved on.'

'I don't think I'll be long at all,' Eline told him.

She rapped on the door and was admitted by Sam.

'Eline,' he said, and a wide smile crossed his face as he took her in. 'Thought you'd gone away.'

'I did, Sam lad,' she said. 'I came back.'

'Nice one,' Sam said, and smiled again to say he meant it. 'Boss is in the back if you want him.'

Eline couldn't imagine why on earth else he thought she would have been there otherwise, but she patted him on the arm anyway and hurried down the hall to Luka's inner sanctum.

'I'm back,' she said as she opened the door.

'I know,' Luka said. 'Thought you were supposed to be going straight to Lan Elenkov's?'

'I am,' Eline said. 'I'm on my way now, in fact. I wanted to bring you up to date first, is all.'

'I know most of it already,' Luka said, and again she remembered that messengers were a lot faster than carriages. 'Leonov told Iagin, and Iagin told me. That's how this works, Eline. Fucking good job remembering his name, though. Reckon that saved your skin.'

'Reckon it did,' Eline agreed. 'There's this, though: I fucked up.'

'Oh, you do surprise me,' Luka said. 'What did you do?'

'I needed to get Bakrylov to come to a private meeting,' she admitted, 'and I'd only met him once. No reason for him to come, or to trust me. I . . . sent him a formal invitation to dinner, of course, but I used his great-uncle the baron's seal. To get his attention, you underst—'

'You fucking stupid bitch!' Luka roared at her. 'You used Lan Elenkov's seal, in *Dannsburg* of all places? You think messengers aren't apprehended on the streets every fucking day? Everyone wants to know who's writing to who, that's how espionage fucking *works*, Eline. You told every cunt in Dannsburg who matters that fucking Lan Elenkov was involved? I could quite happily gut you for that!'

There is always someone better, Eline remembered telling Nama, but she knew instinctively that Luka wasn't one of them and for all his size neither was Sam.

'I'd like to see you try,' she said in a voice like winter.

'You know you got that messenger lad killed, don't you?' Luka said, with what felt to Eline like unnecessary spite.

'Yes, Luka, I fucking well do,' she said. And she'd regretted it ever since.

He met the steel in her eyes, her gaze like ice and torment and impending retribution, and he looked away.

'Aye, well,' he said, in a more temperate voice. 'Best you go and tell your baron all about it then, isn't it?'

'I think it is,' Eline said, and she turned on her heel and stalked out of the room before she said or did anything he would really regret.

Thankfully Gregori and the carriage were still there, and she pulled herself back up into it and told him to take her to the baron's house. He would already know what had happened, she was sure, or at least most of it. The messenger who had called on Madame had almost certainly been his, and would naturally have reported to him first. She dreaded to think how furious he was going to be.

She disembarked as the carriage drew up once again, and was admitted by a footman who had clearly been told to expect her.

'Lady Eline,' he said, and offered her a short bow. 'The baron awaits you in his study.'

He showed her the way as protocol dictated although she already knew it well enough, and opened the door for her.

'My lord,' he said, 'the Lady Eline.'

'Yes, yes thank you,' the baron said, and waved him away. 'Come in, my dear.'

Eline stepped into the room and the footman closed the door behind her. She curtseyed. 'Baron,' she said.

'Yes, yes. Brandy's on the cupboard where it always is, and I'll have a refill while you're about it. My knee is bloody killing me.'

Eline poured a fresh drink into the baron's glass and took one for herself, ignoring his façade. Perhaps his knee really did hurt, she wouldn't know, but she doubted it and even if it did she was fucking sick of hearing about it. His entire personality was a mummer's show except in the rare moments when he was actually *himself*, and then he was quite frankly terrifying.

'Well, that's done, then,' she said. 'Sort of, anyway.'

The baron looked up from behind his desk and met her eyes, then looked pointedly at a chair.

'Sit, for the love of the gods,' he said, and Eline did as she was told. 'What have you done with my great-nephew? He seems to have disappeared altogether now.'

'He's on his way to Messia, leading a regiment to be a new garrison of occupation,' she said. 'Orders direct from the Crown, so I hear, although fuck knows who that even is anymore. I gather the peace has not held. At least his creditors won't be able to follow him there.'

'Indeed not,' the baron said, and smiled. 'Sometimes, Eline, in matters of war or intrigue or espionage, one has to have more than one iron in the fire. It seems His Highness the Prince Regent has come through for me. And my great-nephew's Marodievan creditors?'

'I left at least five of them dead,' Eline said. 'Eight, if you count the three we met on the road. And the rest are hardly going to follow him into what is in all probability by now a war zone, for all that the government are no doubt pretending otherwise.'

Gods, was it so many? she thought, and realised that it was, if not perhaps even more than that. Well, her and Nama and Gregori between them, anyway.

'Yes of course they are,' the baron said. 'The palace will never admit that the Messian truce has collapsed, but that's hardly our problem. Well done, by the way. Was there anything else?'

Eline flushed and swallowed her brandy, then had to confess to having used his seal the same way she had confessed it to Luka.

His reaction couldn't have been more different.

The baron laughed, and clapped his hands together with almost childish joy.

'That was staggeringly stupid of you,' he had to allow, 'but at the same time exactly what I wanted when I gave it to you. No, don't take offence, my dear, you've done well. Very well indeed.'

'I don't follow,' Eline said, irritated. Surely there couldn't be a way in which her foolish act had been of use.

'I wanted the Rose Throne to know I was active not only in Immalia, but in Dannsburg as well. I had hoped your using it at the bank, as I well knew you would have to, would have reached the ears of the Queen's Men at least. But on a letter to Bakrylov, of all people? That was absolutely perfect. He's been in the pay of the house of law for years. It's them backing his debts, because their Provost Marshal owes him an old favour. With him exposed as a relative of mine, thanks to your glorious blunder, he's compromised. That forces the Prince Regent's hand and makes him take action in my favour, which he has evidently already done. Well done, my dear, if entirely by accident. This really is fun now.'

'So . . .' Eline started, completely confused now. 'I didn't fuck up after all?'

'Oh no,' the baron said, 'no, you fucked up magnificently, but in exactly the way I wanted you to.'

'But . . .' Eline said, utterly confused now. 'I mean, if they back-track . . . I didn't have to pay the gate tax to enter Dannsburg, obviously, but they took note of my name and my city of origin. If the Marodievans are at all competent, they'll have someone inside the Guard. They can—'

'Oh, they are, and they will,' he assured her. 'It might take them a day or two, but they will soon work out exactly who you were, where you came from, and what you did when you got there. The same as you and Luka did with your man Milev, and yes I *do* know all about that. I am a *king*, Eline, and I have a *very* good spy network. Much better than Luka's, in fact, and I think he knows that.'

'But then the Marodievans will find you!' Eline said with sudden urgency. 'And I thought you didn't really know Luka?'

'Lied about that, didn't I? Well, I know *about* him, anyway. I don't think we've ever actually met. The Queen's Man in the city I live in? Of course I know about him, Eline,' Lan Elenkov said. 'We can't be seen to speak for obvious political reasons, but rest assured I have him watched as he has recently started having *me* watched. This is the game we play, Eline. And yes, they will find me, and the captain of my Royal Guard and his men will be waiting for them when they get here. And now, thanks to you, I have the Queen's Men on my side whether Luka likes it or not, which I assure you he won't. Not one little bit. I'm going to exterminate these bastards once and for all. With the Marodievans wiped out in this country, I can come out into the open and see about finally getting my country back.'

'Captain of your Royal Guard?' Eline asked, suddenly bewildered. 'You are a king without a country, I didn't know you *had* a Royal Guard. Who is this captain of yours?'

The baron showed her a lazy smile and swallowed his brandy.

'Tell me, my dear,' he said, 'do you perhaps know a man called Marcoss?'

Chapter 33

Oh gods, it was starting to make sense now. Marcoss, and the unreasonable number of guards at the Silver Bells. They were Lan Elenkov's, all of them. They *were* his Royal Guard. Eline had *known* there were far too many guards on the place for a simple brothel, however expensive it was. She had *known* something was off, from the very start. Marcoss, the only man she had ever heard call Madame by her given name. Marcoss was the captain of the Royal Guard of a king in exile, of the Baron Lan Elenkov or the rightful King of Immalia, depending on a certain fucking point of view.

Politics absolutely drove her mad, it really did. Nothing was ever bloody simple, was it? Madame with her 'my good friend the baron'; she fucking worked for him, didn't she? Probably had done since their Poppy Winds days, and only now was Eline seeing it.

'I could scream sometimes,' she snarled.

'Ah, so could I,' the baron said, and reached for the bottle to refill their glasses. 'The trouble is, Eline, screaming does very little good. Ranting and raving at the governing council does even less good, as the vast majority of them are in the pay of the house of law and most of those don't know who else is. They are bribed and blackmailed into voting one way or another, frequently against each other when the house of law wants a motion held up in procedure and nothing decided so they can carry on indefinitely and do whatever they like in the background. That's how the Queen's Men *work*, Eline. Total control. This country is a democratic constitutional monarchy with no monarch, a constitution that's four hundred years out of date, and a so-called democracy where only officers and the gentry get a vote at all. It's a bloody farce, don't you see that? The house of law, the Queen's Men, rule this country. They write the law themselves, and they are themselves above it.'

Eline sighed.

'I'm sure you're right, my lord,' she said, although she couldn't really have given much of a shit about any of it. 'But to bring matters back to the present, what happens next?'

'Next?' the baron said, collecting himself. 'Oh, someone tries to kill me. They'll try very hard, I would imagine, and very soon. Unfortunately, this time I don't know who, or when, or where. We will have to prepare for that in the morning.'

'Will it wait that long?' she asked.

'My spies in the Guard will know when a herd of armed foreigners enter the city, we'll have plenty of warning.'

'And who exactly is *we*, in this situation?'

'Luka,' he said at once, 'and his man Sam, and any other men of violence he can bring to me. Luka may not entirely know it yet, but I have already reached an understanding with his masters in the house of law. As I say, he won't like it but he'll do it. The Provost Marshal owes me now, thanks to you. His Highness himself is backing my actions, if covertly. Who else? Well, Marcoss, of course, and by association, all his men. Gorath knows how the land lies, at least, and the rest will just do what they're told. Madame, naturally. You, Nama. Perhaps Kurt, but I'll allow I'm unsure about that one. He doesn't answer to me.'

'That's quite the presumption to be making,' Eline said.

'Yes,' the baron said, and looked at her over his glass. 'It is, isn't it? But are you about to gainsay me in this, Eline?'

'I could,' she said.

He nodded slowly. 'You could,' he agreed. 'But I don't think that you will.'

'Why not?' Eline challenged him.

The baron laughed and drained his glass, and held it out for another refill.

'You've found something to live for,' he said. 'Your children may be safe now, or at least nominally so, if you take the word of the Queen's Men. If you trust *that* you're a fool, as I think I've told you before, but even so now you have something for *yourself*. A reason to be. A mission, one might say.'

Eline shook her head. 'What if I just want a quiet life?'

'You'd go out of your mind with boredom now that you have experienced intrigue,' the baron said. 'Probably faster even than you think you would. Oh, Eline, you are *born* to this life. Embrace it, girl.'

'Please don't call me "girl",' she said. 'I must be almost your grand-daughter's age, and I'm sure you treat her with more respect than that.'

'That's fair, I suppose,' the baron said, and his face hardened as he dropped the act and turned his gaze on her – really turned it on her. Eline shivered. He had the look of a king, hard as ancient granite. 'So, blade dancer, will you dance for me for your *considerable* retainer?' he said, his voice icy.

Eline swallowed, and made her decision.

'Aye,' she said. 'I think I will.'

'What did he want?' Nama asked when Eline was barely through the door of the Bells.

'To humiliate me,' Eline said. 'To call me "girl", and make me feel like a total idiot.'

'Why would he do that?'

'Because it's fucking *fun*, apparently,' she spat. 'He also wants us and Marcoss and a great number of other people who apparently work for him at his house first thing in the morning. Including Madame.'

'*Madame* works for him?' Nama asked, reeling in surprise. 'And *Marcoss*?'

'Apparently,' Eline said.

'Who *is* he?' Nama demanded, but Eline forced herself to shake her head.

'Some cunt,' she said. 'A rich one. That's really all it takes, isn't it?'

'I thought he was supposed to be all but broke?'

'He is,' Eline said. 'Supposed to be, I mean. He tells *lies*, Nama. A lot of them. Trust me, when he sounds drunk, he's almost certainly lying to you. And when he doesn't . . .' She trailed off. 'He's fucking terrifying.'

'What, the *baron*?' Nama said, and Eline could see that she wanted to laugh. 'That wrinkly old lech? You said he couldn't even get it up!'

'Yes, Nama, the baron,' Eline said. 'Don't underestimate him. That's exactly what he wants people to do.'

'But . . .' Nama started, and then Eline could see her thinking. 'He wanted me to do some sort of magic I've never even heard of, but I refused because it sounded like it would have hurt the horses, and in all truth I didn't know how anyway. How had *he* ever heard of it?'

Eline shrugged.

'From his court magician, I can only assume,' she said. She made herself sound like she was laughing, like it was a joke, so that Nama wouldn't know the truth of it.

'But he's only a baron; he hasn't *got* a court!' Nama protested.

'Quite,' Eline said. 'Think about that, Nama. I'm going to bed now.'

'Eline, wait,' Nama said, and Eline paused in the doorway and turned back to look at her.

'What is it?' she asked.

'I—' Nama started, then trailed off and looked at her shoes for a moment. 'I'm scared, Eline. It was fun to start with, but now? All of this. Magic. Politics. *Courts.* I . . . I don't know what to do with it. Any of it. I thought Luka was bad enough, but *this*? This I don't understand at *all*.'

'No,' Eline confessed. 'I'm not sure I understand all of it either.'

'But . . .'

Nama looked so young, so lost in that moment. Eline went to Nama and put a hand on her shoulder in a way she could only pray to Our Lady was comforting.

'We're a team, remember?' she said. 'What was it you said, back in Dannsburg? "Between us, I don't reckon there's much we can't do", wasn't that it? We just have to remember that, and believe in it.'

'Aye, something like that,' Nama said, and offered her a shaky smile.

Gods, she is so much like my own daughter.

Eline swallowed a tear, and cleared her throat. It had all but broken her heart not to be able to risk seeing her own daughter when they had finally been in the same city again. She regretted that, too.

'So long as we stick together we'll be fine,' Eline said, as reassuringly as she could, and she just wished that she could believe it herself.

With that she went up to her room and put herself to bed, and slept for perhaps six uneasy hours before she was awakened by a heavy knock on the door.

She got up and pulled her robe over her nightdress and opened the door. She found Marcoss standing there.

'Morning,' he said. 'You know why I'm here.'

'The baron,' she said at once. 'He's really called it in, hasn't he? All of it, I mean.'

'Yes,' Marcoss said. 'Me, my lads, you and Nama. Even Marie. He's called the knives. This is serious, girl.'

'Madame,' Eline said. 'Is her name really Marie?'

'Does it matter?' Marcoss asked her. 'That's what I call her, and she answers to it. From me, anyway.'

'And is she your boss, or are you hers?'

'Does it matter?' he asked again. 'We both work for the baron.'

'But why would he want *her* today?'

A ruthless businesswoman Madame might well have been, but dangerous in a fight? Eline very much doubted it.

'You think *you* can dance?' Marcoss said. 'Prepare to take a lesson, gypsy girl.'

'At her age?' Eline asked.

Marcoss smiled, his teeth glinting.

'You'll see. Well, I hope you *won't*, but if it all drops in the pot, and I'm afraid the baron and I both very much think that it will, you will most definitely see. Now have a piss, generally sort yourself out, get dressed and meet us in the hall but don't take all day about it.'

Eline did as he said, and strapped her stilettoes to the inside of her forearms before she pulled her loose-sleeved kirtle on over them and headed down the stairs.

Nama joined them a moment later, then Gorath and Loran and a dozen or so of the household guard – the *Royal Guard*, she corrected herself – whom she had seen sporadically around the house. At least half of them were armed with crossbows with spans for reloading and quivers of bolts, and they all wore blades. Then Madame descended, in a long black gown of ruffled silk with her signature tight waist and low neckline. She had what at first seemed to Eline to be an almost comically long fan tucked through her sash, but she suddenly realised that it wasn't.

It was a scabbarded sword. A very thin one, shaped like a single oversized, elongated stiletto.

'Rapier,' Marcoss muttered out of the corner of his mouth, answering her unasked question. 'Different discipline altogether.'

'What in the world . . .' she started, but he cut her off.

'You'll see, or you won't,' he said. 'Best if you don't, all things considered.'

'But you don't think that's likely?'

'No,' he admitted. 'I don't. I think we're killing this morning, gypsy girl.'

'If you call me that again I may start by killing *you*,' Eline said, and he laughed.

'Aye, that's fair,' he said. 'Don't mean nothing by it. It's just how we talked back in the war, you know? Your lads didn't seem to mind.'

'I suppose so,' Eline said, 'but I'd rather you used my name.'

'Names are earned,' Marcoss said, and he turned away to speak to Madame. 'I think that's all of us, Marie. From here, anyway.'

'Yes,' she said. 'We'd better, then, hadn't we?'

'Aye.'

They travelled in a variety of carriages, carts and on horseback until the lot of them descended on the Baron Lan Elenkov's modest terraced townhouse. Eline had wondered how Madame would fight in that long gown until she climbed up into a carriage and Eline saw it was slit almost to the hip on both sides, giving her perfect freedom of movement. Her legs, which Eline had never seen before, were very white, but they looked surprisingly muscular too. She obviously kept herself in shape, even if it didn't show through her usual preposterous gowns. Eline was still struggling to believe the woman could actually fight though, whatever Marcoss might have said.

Sam waited by the door. Eline wished she was surprised but by then she really wasn't.

'Eline,' Sam said, smiling. 'And all these folk.'

'They're friends, Sam,' she said. 'The boss is on board with this.'

Madame shot her a look at that, but Marcoss had obviously already known so what matter? He, it seemed, had been at least Madame's equal at the Silver Bells all along.

'Aye, I know,' Sam said. 'In with you, then.'

He opened the door, and the crossbowmen immediately headed up the stairs to take up commanding positions in the upper windows without needing to be told. There was a bunch of unfamiliar thugs loitering in the hall whom Eline could only assume worked for Luka the way Sam did.

The rest of the men arrayed themselves around the ground floor, covering front and rear entrances, and Marcoss led Madame, Eline and Nama into the drawing room. The baron was sitting well away from the window with Luka, both of them drinking steaming bowls of tea.

'Marcoss,' the baron said. 'Where are the rest of them? I've received word from the gate, the Marodievans are on their way.'

'My lord, I've brought you the strength we have,' Marcoss said. 'I've had to leave a couple of young lads at the Bells for security, obviously, but other than that . . . I'm afraid this *is* the Royal Guard.'

'What have you brought me, fifteen troops?'

'About that, aye. Several specialists, though, and a cunning woman.'

'Against the might of House Marodieva? I don't suppose we have blasting weapons?'

'Sadly not,' Marcoss said. 'Blasting weapons are illegal outside of the army.'

252

'No bombs then, and only fifteen troops?'

'Against the few men they can have smuggled into the city past the Guard,' Marcoss said. 'This isn't open warfare, sire. This will be a quick, brutal strike on you and your house, and can not be allowed to expand from there.'

'Exactly,' Luka said. 'I could have brought the army and a fucking cannon, but that's not what you'd call subtle, is it? This is an attempt on your life, my lord baron. One we will put down with extreme prejudice, and convince House Marodieva never to attempt it again. Direct order from the Provost Marshal himself. You're not winning your country back today, my lord, but you *are* staying alive.'

'I'll have died of old age before I get my country back at this *fucking* rate,' the baron snarled, and there was nothing drunken and nothing endearing about him in that moment, as far as Eline was concerned. 'The Prince Regent promised me—'

'His Highness promised you protection,' Luka said, 'and that he has delivered, for you and your great-nephew both. Do not, my lord baron, put words in the mouth of the Rose Throne. Don't ever do that.'

'I want my country back!' the baron spat, his face red and his eyes fiery, and in that moment Eline didn't recognise him at *all*.

'I dare say you do,' Luka said, 'and in time careful diplomatic interventions and tactical violence may be able to make that possible. Today, my lord, our only objective is to keep you fucking *alive*. You do grasp that, yes?'

'Yes, yes,' the baron sighed. 'Very well. Please convey my gratitude to His Highness for what he has consented to share with me today, at least.'

'I shall,' Luka said, and he turned and looked at Nama. 'I think I want you by the front door.'

'Why?' Nama asked.

'First person tries to storm it that hasn't already got a crossbow bolt through them, fucking cook him. I gather you like fire, so use it.'

'We're expecting a frontal assault?' Eline asked.

'Aye,' Luka said. 'Wish I could have whistled up my City Guard, but of course none of this is officially happening and can't possibly ever be *seen* to have officially happened, so all I could do was make sure they were somewhere else this morning. This is on us, and our many and various talents. You, guard the baron.'

'And Madame?' Eline asked. 'No disrespect, but why the fuck are you here?'

'You'll see,' the older woman said, and patted the hilt of her strange thin sword, her rapier as Marcoss had called it, with a pale hand. 'You dance one dance, Eline, I dance quite another.'

Eline caught the cold edge in the other woman's words, and they made her shiver. Exactly who *were* these people she had been living under the same roof with for the last however long it had been?

'Do you have any further information at all?' Marcoss asked. 'Any idea when it's going to happen?'

'Soon,' the baron said. 'Soon. Truth be told I thought it would have been before—'

The bomb went off with a crack like thunder.

It seemed it was happening right now.

Chapter 34

Eline heard coughing, yelling, but couldn't see much through the clouds of smoke. Fucking frontal assault? These bastards had used blasting powder to come through the wall from the adjoining house next door, the only direction the baron's crossbowmen *couldn't* cover. Dust billowed down the hall, and she heard shouts and the sound of running feet, boots clumping on the wooden floors.

Eline dashed out of the study to help.

'Guard, deploy!' Marcoss bellowed at the top of his voice.

The men on the doors hurried back into the house to face the incoming threat, just as the front door also blew in behind them with a deafening bang and the stench of burned blasting powder as the flashstone went off outside. More enemies stormed into the hall through the smoke.

Nama met them with an inferno of righteous fury.

'Fuck you and *burn!*' she shrieked, fire haloing her body.

She must have killed five, maybe six men in that initial firestorm, so far as Eline could see. She had her blades reversed in her hands by then, and Madame had drawn her long, slender sword. It looked like an oversized stiletto in her hand, or perhaps a giant needle. Either way, it was like no sword Eline had ever seen before.

Marcoss had a short sword in his right hand and a dagger reversed in his left, and it seemed his fighting style was different again. All the same, she could see his weapons were as perfectly designed for fighting in the close confines of a house as hers were, and Madame's as well. The long army sword that Caromir had sworn by would have been all but useless in the baron's narrow hallway, she knew. Not that Caromir had ever actually used his in combat anyway. The right tools for the right job, she supposed, and when killing was your job then weapons were your tools of the trade.

There are so many different ways to kill, Eline thought, as she danced and spun. She wondered then if there were as many ways to live, and found that she didn't know the answer to that.

This is the way I live, now, she thought. *How the fuck did that happen?*

A man rushed her, no one she knew, and she spun and whirled around his sword thrust, and slid a stiletto into his side with a wild cry of triumph. He stumbled back and clutched a hand to his wet, wounded side, and Madame lunged past her and skewered him perfectly through the heart. Her stance was so long that she was up on the ball of her rear foot and her front thigh was almost parallel to the floor, something Eline had never seen before either, but all the same her strange needle of a sword went straight through the man and punched out of his back in a great gout of spraying arterial blood.

He fell dead at their feet, and Eline nodded in respect to Madame, who met her eye with a deadly glint. Eline advanced.

The fighting was thickest in the centre of the house, where the enemies had torn open the walls. She saw Loran fall to a man with a brutal-looking axe, one arm hacked clean off and his head split open, and she found joy in ending the cunt who'd done it. Loran had always been all right to her, all things considered, and avenging his death felt righteous.

This is Our Lady's plan for him, she told herself as she ripped her stiletto out of the man's eye socket. *Death by my hand.* Aye, the Lady had taken her into Her embrace, and there could be no turning back from that.

Eline was, she realised now, one of Hers. There could be no more wondering on that score, it was simple fact.

She saw Luka and Sam in the fighting too, and as she had predicted Sam wasn't as fast as he should have been, but by Our Lady he was strong. She saw him pick two men up by the backs of their doublets and ram their heads together hard enough to smash their skulls.

He threw them aside like puppets with their strings cut, and laughed as though at a job well done.

Oh yes, she thought then, she could value a man like Sam indeed.

Luka fought competently enough, with the solid skill of a veteran, but he had no real flair for it. Eline supposed that his skills lay in other directions, and that was fair enough. The Queen's Men obviously required a diverse spread of skills, and murder was only one of them.

Lightning flashed past her head and hit a man in the face, and that must have been Nama. It seemed she had found a new toy to play with, something more than fire.

The man dropped, screaming in agony, and Eline dived on him and put him out of his misery with her blades.

'The fuck is the baron?' Luka demanded, shouting through the thick of the fighting.

'Don't know,' Eline yelled.

'Fucking find him, you stupid cow! First rule, never lose sight of the principal.'

Eline almost knifed him then, but she realised he had a point. She *was* supposed to be the baron's bodyguard, after all.

The baron was still in the drawing room, sitting in an armchair with his tea bowl set aside and a glass of brandy in his hand even as war was waged in his house.

'Eline,' he said as she shouldered the door open. 'How are things going?'

'Loran's dead,' she said.

'Who?'

'For fuck's sake,' Eline muttered.

Kings! They knew nothing about those who were prepared to fight and die for them, did they? Not one single fucking thing, and they simply didn't care. She turned to go back to the hall, but the baron raised a hand to stay her.

'Stay in here,' the baron said. 'Keep me safe, in case the others fail.'

'Are you shitting me?' Eline asked, her entire courtesan's façade going out of the window in that moment. 'People are *dying* out there, don't you grasp that?'

'Of course I do,' the baron said, 'and that's why I don't want people dying in here. I most specifically don't want *me* dying in here.'

'Can't argue with that, I suppose,' Eline said.

The baron got to his feet then and crossed the drawing room to a large chest by the wall, which he bent to open. He rummaged inside for a moment then came up with a bundle of old red velvet, which he carefully unwrapped. Inside was a sheathed sword, broad-bladed and slightly curved.

'My trusty old cutlass,' he explained as he drew the oiled and obviously well-looked-after blade. 'I might be old and a bit feeble these days but, believe me, I was bloody good with this once upon a time. If it comes to it, I hope one more sword is still better than nothing.'

His eyes glittered, and there was the old pirate in him, shining through like polished steel.

'I'm sure it will be, my lord,' Eline admitted, if somewhat grudgingly.

He had been a devil back in his days on the high seas, after he'd lost his throne, she had absolutely no doubt about that. It seemed Madame had been no better. Perhaps, Eline thought then, even worse.

The door banged open then and Madame herself backed into the room as if summoned, with her long, slender blade up as a man pursued her with a mace in his hand. It seemed a wildly mismatched contest for a moment as the man swung his lump of steel on a stick at her head and she tried to defend herself with her oversized needle. She ducked and dodged and the savage head of the mace smashed into the door, wrecking one of the ornate panels. Madame threw a hand up behind her and lunged, and her rapier went through the centre of his throat with an almost surgical precision.

'Touché, motherfucker,' she said.

The man slumped to the floor and dropped dead at her feet, and she chanced a look over her shoulder at the baron.

'You are safe?' she asked.

'Eline is looking after me wonderfully,' the baron said, and lifted his glass to her in one hand and his cutlas in the other. 'And I am not completely defenceless, Marie.'

'That,' she said, glancing at his cutlass, 'is from a fucking long time ago.'

'Do the savage tiger's claws fall off in his old age?' the baron asked, and smiled at her. 'Go on, take your pig-sticker back out into the house and stick some more pigs for me.'

Eline exchanged a nod with Madame as she went, and briefly wondered what a tiger was. Some beast they had seen on their exotic voyages, she could only imagine. She knew lions, of course, from heraldry, and perhaps it was something like that, or some sort of bear. She really wouldn't know.

'Get beside the door,' the baron said. 'If anyone else storms in here they won't see you from there.'

Eline nodded and did as he said, flattening herself against the wall beside the open doorway. The baron stayed where he was, standing in front of his chair with his thick, curved sword in his right hand and his glass of brandy in his left. The sounds of fighting from within the house seemed to be dying down now and Eline was almost starting to relax until there was another explosion from the rear of the house.

'That's the blasted back door,' the baron complained. 'This is going to cost me a fortune to repair. Do they think I'm made of money?'

There was more shouting, more dying, by the sounds of it. Eline yearned to join them, but the baron wasn't having it.

'You stay right there,' he cautioned her. 'I think I'll need you right about – now!'

Another Marodievan crashed into the room with his crossbow raised, and Eline spun into action before she even knew what she was doing. The back of her right wrist slammed up into the man's weapon and jerked it up just as he pressed the lever, sending his bolt thudding harmlessly into the ceiling instead of through the baron where it had clearly been aimed, and she ducked into a crouch as she turned again and rammed her other stiletto into his crotch.

The man made a hideous noise of pain and suffering, and the baron moved with surprising speed and swept the man's throat out with a single savage swing of the cutlas that passed a whisker over Eline's head.

Eline felt hot blood splatter across her face as she straightened and blew out a breath, and looked at him.

'I thought your knee hurt?' she said dryly.

'It does,' the baron said. 'Hurting is better than dying, my dear. Now get out there and see the state of things. I need to know what's going on.'

Eline nodded and ducked out into the hall. The worst of the noise was coming from what she could only assume was the dining room, or at least had been. She kicked the door open, and there she found Marcoss and Gorath and Madame fighting in a triangular formation against half a dozen or more enemies. Nama was there too but she seemed reluctant to use her cunning for fear of hitting any of their allies with fire or lightning in the chaos of flashing blades and broken furniture. From the distant shouting voices, she could only assume Luka, Sam and their lads were in the back yard, preventing any more of the cunts from getting in.

Everyone else on both sides seemed to be dead.

Marcoss ripped with his dagger and stabbed with his sword and dropped a man, and Madame's blade flicked like lightning, but she needed a perfect straight-line opening to be effective, and the Marodievans had obviously realised that and weren't giving her any chances. Gorath was fighting a purely defensive action, clearly out of his depth, his skills overmatched by their adversaries.

'Rats!' Eline shouted at Nama. 'For fuck's sake!'

'It's not safe,' Nama shouted back.

'None of this is fucking *safe*!' Eline screamed at her as she threw herself on a man's back and knifed him repeatedly through the neck until her right hand was crimson and sticky. 'Just fucking do it!'

Nama threw her head back and uttered her squeal-howl cry, and Eline heard Luka yelling from the yard as rats no doubt poured past him from wherever the fuck they came from. They were in the room a moment later, swarming over the Marodievans and biting and tearing mercilessly as they came. Rats might not be all that big but there were an awful *lot* of them, and their foes began to fall. Marcoss and Madame waded in and helped them finish the job, while Gorath prayed to the Maiden at the top of his voice and honestly looked like he wished he was already dead.

Eline threw herself into the fray with the others, rats swarming and scampering over her, hot and furry and stinking with their sweat and their fleas, but obviously knowing her for a friend. Her knives did their terrible work even as Madame lanced with her blade and Marcoss ripped and tore with his, until it was done.

Luka and Sam were there a moment later, and Sam's mouth gaped open as he took in the sight before him.

'Lady's sake,' Luka said.

Sam gagged as he took in the torn, half-eaten corpses of the enemy, their ruptured guts exposed and reeking through their opened abdomens. He turned and puked on the floor.

The room was drenched in blood and Eline herself was covered in it, and Marcoss and even Madame didn't look a lot better.

'I think that's all of them,' the baron said from the doorway, his bloody cutlass still in his hand.

He took in the scene of crimson devastation before him, wordlessly.

'Sorry about your house,' Eline managed.

'This is what victory looks like,' he said. 'Same as it ever was. Even on the seas, this was what victory always looked like.'

Chapter 35

There was a lot to do, of course.

This wasn't Dannsburg and Leonov wasn't there, but of course between them Luka and the baron knew enough people even in Drathburg who could make things go away. All the same, it took most of the day, and the baron's house still looked like a battle had been fought there, because of course it had been. Not a battle for the throne of Immalia, perhaps, for all that he would have liked it to be, but a battle for his survival. That, at least, he had won.

'Does this really get me any further forward?' Eline overhead him asking Luka from the drawing room as she waited in the hall, and in that moment the baron truly sounded like the deposed foreign monarch he was and not the drunken minor noble he pretended to be.

'His Highness promised you we would be here for you, and we were,' Luka said.

'Where was the Rose Throne when Immalia fell?' the baron demanded.

'Fighting a fucking war,' Luka said. 'Not Krathzgrad, the one before that, and I don't even know where that was fought, or against who.'

'Why?'

'Gods, how the fuck do I know? I wasn't even born then.'

'Your side started it, as I recall,' the baron said.

'Perhaps we did, I wouldn't know. The queen sanctioned it though, that much I *do* know. Not the last one, the one before her. Her Royal Mother. Must have been over something.'

'Why does anyone invade anyone else?' the baron mused. 'They had something you wanted. Land, gold, iron. I don't know. Meanwhile, your closest ally fell, and was driven into exile.'

'Hardly my fault, or His Highness's,' Luka said. 'Like I say, neither of us were fucking born then.'

'But your country's,' the baron pressed.

'Fuck's sake,' Luka said, 'you can't hold a country's past deeds against the people who run it now.'

'Of course I can. Call it hereditary justice.'

'Call it bollocks.'

'Call it *all* bollocks,' Eline murmured to herself, and went to find the kitchens at the back of the house. Kings and queens, and those who thought they were better than everyone else. Who honestly, at the end of the day, really gave a shit?

As she had expected, she found Nama there. The younger woman had located the house's beer barrel and was greedily drinking from a wooden tankard. She had already drawn one for Eline as well, and she smiled as she saw her.

'Thought you might want that,' she said.

'Aye, thank you,' Eline said, taking it. 'I do. Well, I want a brandy really, but I most definitely don't want to interrupt Luka and the baron to get it. They're having words, as you might say.'

Marcoss came in the back door then, and he gave Eline a nod of genuine respect.

'No, I wouldn't recommend doing that, Eline,' he said.

'Probably not a good idea,' Nama agreed. 'Aren't you going to wash?'

Eline realised her right hand was still coated in blood and she had a great spray of it across her face, and never mind the state of her dress. She also realised that Marcoss had just called her by her actual name for the first time. It seemed that his respect, at last, had finally been earned.

'No,' she said. 'Not until I've spoken to Luka, anyway.'

Nama frowned, then just shrugged as Marcoss walked on into the house.

'Aye, right you are,' she said. 'Look like you work in a fucking slaughterhouse then.'

Eline lifted her beer and drank.

'I do,' she said. 'Work in a slaughterhouse, I mean. What else would you call this? I know what I'm doing.'

'I bloody hope you do,' Nama said. 'I was so scared when the bombs started going off I nearly died of fright. How do you do it? I mean, I only fight from a distance but you could get stabbed any moment at your close range. I'd be terrified.'

'I know I've got you to close me up, if that happens,' Eline said, and smiled at her friend. 'Most stab wounds aren't immediately fatal, and you *are* a cunning woman after all.'

The colour drained from Nama's face.

'*What?*' she said. 'You've been relying on me to . . . I don't know any healing magic, Eline! None whatsoever.'

Eline went positively white. She had been *absolutely* relying on that, she had to admit.

'Oh gods,' she said. 'Then I've been fucking lucky, haven't I? That, or Our Lady has been smiling on me.'

Nama blew out a great sigh, and Eline tried to calm her beating heart. She had been sure, *so* sure, that with the cunning Nama could effectively do anything. Apparently not. She had bet her life on that belief several times now, like a desperate man at the card table, and it seemed that she had been bluffing all along even if she hadn't known it.

'What are you going to do now?' she asked, instead of perusing *that* line of thought any further.

'Me?' Nama said. 'What do whores do? Back the fuck to it, I suppose. I've got money *now*, but I know myself. It'll be all gone by Midwinter. What else have I got apart from the cunning? I can't live off that, Eline.'

'What if you didn't have to?'

'Oh aye, you going to make me a better offer, are you?'

'I don't know,' Eline confessed. 'I hope so, but I could still be wrong about this so don't get your bloody hopes up. Just . . . if I had a better offer to make you, would you take it?'

'Doing what?' Nama asked.

Eline swept an arm out to indicate the half-wrecked, bomb-damaged, blood-splattered house. There were still a couple of corpses lying in the hall.

'This, I suppose,' she said.

'Instead of whoring?' Nama asked.

'Aye, instead of whoring.'

'Fuck, yes.'

Luka came and found her a while later, when he and the baron had finally stopped arguing with each other about things she found she simply couldn't make herself care about.

'Can I see you?' he asked Eline, and looked pointedly at Nama. 'In what's left of the dining room, I mean.'

Ah, he meant alone. 'Aye, 'course,' Eline said, but she refilled her tankard before she followed him, giving Nama a stern look to tell her to stay where she was.

They pushed open the axe-scarred door and seated themselves in the least broken-looking chairs they could find.

Luka sighed, and ran his hands over the patchy stubble that had grown on his cheeks.

'We need to talk,' he said.

'Do we?' Eline asked. 'Why's that, then?'

'I know Iagin offered you a job, when you were in Dannsburg. A messenger came to tell me so. I've still got my own people there, whatever he thinks.'

So the Queen's Men don't even trust each other, Eline thought, and she found that she wasn't remotely surprised by that.

'Didn't take it,' Eline said.

'Not then you didn't, no,' Luka said. 'But in time you will, I know that. And I fucking know Iagin, too. We're on the same side, aye, but . . . look. I can do you one better than that, and I think you've well and truly earned it.'

'I work for the baron more than you, these days,' Eline said.

'And you've his trust,' Luka said. 'As much as anyone has, anyway. He's a wily old bastard, and don't think he trusts you as much as he makes out because of course he doesn't. Old bugger doesn't really trust anyone except Madame and he lies like a devil, but he's also on our side. Sort of, anyway.'

'Where are you going with this?'

Eline could feel the blood drying on her face, pulling the skin taut beneath it. She looked at him.

'That messenger,' Luka said, 'the one who came to tell me about Iagin. Well, she came from the house of law, obviously. She brought me news, and orders, and also something else.'

Luka held the something else out to her, a thick piece of folded leather. She knew what that must be.

'I've been thinking of offering you that something,' he said at last. 'I want to offer you this. The Provost Marshal has read all my reports, and he has already agreed.'

Eline looked at Luka for a long time, and at the thing in his hand. She reached out and took it, and her hand didn't shake. She opened the soft leather slowly and gazed down at the seal of the royal arms, a white-gold rose set upon a golden crown.

The Queen's Warrant.

To be above the law, to answer to no one but the Provost Marshal ever again. To be free, at last. Free to probably spend the rest of her life killing people, for this Rose Throne she had never set eyes on.

No more baron, no more Madame, no more whoring. She could take Nama into her service, and free her too.

Eventually she looked up, and she met the bleak look in Luka's eyes. Oh, he knew exactly what he was offering her: the life of a Queen's Man, and what that meant.

'Sign me up,' she said, and her voice was steel.

Why hope to be happy? That's a fool's errand. Only hope to survive.

That's all Our Lady offers, or so they say at temple.

THE END

Acknowledgements

This isn't the first time I've thanked a dead rock star in my acknowledgements (RIP RJD), but it is the first time I've dedicated a book to one. If you're what passes for a normal person these days you probably have no idea who Wendy O. Williams was, and unless you like KISS, W.A.S.P. or Motorhead you probably wouldn't like her music either, but she was a wonderful woman and a major inspiration for the character that became Eline.

Wendy was the absolute queen of 'fuck you, I'll do what I like'. Punk icon, rock star, stunt woman, Grammy nominee, stripper, sex worker, animal lover, committed environmentalist and absolute badass. Wendy lived and died on her own terms and by her own choice, and I respect that more than I can say.

Legends never die.

I'd also like to thank Theresa Fractale and her amazing steampunk cosplay photos for giving me the inspiration to write about courtesans in the first place. I've never met the lady, but some of her costumes are simply stunning and just set the idea bunny-running in my head.

Thanks are obviously due to my publishing team: my agent Jennie Goloboy at DMLA who I would never, ever want to be without, my editors Anne Perry and Gaby Puleston Vaudrey at Arcadia, and Ghost for the frankly fabulous cover design.

But as aways, the greatest thanks are reserved for Diane, my wife of 30 years, for putting up with all my bullshit over the years and giving me the space to write. Love you babe.

It was an oversight, due to my publishing teams, even family

holder of 1881, who I would never, ever want to be with, and anyone

Aunt Helen and Sally Robinson Andrew at Arundel, and I now feel that it may

fabulous everywhere?!

But even so, the poorest diary is topped up in D, and may well get to

start, me, settling, with all my brilliant over the years and living life, the

space to write, love you Lara.